THE EQUALIZER

THE EQUALIZER

Midge Bubany

NORTH STAR PRESS OF ST. CLOUD, INC.
St. Cloud, Minnesota

For Tim, Stacy, and Shawn.
My loves, my life.

Printed in the United States of America

Published by
North Star Press of St. Cloud, Inc
PO Box 451
St. Cloud, MN 56302

www.northstarpress.com

Be not afraid of any man,
No matter what his size;
When danger threatens, call on me
And I will equalize.

~Inscription of the nineteenth-century
Winchester Rifle

1

DAY ONE

Friday, October 7th

A BODY HAD BEEN DISCOVERED in Emmaline Ronson County Park and because this was my first major case as an investigator, I was anxious to get to the scene. As I was approaching the red light on Ash and First Avenue, I noticed a black Toyota coming up from behind way too fast.

"Oh, no! No! No!" I hollered laying on my horn.

WHAM! I was pushed into the intersection—and at that exact moment a vintage Grand Marquis crashed into my driver's side front fender. All three cars moved like a single mass back toward the stoplight. The sound of metal and plastic slamming, buckling, and crunching was unbelievably loud, and then came—the quiet.

"Of all fricking mornings for this to happen. Thank you," I said looking into rear view mirror at the driver of the Toyota. Wait—do I see her *smiling*?

My concern turned to the driver of the Grand Marquis, a woman who looked to be about a hundred years old—and frankly if the crash didn't kill her—time was not on her side. Her front end blocked my driver's side door, so I dragged my six-foot-three frame across the seats and out the passenger side. Lucky I could even get out, as the back door was jammed up against the stoplight. I walked around to check on the woman. She rolled down the window, and I got a whiff of her perfume. She must have used half the bottle and whew . . . I wouldn't put that shit on a dog.

When I noticed tears rolling down her face, I showed her my badge and said, "Deputy Cal Sheehan. Are you injured, ma'am?"

"I'm okay," she said, as she bobbed her head and dabbed her eyes with a thin embroidered handkerchief. She said her name was Agnes Salmi and was on her way to help with the Finnish Lutheran Church rummage sale when my car suddenly appeared in front of her. "I had the green light," she said.

"Yes, ma'am, you did," I said. "The Toyota driver rammed me into the intersection and your beautiful car. What year is this beauty?"

"It's a 1978 Mercury Grand Marquis," she said proudly. "Is it badly dented?"

"Not badly."

The driver of the Toyota had exited her vehicle and joined us. She was a tall brunette and looked to be in her early twenties. I knew most all the women ages twenty to thirty-five in this town for one reason or another. So, she was either new in town or passing through.

"I'm so sorry!" she said. "I couldn't stop."

"Why?" I asked. Hmm, she was definitely a looker, long legs, cute little behind.

"My brakes didn't work," she said.

"Like I haven't heard that a thousand times."

She ignored my comment and leaned into Mrs. Salmi's window. I could hear her speaking sweetly—trying to fend off a lawsuit with a load of fake concern. Trouble is, I think it was working. Mrs. Salmi was smiling adoringly up at the young woman who towered over her. We all were suckers for a pretty face and a little attention . . . or was that just me?

First, I called dispatch then my sergeant, Ralph Martinson, to let him know I'd be delayed. By the time I hung up, I already heard a siren. My attention then turned to Old Red. I took a cruise around her to assess the damages. Not good—not good at all. The driver's side wheel had collapsed and was now underneath the car. I'll admit rust may have been a contributing factor.

"What happened? You didn't see me or the red light?" I asked the driver.

"I told you, my gas pedal stuck," she said.

I eyed her suspiciously. "You sure you weren't texting?"

She shot me a look of indignation. "No, of course not."

Yeah right . . . but I couldn't testify to that fact. I looked inside her vehicle spotting a brief case lying open, no mobile phone visible.

Within a few minutes, the department's only African American officer and a friend, Tamika Frank, rolled up. She was large in stature: solid muscle, six foot even, quick and strong. She'd played college basketball, and I'd seen her throw guys down to the ground like a professional wrestler. After asking the gathering crowd to back up on the sidewalk, Tamika approached me.

"Well, well, well, I thought you had something better to do this fine morning?" she said, chuckling.

Through clenched teeth I said, "I'm supposed to be at a scene."

"Heard about that. We'll get you going as fast as we can, but to expedite matters, you'd better call for a tow truck because you won't be driving this piece of shit anywhere."

I gave her the eye. "Tamika, a little respect, please."

She tried to suppress another chuckle, but was unsuccessful. "So what happened?"

"Toyota driver rammed me into the intersection just as Mrs. Salmi's boat of a Grand Marquis entered! I believe the Toyota driver didn't have her full attention on the road, probably texting."

"Uh huh," Tamika said. "You okay?"

"Yeah, but I gotta get moving."

"I understand." Tamika cocked her head. "Toyota driver's a pretty thing."

"Didn't notice," I said.

"Right. Shall we find out what the stories are?" she said as she walked over to the other two drivers.

"Deputy Frank. Anyone injured?" she said.

Both drivers shook their heads.

I used my personal iPhone to call for a tow and then joined Tamika and the two women who were arm in arm. Cozy.

Siren blaring, lights flashing, the ambulance entered the intersection. More locals were joining the spectator event. After the EMTs briefly questioned all of us, I encouraged them to check out Mrs. Salmi. Tamika asked the drivers for their licenses and registration then after checking both on the computer, she came back and approached the young female. "Victoria Kay Lewis, what happened here this morning?"

Ms. Lewis's behavior seemed off to me. She didn't seem upset or nervous, like most people when involved in a crash. As she spoke to Tamika about her accelerator pedal, she had kept glancing back at me, smiling. But I was not in a smiling mood. She said she'd just moved and was planning to put in a change of address on her license. Tamika busily wrote in her notebook, examined the Toyota's interior, taking more notes. When she moved on to question Mrs. Salmi, I was too angry with Ms. Lewis to make small talk. She pulled a mobile phone out of her pocket, made a call telling someone she was going to be late.

Well, you're not the only one, lady.

My insides churned. I wanted—*needed*—to get the hell out of there ASAP. While Tamika seemed to take her merry old time snapping photos, I tried to expedite matters by suggesting we three drivers exchange insurance information. With gnarled fingers, Mrs. Salmi wrote hers on tiny notebook pages—the writing nearly illegible from her shaky hand. Victoria Lewis wrote her information including her cell phone number and email address on Post-it notes, and handed one to both of us. When I handed her my card, she looked at it and laughed. "Wow, it's not everyone who rear-ends a deputy sheriff."

You didn't get a clue from my brown jacket with the big yellow SHERIFF written across it?

The tow truck arrived with a flat bed and began loading my car.

Tamika printed police reports for our insurance companies and both of the other drivers were able to drive off in their vehicles. After the tow truck left, Tamika gave me a ride to the Birch County Sheriff Department complex in the center of town on First Street.

"Looks like those two women got the best of your Civic. Grand Marquis got a tiny scratch, and the Toyota a minor dent."

"Figures."

"I think Snow White has a crush on you," she said with a mischievous grin.

"Snow White?"

"Uh huh—doesn't she look like Snow White with her *creamy*, white skin and dark *shiny* hair."

"Should Anton be worried about you talking about women resembling princesses?"

She snickered. "We've just been through a fairy tale movie marathon at my house," she said. "It's making me crazy. But you gotta admit, the girl is Snow White."

"I wouldn't know. She's not my type."

Tamika's eyes were on me, not the road. "Seriously Sheehan? She's *exactly* your type."

I pointed at the car braking in front of us. "Brakes!"

She did quick stop.

"Oh, so you think you know my *type*?"

She looked at me and said, "Tall, skinny brunettes—no use denying it."

"That's crazy," I said, as I wracked my brain, trying to remember a woman I'd dated who *wasn't* brunette. "Suzy Williams—my freshman year in college—she had red hair and . . . and . . . Becca, my high school girlfriend, was short with light brown hair. So there."

"With Adriana out of the picture, I don't get why you and Shannon haven't hooked up. Or maybe you have and just aren't telling anyone."

Shannon Benson was a deputy who joined the department just before I did. Five years ago a drunk driver killed her husband, Evan, while he was jogging. She said Evan was the love of her life and no man measured up—so I never pushed a relationship beyond friendship. I avoid rejection whenever possible.

"Hardly. We both agree it would ruin our friendship," I said. And to get her off the subject I asked, "By the way, do you believe Ms. Lewis's sticky accelerator story?"

"Well, maybe she used that as an excuse so I'm requiring her car to be examined by a mechanic."

"Good. Did she have anything on her record?"

"A speeding ticket a couple years ago."

Tamika pulled up in front of the department to let me out.

"Well, thanks for the lift, Tamika. Tell your lucky husband hello from me."

"Oh, if I say that, he'll misinterpret thinking he's gonna *get* lucky. My man has a one track mind . . . over production of testosterone or something."

"Nah, we're all like that," I said.

Her husband, Anton Frank, owned the twenty-four hour gas station in town and had the city and county fuel contracts. Most patrol officers took breaks at his place because Anton gave law enforcement free drinks—that's how Tamika and Anton met. Anyway, it was a win-win—we got freebees and our presence helped deter robberies. Took a while for the white bread town folks to get used to the biracial couple—besides, she's ten years younger, four inches taller and has a good thirty pounds on him.

Immediately after signing in at the department, I grabbed my gear, picked up my assigned department Explorer and called Ralph to notify him I was finally on my way.

"You okay?" he asked.

"I'm fine, just frustrated not to be on the scene."

"You haven't missed much. These things are never quick."

"See you soon."

But I wasn't fine. My stomach ached and I was hoping it was just the jimjams and not the suspect cream cheese I'd smeared on my stale bagel this morning. Now that I was on the road again, I realized I hadn't even asked who the victim was.

2

AUTUMN IS MY FAVORITE SEASON and today, the first Friday in October, the drive south on County 51 was a sight to behold. The sun shone on the fall foliage, making the ambers, oranges, and reds even more brilliant.

After six miles I turned left on South Lake Road, and three-fourths of a mile later, I parked on the side of the road behind three department SUVs and the sheriff's new cruiser. I gathered up my evidence kit and made my way to the two deputies guarding the park entrance. We made small talk as I signed the login sheet, then stepped over the yellow crime scene tape and headed in to the scene.

Most of the southern half of the square mile was part of Lake Emmaline County Park. The Ronson family donated the land years ago. A public access to Lake Emmaline was built and hiking trails were established through the forested area to the west. As a patrol officer, I always felt this park was a real pain in the ass. Kids thought it was a great place to party, and we had umpteen noise disturbance calls every year from the four families who lived in the small neighborhood directly east.

Leaves were already gracefully drifting to the ground as if performing a waltz. I could picture the scene as a painting or photo on a calendar for October—minus the dead body, of course. A few yards in, several crows startled me as they screeched and flapped skyward. *Whoa, settle down, Cal.*

I walked the quarter mile on the narrow paved road leading into a large parking lot where two squads, a county parks' department pickup truck, and the Birch County Crime Scene Lab van were parked. Also, parked along the east edge of the parking lot next to the large white storage building was a late model dark-blue SuperCrew Ford F150 with a Shorland'r trailer.

Five people hovered near Sheriff Jack Whitman: Sergeant Ralph Martinson; Betty Abbott, one of our lab specialists; Deputies John Odell, Greg Woods, and Shannon Benson. Shannon flashed a smile as I approached. I winked back.

I moved in next to Ralph. He wore his department brown stocking cap over his salt-and-pepper buzz cut, and this morning a green parka, gray sweatshirt and jeans had replaced the ill-fitting warehouse suits he usually wore. He was one of my favorite people. He smiled and laughed easy, was a team player, and had a calm, disarming demeanor.

"You okay?" he asked.

"Yeah, but the Civic's totaled."

He shrugged. "Just be thankful *you're* not totaled."

"Well, true. So who's our vic?"

"Turns out we have *two*. Both died from multiple gunshot wounds."

"Whoa, two? That changes things. Who are they?"

"Ted Kohler and Ronny Peterson."

I made a face. Our vics were polar opposites. Kohler ran a successful accounting business. Peterson worked for the Birch County Parks Department. He was young, single, with a big mouth that got him into his share of bar fights.

"Why were they out here so early in the morning?" I said.

"For different reasons. Ronny Peterson's boss, Naomi Moberg, said he was here to pull in the dock. He was found farther in the woods. Ted was found in his boat. I would guess he was trying to get in his last fishing trip."

"Yeah, well, he succeeded."

I followed Ralph the short distance to the black sixteen-foot Lund fishing boat bobbing up against the dock. Kohler's body, clad in tan coveralls, was sprawled face up on the rear bench seat of the boat. He was shot twice: once through an eye and also in the chest. His remaining eye was blue and still clear—he hadn't been here long.

"Did you know him?" I asked.

"Not well, but he seemed like a friendly guy. Hope we can find a bullet because if not, it could be way the heck out in the lake," Ralph said.

"And probably unrecoverable," I said, glancing out over the lake. This morning the view was remarkable: fingers of mist drifted up from the dark-blue lake waters, framed by the vibrant autumn colors. "Ironic to see the beauty of Mother Nature side by side with ugliness of violence."

"Huh? Oh, yeah, it's real pretty out this morning," Ralph said.

"So, where's Peterson?"

"Follow me," he said.

Ronny Peterson lay face down about a hundred yards west into the wooded area, a good fifty yards from the trail. He was a brick: short and broad. He wore a green county jacket and blue jeans—his white cap with the county logo lay a foot forward from his head. Two small bloodstains were located within two inches of each other in the center of his back.

"Shot twice," I said.

"Hopefully, we can find these bullets," Ralph said.

I noticed Ronny's wallet bulge in his back pocket. I leaned down and pulled it out and looked through it.

"ID says he's twenty-two. Has thirty-two dollars and two credit cards on him—not a robbery."

"Might as well bag the wallet now," he said.

Ralph rolled Peterson slightly. "Hey, one bullet didn't exit."

"That's very good."

He searched his front left pocket, then the right, but came up with nothing. "No phone. The truck keys are in the ignition." He looked back at the landing, then back at me. "Why would anyone do this?"

"Maybe these two saw something they shouldn't, or maybe one was a primary target and the other just unlucky—wrong place at the wrong time."

The sheriff approached. Not a particularly handsome man with his beak of a nose and ruddy complexion, an extra forty in his belly, but Jack was a commanding figure who tended to dichotomize the staff. People either loved or hated him.

"Jack, any idea when BRO will be here?" Ralph asked, referring to the Bemidji Regional Office of the Minnesota Bureau of Criminal Apprehension (BCA).

Jack looked at his watch. "Should be any minute."

"Naomi said she'd notify Ronny's folks. Want me to send someone to Kohlers' to notify Eleanor?" Ralph asked.

"No! I'll tell her myself," Jack snapped.

"It's probably best to have someone tell her before she finds out . . ."

Jack enunciated each word as he said, "She isn't going to find out *until* I tell her. Period."

Ralph and I exchanged glances. *Okay then.* Two BCA Vans rolled in breaking the uncomfortable moment, and we all made our way back to the parking lot. Ralph introduced Leslie Rouch, an investigator with the BCA, and she in turn introduced three technicians who all looked fortyish: Helen, Christopher, and John. Leslie, also in the same age range, was a blue-eyed blond, five-foot-seven, average weight. She wore a heavy, navy-blue Columbia jacket and stocking cap. Smart. Over night the temps had dropped into the upper thirties and my ears were getting cold. I pulled out my orange hunting stocking cap I'd stuffed in my pocket this morning—the only one I could find in a hurry.

The sheriff gathered the group together back at the landing. "Okay, just to recap for the new arrivals. At 7:56 a.m. the 911 came in. Bob Brutlag, who lives out here on the peninsula, found Ted Kohler in his Lund. Ted's a CPA in town—father-in-law is Hamilton Fairchild, a county commissioner and president of Prairie Falls First National Bank. We thought we just had the one victim until the deputies found Ronald Peterson, a park maintenance employee, when sealing off the crime scene."

Ralph jumped in. "According to Naomi Moberg, the Parks Department director, Ronny was scheduled to roll the dock in. Stan Haney, manager of the maintenance garage, said Ronny checked out the county truck unusually early, 7:15. If he drove right to Emmaline, he could've been here as early as 7:25 a.m."

"I didn't think maintenance started that early," I said. "And pulling a dock in can't be a one man job."

Ralph nodded. "You're right on both. Naomi didn't know why he checked in so early. In fact, she thought he was going to be late. Naomi said Gus Taylor was going to meet him out here, but got turned away by a deputy."

"What time was that?" I asked.

Ralph looked at his notes. "Eight-twenty."

"What time did the first responder arrive on scene?" Leslie asked.

Shannon's strawberry blonde ponytail hanging out of the back end of her cap bounced as she stepped forward. "At 8:04, ma'am. The caller reported a body with a gunshot wound in a boat at the park. When I arrived on scene, there were two vehicles in the parking lot, the Ford pickup with a boat trailer and the county truck #13. I waited for backup before I rushed out into the open. Deputy Woods arrived followed by Deputy Odell and the EMTs. We secured the area before we allowed the paramedics to check out the victim in the boat. At the same time we looked for the driver of the county vehicle and that's when we found Peterson."

"So if Gus Taylor and Ronny Peterson were supposed to work together, why didn't they ride out together?" I asked.

"I wondered the same thing—save the taxpayers gas money," Ralph said.

"Park workers don't give a crap about saving the county money," Jack said.

"Kohler must have been here first. Ronny would have told Ted he couldn't put his boat in because they were pulling out the dock," I said.

Ralph nodded. "Makes sense."

"Did the 911 caller enter the boat?" Leslie asked.

Jack shook his head. "I don't know. I haven't had a chance to speak with him. Leslie, we've got acres of county land to the west and residential property on the east. Do you need my deputies to help search?"

"Normally, we like as few people as possible tramping through the crime scene, but considering the scope of the area, we can use them. We'll assign teams of two to specific areas. But first, John'll videotape the area and draw up a sketch."

The waiting around was getting to me, but there was nothing I could do to make this thing move any faster. As crows and jays argued off in the distance and squirrels dashed about in the leaves, it struck me the wildlife was totally unaffected by death's hand. I stepped back and took in the area surrounding the scene, trying to picture what went down.

Shannon Benson approached me. "Penny for your thoughts."

"I was just trying to imagine what occurred. It's possible one or both were part of some illegal activity or they interrupted something. Could be more than one shooter. If Ronny was shot first, Kohler wouldn't have seen the body. He pulls up and puts his boat in. Shooter's still here and Kohler sees him. Boom. Shooter takes out his witness. Or two, the shooter kills Kohler first, Ronny drives up and finds Kohler dead, sees the shooter and when he realizes the situation he's in, he panics and takes off running, and is shot in the back."

She bobbed her head from side to side, "So, which makes more sense?"

"Sometimes sense has nothing to do with it. I want to ask Jack something."

He was with Deputies Odell and Woods by the BCA van.

"Have the neighbors been interviewed?" I asked as I approached him.

Jack looked up, said "Not yet."

"Want me to—"

He looked annoyed. "No, I don't. Just hold your damn rookie horses."

I know he snapped at Ralph earlier, but it embarrassed me to have him speak to me with a tone he'd use on a kid, especially in front of my colleagues. Asshole. Odell, who had no love for Jack, looked my way and rolled his eyes. I walked back over to Shannon.

"What's his problem?" she whispered.

I shrugged. "This case is a huge deal for Jack. But the inefficiency really gets to me. I'd have deputies out interviewing the neighbors."

"They're probably all at work anyway. Doesn't Jack's son, Ben, live out here?"

"Yep, second lot over from the park."

I returned to the dock where Leslie stood with our lead county lab technician, Betty Abbott—fifty something, heavy in the hips and thighs. This morning she wore a white wool beret over her stick straight, brown hair, and an olive-green parka over her white lab coveralls. She was photographing the blood spray on the motor, boat, and Igloo cooler. I overheard her talking to Benson once about why she didn't wear makeup. She'd said, "No make-up of any kind has ever touched my epidermis. I don't want to clog my pores with chemicals." Makes a whole lot of sense to me.

"Too bad they got Kohler in the face. He was a looker," Betty said.

Leslie's head bobbed in agreement. "I'll say."

I looked at the two women and shook my head. "No one looks too good dead, especially with an eye shot out."

Leslie's mouth turned up in a smile. "Did you know the victims?"

Betty spoke up. "Everybody liked Ted. He must have at least five kids."

"What about Ronald Peterson?" Leslie asked.

I took this one. "Single guy. Twenty-two, but he still lived with his parents. Hung out in Buzzo's Bar. I first encountered him when I worked patrol. He liked a fight."

"He had enemies then," Leslie said.

I shrugged. "You could say that. One of the bullets didn't exit his body, but Ralph worries Kohler's went through," I said. I went to check the back of the boat for dings or bullet holes.

"We'll get a better look when the body is removed," Leslie said.

A metal bait bucket sloshed its contents as the boat rocked with the waves lapping the rocky shoreline. The sandy bottom started about five feet out. I noticed an indentation in a post at the end of the dock. I walked over and said, "Lookie here. I think we have a bullet."

Leslie came over to examine it. "Well, my, my. It's unlikely to be it our fatal bullet, though."

After she flagged it with an evidence number and snapped several photos, she tried to wedge the bullet out of the wood.

"It's not budging and I don't want to take a chance and drop it in the lake. We'll have to saw off the top of the post," Leslie said, and directed me to get the saw out of the van. I also brought a large evidence bag to place it in.

As I was entering the post on the log, Doc Swank, the county medical examiner, pulled up in his vehicle. After he shook hands with the sheriff he proceeded to the boat. Doc was known for his professional, efficient, and respectful approach to the living and the dead. He has a full head of white hair, and I'd guess him to be nearing sixty. After Doc and the crime lab team finished with the bodies they'd be transported to Bemidji to BRO for autopsy.

Completing the initial tasks of documenting the scene, Ralph gathered the group together. "Okay, we have four teams of two to cover specific areas. We've made maps for each team and assigned a zone. Work it like a grid, crisscrossing to make sure we don't miss anything. We're looking for shell casings, footprints, cigarette butts, wrappers, a confession . . ."

Everyone laughed.

Leslie added, "Try not to trample any evidence, and if you find something, mark it, and you can take your own photos but let John know so he can also photograph and document the exact location on the grids. Be thorough when you fill out the information on the evidence bags. We'll collect and log in all the evidence in the van. Metal detectors are available for your use."

Leslie showed us a hand-drawn map and assigned teams of two to specific quadrants. Shannon was my partner. Our area was within the perimeter of the landing and open area back to and including the road. We began by running a measurement of our area so we could track any evidence we would find. We would work the area south to north, then east to west. The grass surrounding the parking lot was long but sparse and easy to see through to the sandy soil. On the first pass through, a hundred yards from shore, along the western edge of the clearing, Shannon found a marijuana stub ground into the soil. The grass surrounding it looked a little trampled but there were no visible shoe prints. After we donned gloves, we labeled and photographed it, called John over to do his thing, then we bagged it.

The metal detector sounded near the center of the clearing. I was pumped when we found three bullet casings within a ten-foot radius. We followed procedure for handling the evidence, then turned it over to Leslie in the BCA van. Besides the casings and the one roach, Shannon and I recovered a Pepsi can near the building.

"Let's check out the vehicles," I said.

The door to Kohler's pick-up was locked. Through the windows it looked showroom spotless. We took photos of the exterior, then made our way to the county vehicle and searched it. The county vehicle was unlocked with the keys still in the ignition. Sitting on the driver's seat was a clipboard with Ronny's log. He hadn't marked the time he entered the park. I looked for his cell phone, but it wasn't in the truck.

I asked the sheriff if we could get in the storage building where the county stored the dock. Jack said the code for all the park maintenance buildings was one two three four. How stupid was that? As I opened the double doors, dead leaves danced across the concrete floor. The only light came from four small dirty windows. Shannon swatted at cobwebs.

"Man, you wouldn't want to have arachnophobia and search this place," she said.

"You afraid of spiders?"

"No, bats."

"They eat a lot of mosquitoes."

"Yeah well, I had a bad experience with one at Scout Camp—one got into our cabin at night and was dive-bombing our heads." She shuddered then shined her flashlight around. "How 'bout you, Sheehan? What gives you the willies?"

"Not much." Yeah, I'd never tell.

She pointed to the sand on the single shelf in the rear then up to an access panel. "Why would they put a ceiling in this building?"

"Storage?"

She crawled up onto the shelf, pushed the panel aside, and her head disappeared inside.

"Look out for the bat!" I said.

Shannon ducked out.

I grinned. "They like attics."

"Damn it, Sheehan. I knew as soon as the bat story came out of my mouth I'd regret it."

"See anything furry with wings?"

"Ish, no, but I do see something here. Hand me the camera. Still got your gloves on?"

"Yep."

"Good, because I'm gonna hand it down."

After snapping photos, she handed me a black vinyl case. I waited until she crawled down so she could open it. Inside were two pipes, a plastic bag containing what looked like less than an ounce of heroin—plus a sandwich bag of weed.

"Who would store their drugs in a county building?" she asked.

"A *county* worker? Maybe Ronny? Hope we can get some prints off of it."

After we relocked the storage building, Shannon beat it to the van to log in her find, and I walked back to check out the unisex toilet. There was nothing on the floor or trash can—not even the usual paper towels or strips of toilet paper. Two rolls of toilet paper were placed on a shelf above the toilet but the paper towel dispenser was empty.

As I rejoined the group who had gathered, Ralph said, "Good news. Looks like we have five casings all the same type. Odell recovered a bullet in a tree near Peterson's body and Cal found one in the dock. Good work."

It was then I noticed Bob Brutlag standing to the east outside the taped area. "Bob's here."

"Leslie, he's the 911," Jack said.

"Good. I want to speak with him."

"Set up a time for him to come in to the department for a formal statement later," Ralph said.

As Leslie, Jack and I walked toward Brutlag, Jack said, "Even though he looks like a hippie, don't underestimate him. Guy's a gear head. Best mechanic at Daniels Ford."

Hippie? My mother's a hippie. This guy looked like a typical red-neck biker—with his untrimmed beard; long, brown hair pulled back into a ponytail; a Harley Davidson jacket and baseball cap, dirty jeans, and work boots. He saluted Jack as we approached.

"Mornin', Bob," the sheriff said.

"Mornin'," Brutlag answered readjusting his cap. Standing along side of Jack whose belly mounded from chest to groin, the guy looked scrawny. He was maybe six foot, but he couldn't weigh more than 160 pounds soaking wet.

Jack gestured with his hand from Leslie to Bob. "Detective Leslie Rouch from the BCA, this is Bob Brutlag, our 911 caller."

Brutlag nodded to Leslie.

As an afterthought, Jack added, "Bob, you know Cal Sheehan?"

"Sure do," Brutlag said, and extended his hand first to Leslie, then to me, but avoided eye contact with both of us. Brutlag sniffed a couple times. His eyes were glassy and blood-shot. Maybe it was *his* stash in the storage shed—anybody could know that idiotic code.

I first met him when I responded to a noise complaint he'd made when a group of college kids had a kegger here in the park. He'd probably have been partying with them if not for his pretty Hispanic wife who'd just had a baby. She used to work at Buzzo's Sports Bar in town.

Jack lit a cigarette and offered one to Brutlag, then lit both. Bob sniffed again, took a drag of the cigarette, leaving it precariously perched between his lips. He squinted as the smoke drifted into his eyes. He took the cigarette into his fingers, and flicked ash.

"I understand you made the 911 call, Mr. Brutlag?" Leslie asked.

"Yes, ma'am." He took another drag then spit on the ground. Leslie made a face and stepped back.

"Did you hear gunshots this morning?" I asked.

He shook his head slowly as he took the last drag of his cigarette before he ground it out with his boot.

"Living so close, I'm surprised you wouldn't have," I said.

He glanced at me before looking at Jack. "I sleep like a rock."

"How far away is your home?" Leslie asked.

He pointed to the northeast. "It's on the peninsula, maybe five hundred yards." A copse of pine blocked the view to his property.

"What brought you to the park this morning?" Leslie asked.

"I walk the trails. Guess I'll think twice about it from now on," he said, snorting, twitching. He twitched a lot.

"Is this landing busy?" Leslie asked.

"Not at all, especially this time of year," Bob said.

"Did you see anyone else or any other vehicles in the area?" I asked.

"Just Kohler's pick-up and the county truck."

"Did you enter the dock or boat at any point?" Leslie asked.

Bob focused on Jack as he spoke. "I could see from shore he was dead. Dint 'spect there was any use going in the boat to try to save him."

"You're not working today?" I asked.

"Second shift."

"You ever see anything suspicious, like illegal activity, going down out here?" I asked.

Bob puffed out his lips and said, "Just kids partying."

"Were you wearing those boots this morning?" I asked.

He nodded.

"We'll need a photo of the bottoms to ID your footprints," I said.

Bob screwed up his face and got a nod from Jack before he complied. He placed his hand on a tree for balance and lifted his feet one by one so I could snap the photos of soles of his brown boots. Standing close to Bob, I detected the odor of marijuana.

"The soles have a distinctive pattern. What kind are they?" I asked.

"Redwing, steel toe," he said.

Jack took a cigar out of his front shirt pocket, cut the end, lit it, then produced puffs of smoke. He spat a speck of tobacco off his tongue. *These guys ever hear of lung cancer?*

"So, what do you think happened, Jack?" Bob asked.

"Well, what I think and what I know are two different things. We have two victims, and that's pretty much it, at this point."

"*Two?*" Bob asked. He seemed genuinely surprised.

"We found Ronny Peterson in the woods," the sheriff said.

Bob grimaced. "Nooo. What the hell?"

Jack shrugged. I was surprised he gave him any information at all.

"We'll need you to come in for a formal statement, Mr. Brutlag," I said.

"Be at the department tomorrow at 10:00 a.m.," Jack said.

"All right, I can do that," he said with a crooked smile.

"You can go on home now, Bob," Sheriff Whitman said, "and keep this under your hat. We've got next of kin to notify before it's spread all over town."

"I hear ya. Mum's the word," he said crossing his lips with his index finger, then walked away.

"Seems like you know him well," I said.

Jack said, "Since he was born. His dad, Pete, is a good friend of mine."

"Pete live here in the area?" I asked.

"He moved to Arizona a few years back," he said. "Gave the place to Bob."

As I watched him walk off I put Bob on my suspect list.

AFTER THE TWO BODIES were placed in the BCA van for transport, Ralph gathered the investigators and deputies. He said he would question the four Lake Emmaline residents, but we also needed to canvas area motels and resorts to interview duck hunters or fisherman who may have been in the area. Jack said he'd have his secretary call in additional personnel. We would meet back at the office at 6:00 p.m. It was already closing in on 2:00 p.m.

Ralph grabbed my arm. "I'm gonna stay and finish up out here. Cal, Jack's going to notify Mrs. Koehler now. Why don't you go with to question her?"

"Sure," I said.

"Listen, mention we have a substantial search warrant. Georgia has it."

"Okay, see you later," I said.

As I followed the sheriff's new cruiser back into town, I played out how the family notification would go. I'd never gotten used to giving families the worst news they would ever have. If I ever did, it'd be time to quit.

3

A S THE SHERIFF AND I walked into the administration office, his
secretary, Georgia, handed him search warrants for the victims' homes,
office, computers, vehicles, credit cards, and bank and phone records.
Hopefully, we'd find a motive somewhere for these senseless killings.

Jack disappeared into his office, while I got a cup of coffee from the squad
room. Tasted like shit but it was hot. When Jack came out of his office, he handed
me his keys and ordered me to bring his cruiser around to the back entrance.

The sheriff's cruiser was one of the last Crown Vics off the production
line and loaded with all the bells and whistles. I turned up the heat and
directed a vent toward my hands. When I pulled around, he climbed in the
passenger side and began pointing out the car's features, but the only one I
cared about was the heater. It was thirty-eight degrees according to the
cruiser's readings, and my hands and feet were ice cubes.

The sheriff directed without talking. Instead, he used two flops of his right
hand to indicate the two right turns. Kohler's home was located on a street
of highly desirable remodeled homes in "old town." When we came to a light-
blue two-story with a big wrap-around porch on the corner of East Sixth
Street and Morris Avenue, a single finger pointed to the correct driveway. I
had to avoid two bikes dropped on the edge of the concrete drive as I parked
next to a white Honda Odyssey minivan.

The sheriff turned to me. "Ya want to pull off the orange cap? Not too
professional."

I took it off and stuffed it in my pocket, then finger combed my hair.

The sheriff walked around in front of the cruiser making a detour to peek
in a window in a side door front of the three-car garage.

"Huh, Ted's Town Car isn't in there."

As we walked up the steps to the back porch, Eleanor Kohler flung open
the door.

"Sheriff? What's wrong?" she asked.

"Eleanor, I'm afraid I have some bad news for you," he said.

18

Her eyes widened. "What is it?"

"Can we come in?" he asked.

"Of course," she said.

We followed her across the porch, stepping around an obstacle course of large toy trucks and through a mudroom. As soon as I entered the kitchen, I was hit with the aroma of fresh baked goods. It took me back to my childhood with my Grandma Sylvia's ritual of Saturday baking. We entered a large, gourmet kitchen complete with professional-quality stainless steel appliances and cherry cabinets. Several freshly baked loaves of bread and two batches of cookies lined the granite counter—a small smudge of flour dotted her right cheek. I didn't know anyone under sixty baked like this anymore.

Eleanor gestured for us to sit at her large oak table, but stayed standing, her hands braced on the top of the chair. The bright kitchen light shone on her copper-red hair that accentuated her fair skin and striking green eyes.

"This is Deputy Investigator Cal Sheehan."

She made brief eye contact with me. I nodded, forcing a smile.

"Tell me what's going on," she said.

Jack cleared his throat. "It's best you sit down," he said softly.

Her eyelids blinked rapidly as she hesitated before she sat. My stomach lurched to my throat. This was heart wrenching.

"I'm very sorry to have to tell you Ted was found dead this morning out on Lake Emmaline. He'd been shot," Jack said.

Her jaw dropped, color drained from her face. "Oh, my God," she said. She leaned forward and suddenly pushed herself up from the table. "Excuse me," she said as she disappeared through a doorway in the hallway on her right.

Jack surveyed the room until his eyes came to rest on the baked goods. I could hear Eleanor vomit. The toilet flushed. After a full minute, she returned, her face still damp.

"Sorry about that," she said as sat in her chair. Her hands were trembling.

"No problem," Jack said.

"So who . . . shot . . . ?"

"At this point we don't know. He was found in his boat still tied up to the dock at the public landing on Emmaline," Jack said.

"Did he intend to go to work today?" I asked.

"Yes, and when he didn't come home, I thought he might have gone straight in instead of stopping back at the house. He does that sometimes."

"A local resident found him this morning, but I wanted to notify you in person," the sheriff said.

She whispered, "Thank you for that, Jack. Did they take him to Nelson's?"

"No, he's on his way to Bemidji," he said. "An autopsy is required. Would you like me to let them know your preference for funeral homes is Nelson's?"

"Yes."

I could hear the TV and kids' voices in the back of the house.

The sheriff then asked, "How 'bout I call your dad?"

She nodded. Jack pulled out his cell phone and walked into the dining room.

Eleanor closed her eyes then placed a hand over her mouth. She moved it to her cheek and said, "This feels surreal. Forty-year-old healthy men shouldn't die. Did he suffer?"

"No, I'm sure it was instantaneous."

Eleanor gasped. "Do you think it was an accident?"

"I doubt it. Another man was also killed—a parks worker."

"Oh, my God. Why?"

"That's what we have to figure out."

Jack returned to the kitchen. "Your dad said they'd be right over."

Eleanor nodded.

"Would you'd like me to notify Ted's mother?" Jack asked.

"Yes, maybe that would be best."

"What time did your husband leave this morning?" I asked.

"I'm not sure exactly. He was gone by the time I got home at 7:45," she said.

"Where were you so early?" I asked.

"At the dairy," she said.

"What time did you leave?"

"After 6:30."

"Did your husband go fishing often?" I asked.

Jack said, "Humph. Every morning."

"Almost—never on Sundays," Eleanor corrected, "but, yes, he's a fishing fanatic. He goes out year round—pulls an ice house out on the lake as soon as the ice is thick enough."

"Do you know if he always used the public landing on Emmaline?" I asked.

Two nods.

"And that was well known?" I asked.

"Yes, I suppose it was," Eleanor said.

"Do you know of anyone your husband had a quarrel with?" I asked.

She hesitated, looked at us deliberately before she said no, which made me believe she wasn't telling us something.

"Does Ted have an appointment book, briefcase, or address book here at home?" I asked.

"His briefcase might be in his office upstairs. I'll check."

Jack started rapping the table with his beefy fingers until he lapsed into a small coughing fit. A couple minutes later Eleanor handed Jack a soft black leather briefcase.

"His appointments are all on the computer at the office," she said.

"Does he have many employees?" I asked.

"Just Lisa Kelly, his secretary. I'll call her," she said.

"I'll need to talk to her. I'd appreciate the number and her address, if you have it handy," I said.

She wrote the information on a Post-it and handed it to me.

"How long had she worked for Mr. Kohler?" I asked.

"About a year."

"Did your husband ever mention problems with a client?" I asked.

"No, never."

"Any issues with alcohol or drugs?"

"No."

"How about finances?"

"No problems there," she said.

"Any marital problems? Affairs?"

"No."

"You're sure that there wasn't a conflict of any kind with an individual or within in an organization or . . ."

"She already answered that," Jack snapped.

Then in the doorway appeared a cute little girl about age five. She disappeared, and three seconds later, five children entered the kitchen. The tallest girl, who looked like her father, said, "Mom, what's going on?"

It was at that moment I first noticed Eleanor blinking away tears.

"I'll tell you shortly, Alicia. Now, please wait in the living room until our business is completed," Eleanor said.

"Why? What's happened?" Alicia persisted.

"Alicia, do as I say."

Surprisingly, all five left, but I suppose if a sheriff and a deputy are sitting in your kitchen, even the smallest child knows to comply.

"Kids don't have school today?" I asked.

"Teacher workshop day," she said.

Jack pulled out the warrant. "Eleanor, we have a search warrant for your house, vehicles, and office."

I added, "Phone and bank records, too. The crime lab will stop by the house today. There could be items taken as evidence. You can certainly leave if it's easier on the children."

She looked alarmed. "What would be here?"

"It's just routine, Eleanor," Jack said. "And do you have a key to the office we might borrow?" Jack asked.

"There should be a set in the briefcase," she said.

Jack opened the case, fingered through, and brought out a set of keys.

"Office keys?"

Eleanor Kohler examined them and pointed out the office front door key.

"We'll return these as soon as possible," he said jingling the keys, "and I'll get back to you as soon as we know anything. We can stay until your folks get here," Jack said.

"No, I'm sure you have a lot to do," she said.

I said, "We'll probably need to speak with you again, Mrs. Kohler. I'm so sorry for your loss." I handed her my card and told her if she thought of anything else, to call me.

Jack rapped his knuckles once on the table. "Okay then."

As we left the kitchen, Jack turned to Eleanor and said, "Did I see a new minivan in the driveway?"

"We just got it this week."

"Did you trade the Town Car in? "Jack said.

"No, it's in the body shop. There was a small dent in the driver's door."

"How did he get the dent?" I asked.

Eleanor looked at her feet. "I'm not exactly sure," she said.

And you wouldn't ask?

She was chewing her lower lip. She just wanted us out.

Jack said, "Eleanor, sorry about this. Ted was a good man."

Eleanor nodded, tears resurfacing.

She closed the door behind us.

When we left the house I walked over and briefly looked inside the Odyssey. The exterior was immaculate. I knew crime lab would look through it so I walked around to the sheriff's car and noticed a few pebbles of gravel in the tires. I popped a couple out and placed them in an evidence envelope I had in my pocket.

I still had the cruiser keys and saw that the sheriff was already sitting in the passenger seat. The man likes a chauffer. I backed out of the driveway. "Now that was the calmest reaction I've seen," I said.

"You don't suspect her, do you?" he asked.

"Most people break down. Her tires had gravel stuck in the treads. Where would she pick up gravel in town?" I said.

"People react differently to sudden death. You can always run by the dairy to check if she was there."

"I will."

He shook his head and said, "Let's go back to put the briefcase into evidence and pass the warrant and the keys off to the Rouch woman. I'd hoped they'd send Jim Wilson instead of her." He sighed.

"Shouldn't we notify Mrs. Kohler of her son's death first?"

"I'll do that after you drop yourself off."

He didn't want me along. I glanced up at the house and saw the youngest boy looking out a window. He couldn't be more than six. I was determined to find his daddy's killer.

4

W HEN WE PULLED INTO the sheriff's reserved parking spot, I spotted
the local media vehicles. Mac Simmons, editor of the local weekly
paper, *Prairie Falls Times Journal*, and Jim Logan, from WRPF, the local radio
station, exited the front doors of Simmons's car. Then who should pop out of
the *Birch County Register* van—but the Lewis woman who rear-ended me. She
presented a press credential for the county's only daily paper, and introduced
herself as a reporter. Huh. Vince Swanson, a photographer for the paper stayed
in the vehicle. The three reporters began firing questions at us.

Jack held up his hand. "No comment yet, folks. You'll be the first I'll notify."

Ms. Lewis smiled flirtatiously at Jack and handed him a card. "Victoria
Lewis. I look forward to your call, sheriff."

As we walked into the Sheriff's Department building, he looked at her
card. "She's new."

"Yes, I believe she is."

"She's . . . what you kids call . . . hot?"

"She is that."

"Well, she must be a member of the Lewis family who owns the *Register*
and several other newspapers across the country. Things are changing."

I didn't even bother to ask what he meant by that because I had a feeling
it was sexist.

Jack took the elevator to the third floor and went directly to the evidence room.
I wanted to check the contents of the briefcase after the deputy in charge logged
all the items into the database. He'd attach a barcode label to each and as we
wanted to examine items, we'd need to sign them out on the chain of custody
log.

Jack emptied the contents of the briefcase and fingered through it. "Doesn't
appear to be anything significant. Go have something to eat," said Jack.

AS I MADE MY WAY to my assigned Explorer, Ralph drove up and rolled down
his window. "So, you're gonna need a new vehicle."

"I drove the Civic one hundred eighty-three thousand miles and never had a collision—until today."

"Impressive. If I were young like you, I'd buy the red Mustang convertible Daniels has in the showroom. The ladies like those."

I smiled. "But the gas mileage . . ."

"Screw the gas mileage. Buy something fun. You can be practical when you're old like me."

I laughed. I was born practical.

"You should get pre-approval on your car loan. First National will cut you a deal if you mention you're with the department."

"Good to know."

"Did you get anything from any of the neighbors?" I asked him.

"Only caught the Albrights at home. They're newly retired. Going back out later this afternoon. Have you eaten yet?" Ralph asked.

"Just goin' to get a bite," I said.

"Hop in."

"Things winding up out at the scene?" I asked.

"Pretty much. They were bringing the trucks, boat, and trailer into the county garage when I left. So, tell me about your accident," Ralph said.

I gave him the condensed version.

"Victoria Lewis, eh? Don't know the name."

"She's a new reporter for the *Register*."

"Ah," he said. "You can bet if you rear-ended her, it'd end up on the front page."

I laughed. "You're probably right."

We drove one block south and down old Main Street. Within the last two years, the exterior of most shops received a facelift with the help of grants. The city adopted new strict guidelines on storefronts and signage, invested in banners that changed with the seasons and holidays, and hung large flower baskets in the summer down Main. Prairie Falls was ready for an influx of tourists.

"Downtown looks nice with the changes," I said.

"Thanks to the new progressive city council members willing to spend a little money. For several years running, we fought a few old-timers and their don't-change-our-town policies. Did you read the article in the paper noting downtown retail sales were already up this year?"

He pulled up the side parking lot of Dotty's Café on east Main Street. It was a short block from the Birch River that used to border the north and west edges of town before the newer developments were built. The yellow, freestanding cafe had an old Ski Doo perched on the roof. Legend has it that the snow was so deep one year, Dotty's husband drove it right up on the roof, and there it stayed.

The council didn't ask Dotty to change. They knew it'd ruin the ambiance. Entering the restaurant was like walking back in time—I'm talking decades. A combination of grease, food, and cigarette odor lingered from a time when customers could light up with their morning coffee. Sunlight spilled through the storefront windows onto the black-and-white tiled floor. Dark-red Naugahyde booths lined the right side of the café all the way to the rear wall. On the opposite side was a long counter. Four retired locals sat on stools drinking coffee and rolling dice. Several empty tables for four filled the area between.

It was late for lunch, after 3:00 p.m. Ralph and I sat a booth in the center of the restaurant. Ida, undoubtedly the skinniest person in Prairie Falls, approached with two laminated menus edged in red tucked under an arm, and two red plastic glasses of ice water balanced in one hand. I drank my water down without taking a breath.

Ida was pushing seventy. Her black hair was pulled up into a knot on the top of her head—the ends, darker than the rest, stuck straight out like pins in a cushion. Her eyebrows were drawn on in black, thin arches giving her a look of surprise. She set the menus in front of us.

"Special today is the hot beef sandwich with a side salad." Her bass voice reflected way too many cartons of cigarettes. She stayed, waiting for us to make up our minds on the spot.

Ralph said, "Well, then, that's what I'll have—with blue cheese and coffee." She stared at me tapping her order pad with her pencil.

"I'll have chili, a grilled cheese, and milk, please."

Ida could write and chew gum at the same time. She'd had lots of practice. She briefly scribbled on her pad and left.

Dotty, an extra large blonde and owner of the establishment, came from kitchen, scraped a chair across the floor from the table next to us, plopped her generous behind down and said, "Hi, Ralph." She then turned her attention to me and said, "Hello, Deputy Eye Candy." I blushed every time.

"Yeah, that's what we call him at the department, too," Ralph said.

"Oh, I'd lift my nightie for you too, Ralph honey."

Whoa! I don't welcome that image. But I did enjoy seeing Ralph blush.

"Now, what's this I hear about murders out on Emmaline?" she asked.

"You know my lips are sealed, Dotty," said Ralph.

"Well, rumor has it one's Ted Kohler. It's got everybody scared so you better find the killer real fast so the town business doesn't dry up."

"Way to put the pressure on, Dotty," I said.

She nodded. "I'm serious. It could be bad for us." She scraped the chair back to the other table and waddled back to the kitchen.

"See, she'd lift her nightie for you too," I whispered.

He snorted. "Shoot, I had to think of cleaning fish to knock that picture out of my brain."

I laughed. "I won't let you forget that one."

"I'm sure you won't."

"Man, news travels fast."

"News is in the paper before it happens," he said, chuckling.

"People say Kohler was a nice guy."

"Yeah, real friendly. Always had a smile and a wave for ya. Model citizen— did a lot of community work, sponsored a Little League team, active in Lions Club and in his church."

"His wife says he didn't have any problems with anyone. Way I figure it, if you're alive you have some kind of conflict. Now for Ronny, conflict was normal. He was always riling somebody."

Ralph nodded. "You're right. The Kohlers are really respected in town so this is going to hit the community hard."

Ida refilled our water glasses and sashayed off.

He sat back. "So, are you seeing anyone now?"

I screwed up my nose. "What was that segue?"

"I don't know. I guess all that eye candy talk made me think about how you and Adriana were a good-looking couple. So, if you're not seeing anybody, Liz could set you up again," he said.

Here we go again. Since Adriana Valero and I parted ways last summer everyone seems to feel the need to set me up.

"Frankly, I'm on blind date overload. So, no thanks," I said.

"Maybe you're just too damn picky. What was wrong with Heather?"

"Have you ever been to her house?"

"Can't say that I have," he said.

"She's a doll collector"

"So?"

"So she has like a thousand of those suckers everywhere on shelves—staring down at you with their beady little eyes—like Chucky. No more set ups, Ralph."

He sat back and gave out a good belly laugh. "So, you've had enough?" he said. "Oh yeah."

Ida brought our food. After we'd finished, she walked back with two pieces of pie a la mode and the check. "Dotty says these are on the house. Fresh blueberry just baked this morning."

My belly registered full, but when I looked at Dotty's blueberry pie, my brain said there was topping-off room.

"Tell Dotty thanks," Ralph said.

Dotty was at the pass through window from the kitchen. I lifted my fork and said, "Thanks, Dotty. You're the best!" I took another forkful. "You need to wear sweatpants when you eat in here."

As Ralph finished his pie, he patted his paunch. "That was good eats." He picked up the check. "This is on me today. Celebrate your first two months on the Investigations Team."

"Thanks, Ralph, and thanks for bringing me in on this one. Troy will be pissed he was in Vegas."

"He has his hands full with the Drug Task Force, anyway. I just hope we can solve this, period."

"But don't you think we have some pretty good evidence?" I asked.

"What seems like good evidence can take us nowhere fast . . . but yeah, I think we have a little to help us."

He gave me a ride to Daniels Ford so I could pick up a rental, then I drove the gold Taurus back to the department, parked it, and signed out my assigned tan Explorer. I drove over to Stillmans' Dairy on the west side to confirm Eleanor's story, and the first thing I noticed was that the parking lot was graveled. Now why didn't Jack just tell me that?

I'd never been in the dairy. They sold many different items beside dairy products: poultry, eggs, bread, some canned goods. The woman behind the counter wore a white shirt with CANDY embroidered in red above the pocket. I showed her my ID and asked her if she could verify Eleanor Kohler's purchases.

She narrowed her eyes, pursed her lips, and her arms crossed across her chest. "What in the world for?"

I smiled politely and asked her to show me the cash register receipt.

"For heaven sakes," she said, staring me down. "I didn't know it was a crime to buy milk and butter." She finally gave in and opened a drawer and fingered through the receipts.

"This is hers, she always pays with a debit card. Never a problem." She handed the receipt to me. I checked the time. 6:51 a.m. I took a photo of it.

"Could I please have your name, ma'am?" I asked.

She glared.

"For my records," I said.

"Candy."

"Last name?"

"Stillman," she said, disdainfully.

"Thank you. That wasn't so hard, was it?"

I forced a smile and walked out thinking they should keep Candy Stillman in the back killing chickens. As I stooped to pick up gravel samples, I glanced back to see her watching me through the glass door. I gave her a finger wave, but she didn't lift a hand off her hefty hips.

BY THE TIME I RETURNED to the department, several media crews from across the state were parked in the front lot. I drove on by and pulled around to the back lot, and entered through the back security door. I stopped by the evidence room to check in the gravel sample. I called Larry Sauer, my friend and apartment manager, to ask if he'd feed and let out my yellow lab, Bullet. Because he considered himself Bullet's co-owner, he jumped at every opportunity. He had a dog bed, treats, and a bag of food both in the office and apartment above mine.

We had our case meetings in the large, third-floor conference room, across from the investigations office. I spent time sketching the crime scene on a corner of the white board that covered most of the north wall. I noted the location of both bodies. Betty brought me photos of the victims. I placed them at the location on my sketch where the bodies were found. As I started a list of what I knew about each victim, Dotty's comment came to mind: "Everyone's scared."

People are worried there could be more killings. So am I—we don't know what went down.

5

A T SIX O'CLOCK, Leslie Rouch, Betty Abbott, and I were chatting in the conference room, waiting for Ralph and Jack. When they entered together, Jack threw down his brown-leather Franklin Covey on the large oak table. The *whack* silenced the room. He ran his fingers through his thinning hair and said, "As I thought would be the case, the press is hot on this one. I don't want anyone giving out any statements, except Oliver Bakken or me." Bakken was the county attorney.

No problemo.

Ralph began by stating the case number and victims. "Cal, thanks for starting things on the whiteboard. Leslie, how about you start?"

"Okay. The doc doing the autopsies called me with something he thought we should know—Kohler has some contusions on his chest, back, and abdominal areas—possibly a week old."

"Did Eleanor mention anything about that?" Ralph said, looking at me.

"No, not a thing," Jack said. "Maybe he fell or something."

Ralph wrote in his notebook. "We'll have to find out. Okay, by way of evidence, we have five casings and three bullets—one recovered from the dock, one in a tree trunk, and one still in Peterson. I don't suppose the bullet in the dock passed through Kohler." Ralph said.

"Not likely with the point of entrance, but the two recovered are Winchester .30-30, 150 grams," Leslie said. "Those that passed through Kohler's body and are most likely in the lake."

"We need authorization to order a dive team to search the lake for the bullets, Jack," Betty said.

"I won't authorize funds for that," the sheriff said.

Betty looked at Jack like he was crazy.

Ralph said, "I suppose that'd be quite an undertaking. Who knows how far that bullet traveled?"

"You have three other bullets to work with. When we gonna get the one in Peterson?" Jack said.

"I'll ask. We should have the final autopsy reports in a few days, toxicology screens in a week, " Leslie said.

Ralph cleared his throat. "Good, it's just that we'd like everything *yesterday*."

"Understood," she said.

He continued. "Well, I talked to a few residents. Jack's son's wife, Sarah, and the Albrights were home. They agree they heard six shots: three, then approximately ten minutes later, three more. Bob Brutlag was home but didn't hear the shots. Martins weren't home, but Del says during duck hunting nobody thinks much of hearing gunshots."

Even though shotguns used for waterfowl (now in season) and rifles used for large game (not in season) sound completely different—the *pow* of a shotgun verses the *crack* of a rifle.

"And Jack's son Ben was at Cadillac Jack's by then," Ralph said.

The restaurant was co-owned by Jack and Ben, but since Jack was elected sheriff, Ben took over as manager.

"Now, let's discuss who we need to interview and what direction to go. Cal, write down the list on the whiteboard. I'll take notes, then make copies for everyone."

Ralph pulled out his laptop, and I stood, grabbed a marker and turned to the whiteboard.

"I had both victims' home and work phone records run but haven't had time to look at them," Ralph said. "We'll get bank records on Monday. Let's get our interview list started."

As I wrote on the white board, Ralph assigned interviews to either himself or me. I was to take Bob Brutlag, Ronny's boss, and co-workers. I wasn't exactly overjoyed when Jack said he'd be sitting in on the Brutlag interview. Ralph was looking into Kohler's business records and interviewing Kohler's family, in-laws, and secretary. Since I saw his kids and heard about the bruising in his mid-section, I had more of an interest in Kohler, but it wasn't my decision.

"We'll meet back here tomorrow at 8:00 a.m. and see what we've got at that point."

After, I went into the office to check my phone messages. I'm a rule follower so I don't use my department cell phone for personal use, which means I carry two and have to check both for messages. My own iPhone had no messages. The department cell included a message from V. Lewis. Not sure if it was an attempt to pump me for information or about the crash, I returned her call.

"Oh, hi! Thanks for calling back," she said. "Look, I feel so awful about the accident, I'm going to buy you dinner."

That was unexpected—and presumptuous. Yeah, I suspected she wanted to pump me for information.

"Thanks, but that's not necessary," I said.

"But I *want* to."

"Sorry, I already have plans."

"Oh."

To fill the silence that followed I asked if she'd contacted her insurance company.

"It's all being taken care of. Another time for dinner?"

"Ah . . . maybe," I said and hung up. That was weird—but the invitation fed my ego and I found myself smiling.

NO ONE ANSWERED Peterson's doorbell or phone. I left a message expressing my condolences and requested an interview at their earliest convenience.

I then drove over to the department garage where they'd taken Kohler's truck, trailer, and boat, and the Parks' department truck Ronny had driven. I found Leslie lifting prints off Kohler's door handles.

"This truck's the cleanest vehicle I've ever seen in my entire life," she said. "Only thing out of place, a Prairie Falls First National Bank pen under the passenger seat, but I found something tucked in the owner's manual you should see."

She handed me a piece of computer paper in a plastic evidence bag. I read it aloud.

"The day one dies is better than the day one is born! It is better to spend your time at funerals than at festivals. For you are going to die and it is a good thing to think about it while there is still time. Kyrie Eleison"

"Holy shit. You found this in Kohler's truck?"

She nodded.

"Kyrie Eleison. Latin?" I asked.

"Yes, it means 'Lord have mercy.'"

"That's interesting. You didn't find Peterson's cell phone?"

"No."

"Strange, he didn't have it on him and it wasn't in the truck. I'll ask his boss about it when I talk to her."

"That would be good to find."

"Did you take prints from the park restroom?"

"We tried. Strangely, there were none."

"Really?"

"We expected to see at least smudges, but the surfaces were all wiped clean."

"Maybe the killer waited in there and wiped it down after."

Immediately after I left Leslie, I called Ronny's boss, Naomi Moberg, who agreed to meet me at her office in fifteen minutes. Naomi and her ex were in my golf couples league. She'd had a rough year. After her mother died, her husband, Jeremy, left her for his young secretary. Personally, I always liked Naomi more than her arrogant prick of a husband.

The County Parks offices were located on the west side of town near the County Maintenance Buildings. The parking lot was empty except for Naomi's blue Prius. She was waiting for me just inside the glass doors. She always looks like she'd just walked out of a beauty salon. She claims she's an outdoorsy kind of gal, but her jeans, black V-neck knit top, and black high-heeled boots were as outdoorsy as I've seen her wear.

I followed Naomi a short distance through a door behind the receptionist's desk down a hall.

"Isn't this absolutely horrible?" she said. "You never think it'll happen in your town to people you know."

"Yeah, it's a shocker. How's your staff handling it?"

"Everyone's pretty upset and rightly so. I called a meeting early this afternoon to let them know before they heard it on the news."

"Good idea."

When we entered her large corner office, she gestured for me to sit in a gray fabric armed chair across from her desk. She smiled faintly, tapping her long, red fingernails on the wood desktop.

"Your desk is as tidy as mine," I said.

"I'm a bit of a perfectionist," she said laughing.

"Me, too."

I pulled out my recorder and notebook and turned on the recorder, giving the date, time, place, and case number, then asked Naomi to give her full name, position—that sort of thing. She sat straight in her chair like she had a rod up her back. I gave her a little smile, trying to put her at ease.

"How long had Ronald Peterson worked under you?"

"I hired him two years ago."

"What kind work did he do?"

"Park maintenance."

"Why was he out in Lake Emmaline County Park this morning?"

"He was going to be taking in the dock."

"Was he going to do this himself?"

"No, Gus Taylor was supposed to help, but when he got to Emmaline, the Sheriff's Department sent him away. He called to tell me the park was closed for an investigation, and at that point, I didn't know what it was about. No one would tell me anything. Later, Ralph called me."

"What sort of a worker was he?"

She hesitated. I waited. Then she sighed and spoke quietly. "All right."

"Meaning?"

"Meaning sometimes he showed up late for work, but always managed to quit on time, and didn't always follow directions."

"Employee of the month?"

She sat back and smiled. "Not exactly."

"Did he get along with the other workers?"

"Usually, but there were some complaints, especially from the veterans."

"An example?"

"Okay, here's one: Ronny and Gus Taylor were supposed to pull the dock at Emmaline *yesterday*. I just happened to drive out late in the afternoon to check if the trails were holding up, and I saw the frickin' dock was still there, so I called Gus and asked him why. He said he was waiting on Ronny, who was supposed to be done clearing brush at Birch County South with Harvey Kling. Then it got late, so Gus said they might as well wait until this morning. The whole thing was ridiculous. That job at South was a two-hour job at most. After I chewed Gus out, I called Ronny and told him he needed to get his sorry ass where and when he was assigned. I feel really awful—those were my last words to him."

"You had a job to do, Naomi."

She looked at her fingernails then up at me. "That's probably why he was there so early this morning." The pain in her eyes told me she was having trouble forgiving herself.

"I thought he was going to be late because of a dentist appointment. So when Ralph Martinson called to tell me Ronny had been shot out at Emmaline, I checked the log to make sure he had the right guy."

"Quick dentist appointment?"

"No, it was canceled. The hygienist had called in sick. When I went over to tell his mother, she was *sure* I was mistaken—she immediately called the dental office to prove me wrong. So then she blamed the hygienist. She said *if* she'd come to work, her son would still be alive."

"Unless he was the primary target, then it would have happened later."

"Geez, I hadn't thought of that," she said.

"So, did Ronny have a department cell phone?"

"Yes, all full timers do."

"It wasn't on him or in his truck."

She looked puzzled. "Huh. Maybe he left it at home."

"Maybe. Can you give me the number of his phone?"

"Sure," she said. She opened her desk drawer, and pulled out a sheet, then wrote the number on a Post-it for me.

"Did Gus and Ronny work together a lot?"

"When the job called for two guys, I paired Ronny with either Harvey or Gus because they kept Ronny in line better than anyone."

"Did Ronny have a drug problem you're aware of?"

"I thought I smelled marijuana on him once and warned him if I ever smelled it again I'd not only fire his ass, but I'd call the sheriff as well. Then I put out a memo that we would be doing random drug tests."

"How long ago was that?"

"Maybe six months. I documented it just in case." She pulled a file out of her desk drawer.

"And did you do the drug testing?"

"No."

"This is his file. Do you want a copy?"

"Let me take a look." I glanced through the pages.

"I can't see anything that'd help, but I'll give you a call if my boss thinks it's necessary. What are the maintenance workers' hours?"

"I'm flexible on hours as long as they get in eight hours, but most work eight to five with an hour off for lunch," she said, as she played with a hoop earring.

"Do you know what time Ronny signed out the truck this morning?"

"Seven-fifteen."

I handed her my card. "Look, if you think of anything else that might help us, no matter how insignificant it seems, give me a call."

"I do have one question."

"What is it?"

"Have you had dinner?"

"No, but Benson asked me over for pizza. Her kids want to see my dog."

Naomi smiled. "Is that right?"

"Yeah ... you know we're just friends." Why I felt compelled to explain, I wasn't sure.

"Would you consider going out for dinner with me when you're not bringing your dog over to see Benson's kids?"

"Sure, sounds good."

"Tomorrow night?"

I nodded, "All right."

I accepted because I didn't want to hurt her feelings, or maybe Tamika's remark about "my type" struck a nerve and I wanted to prove her wrong— though I usually don't date women with kids because they complicate things.

Naomi drummed her nails on her desk.

My phone signaled a text message: It was from my mother: *R U on the big murder case?* I answered: *yes can't talk now.*

"My mom."

Naomi looked like she didn't believe me. "Anyway, call tomorrow night when you're ready for dinner—no matter how late. I'm thinking it's time I start getting out there again, and I can't think of a man I'd rather be with than you."

I felt my face flush from the flattery. "Okay. Is a half hour's notice okay?"

"I'll be waiting."

Why is it feast or famine where women are concerned? Wonder what Adriana would say if she knew I had a date with Naomi. And why did I care?

THE KLINGS LIVED in a small rambler on the north side of town still referred to the "new side" even though the homes are circa 1970s. I passed Shannon Benson's house on the way.

Only a few leaves remained on the Kling's manicured lawn. Harvey's wife answered the door, and, after I introduced myself, she brought me through the immaculate house to the basement family room where Harvey sat in a brown-leather recliner. First thing I noticed was his large, bulbous nose. He was holding a beer and watching a poker tournament on TV. He stood to shake my hand—he had big hands for an average size guy.

He held up his beer and asked, "Want one?"

"No thanks. I'm on the clock."

He nodded, then pointed to a clean but dated turquoise-and-magenta plaid couch where Mrs. Kling was already seated. She wasn't going to miss this.

"Harv, turn off the TV," Mrs. Kling demanded.

Harvey lowered the volume but defied the order to shut it off. He was slim like his wife. Both looked to be in their mid-sixties, so "Harv" must be near retirement.

"I understand you worked with Ronny Peterson yesterday."

He nodded. "We cleared brush at South until 1:00 because he worked so damn slow. I wouldn't break for lunch until we were done. He didn't like that."

"Did he ever indicate any problems he was having with anyone?"

"Nah, but he wouldn't tell me if he did because he knew I didn't want to hear it."

"You know of anyone who had a grudge against him?"

"I 'spect he ruffled feathers wherever he went."

"Did he ruffle your feathers?"

"I didn't like him enough to let him get to me."

"Harv," his wife scolded.

"Just telling the truth."

"What truck did you sign out yesterday?"

"I always take 20."

"Today as well?"

"Yep."

"Did you notice if Ronny left his cell phone in it?"

"I clean out the truck everyday when I'm done, and don't let him leave so much as a crumb. I don't like clutter."

"Me neither. And where were you this morning from approximately 6:30 a.m. to 8:00?"

"Me and the missus walked to Dotty's where we meet some friends every Friday morning for breakfast. After, I went straight to work."

The missus nodded her head.

NEXT, I DROVE OUT to the Taylor farm on the western edge of town to speak with Gus Taylor. As I parked in the gravel yard, a mixed-breed dog came running off the porch of the old white farmhouse. He barked twice then wagged his tail when I exited my vehicle.

"Some watchdog," I said as I leaned over and let him sniff my hand. I gave him a good scratch behind the ears. When I stood, he ran ahead, escorting me to the front door. I knocked. Exterior lights flicked on and Gus opened the door. He wore a faded red sweatshirt that barely stretched across his gut—his jeans hovered just below that. A bachelor, probably fifty, he looked ten years older.

"Hi, Gus. Sorry about Ronny."

"Yeah. What the hell's this world comin' to, eh? A guy gets shot at a park just doing his job?"

"I know, right?"

His dog bumped my hand with his snout. I reached down to pet him. "Nice dog. He probably smells mine on me. What's his name?"

"Spinner."

"Mind if I ask you a few questions?"

"Nope, come on in."

He led me through the cluttered porch and living room and into an equally cluttered kitchen where we sat at an oval table stacked with newspapers and magazines. He cleared a place by making higher stacks.

"Want a beer?" he asked.

I did, but still declined.

His eyes widened as I turned on the recorder and stated the necessary information. He sat back and crossed his arms over his belly.

"Gus, I understand you and Ronny were to pull the dock from the public landing at Lake Emmaline this morning?"

"Yeah, we was gonna go out there after his dentist appointment but he called and said they canceled it and he was ready. I told him I was having my breakfast and if he didn't want to wait for me he could start without me."

"Were you home?"

"No, McDonalds."

"So was the original plan to meet at the garage or at the lake?"

"At the garage so we could ride together, but he was always trying to change things to his liking. It sorta pissed me off. I ain't proud to say I took my time."

"Driving separately today may have saved your life."

Gus nodded. "Man, I'll be honest with ya—that thought crossed my mind."

"So, what time did you leave for Emmaline?"

"After eight, but when I got out there the deputies turned me away. Wouldn't tell me why. I figured it was a drug bust or something. Maybe even Ronny."

"Have you evidence he used drugs?"

"Just what I've heard, but he knew better than to try that shit around me."

"You know of drug activity out at Emmaline?"

"We'd find drug paraphernalia—needles, aluminum foil, glass tubes—in all the parks."

"Tell me about Ronny."

Gus's forehead furrowed. "I hate to speak ill of the dead, but he was one of those guys who made his own trouble. He was a bully and lazier than shit. I thought it kinda funny he didn't seem to know he didn't get along with people."

"Explain."

"Tried to tell *me* how to do *my* job. I had to let him know he wasn't the boss. Then he backed off."

"How did you accomplish that?"

"One day I'd had enough of his mouth, so I told him to shut the fuck up or I'd take him by the balls and throw his ass out the moving truck. O'course, I'd never do it, but he didn't know that. Worked." He winked.

"Did he tell you about any recent incidents with others?"

"He was always jabbering. I just tuned him out."

"Did you know Ted Kohler?"

"He belongs to St. Stephens too, but he didn't talk to me or nothing. You know Ronny went there too?"

"No."

Harvey and Gus had no love for Ronny. If their alibis checked out, both would be off my suspect list.

IT WAS ALMOST NINE when I called Shannon to ask if it was too late to come over. She said the boys would have a bloody fit if we didn't. So, I stopped to buy a six-pack of Miller Light Lime and Clamato juice before the liquor store closed, then picked up Bullet.

As I pulled up into the driveway, both boys ran out to greet us. Luke, the eight-year-old, grabbed Bullet by the collar and led him into their fenced backyard. Colby, the six-year-old, bounded after.

I walked through the opened door. "Benson?"

"Hi," she said meeting me in the entryway.

"Sorry I'm so late. Brought beer, Clamato, and limes," I said following her to the kitchen where I put the bag on the counter.

"Ahh, that's nice of you! Thanks. I already fed the boys, but I kept the pizza warm for us."

After she opened a couple beers and made a Clamato for herself, we moved into the family room and ate pizza from her coffee table. The family's two orange tabby cats, Roy and Dale, sauntered in and rubbed up against my legs, then both jumped up on an arm of the chair.

"You're surrounded," Shannon said. "They love you. Want to trade pets?"

"I think they just want pizza, and besides Bullet's my running buddy. Cats aren't exactly eager to jog."

"They're easier to take care of, but suit yourself."

"You had first pick, Benson. Besides you'd have to fight Larry for him."

Bullet and the cats were rescued from a hoarder's home a couple years ago. Shannon and I had taken the call that Fred Paisley was passed out on the sidewalk. He'd lost his wife two years ago and in his grief stuck his head in a whiskey bottle and never came out. When we gave him a ride home, we discovered the horrid conditions he and his three pets lived in. Amazingly, the dog and cats were still in good health, but Fred was placed in a chemical dependency treatment center—and his house was condemned. Currently, he's doing well living in a senior apartment building. I check on him every now and then and bring Bullet along for visits.

After a while the boys and Bullet came running in and tore upstairs. From above we could hear bumps, thumps, screams and shouts, but Benson's philosophy was as long as there's no blood or broken bones, ignore it.

"How's the case stacking up? Do you have any leads?" she asked.

I sighed. "Nothing yet. Did you know Kohler?"

"Not personally, but I used to work out with Eleanor at the Y before the department built our gym."

"What's she like?"

"She's all about organic and home-grown foods. I know they're active in their church. She seems really down to earth."

"And what do you know about Bob Brutlag?"

"Good mechanic, rough exterior. Is he a suspect?"

"Everybody's a suspect. Ever hear of him being violent?" I asked.

"Nah, he's a pretty amiable guy," Benson said.

"Not Ronny."

"God no. Remember a year ago I arrested him for battery at Buzzo's?"

"What was the deal again?"

"He picked a fight with a pal of Nevada Wynn's, by the name of Pierce Redding. The charges were dropped when Redding skipped town."

"What do you know about Redding?"

"He was in town only a short time. I had a feeling he was a real bad guy and Ronny didn't know who he was messing with."

"Was Ronny a user?" I asked.

"Never caught him, but that doesn't mean anything. So, you seem like you were in your element today—investigating these murders."

"My juices are flowing again. Up until now, the investigations have been kind of routine."

"It got you off dog-watch." She smiled.

I laughed. "You know I loved dog-watch—more action. It was Adriana who didn't like me bidding on night shift."

"Hard to manage a relationship with those hours."

"But now I can get called in anytime, even days off."

"Would you give it up for a woman or a family, Cal?" she asked.

"What kind of question is that?"

Screeching from above saved me. We both looked at the ceiling as if we had x-ray vision. Predictably, the boys bounded down the stairs, one brother accusing the other of not sharing Bullet.

"Maybe it's time to say good night to Bullet," I told the boys.

"Can he sleep over?" Luke asked.

"Not tonight," Shannon said. "Now, go get your pajamas on and Uncle Cal and Bullet will come up and say good night before they leave."

When they'd disappeared up the stairs, I teased Shannon by saying, "We could both stay."

She made a dismissive face.

I pointed my finger at her. "Hey, you should be so lucky. I'll have you know I got hit on twice today."

"Oh, yeah?"

"You sound surprised."

"Not at all. You have women waiting to pounce on you like black flies."

"Black flies? *That's* the simile you come up with?"

"Bees to honey?"

"That's better."

"So are you going to tell me the honeybees' names?" she asked.

"The woman who rear-ended me—and Naomi Moberg."

Her lips curled in a slight smile. "Neither surprises me. Tamika said that young woman was falling all over herself trying to get your attention, and just last week Naomi asked me about you."

"What did she say?"

"Wanted to know if we have 'a thing' going on."

"What did you say?"

"That we were just friends."

"Why would she ask that? Everybody knows we're friends."

"That's what I wanted to know. She said because we golfed as a couple on the league last summer. She asked me if we were friends with benefits."

"Seriously? Were you girls tipping cups at the time?"

"Actually, we were. Girls' night."

"Was Tamika there?"

"Yeah, why?"

"Today she said she didn't understand why we never got together."

"What did you tell her?"

"I said we both agreed it'd ruin our friendship."

"I'm a firm believer no one I work with should cross my Mason-Dixon line."

"Oh, really? Your Mason-Dixon line? Well, there was that once," I said—and at once regretted it.

She looked embarrassed. "I don't know what you're talking about. So, is the woman who rear-ended you using her feminine charms to help you *forget* all about the accident?"

"Ha, ha. No, she said felt bad about the crash. But since she's a reporter for the *Register*, I figure she just wants to ply information out of me while having hot sex. Now, getting back to this Mason-Dixon line—where is that exactly? Your belly button?" I touched her waist.

She shoved my hand away. "What's with you tonight? Don't you have to get on your way?"

"Not before I whistle some Dixie—I'm a Dixie Doodle Dandy."

"That's Yankee Doodle Dandy, stupid."

"I have a dandy doodle."

She gave me a shove. "Get upstairs and say good-bye to the boys."

I did as I was told. On the way down stairs I whistled *I Wish I Was in Dixie*, and Shannon escorted me all the way out the door. I heard the lock click. Geez.

On the drive home I thought about the night Shannon and I made love. It was a week after Evan died. We were sitting on her couch. I had my arm around her, comforting her, and before we knew it clothes were flying off. She wept afterward, and I felt like a shit. I shouldn't have brought it up. I also thought about her question: *Would you trade it all for a woman or a family?* I'd like to think I wouldn't be with anyone who'd ask me to.

6

DAY TWO

I T WAS LIKE THE MEDIA vans had procreated overnight, doubling in number. I again took the back security entrance and headed straight to the Investigations office. Ralph was already at his cluttered desk.

"Morning. Get your interviews in?" he asked.

"Naomi Moberg, Harvey Kling, and Gus Taylor. The Petersons weren't answering doors or phones."

"Don't blame 'em—they just lost their boy, and I'm sure the media is bugging them. Well, we better head to the meeting."

"Do I have time to try the Petersons again and see if I can talk to them today?"

"Sure, I'll be in the conference room."

Mrs. Peterson answered and agreed to an interview at their home at 1:00.

Ralph and Leslie Rouch were in the conference room, both paging through notes. Jack Whitman entered and tossed two plastic bags of cake doughnuts on the table.

"Dixie sent these," he said.

Georgia, Jack's secretary, was right behind him wheeling in a cart with two coffee carafes and a pitcher of water, and cups. She was a pleasant woman in her fifties with pure white hair she said turned by age forty when her daughter turned fifteen.

"Thanks, Georgia, you're a peach," Jack said—as he always did. She gave him a tiny smile.

"Do you need me anymore, Sheriff?" she asked.

"Nope, you can go."

Georgia nodded. "All right then. We have a choir rehearsal this morning—we're having a special prayer service tonight for Ted and Ronny. They were both members of St. Stephens, you know. Such a sad time for everyone."

"That it is. Thanks for coming in this morning. See you Monday," said Jack.

Then he turned to us. "Austin Spanney called me last night. Said dozens of people broke through the tape at Emmaline—singing, holding candles. He wanted to know what he should do."

"What did you tell him?" Ralph said.

"Let them be as long as they were peaceful. Figured BRO had what they needed."

Ralph continued. "Hopefully. Anyway, let's get started. I spoke with Kohler's in-laws, Hamilton and Ruth Fairchild. The last time they saw Ted was on Sunday for dinner. He acted like himself and never mentioned any problems. They couldn't think of anyone who would want to harm a well-liked and respected man such as Ted. Ham mentioned all the community service and charities he contributed to." Ralph paged through his notes. "And they were at mass Friday morning when the shootings occurred."

"What time was mass?" I asked.

Ralph checked his notes. "Eight o'clock. I confirmed their attendance with Father Moran."

"Maybe they went to establish the alibi," Leslie said.

I think I just heard Jack say "Bullshit" under his breath. Leslie either didn't hear or was too classy to respond.

"Leslie, I understand you found something of interest in Kohler's truck," Ralph said.

"Yes, in the glove box. Here are copies of the Bible verse I found. We're going to try and pull prints and DNA from it."

"Did you ever locate Ronny's phone?" I asked.

Leslie paged through her notes. "No. It wasn't at his home. Kohler had his on him. We did a quick check and no calls were made or received that morning."

Ralph wrote in his small notebook. "Has your doc looked at Ronny yet?"

"He retrieved the bullet from the spine but that's all. He'll perform one autopsy at a time."

"What did you find out, Cal?" Ralph asked.

I gave a summary of my three interviews.

Ralph said, "So, now we have to reconstruct what may have happened. Anyone have any thoughts?"

"Either one victim was an intended target and the other was an unlucky bystander, or both victims were in the wrong place at the wrong time," I said.

"So what's logical considering what you know about the victims," Leslie asked.

Ralph sat forward. "Kohler was a model citizen. He was just out there fishing before he went to work like he did most mornings."

I said, "And Ronny was a wise-assed kid who shot his mouth off and never turned down a fight, and was a possible drug user. But of course people's lives are often not what they seem and we need to look into *both* victims': their workplaces, relationships, finances, bad habits, secrets, etcetera."

"Exactly," Leslie said.

Jack sat back and crossed his arms. He had a disgruntled look on his face like we were doing something wrong. I wanted to ask him what he was thinking but thought better of it because I wasn't sure I even wanted to know. He had less experience with homicide than Leslie and Ralph did.

We added to our interview list and Ralph adjourned the meeting. "Okay, try to get your interviews done today and tomorrow. Call me with anything new and significant, otherwise we'll meet bright and early Monday morning," Ralph said.

When the room cleared and Ralph and I were alone, I asked him if he heard Jack's "bullshit" remark.

"Yeah, he's under a lot of pressure, but that's no excuse for rudeness."

"Ralph, I didn't mention in the meeting that Eleanor Kohler had fifty-six minutes of unaccounted time but I haven't checked it out."

"Eleanor's on my agenda for today. I'll ask her about it," he said.

7

B OB BRUTLAG WAS my only suspect, and he was due in twenty minutes. While I waited for his arrival, I looked over my notes and questions I'd written on note cards. Jack forged into Interview Room 3, dropping what was left of the doughnuts and a carafe of coffee on the small table, then left without a word. *I guess we're having a coffee party.* Man, I had a bad feeling about Jack being in on this interview.

At 10:03 a.m., a deputy escorted Bob Brutlag in, and I asked if he'd let the sheriff know we were ready. I shook Bob's clammy hand. He smelled of cologne and Listerine. His beard was trimmed down to about a half-inch, and his hair, still damp on the ends, was pulled into a ponytail. He wore a black down jacket, black slacks, and cowboy boots. No Harley gear today.

"How are you this morning, Mr. Brutlag?" I said.

He smiled crookedly. "I'm good. And you?"

"Dandy, thank you."

"There's a real media circus outside, huh? Jack warned me not to say anything to the reporters."

Jack entered carrying three white mugs that clanked as he placed them on the table. Nothing quiet about Jack.

"Take off your jacket and stay a while, Bob," Jack said. "Coffee?"

Bob gave him a wide smile and nodded. Jack poured coffee into a mug and pushed it across the table toward our interviewee leaving a wet streak. Bob took off his jacket revealing sweat stains under the armpits of his blue cotton shirt. He slung the jacket on the back of his chair.

"Those Dixie's doughnuts?" he asked flashing a smile.

"Help yourself," Jack said.

"Great. Dint have breakfast this mornin'," he said as he reached across to grab a doughnut out of the bag. He left a trail of cinnamon sugar and as he lifted the doughnut to his mouth, more dribbled down his shirt. He bit off half in a single bite. He brushed the sugar off the table and from his shirt onto the floor. He sniggered and said, "Sorry 'bout that."

The second bite finished off the doughnut. I impatiently waited until he chewed and swallowed before I started furnishing the case information for the tape. I turned on the small recorder on the table and while I stated the case number, those present, date and time, Bob grabbed another frickin' doughnut. I was pissed Jack brought them into the interview.

"Dixie makes the best damn doughnuts. Don't she?" he said.

He's trying too hard to cover his nervousness—or he's an idiot.

I ignored him and shuffled my note cards.

"Investigator Sheehan will be taking your statement," Jack said.

Bob nodded, his mouth still stuffed with doughnut. Ridiculous.

I said, "We're also video recording for future reference. When you're finished chewing, Mr. Brutlag, we'll start with your name and address."

Bob looked for a camera as he swallowed. He took a sip of coffee, cleared his throat, and then complied, giving his name and address.

"Where were you Friday morning, October 7th?" I asked.

A corner of his mouth turned up—as if the question was humorous. "You know where I was. You saw me."

Jack leaned forward and whispered, " Just part of the process, Bob. Answer the questions even if you think we already know the answers."

Bob snorted. "Gotcha. I was going to go for a walk in the park."

"The park meaning?"

"Emmaline County Park. That what you want me to say?"

"I just want you to answer the questions. What time did you leave your house?"

"Maybe quarter to eight."

"You said you were going for a walk. Where exactly did you plan to go?"

"I walk the trails."

"How often?" I continued.

"Most days, but not always in the morning."

"On October 7th specifically, where did you walk?"

"Down my driveway a ways then I cut across to the landing. I was going to take trail loop and back, but then I saw Ted Kohler laying there in his boat . . . so I stopped and walked home to call 911. Well, actually, I ran." He gave out a little hoarse laugh.

"No mobile phone with you?" I asked.

"I usually carry it, but wouldn't ya know, that morning I forgot the damn thing."

"How close to the victim did you get?"

"On shore next to the boat."

"Did you enter the boat at anytime?"

"No."

"Did you see anyone else in the vicinity?" I asked.

Bob shook his head and said, "Nope."

"Did you hear the gunshots that morning?"

"No, sir."

"You live what? Five hundred yards from the park? And you didn't hear rifle shots?"

"No. I sleep pretty sound."

I stared at him and watched him fidget. "Every little sound could be important. What do you remember seeing or hearing as you approached the park?"

Bob moved his head back and forth in little movements, his eyes cast upward as if he were trying to retrieve the information. His shook his head. "Nothing. Sorry I can't be of more help to youse."

"Do you own firearms?" I asked.

Bob's face dropped as if it was the first time he considered he might be a suspect. "I have two rifles, a Winchester and Remington, plus I have a Browning 410 shotgun."

"Caliber of the rifles?"

"Both .30-30s."

"Would you be willing to surrender your rifles so we can eliminate them as the firearm that killed Mr. Kohler and Mr. Peterson?"

He nodded assent.

Jack sat back in his chair. Bob took another slurp of coffee.

"Did you know either victim?" I said.

Bob eyes jumped to Jack, then me. "Sure, I knew 'em both. I've seen 'em both at Buzzo's and Cadillac Jack's. Plus, Kohler always requests me as the mechanic to service his vehicles."

Buzzo's was a popular sports bar hangout on East Main. Cadillac Jack's was located on Clooney Lake two miles north of town, adjacent to Jack's home.

"Tell me about your relationship with the men."

"What's to tell? Ronny and me got along okay. We weren't pals if that's what you mean."

"And Mr. Kohler? How well did you know him?"

"Talk to him about his cars is all."

"What was your opinion of Mr. Kohler?"

"He wasn't exactly my favorite person."

"Why?"

"He was a hypocrite, you ask me."

The sheriff adjusted in his chair. He was staring at Bob.

"How so?" I asked.

"He acted all superior and churchy, but I think underneath he was a prick."

Jack shifted in his chair.

"Can you be more specific?" I asked.

"Yeah, he went after Lisa Kelly, his secretary."

Whoa. Our model citizen went after his secretary? "You know this for a fact?" I asked.

Jack brought his hand to his forehead and sighed. He didn't look happy.

"Sure! Jack knows too."

Jack sat forward and rapped his knuckles on the table. "No basis. Move on. We'll discuss that later, Cal."

Bob's eyes flickered. I couldn't let that kind of information slide.

I avoided eye contact with Jack as I leaned forward. In my peripheral vision, I saw him lean back. "Tell me what you know about it."

"Well, about a week ago, Lisa came into Cadillac Jack's all upset. Said that Ted trapped her in the file room and felt her up."

"How did you feel about that?" I asked.

"It pissed me off. She was young." Bob had raised his voice and started using his hands. "He was all fatherly toward her at first. Helped her find an apartment and all. Then he come on to her like that?"

"That kind of behavior would make a guy angry," I said.

"Definitely."

"Where you were yesterday morning when you heard the shots?"

"I told you I dint hear no shots."

"Who did you see?"

"No one . . . see that's why I walk there," said Bob with an edge to his voice—just what I wanted.

"Mr. Brutlag, two men were brutally murdered and you're the only person we know who was at the scene. You live a short distance but didn't *see anything* and didn't *hear* rifle shots. You stated you didn't like Kohler and his behavior made you angry. Now, I put that all together and well . . . I've got a suspect."

Bob drew his head back and said, " A suspect? Pftt."

"Bob, answer the question," said the sheriff in a patronizing manner.

"Was there a question there?" Bob said. A corner of his mouth turned up. His tone was like a sassy kid's. I believed he was fueled by Jack's attitude.

"I don't have to prove I'm innocent for Christ's sake. *You* have to prove me guilty, and that's gonna be pretty damn hard, 'cause I dint shoot nobody."

With that, he sat back and crossed his arms over his chest. Jack stifled a smile with his hand. I felt a spike of anger, but I tried not to react. Jack was undermining me. His face would not be caught on camera, but mine would. Jack began tapping the eraser tip of his pencil on the table. Tap, tap, tap, tap. I wanted to grab it and break it in half and throw it across the room.

Brutlag's expression made me think he'd become overconfident. "Ted was already dead when I found him. End of story."

I had to regain control. "Not quite. What did you do after you saw Kohler in the boat?"

He punched his words out: "I went home to call 911."

"You a married man?"

"Yeah."

"Can your wife verify when you left the house and returned?" I asked.

"No, she's in Texas visiting her mom."

"Your wife's name is?"

"Juanita."

"She works at Buzzos. Is that correct?" I asked.

"Yes," said Bob.

"Did she ever have problems with either man?" I asked.

"I know Kohler flirted with her and the other waitresses," said Bob.

"More reason to not like him, right?"

"Right. Look, I'm not hiding anything here."

"He flirted with your wife and molested his own secretary, which made him a hypocrite in your eyes."

"Yeah, so?" Bob said.

"So he should have been stopped, right?"

"Damn right!" he shouted.

"And you stopped him!" I said.

"No!" Bob shouted. He sniffed, jerked his head, and glared back at me. After a few seconds, he said, "I know what you're trying to do. It wasn't *me* who killed either one of 'em."

Bob was like a rubber band pulled tight. I remained silent and kept eye contact. He'd look at me for a few seconds then down at his hands, then back at me. It was only about fifteen seconds before he looked at Jack and asked, "Can I have some more coffee and another doughnut? Damn they're good." He laughed a little. Jack was right. I would not underestimate this man.

"Sure," Jack said. "Help yourself. I have to go to the can. I'll be right back."

As soon as Jack left the room I pulled the bag of doughnuts away and said, "Let's hold off until we're through."

He nodded.

"So, did you ever confront Kohler about your wife or his secretary?"

"No. I seen him out at Cadillac Jack's about a week ago but I dint say nothin' to him about anything. Didn't think it was my business."

"What night was that?"

"Actually, it was the night after Lisa's trouble with him—toward the end of September sometime."

"Did you see him talking to anyone that night?"

"No, he didn't stay long—dint even have a drink."

"Why do you suppose he was out there?"

"I think he was lookin' for somebody."

"Lisa?"

"Didn't seem like it."

"Do you have a good marriage?"

"I don't see how that's any of your business."

"Yes, actually it is. I'm entitled to ask you any question that I think necessary to help bring this investigation to a conclusion," I said.

Bob shifted in his chair and said, "We've been working on our marriage."

"Did she go to visit her mother because of that?"

"Guess so."

"Did you ever fight with Peterson or Kohler?"

"No, sir."

Jack walked back in Bob said, "Hey, you ever go out to Jack's restaurant on rib night? They have the best ribs. Good steaks, too," said Bob.

What?

"That's quite a commercial, Bob," Jack said.

Bob had a real knack for diverting the focus. This behavior was absurd and I was done with Bob and Jack's tag team.

"Mr. Brutlag, that's all I have for now, but I may need to speak with you again," he said.

"Anytime," he said as he grinned. "Maybe I'll see you out at Jack's place sometime," he answered.

I handed him my card. "Just in case you might remember or hear something that would help with the investigation."

I watched Bob walk out of the conference room and signaled for the recording to be terminated.

"Sheriff, what's this about Kohler and his secretary?"

"Cal, first thing you better learn is to sort out facts from hearsay."

"You mean about Kohler molesting his secretary?"

"I talked to Kohler and he said it never happened."

Unbelievable. "Like men don't lie about things like that?"

"Trust me. Kohler wouldn't have touched her. He was a real Christian."

"Right."

"Why did you go at Bob like *he's* a suspect?"

"The person who discovers the body is always a suspect until eliminated."

"That what you learned at those classes I paid for? A good investigator intuits who he needs to look at and so far you're batting zero as far as I'm concerned," he said and stalked out of the room.

This investigation was the first time I'd experienced the controlling, demeaning, manipulating side of Jack, and I didn't like it.

"Don't you worry, Bulldog, I can sort out facts from hearsay," I mumbled as I gathered my things together.

Jack popped back. "Calvin, I see where you're going with this. Don't waste time on Bob or Eleanor Kohler or Ham Fairchild. They aren't responsible. Period."

I said nothing and he left without waiting for my comment. "Okay you figure it out, asshole," I whispered.

Every muscle in my body felt tense. I needed a workout so went down to the gym in the basement of the department next to the firing range. I normally run and work out opposite days and had missed a couple. My muscles were complaining. I changed into my sweats and pushed the machines with a vigor that came from pure frustration.

What the hell was Jack doing? Why did he chastise me for questioning Brutlag as a suspect? Was something else going on? I wanted Ralph's feedback after he viewed the tape. Regardless of Jack's opinion about Kohler's alleged sexual impropriety with Lisa Kelly, if she had a boyfriend and she told him Kohler molested her, the boyfriend was definitely a suspect.

After showering and changing, I gave Ralph a quick call to brief him how the interview went. He said he'd review the tape and would contact Ms. Kelly and her boyfriend, if she had one, and set up interviews. Shortly after, I received a text that he'd set them for 1:00 p.m.—the same time I was talking to Ronny Peterson's parents.

8

PETERSON'S TWO-STORY HOUSE was on Eighth Street, a couple blocks north of Kohler's. More and more of early twentieth-century homes in this area were refurbished, Peterson's included. A round, middle-aged woman who stood about five feet tall let me in the front hallway. Dark circles underscored her red, puffy eyes. When I introduced myself, she said she was Ronny's mother but to call her Ellen. She showed me into the living room and introduced an older, heavier version of Ronny as her husband. He stood as I moved across to shake his hand. Like his son, Mr. Peterson was five-foot-seven at most.

"Ron Senior," he said.

"Sorry to meet you under these circumstances," I said. "You both have my deepest sympathy on your loss."

"Just find the maniac that killed my boy," he said.

"We're doing our best, sir."

As Senior went back to his Lazy Boy, he gestured for me to be seated as well. I sat on a high-back chair and Ellen the sofa.

"He shouldn't have even been out there," she said, dabbing at her eyes. "He was supposed to be at the dentist, so when Naomi Moberg came by to tell me he'd been killed, I didn't believe her."

Senior waved his finger at me. "I think they walked into something bad going on out there—a drug deal, or something."

"We'll certainly look at all the possibilities," I said. I thought of the drug stash and paraphernalia in the storage garage that could be their son's.

Ronny's clone came in and sat down on the other end of the sofa. Senior introduced him as their son, Kevin.

"I lost a brother too." I said.

Kevin nodded.

"Then you know how we're suffering. Our boys were eleven months apart and were always very close," Ellen said.

Kevin put his arm around his mother.

"I know this time is very difficult for you all. Thank you for taking time to answer my questions this afternoon."

I pulled out my small recording device. The family sat quietly as I recorded the date, time, place, and those present, then placed it on the coffee table.

"Did Ronny mention anyone he was having a conflict with?"

The three Petersons looked at me blankly, as if they didn't understand my question.

"The more information we get, the faster we can solve the case," I said.

"You think our Ronny was a target?" Senior asked.

Your son was an asshole, so yeah, could be. "We don't know what happened out there, so if you can give us any information as to who he may have had problems with, we'll be able to make more informed decisions."

"People liked Ronny," Mrs. Peterson said, "He was a good boy."

Kevin pointed at me. "Snake."

His parents' heads whipped toward their son.

"Do you mean Nevada Wynn?" I asked.

Snake was the street name for a known drug dealer—an all around bad guy. I'd heard he'd moved to Minneapolis when the multi-agency task force turned the heat up on the dealers and traffickers doing business in the county. His name had been mentioned in connection with Pierce Redding the guy Ronny had a fight with.

"Yeah, that's his name."

"Tell me about it."

"All I know is Snake and a buddy of his didn't like Ronny for some reason and picked a fight with him last summer."

"What was it about?"

"I guess he looked at them wrong, or something."

Or something. "Ronny buy from him?"

"What do you mean *buy*?" Mrs. Peterson asked.

"He means drugs, Ma," Kevin said.

Mr. Peterson stiffened. Mrs. Peterson shook her head. "Ronny didn't use drugs. He was a church-going boy."

Right. The other days he drank himself ornery and looked for fights. "Anyone else come to mind who might have *picked* on him? Any coworkers, for example?"

"Everybody loved him at work. His boss said he'll be highly missed," Mrs. Peterson said.

"Would you write down a list of his current friends so I might question them?"

"Kevin, you do that. There's a pad of paper on the counter in the kitchen," Mrs. Peterson said.

Kevin lumbered out of the room. I was curious how long that list would be.

"I understand he lived with you," I said.

"Both boys do because they take classes at the Community College."

I nodded. *And I'll bet mama takes mighty good care of her boys so they didn't ever think about moving out.* "Did Ronny leave his mobile phone home by any chance?" I asked.

"No, I'm sure not. That thing is glued to his hand."

"Does he have another cell phone beside the one the county provides?"

"No, he said he didn't need another," Mrs. Peterson said.

"May I look through his things?"

"The lab people took a bag of stuff from his room last night, but you're welcome to have a look."

I nodded then followed his mother down to the lower level. She said the boys' bedrooms were across from each other. Both were very neat, vacuumed, and dusted. Mrs. Peterson stayed to watch as I went through Ronny's closet, searched pockets of clothing, and tidy drawers. Hunting magazines were stacked neatly on his bedside table and photos of hunting and fishing trips were taped to his mirror.

"I don't know what they took in those bags that could possibly help to find his killer," she said.

"Did you clean up his room before the lab people got here?"

She hunched her shoulders. "How did you know?"

"Because I know moms—and this room is too tidy for most guys in their early twenties."

"I just got rid of garbage—nothing that'll help you."

"I'd like to see it."

I followed her upstairs and into the garage. She didn't seem happy to hand me the stuffed white kitchen garbage bag.

"Those BCA people already took our garbage from the cans."

"You never know what clues can be found in trash."

I grabbed the list from Kevin, told the family we'd do everything we could to find their son's killer, and drove back to the department.

I FOUND RALPH in the hallway near the interview rooms. "Whatcha got there?"

"A bag of trash from Ronny's room that his mother hid from the BCA, and a list of his friends."

"First, let's have a quick look at the bag," he said.

"Three Playboys, beer cans, a half eaten bag of Cheetos and Little Debbie wrappers. No wonder she picked it up," Ralph said. "Ah, just dump it."

Then I showed him the list Kevin had written: Max Becker, Aaron Young, and Todd and Chad Hackett. The first two must manage to stay out of trouble because I didn't know them, but the Hackett brothers had juvenile records and connections to Wynn.

"How'd it go with the secretary and her boyfriend?"

"Surprising development," he said, wiggling his eyebrows. "Come watch her interview then we'll take Johnston on. He can sit and cook a little longer."

LISA KELLY WAS ATTRACTIVE and looked younger than her years. For a petite woman, she had voluptuous curves emphasized by her clothing: a short jeans skirt and a white blouse that pulled across her full breasts. Her curly, light brown hair was cut just below chin level. When Ralph mentioned to Ms. Kelly he was video-recording the interview, her eyes nervously darted around the room. When he turned on the small cassette recorder on the table, she began to chew on her lower lip.

"I understand you were Mr. Kohler's secretary, Miss Kelly."

She leaned in toward the small recorder to speak. "Yes, sir."

"When did you first find out about his death?"

"Yesterday afternoon. Mrs. Kohler called and told me. I was so shocked, but I'd been wondering where he was because he didn't show up at the office. I almost called his home to find out if he was sick or something."

"How did you get the job with Mr. Kohler?"

"I answered an ad in the paper last year. He hired me on the spot—even helped me find an apartment."

"In that time, have you witnessed any instances of conflict or confrontations he had with anyone?"

"No. He was very friendly and had good relationships with all his clients. Is that what you're asking me?"

"Yes. It's been reported to us that Mr. Kohler molested you. Is that correct?"

Lisa looked startled and immediately blushed a deep red. "Um . . . yes."

"Tell me what happened."

She swallowed. "Well, late one afternoon . . ."

"The date?"

"Uh, it was Thursday, September 29th, just before I was ready to go home and change for work out at Cadillac Jack's. I work out there to earn money for my wedding. Anyways, Mr. Kohler asked me to get the Olson's file, but he followed me right into the file room. He came up very close behind and . . ." Lisa Kelly broke into sobs.

"It's okay. Take your time," Ralph said.

"You don't understand," she said through her tears.

"What don't I understand?" Ralph asked.

"I—I made it up. I was trying to make Mike jealous and it worked."

Oh, boy.

"Mike?"

"Mike Johnston—my fiancé."

"Does he know you made it up?"

"Not exactly," she said.

"Why did you feel you had to do that?"

"Mike was going out drinking with the boys again. I called and told him. I needed him, then the words tumbled out of my mouth . . . that Mr. Kohler had touched me—you know—inappropriately."

"What did Mike do at that point?"

"He was really mad, wanted to come right over—but I stopped him—calmed him down."

"Then?"

"Then he said he'd be at Cadillac Jack's later. He proposed to me that night."

Holy shit.

"Did you tell anyone about the molestation?"

"Molestation? Well, I sorta told Ben, my boss, and right away he insisted on calling his dad, you know—the sheriff. I got real nervous when he came over from his house next door and talked to me. I didn't want to get Ted in trouble with the law so I told the sheriff I needed the job, so maybe I should just forget it."

"Anyone else you told?"

"Oh, I think Bob heard me too, but I did tell everyone to forget it," Lisa said.

"Bob who?"

"I don't know his last name."

"Where were you on the morning of Friday, October 7th? The morning your boss was killed" he asked.

"Mike stayed over on Thursday night. Then we went to Dotty's for breakfast, and then I went to work."

"What time did you get to work?"

"About 9:00," she said.

"And Mike was with you all that time?"

"Yes."

"Didn't he go to work that day?"

"He had a doctor's appointment at ten, so he took the morning off."

"What for?"

"Huh? Oh, the appointment . . . he had a mole removed."

"Miss Kelly, were you aware of any relationships Mr. Kohler might have had? Any women happen to drop by the office? Call him?"

"Just business appointments."

"Did the Kohlers seem to get along as far as you know?"

"Yes . . . well, sometimes I could tell they were fighting, but doesn't everybody?"

"Can you think of any instances where he had irate or upset clients?"

"No, not really," she said.

"Well, that's all I have for you at the moment. Mind waiting here?"

"No."

Ralph stopped the tape. "Unbelievable eh?"

"Who lies about that kind of thing?"

"It happens."

"You know even if it wasn't true, Johnston doesn't know that and he has motive."

"My thought exactly. So now, it's Johnston's turn. You want to take it? I'll sit in. I'd like to bring these two together for the end of the interview."

"Okay."

HAVING RALPH SIT IN was a whole lot different than having Jack there. Johnston was already waiting for us in Interview Room Number Three. At first glance, I thought he was bald, but his blond hair was buzzed to maybe a sixteenth of an inch long. He was dressed in a body-hugging plaid shirt and black slacks. He was about five-foot-ten, weighed at least 225 pounds, and had a neck the size of Colorado. This boy was a body builder and definitely could do someone physical harm.

I explained the taping process and gave the case number, time, date, and then asked him to state his personal information. He said he worked at the tile plant in Brainerd and lived with his parents. Lot of that going around.

Johnston leaned forward, elbows on the table. "Let's get on with it. I have things to do."

Jesus Louise. Things to do? I leaned forward, cocked my head, and stared into his eyes. "Is that right? Well, Mr. Johnston, I think you just better sit back and relax, because you'll be here answering questions for as long as needs be. Understood?" I asked.

Johnston didn't acknowledge he understood and he didn't move a muscle except to clench his oversized jaw.

"Why don't you tell us why you're upset?"

I heard foot tapping. "I'm not upset. I've just been sitting in here for a goddamn hour."

"Golly, sorry to keep you waiting while we question others in a double murder investigation. So, what's your relationship with Ted Kohler?"

"He was my girlfriend's boss."

"How did you feel about him?"

He looked at me for a good ten seconds before he answered. "He was okay."

"Ted had a reputation for being a real nice guy, but I suspect not everyone held that opinion. How about you? Did you have any reason to dislike the guy?"

"Maybe."

"Why don't you enlighten us?"

"What am I? A suspect or somethin'?"

"Why would you be a suspect?"

A red hue creep swept across Mike Johnston's face and down his tree stump neck. "Why else would you haul me in here?"

"So *did* you kill Mr. Kohler, Mr. Peterson?"

"No!" he said and pushed back in his chair.

I waited a few seconds then said, "I understand Kohler molested your girl in the file room."

Johnston's legs started bouncing. "She tell you that?"

"Yes. So, what did you do about it?" I asked.

"Nothing," he said.

"So, let me get this straight. He feels your girlfriend up and you do nothing?"

"Sure, I wanted to beat the crap out of him, but Lisa made me drop it."

"Mr. Johnston, Mr. Kohler sustained injuries around his midsection approximately a week ago. That would be about the time of the file room incident on Thursday, September 30th. You want to know what I think? I think you taught him a lesson. I believe you had a fight with him and didn't tell your girlfriend about it."

Johnston's forehead started showing beads of sweat. "No, sir, I did not." He moved his head in tiny jerks he spoke as he spoke. He was lying.

"So, you didn't defend your girl?"

"I let it be because she promised me if it happened again she'd quit the job and sue the bastard," he said.

"Where were you on that Thursday?"

"I worked late. Afterward, I went home to clean up, then drove to Cadillac Jack's."

"Weren't you going to go out with the boys?"

"I changed my mind when Lisa called."

"What time did you see Kohler that night?"

"I didn't."

"Where were you on Friday morning, October 7th?"

"I took Lisa out to breakfast. Then she went to work and I went to the doctor."

"Did you know Ronald Peterson?"

"No."

"How did you learn about Kohler and Peterson's deaths?"

Lisa called me. She was upset because there were reporters trying to ask her questions, so I told her to go to my parents' house until I got off."

"How did you take the news?"

"Look, I didn't like the guy, but I wouldn't wish anybody dead," he said.

I let some silence pass before I asked, "What would you say if I told you Lisa made up the story about Kohler molesting her to get your attention?"

Johnston jaw muscles slackened as he stared at me. After a few seconds his jaw started pulsing. Finally he said, "I'd say you were wrong."

With that, Ralph said, "Excuse me," and left the room.

I let Johnston sit and stew.

"Are we done here?" he asked.

I smiled. "No."

Johnston fidgeted in his chair and studied his fingers.

When Ralph brought Lisa into the room, Johnston looked meaner than a junkyard dog. She sat on the edge of her chair across from him looking extremely uncomfortable.

"All right, Lisa. Suppose you tell Mike what you told me?" Ralph said.

She immediately started sobbing.

"Lisa, they said you made that whole thing up about Kohler. That true?" Mike asked.

She nodded.

He tossed his head back and said, "Why would you do that?"

"Because you wanted to be with the boys more than me!" she said through her tears.

Johnston looked confused, then looked at Ralph and me. "You think I killed Kohler—because of what she told me. Don't you?"

"This is what I think: I think you were so angry that Kohler touched your girl you confronted him. Punched him a few times but that wasn't enough, so you took it further. Lisa knew her boss went fishing every work morning, so you knew. Emmaline is an isolated area. You went out there and shot him. Unfortunately, the park worker shows up and you had to shoot him too," I said.

"No, sir. I've never even been out at that park. Tell him, Lisa."

"I told you he was with me until nine o'clock. Eleanor told me the shooting was before eight," Lisa said.

"Don't you get it? They think you're covering for me."

"It happens," Ralph said.

"All the time," I said.

She looked stricken, "I'm not covering for him!"

"You don't want to protect your man?" I asked.

"No . . . I mean, yes . . . I mean I didn't lie when I said he was with me."

"We know you are capable of telling lies, now don't we? You felt guilty for telling the whopper about Mr. Kohler, and you know in your heart that Mike wouldn't let him get by with that behavior."

"No, he'd never hurt . . ."

"Forget it Lisa. Look, I didn't kill anybody. I'm not crazy," Johnston said.

"We'll find out shortly. We have a search warrant and we've already confiscated your rifles, and running DNA evidence found on paper, vehicles, etc."

"What? Are you arresting me?" Johnston asked. Then he looked at Lisa like he wanted to punch her lights out.

"No, Mr. Johnston, for now you're free to go, but as they say in the movies, don't leave town. Deputy Sheehan will walk you out," Ralph said.

Johnston got up with a huff. "Stupid bitch," he murmured, leaving his girlfriend behind. I walked him out and just before we reached the door he said, "This is so un-fucking-believable."

"She gets hurt, I'm coming for you," I said.

He turned and faced me. "Look, I'm mad, but I'd never hurt her. Okay?"

"Just a warning," I said.

Johnston's eyes were focused on something behind us. I turned and saw Ralph and Lisa entered the lobby. Johnston shoved the door open and took off.

"I think you may need a ride," I said to Lisa.

Her eyes were full of tears, as she said, "No, thanks."

As Ralph and I walked back to the Investigations Office I said, "Wow, that was quite the revelation. Yeah, I'd say that relationship just crashed and burned."

"Glad to help," he said laughing, which made me laugh.

"So, what do you think?" I asked.

"I think he could be our man but we need to tie him physically to the shooting."

"Have they run ballistics on the rifles yet?" I asked.

"It's on for this afternoon."

"Trouble is one can always get rid of the murder weapon."

"You just had to say that, didn't you?"

9

ABOUT FOUR O'CLOCK, Ralph and I drove to Buzzo's to question the patrons. Everyone was willing to turn away from the football game on the big screen to give their opinions—and some were bizarre. One local concluded it was a mafia hit because he saw *Soprano* types at the Sportsmen's Café.

Connie Hackett, one of the barmaids, called Ronny a "doll" and Kohler a "charmer." According to her, neither victim had any conflicts—despite the fight she'd admitted she'd witnessed in July. "Boys will be boys," she cooed.

I asked her how her sons, Chad and Todd, were.

She smiled and said, "Real good, do you know them?"

I nodded. Every law enforcement officer in the county knew them.

She smiled. "They've both straightened up their act, take classes at Community, and have real good jobs, now. I'm so proud of them."

The woman never did think her sons did anything wrong. She lives off and on with their abusive loser of a father. I remember the night one of her neighbors in the trailer park had reported hearing screams and loud noises coming from next door. Even though Connie needed six stitches on the top of her head, the result of a "little shove," she begged me not to take Kent Silva in. It was out of her hands.

LAKE EMMALINE WAS my last stop for the day. It was after five o'clock when I knocked on the front door of Brutlag's large log home. Bob looked caught off guard when he saw me standing on his porch stoop.

"What's up?" he asked.

"I need to speak to your wife," I said.

"Did ya think I was lyin' when I told you she was in Texas?"

"No, I was thinking you could give me a phone number where I can contact her."

He sighed. "You drove all the way out here for that? I don't even get why ya need to talk to her."

65

I want to tell her she's married to an asshole jerk. "She worked in a bar both victims frequented. She may know something that can help us," I said.

Bob waved me through the door and into a large great room open to the kitchen. Although there were a few dirty dishes in the sink and a couple empty beer cans on the counter, the place was orderly. As I moved further into the room I caught a whiff of marijuana. He walked to a built-in desk on the edge of the kitchen cabinets, pulled out a Post-it note from the top drawer, and wrote down two numbers.

"Top one is her cell phone and the bottom is her mom's. Personally, I think it's a waste of your time."

"I also drove out to get your rifles. Hopefully testing them will also be a waste of time. I don't have a search warrant, but I figure you won't mind surrendering them."

"When will I get 'em back? It's huntin' season pretty soon."

"As long as one isn't the murder weapon, it shouldn't take long. They'll give you a call."

"I've got nothin' to hide." He walked over to a gun cabinet, unlocked it, and pulled out two rifles. They were both beauties, each with scopes. First, I examined the Remington, then the Winchester: both cleaned and oiled.

"I haven't shot either since last hunting season."

I smiled and said, "Thanks for your cooperation, Bob."

He put both guns in cases and handed them to me, and as I walked toward the door he asked, "Hey, do you want a beer?"

What?

Bob went into the kitchen and pulled open his refrigerator. It looked emptier than mine: beer, soda, jam, ketchup, and not much else. He pulled out two Buds.

"No thanks, Bob."

"Coke then?"

"All right, thanks," I said.

He handed me a can of Coke and gestured toward the matching dark-red leather couches parallel from each other. He stoked the fire in the large stone fireplace then put another log on. He took a seat across from me, picked up a pack of Camels, lit one, shook the match and threw it in a colorful ashtray on a large oak coffee table. He took a deep drag and after exhaling he said, "Mind if I smoke?"

"It's your place," I answered. Actually, I did mind, but didn't say so.

"Do I come across as an asshole to you?" he asked.

Didn't expect that—I had to laugh. "Yeah, you do."

"Well, sorry 'bout that. I apologize. I just don't get why I'm a suspect?"

"Because you were at the scene."

"So what?"

"So maybe Kohler and Peterson saw something you didn't want them to see. Maybe there was some transaction going down in the parking lot."

"You're kidding me."

"No, I'm not. You're a pothead, Bob."

"I've been straight since Enza was born. Pretty much, anyway."

"I smelled marijuana on you yesterday, and again when I came in your place today."

His mouth pulled up into a crooked grin. "You gonna arrest me?"

I shook my head. "I'm here regarding the murders, not your pot habit. But I suspect you have to keep your stash outside the house so your wife doesn't throw it."

He laughed hoarsely. "You're right. I hide it in my garage. I'm out now anyway. You can check if you want."

I shook my head.

"Guess I better air out the place before Juanita gets back."

"Good idea. Did you ever buy from Nevada Wynn?"

"Ah, no. I stayed away from that dude."

"You said you saw Ted Kohler out at Cadillac Jack's on September 30th. What time was that?"

"Late afternoon. Maybe around 5:00 or so."

"Anyone follow him out the door when he left?"

"Not that I remember."

"Mike Johnston around then?"

"Didn't see him that night until much later," he said. "You know, all this makes me nervous. You hear of innocent dudes spending years in prison."

"The rifles can eliminate you."

Bob changed the subject by reaching under the table to get a photo album of his family. As he showed me the pictures of his wife and daughter, his eyes filled with tears. He turned to a picture of him as a little kid with his parents. He said his mother died from breast cancer on Christmas Eve when he was six. Then gave me a brief history of his childhood and all the trouble he gave his dad. I sort of related to him and left liking Bob a whole lot more.

ON THE DRIVE BACK into town, I thought about my date tonight and how my life was simpler when I was in a committed relationship with Adriana Valero. For some reason, I wasn't up for this dinner date with Naomi Moberg. Maybe I'd cancel—say I have to work too late. After I checked the rifles into evidence, I drove the Taurus to my designated parking spot in front of my apartment building.

Adriana had urged me to move out of my cheap efficiency on the east side of town, to a condo in West Wind on the southwest side, so she could be more "comfortable" when she stayed over. Seems like I'm paying a whole lot more money because of Adriana, and now she's living in Minneapolis working for a high-powered law firm for double the salary. When she'd accepted the job, she'd just assumed I'd move down with her. I briefly considered it, but there were no job openings and even if I had been offered a position, I'd be starting all over seniority wise. That's when we amicably parted ways.

West Wind, two L-shaped buildings, enclosed a well-landscaped center courtyard with an outdoor pool with a waterfall feature, and a Jacuzzi. The buildings had interior corridors and each large apartment had either an exterior small patio or balcony. My one bedroom was a large corner unit on the ground floor with an open patio facing the street. I did like my apartment, but unfortunately now I couldn't save as much money each month for my house fund.

After I took Bullet out for a walk and fed him, I called Naomi. I had intended to renege, but when I heard the anticipation in her voice, I couldn't do it. We agreed to meet at the small restaurant called Minnesota Fare in Birch County Park South. I'd eaten there only once. They featured organic and local foods, especially fish. Naomi was instrumental in building the new and successful restaurant in the park near the falls.

I took a shower, shaved, dressed, then cracked a beer to relax before leaving. I was about to take off when my cell phone rang and Caller ID displayed Hope Sheehan, my mother. *Oh, boy.* If I picked up—I'd be on the phone for an hour. I decided to let it ring over to voice messaging.

Before I went into the restaurant, I sat in the parking lot and listened to Mom's message: *"Cal honey, this is your mom. How's the murder case going?*

When you get this, call me back on my cell. It's important. Please!" Since hangnails are important to my mother, I figured it could wait.

Then my mind flipped to our suspects: Bob Brutlag and Mike Johnston. I was leaning more toward Johnston at this point but we needed strong evidence, like a positive ballistics report. Then I realized I'd forgotten to mention to Ralph about Kevin Peterson's comment about Nevada Wynn. With all this rolling around in my head I wasn't going to be a good date.

10

NAOMI, ALREADY SEATED at a table, gave me a big smile when she saw me. She was wearing a red v-neck sweater revealing more cleavage than I was aware she'd had. When she stood to give me a brief hug, she almost spilled her water glass. "Can you tell I'm nervous?" she said. "I feel like a teenager again."

"You've not dated for quite some time. Feels weird, huh?"

"Actually, it feels good." She took my hands, looked me in the eye and said, "Thank you for agreeing to go to dinner with me."

Although the moment felt a bit awkward, I said, "My pleasure," and felt compelled to give her a kiss on the cheek.

When the server approached with menus in hand, Naomi dropped my hands. I suddenly realized I was dressed like the wait staff: black pants and white shirt. He said his name was Rex and asked what we'd like to drink. Naomi asked me what kind of wine I liked—I told her the truth—anything's fine by me—except that wine Zinfandel crap. She suggested a bottle of Pinot Noir to the waiter and off he went.

She appeared to have relaxed a little. "So, how's the case coming?"

"It's early. We're gathering evidence, interviewing everybody and anybody."

"What the heck happened out there? Some drug deal or something?"

"That's what everyone seems to think. Time will tell."

"Yeah, and let's agree not to talk about it tonight."

"Thank you. So what should I know about Naomi Moberg?"

She blushed. "I've never been asked that before. Um, maybe that I'm a perfectionist."

"I think I could say that of myself as well. Where does that come from?"

"I always thought it was because I was an only child and I had to be perfect for my parents."

"Really? I think we perfectionists are born that way."

A smile crossed her face. "Yes, maybe. My room was the most organized room in our house."

"Mine too. My mom enjoys clutter. I do not."

She sat back and laughed. "Boy, me either."

"So, what would Jeremy say if he knew we were out?"

She wiggled her brows. "Maybe I should call and tell him."

"Nah."

"Were you aware that he's always been jealous of you."

"Me? Why?"

"Look at you. You're gorgeous—and he's so—average. If I so much as looked at another man, he'd accuse me of having an affair, but as it turns out, I was the one who should have been worried."

"Maybe he left you before you could leave him."

She appeared to be digesting that notion, then smiled. "Never thought of it that way."

"So you're living in your mom's house?"

"Yeah, the only house on the block that hasn't been remodeled."

"You haven't been there that long. You can always fix it up later."

"When Mom found out she had pancreatic cancer, I moved in to take care of her. It was only three months before she died. Two weeks later, Jeremy announced he wanted a divorce."

"What an asshole," I said. "So he got the house?"

"No use in fighting for it. We're upside down on it anyway—and with the repressed housing market, he can't put it up for sale. At least, we share custody of the kids."

"How old are they now?"

"Jackson's five and Maggie's three. They're sweet kids. I miss them when they're with their dad."

"I bet you're a good mom."

"I try to be. So, Tamika told me you had an accident on the way out to Emmaline."

"Yeah, someone rear-ended me into the intersection just as poor Mrs. Salmi was driving through with her tank of a car."

"What are you going to replace it with?"

"I have no idea. I'm too busy to car-shop. Man, I don't want car payments."

"I know what you mean," she said.

After a bit of an awkward silence, I moved the conversation into typical first date topics. Turned out we had a lot in common: we both enjoyed being outdoors, golfing, biking, hiking, and fishing. She also liked most kinds of music, reading thrillers and mysteries.

Naomi grew up in Prairie Falls. I grew up in the Brainerd area. She was a single child and I grew up as one—after my little brother, Hank, drown at age six. I shared that my mom and Grandma owned a gift shop. Her mother, Neva Hunt, owned and operated Hunts' Cleaners until she got sick. Naomi went to U of M Crookston for her bachelor's and master's degrees. I went to St. Cloud State University, then the Police Academy in St. Paul.

By the time we'd finished our walleye dinners it was ten thirty. We'd been listening to a singer/guitar player who'd been playing all evening. But I was tired and thinking of leaving when and Naomi took my hand and led me to the small dance floor. As she snuggled in close, I smelled her light cologne.

"You smell good," I said.

"I feel even better."

Whoa.

After a couple slow dances pressed up next to Naomi, my Mason Dixon man parts were thinking they were being called up for duty. After I insisted on paying the check, I asked her if she wanted me to follow her home.

She said, "No, not necessary."

Really? What was all that rub-a-dub-dub on the dance floor?

After I got home, I sat and made notes of everything I wanted to get done tomorrow, including check out Johnston's story. But even if he had been at Dotty's, it didn't mean he didn't kill before breakfast.

11

DAY THREE

BY SEVEN-THIRTY SUNDAY MORNING, I was standing in a short line at Northwoods Coffee Shop fantasizing about what *didn't* happen last night, wondering if Naomi and I would be even good for one another, when I felt a tap on the shoulder. I turned to find *Snow White* grinning at me.

"Remember me?" she asked. "I'm the one who bumped you."

"Don't you think 'bumped' is an inadequate word when my car gets hauled off to a junkyard, Ms. Lewis?" I asked.

She giggled. "Victoria. So, that means you're getting a new car?"

I made a grim face. "That's what it means, *Victoria*."

"Well, that's a good thing. Your car was a real piece of junk. Oops. Sorry." She giggled again.

My eyes narrowed. "A crash is never good," I said.

"No, of course not. I'm *really* and *truly* sorry. The dinner offer is still good. Are you free tonight?"

I shook my head. "Nope, sorry."

Her smile remained fixed. "At least let me buy you a coffee."

"Okay, sure," I said hoping it might end her guilty suffering.

While we waited for our order to be filled, she told me the auto-body shop promised her car would be ready in three days.

"How *nice* for *you*," I said.

When I picked up my coffee, I thanked Victoria for the coffee and made for the door.

She came up behind me and grabbed my arm, causing my coffee to splash through the hole in the lid.

"Wait. You're leaving?" she asked incredulously. Her look of disappointment gave me a jab of guilt so I stopped to explain.

"I'm working a big case. I should think you'd get that."

She continued to follow me out to the Taurus. "You're afraid I'm going to pump you for information. Aren't you?"

I liked her directness. "The thought did cross my mind."

"That's not what this is about. Look, I'm new in town and lonely for some companionship."

God, she was pretty. "Okay, how about dinner one night this week?"

A grin erupted revealing her white, perfect teeth. "Okay, give me a call. You still have my number?"

"Yes."

What was I doing? I don't date two women at a time. But what was one date?

BACK AT THE OFFICE, I called the county's cell phone provider and asked them if Ronny's cell was active, and if so, to find its location. I was on hold for at least fifteen minutes before they gave me a general tower location but recommended I use the Find my Phone application. Good point. I entered his number in my phone and discovered Ronny's phone was in the area of the Parks Department. I drove over and pulled into the lot where the parks' department trucks were parked.

As I walked through the lot, I called Ronny's number. A ring sounded leading me to county pick-up truck #10—not the one Ronny was driving the morning he was killed. I copied down the vehicle number and left Naomi a message.

I went back to the office to research Ronny Peterson's friends. Within a half hour, I learned Aaron Young was in Madison, Wisconsin, and hadn't been home since August, and Max Becker lived in a house on Fourth Street owned by his father, Dennis Becker. Nothing showed on the Hackett brothers' latest address. When I called their mother, Connie, I didn't get an answer.

At nine o'clock, I got in my assigned Ford Explorer and made my way over to Fourth Street. No one was parked in the street in front of Becker's house, so I drove around and down the gravel alley. A black Ford Focus was parked alongside the garage behind the Becker house. I did a quick check and found the registered owner was Maxwell Lee Becker. By the looks of the state of the lawn, the occupants used the back yard for a parking lot. I blocked the Focus in and got out to check the garage through a dirty side window. It was piled high with junk.

I knocked several times on the front door before a guy with bed hair and sleep wrinkles on his face stuck his head out the door. The daylight made him squint.

"Maxwell Becker?"

"Yeah," he said.

I flipped him my badge. "Deputy Investigator Sheehan. May I come in?"

He scratched his head. "Ah, sure. Just let me grab some pants first."

I waited outside the door, my ears keen for sounds of someone splitting out the back, but a few seconds later, he reappeared and let me in. He was wearing a soiled white T-shirt and a rumpled pair of jeans, and no shoes.

The odor of marijuana lingered in the air. Beer cans, pizza boxes, and nasty, over-filled ashtrays were scattered across the room. I ignored it all, moved some game controls off a chair that looked like it could tattoo its unusual stain pattern to the seat of my pants. I took a chance.

Max sat on the equally disgusting sofa and lit a cigarette. *I can't believe how many young people smoke.* I turned on my small recorder and placed it on top of a *Hustler* magazine on a wobbly coffee table. "I'm investigating the shooting out on Emmaline. Your name was given as a buddy of Ronny Peterson's," I said.

Max took a drag of his cigarette. "He's not really a buddy."

"Oh?"

"Maybe they said it because we played sports together in high school, but I haven't hung out with him all that much since we graduated."

"What was he like?"

He cleared his throat and looked at the recorder. "I dunno. Just a regular guy."

"Why didn't you want to hang out with him then?"

He uttered a small snort. "Because he was a jerk."

"Tell me about it."

"Let me put it this way, he was always trying to prove he was tougher than the next guy. It was like the dude was back in high school. He still talked about the state wrestling tourney four years ago and how the ref was dirty and had it out for him. He lost. Get over it, right? Anyway, after that he changed. Never saw the dude turn down a fight."

"You know of anyone he pissed off?"

"I don't know of anyone he *didn't* piss off—but enough to kill him? No."

"What do you know about Snake and his pal, Pierce Redding? I heard they had a run in with him?"

"I wasn't there, but the way Ronny talked, he got the best of him."

"Do you know where the Hackett brothers live? Heard they moved out of their mom's."

"Uh, they're living here."

"What a coincidence. Are they home?"

"No, they're at work."

"What do they do?"

"Janitors at the hospital."

I was surprised the hospital had hired them considering they were skinheads, neo-Nazi wannabes with tattoos, piercings, and bad attitudes. Seemed to me they'd frighten the patients.

"And you, Max?"

"I go to Birch County Community College and work part time at the Quick Stop."

"Aren't Todd and Chad going to Community as well?"

"Used to."

Their mother wasn't informed about the "used to." "Where were you Friday morning?"

"Working at the Quick Stop. You can ask my boss."

"You read the Bible?"

"Huh?"

"Do you read the Bible?"

"Why you asking me that?"

Yeah, he didn't seem the type to be into scripture reading and quoting. "Did you know Ted Kohler?"

"He the accountant killed with Ronny?"

"Yes."

"That's all I know 'bout him."

"Max, we'll figure out what happened to Ronny." I stared him down for a few seconds see if I could catch a reaction. He nodded and looked at the floor.

"One more time. Do you know anything at all about Ronny that would help us find his killer?"

"No, sir."

He knew something he wasn't telling me and was purposefully distancing himself.

I DROVE TO BIRCH COUNTY Regional Hospital and was directed to Neal Howard, the custodial services supervisor. Howard said both brothers were working today seven to three—and confirmed they worked the same shift last Friday. That should clear both but I still wanted to talk to them. Howard let me use a small conference room. I asked Neal to call them down one at a time.

Chad, the older brother, entered the room first. He knew me, but I introduced myself anyway. I'd placed the small recorder and my notebook on the table and pressed the *on* button, explaining I was gathering information about Ronny Peterson. He folded his arms across his chest, slumped back, and gave me a belligerent look.

"Too bad about your friend, Ronny," I said.

Stoned faced he said, "Not my friend."

"Hmm. That's weird. I heard he hung out with you guys."

"Not with me, he didn't."

"You go to high school with him?"

"He was in my brother's class."

"You know of anyone that had problems with Ronny?"

"Nope."

"Nevada Wynn or his buddy, Pierce Redding?"

A steely look crossed his face as crossed his arms and sat back. He refused to answer any more questions. Now, I was beginning to think this had everything to do with Wynn and Redding.

"Thanks for all your help." I turned off the recorder before I said, "Be careful now, you don't want to piss off whoever Ronny pissed off."

He stood defiantly and left the room without a word. I asked Howard to send Todd in. Five minutes later he took the chair across from me. I repeated the introduction and purpose of our talk.

"Too bad about your friend, Ronny."

"Yeah," he said.

Hey, I was getting somewhere. "So, who had a grudge against Ronny?"

He smirked. "Why?"

"Why do you think? To help find his killer, of course," I said. Then I leaned in and looked really serious. "Well, especially since you could be next on the list. Know what I mean? Your giving me a little information might save your own ass."

His eyeballs zigzagged as he thought it over. "You think somebody killed that accountant because they had a grudge against Ronny?"

"What I think is that you know something."

He blinked repeatedly. "Maybe he pissed off the wrong guy."

"My thoughts exactly. You have a name for the wrong guy?"

"Nah."

"Nevada Wynn, perhaps?"

Todd's expression hardened. He looked at the ceiling. "I don't know him."

I laughed. "Like hell you don't," I said. "He was a passenger in your car last year when I stopped you for speeding."

"That was you?"

I smiled. "Yes, 'twas me."

He leaned back and grinned. "You thought you caught our asses with something big."

He was right. The Multi-jurisdictional Drug Task Force (MJDTF) thought the Hacketts were running drugs. When I made the stop, Troy had heard the call and showed up on scene. He said the driver and passengers were acting suspicious and he had probably cause for bringing out the drug dog. Todd walked away with a speeding citation. I stared at him and let the silence eat at him.

"So what if I do know Wynn. Haven't seen him since he moved to the Cities."

"Wasn't it one of Wynn's buddies that Ronny beat the shit out of last summer?"

"I don't know nothing 'bout that."

"Yeah, you do. Guy's name is Pierce Redding."

He shook his head and pulled his lips in.

I moved two fingers from my eyes to his. "I'll be keeping an eye on you."

He copied my gesture. "Maybe I'll be keeping an eye on you," he said.

"Now that may have been the stupidest thing you've ever done. Threaten a law enforcement officer—and on tape."

"We through here?"

I nodded.

He looked at me, the tape recorder, then got up and left. The Hackett brothers both had the same empty blue eyes—cold little bastards like their sperm donor.

I WAS ON MY WAY to the office when Naomi called back. She said she'd meet me at the vehicle lot. On a Sunday it was full with the fleet of county vehicles.

Soon Naomi rolled up in her Prius and parked near the Explorer. I was standing next to the truck that contained Ronny's phone. When she hopped out of the car, I noticed she was wearing running gear.

She gave me a big smile. "Sorry, I'm all grungy. I was jogging and turned off my ringer. When I listened to your message, it sounded urgent so I came right here."

"You look great," I said. She did—hair still perfect—maybe less make-up than usual.

"How many miles?" I asked.

"Only five."

"*Only* five? What do you usually do?"

"Between five and ten."

"Wow," I said, suddenly feeling like a wuss. "Sorry to bother you on a Sunday morning."

"No problem at all. I'm glad to help."

"I'm pretty sure Ronny's phone is in this truck." I redialed the number so she could hear it ring.

She glanced at the number on the truck. "Number ten? I'll get the keys from the office."

After she unlocked the door to the large building, I followed her in and waited while she located the truck key in a large cabinet on the wall.

"Can you tell me who had it checked out on Thursday and Friday?"

She went behind the desk and sat at the computer. She tapped the keys for a while then looked up at me and said, "Okay, Gus Taylor on Thursday, and Mark Norland on Friday."

"What time did Norland check it out?"

"At 7:55."

"What time did Ronny signed out #13?"

"Just a sec ... okay looks like 7:15—which is unusually early—Gus signed out #21 at 8:05. They were supposed to work together."

"Do you have the pass codes for the phones?"

"Yes. Just a sec."

While she was looking it up my cell phone chimed. It was my mother. I walked outside to take the call. Mom wanted me to come for noon dinner, and since I had my interviews in, and there wasn't another meeting until tomorrow morning, I agreed. She sounded ecstatic. I guess it'd been a while since I've been home. I hung up and reentered the office to find Naomi running something off on the printer.

"My mom," I said after reentering the building.

Naomi smiled and handed me the paper. "This is what you need."

We walked back outside and to the truck, and she unlocked the driver's door. I called Ronny's number again so we could locate the phone faster. It was down between the driver's seat and the center counsel. I put on a glove to pull out and dropped it in an evidence bag.

"I find it odd it's in this particular truck," she said.

"Maybe it fell out of his pocket sometime Thursday and he didn't know it," I said. "Wouldn't he have missed it?"

"You'd think."

"Well, thanks for helping me out this morning."

"Happy to help. Want to grab a bite to eat?" she asked.

"Can't. I just agreed to go to my mom's."

She looked disappointed. "Okay. See you soon?"

"I'll call you."

"You'd better," she said with a sexy smile.

I DROPPED OFF THE PHONE at the evidence desk then sent an email to Betty to check it for fingerprints. After I picked up Bullet, I took off for Gull Lake where my mom and Grandma Dee live together. When I was six, Mom and I and my baby brother moved in with my grandparents, Grandpa Arnie and Grandma Dee Riggens, after my dad left us. They also worked together at their gift shop, North Country Gifts, in Nisswa. The two were polar opposites in every way and seem to tolerate each other views and ways, except Grandma Dee put her foot down and refused to ride in my mother's white '98 Dodge van not because it was an old, rusty heap, but because it still had *GORE/LIEBERMAN* and *OBAMA/BIDEN* bumper stickers.

Both grandfathers tried hard to be a father to me. The two men were friends and often the three of us would hunt and fish together. They died within a year of each other.

Mom's dad, Grandpa Arnie, had been in the Marines. He taught me how to defend myself and how to kill a man before the police academy did. He was drafted after high school and when he got out of the service, he worked as a carpenter. He made me wood toys: trains, trucks, and marble runs. He was a good man but every couple years he went on a drinking binge and morphed from a likeable character into a verbally abusive man. Once when I was about seven, I heard him tell my Grandma Dee to "go piss up a rope." The next day she caught me trying to pee *up* a rope that Grandpa had hanging in the garage. Naturally, she had asked why, so I told her. That rope disappeared and I never heard him use that expression again. Ten years later, he got plastered at the municipal liquor store, came home, fell down the basement stairs and broke his neck dieing instantly.

My other Grandparents, Sylvia and Gordy Sheehan, lived on the northwest edge of town where I'd spend most summer days and school vacations while my mom and Grandma Dee worked in their shop. Grandma Sylvia still worked out of her home as a seamstress, and Grandpa Sheehan worked for the County Highway Department. He taught me how to play poker and drive a car when I was twelve. I remember his one-liners like, "If God is watching us the least we can do is be entertaining," and "Going to church doesn't make you a Christian any more than standing in a garage makes you a car." Grandpa Sheehan died of a massive heart attack, sitting in his recliner watching TV. I missed both men. Their sudden deaths took a toll on me as much as my little brother Hank's death did.

WALKING INTO THE GULL LAKE house, smelling the food cooking, always made me feel like a kid again. The three women in my family had always doted on me, and it was carried over to my adulthood. Bullet trotted right up to Grandma Dee to receive his dog biscuit. She said, "Bullet, when is your dad going to get married and make me a great-grandma?"

I ignored all such comments.

"Oh, I'm so glad you could get away from that big case! How's it going?" Mom crowed as she hugged me tightly.

"Just getting started."

It obviously was some kind of special occasion because she was wearing lipstick and her dress-up hippie clothes: suede boots, long colorful skirt, and fringed calfskin suede jacket. Today she wore her hair down in soft curls, more gray creeping into the brown.

"Who's minding the store?" I asked.

"Crystal, our new girl we hired last summer," Grandma Dee said.

At fifty something, Crystal was hardly *a girl*. In my opinion, she was scary—like a gypsy medium with her big hair, heavy make-up, abundance of bangles and flowing garments.

As my two grandmothers moved in for hugs, I noticed a tall man dressed in khaki pants and a blue shirt, standing against the kitchen counter. At first, I thought this whole thing was about mom wanting me to meet a new boyfriend, but then I realized *who* he was—Patrick Sheehan—my adoptive father, the man who abandoned us. I did the math . . .twenty-six years ago.

"You remember your dad?" my mom said. Her absurd question made me laugh.

I looked at the man with salt-and-pepper hair and a smile that didn't match his sad eyes. Patrick apprehensively moved toward me, arms extended expecting a hug I couldn't give. He withdrew his arms.

My shock was quickly replaced with anger. I turned to my mom. "You totally blindsided me. How could you not tell me Patrick was going to be here?"

Her mouth opened as if to speak but no words came out.

I glared at Patrick. "So, after twenty-six years, what the hell are you doing here?"

He looked like he was going to cry.

"He's visiting your Grandma Sylvia," Grandma Dee said, obviously trying to be helpful.

"It was time," Patrick said.

I laughed. "For what? To make sure you get your inheritance?"

All three women gasped. Mom turned her back to me and placed her fingers to her temples.

Patrick said, "I told them you should have the choice whether I join you for dinner or not."

"Yeah, well, they knew what I'd say. And personally, I can't imagine why my mother would even let you in the door."

After a few seconds of awkward silence he said, "I don't blame you for your feelings, Cal, but I do want you to know I've loved you all these years."

I had to laugh again at the ludicrous statement. "Fine way to show it, Patrick."

Grandma Sylvia put her hands on her hips. "Oh, my gads, I thought you'd be happy to see your dad."

"Whatever made you think so? He deserted us. Now, he's standing here like he's done nothing wrong, and you're all cheery and weird."

"He's my son!" Grandma Sylvia shouted.

I glared at her. "When was the last time you've heard from him?"

She shuffled her feet. "We've been talking."

"Really? Nice if someone would have let me in on it," I said.

"I'm sorry, dear. I realize now we shouldn't have surprised you." Grandma Sylvia said.

"Ya think?" I said.

My mother turned around. Her face was crimson and tight. "Can we all agree that this is a difficult situation for *everyone* and just try to be civil and have a nice meal together?"

"You have got to be kidding me. No, if you want to have a nice chummy meal with Patrick, go right ahead," I said and called for Bullet.

"No, no. I'll go," Patrick said, grabbing his jacket from the hook bar by the back door. He picked up a briefcase from the floor and said, "See you later, Mom."

After Patrick left—came the silence. The women stood motionless until my mother went for the wine.

"What the hell did you all expect?" I asked.

"I asked Patrick to be here when I talked to you," she said.

"About what?" I asked.

"There are some things you don't know and I wanted you to hear the truth from both of us together," she said.

"Yeah well, it's all yours now." If I were a cartoon, smoke would be coming out of my ears. It took everything I had not to put a fist through something.

Just then the doorbell rang. "Oh, that's just George," Grandma Dee said as she hustled to answer it.

"Just *George*?" I asked.

"George Dobowitz, her new boyfriend."

What the fuck? "Boyfriend?"

Grandma Dee walked back arm in arm with a man who could be her male twin—a slender, silver-haired man. They were about the same height and build, even wearing similar clothing—dark slacks and sweaters over white shirts. She introduced us. We shook hands. Firm grip.

"Wine?" she asked, as she poured several glasses of red. She handed me one.

"What's this? Liquid courage?" I asked.

"I definitely need it," my mother said picking up her glass and chugging it.

"What the heck is going on?" I asked.

Grandma Sylvia gestured with her hand to move. "Go talk! We'll get the dinner on."

When Mom and I made our way into the living room, I was shocked to see the beige walls had been painted dark red.

"Don't you just *love* the new color?" mom asked.

"What's not to love about the color of blood?" I asked.

"So warm, don't you think? What about the new vertical blinds? And try out the new cream leather couch and matching chair. They are real comfy," my mother said chirpily.

"Yeah, yeah—everything looks great. Now, quit stalling. Tell me what I *need* to know," I said. I took a big gulp of wine and quickly realized it was a cheap vintage but not terrible. I sat in the new chair—surprisingly comfortable. Bullet, sensing something was going on, lay down at my feet.

Mom took another gulp of wine then sighed deeply before she began. "You know some of this. When your Aunt Grace finished her senior year of high school, she was just eighteen and six months pregnant with you, but what you may not know is that . . . Patrick . . . is your *biological* father."

"Oh, Christ."

"Why don't I start at the beginning?"

"Why don't you?" The anger began to seep into every fiber of my being. I took a big breath and counted backwards from ten, trying to transfer the rage to the cognitive centers of my brain. "That means your husband screwed your sister when she was underage."

Mom bobbed her head back and forth a few times. "Well, yes. Can I just tell the story?"

"By story, I suppose you mean the long version?"

She ignored my comment. "Grace wasn't really dating anyone at the time and wouldn't tell us who your biological father was, so I had no idea it was Patrick and when he insisted Grace move in with us until she delivered, I thought he was the most *sensitive* and *supportive* husband in the world, taking in my little sister like that." She took a quick breath and another sip of wine. "The plan was she'd put you up for adoption, but she couldn't do it. She wanted to take care of you. When it was time for her to start classes at the

State University, we moved you both into a small apartment in St. Cloud. About two weeks later, she called, sobbing. Patrick *insisted* we drive right down and talk to her. Grace was hysterical because she said she couldn't be a good mother and a college student at the same time. When he suggested we adopt you and raise you as our own, Grace agreed, and I was delighted."

"And why in hell did you wait until now to tell me all this?"

"Can I finish my story?"

"Go ahead." I couldn't imagine being any more pissed off, but hey, who knew.

"Around that time, Mom and I had opened our shop, and your dad was teaching biology at Prairie Falls High School and because he worked summers as a house painter, we paid Grace to be your nanny so she could earn money for college. Well, by then Hank came along, Grace graduated that spring and hadn't found a job, so she continued to nanny for us during the day, but lived with my folks. One day when I was making supper, you told me that your daddy and auntie took naps together."

"You got mad at me and stopped cooking my macaroni and cheese."

"Oh, sweetheart, is that how you remember it? Of course, I wasn't mad at you. Well anyway, when I called Grace and told her what you said, she told me everything—that Patrick was your father. When he walked in the door that night I immediately confronted him—he couldn't even look at me. I told him to get out. He went over to my parents to try and talk to them about Grace, but by that time mom and I had already talked. Dad threatened Patrick with statutory rape . . . told him if he ever saw him near either of his girls or grandkids he would have him arrested, and if that didn't work, he'd kill him. Next thing I knew, he resigned and moved to California. Dad never figured on Grace leaving with him.

"Anyway, Grace would call every so often and want to talk to you, but because it was upsetting, Dad put his foot down and told her not to call again."

"So, Grandpa disowned Grace."

"Well, yes. Cal, there were so many times when I almost told you the truth. But at first, you were just too young to understand, then the longer I waited, the more awkward it became. I know it was wrong not to tell you," she said.

"Ya think?"

As Mom started to cry, she wiped her tears with her sleeve. The only times I've witnessed her crying was the first day of kindergarten, when Hank and my Grandpas died, and right then.

"Grace died a short time ago from cancer. She left you an inheritance."

"I don't fuckin' want it," I said.

"Don't be so hasty. It's quite a sum."

"They never contacted me in all those years. Screw it. I don't want their money."

She put her fingers to her mouth. "Well, that's not exactly correct."

"What do you mean?"

"They sent you letters," she said.

My mouth dropped open.

"I saved them all for you," she said.

"Why would you hold back letters?"

"Because I was afraid they'd entice you with Disneyland and you'd want to go live with them and the court would agree—There, I said it. I was afraid of losing you, too." By this time she was sobbing.

I didn't react for a while—maybe as long as a minute or two.

"I'm absolutely stunned to find out you're not who I thought you were."

"I'm so sorry. Can you ever forgive me?"

"See, that's tricky. I'm just not sure. But now I can adjust to the fact that you're a liar and I can never really trust you again."

"Don't say that. You're just mad. You'll get over it."

"You know I'm not so much mad as I am extremely disappointed . . . in all of you. What a bunch of . . ."

"Fuck ups?" she offered.

"Took the words right out of my mouth."

And at that moment, Grandma Dee entered to tell us cheerily that dinner was ready.

"I'm leaving."

Grandma Dee grabbed me. "Honey, I know this is hard for you. We haven't been together in such a long time and I want you to get to know George a little bit. Please, at least stay for dinner."

I have trouble saying no to my Grandmas because they've always gone out of their way to make me happy.

"Didn't *you* think I deserved the truth, Grandma?"

Mom spoke up. "Your grandmothers didn't know much of it. Don't punish them."

So, she guilted me into staying for dinner. George pulled Grandma Dee's chair out for her. They grinned like a teenagers in love—*oh, man, this is so bizarre.*

My grandmas had put together my favorites: chicken, mashed potatoes, corn, cole slaw, fruit salad, and lemon meringue pie. I picked at my food while George told lame jokes, and laughed at all the stupid stories my family told about me—like the time I asked my first grade teacher how long it took to grow boobies that big. So, I thought I'd give it back to the old boy while mom and the grandmas were in the kitchen serving up the pie. I sat back in my chair and looked him in the eye.

"So, George, what exactly are your intentions with Dee?"

He looked caught off guard, but replied, "Why, she's a very fine lady and we are having the time of our lives."

"So how did you two meet?"

"My neighbor introduced us. She works in your grandmother's store and I stopped by one afternoon to say hello."

"You mean Crystal?"

"Yes, Crystal."

"What's she like anyway? You hear strange bumps and noises coming from her house, visitors coming and going?"

"What are you insinuating? She's a fine, respectable woman."

"Oh, I heard she talks to spirits and gives palm readings or something."

An indignant look spread across his face. "Certainly not."

My thought was he might be doing Crystal. "Are you using protection?"

Having just taken a swig of his wine, George had an awful coughing fit. Grandma Dee came out to ask him if he was okay and pat his back. After it subsided, she went back into the kitchen.

"Sorry, George," I said. "I'm just messing with you."

He smiled faintly.

"Seriously though, condoms aren't just to prevent pregnancy, there are diseases out there you don't want to share with the golden girls."

He mumbled something that included the word "monogamous" and excused himself to the restroom.

After dessert, Grandma Dee insisted we played a few hands of blackjack so they could practice. *Practice* my ass . . . they cleaned our clocks.

"Are you two living at the casino?" I asked.

"We take the senior citizen bus every Friday to the Grand Casino in Mille Lacs," Grandma Dee said proudly.

"Terrific," I said wondering how much of her savings she'd gambled away.

Shortly after, George and Dee excused themselves—they were playing in a blackjack tournament at the Senior Center in Brainerd.

That's when my Mom handed me an envelope. I was a bit taken aback when I saw an insurance check in the amount of $750,000.

Next, she handed me a large, stuffed manila envelope. I pulled out an envelope postmarked 1982 that appeared to have been opened and re-glued. *Good grief.*

"I'll read these at home. I'm taking off."

"You're leaving so soon?" my mother asked.

"I stayed for dinner to spend time with my grandmothers and now I really don't care to be around you."

"Well, you did get a surprise today."

"That's what you call it? A surprise? I'd call it a fucking mind-blowing revelation . . . and not in a good way."

"Oh."

I shook my head and headed for the door.

"I've packed leftovers for you," Grandma Sylvia said.

"Thanks." I grabbed the bag of food, called Bullet, and left. I seriously didn't know if I'd ever get over this deception.

12

I WAS TWO MILES from Gull Lake when I turned around and headed to Brainerd to Grandma Sylvia's house. I found Patrick in the living room watching television in my grandpa's old recliner. He looked surprised as I walked in sat down on the couch. Bullet walked off sniffing and exploring. I threw the check down on the coffee table.

"I don't want your money," I said.

"Don't punish yourself for what I did. It's yours. Grace wanted you to have it."

"I guess you were supposed to help with the big announcement."

"That Grace passed?"

"Ah, no—that you were my sperm donor."

"Well, I *was* shocked Hope had never told you. It would have furthered her case against me."

"It slipped her mind." A few seconds of silenced passed before I added, "This afternoon she gave me all the cards you sent me when I was a kid. First I knew about them."

"She told me she was going to. I understand why she kept them from you."

"Isn't that big of you? What I want to know is why you thought a card a year was enough?"

Patrick winced. "You're right . . . it wasn't. This may sound like an excuse, but when we tried to call and talk to you, we were threatened and told never to call again. Then they changed to an unlisted number."

"Here's the thing. If I have children, nothing will ever separate them from me. Nothing. It was your Goddamn choice to leave the state and not fight for me. So, don't give me any more of that 'I tried' shit."

Bullet came to nudge me with his head. I stroked his head and told him it was okay.

Patrick held his hands as if in prayer. "You're absolutely right, but I knew a custody battle wouldn't be good for anyone."

"You knew you'd lose. Statutory rape and all that." I was firing below the belt and it felt good.

"Maybe, but we also knew it would have devastated Hope."

"Yeah, you were thinking of Hope the whole time you fucked her under-aged sister."

He shook his head. "I must be a monster in your eyes."

I nodded, "Yeah. Child molesters are."

We sat in silence for a few moments before I said, "You all handled this just about as poorly as three people could. You know that?"

"I do. We tried to find you when you were college age, but no one would give out your information."

"About that time, I'd thought about trying to find Grace. I'd asked Mom if she knew where she was. She said she didn't. I had no desire to find my adoptive father who deserted us."

We sat in uncomfortable silence for a time before Patrick said, " I drove out to the cemetery today to see my dad and Hank's graves."

"You didn't come to either funeral," I said accusingly.

"Actually, I was here for Hank's but your Grandpa Riggens convinced the cops I was going to kidnap you and had me thrown out of the town the morning before the funeral."

"You were there?"

"You don't remember that we talked at the funeral home the night before?"

"No. I probably blocked it out."

"Well, we didn't talk long before Hope spotted us and yanked you away. I have a lot of regrets, Cal. I never wanted to hurt Hope, but what I had with Grace was overpowering. She was my whole life—and now without her—I can hardly breathe." He began sobbing. He cried for a good two minutes, but I couldn't bring myself to comfort him.

When he stopped I said, "It's hurts to be left, doesn't it?"

He looked at me heavy-heartedly. "I have something for you," he said. He left the room and came back with the briefcase and sat in the recliner. He pulled out a five-by seven headshot of two women and handed it to me.

"That's Grace and your sister, Angelica, taken a couple years ago, before Grace got sick," he said. "You can keep it."

"I have a sister?" *Why hadn't I thought about the possibility of a sibling?*

"You didn't know?"

"No."

"You resemble each other. I hope you'll agree to meet her some day."

My cell phone rang. I looked on the display to see Naomi Moberg's name. I picked up. "Hi."

"It's Naomi. Hey, I need to get out of the house. Want to go to a movie tonight?"

"I'm still in Brainerd."

Silence. "Oh, sorry to bother you."

"No, no it's fine. How about I drop by when I get back?"

"I'd like that," she said.

After I'd hung up, I noticed an Angels' baseball cap on the side table. It triggered a memory.

"I remember the three of us together," I said.

He looked at me hopefully. "Yeah?"

"You, Grace, and me. It was a rainy day, Hank was napping, and Grace was reading a children's book to me about a cap peddler who had all his caps stolen by monkeys. She gathered a bunch of caps and stacked them on my head and when you came home, we showed you our game and you joined in. We all fell to the floor, rolling around, and laughing. There was something very intimate about that day and I never told mom about it. I think it was the next day I saw you in bed together. I told mom. Why didn't I tell her about the caps instead?"

Tears rolled down his cheeks. He took out a handkerchief and wiped them away. "I'm sorry," he said. He leaned down and reached into the briefcase then pulled out an envelope and handed it to me. "This is from Grace. She wrote this when she knew she wasn't going to make it. I was going to give it to you after dinner when your mom and I talked to you."

"What did she die of?"

"She had an aggressive form of breast cancer called metaplastic carcinoma. It had already metastasized by the time she was diagnosed."

"I'm sorry for your loss." And at that moment, even though I didn't really know Grace, I felt a loss too.

"I hope you'll agree to meet your sister. Both of you are innocent in this thing. She's studying in London this year, but she'll be back in May."

"I'm truly overwhelmed by all of this shit."

"Cal, we won't pressure you." He reached for the insurance money envelope and stood to hand it to me. "Look, this money sure as hell doesn't remove the guilt we all share in hurting you. I just think you deserve something."

Both envelopes in hand, I said good-bye, not knowing if I'd ever see him again. He moved in for an awkward hug, and I didn't stop him but didn't reciprocate.

He got tears in his eyes again. "Do you have someone special in your life?"

Adriana flashed through my mind. "No," I said.

"Don't settle for anyone that doesn't knock your socks off."

"I find it amusing—you giving me relationship advice." I stood. "I'm gonna take off."

"Bye then," he said, patting my back.

I whistled for Bullet. He came running and we left. On the drive back I muttered to myself the entire way. I couldn't fucking believe my fucking family.

NOT KNOWING HOW SOMEONE as supremely groomed as Naomi felt about dogs, I dropped Bullet off at home and fed him, before I drove to her house.

When she opened the door my face must have revealed my emotional state because she said, "What's wrong?"

"Bad day with the fam."

"Come in." When we were just inside the door she asked, "Beer or wine?"

"Whatever you have, as long as it's alcohol," I said.

"Merlot all right?"

I nodded.

"Family gatherings can be a bitch," she said.

"You have no idea."

After she poured us both a generous glass of wine, we went into her living room and back into the seventies—gold brocade matching chair and couches that looked brand new.

"New vintage couches?"

"I pulled off the plastic after Mom died. I hate them, but I can't afford to buy all new furniture yet."

Naomi picked up the remote and turned off one of those Jersey housewives' shows. She put her wine glass on the glass coffee table, sat on the couch, tucking one leg under her. She patted the sofa and said, "Take a load off. You look like you need to talk."

I sat next to her and said, "I almost don't know where to begin."

"Doesn't matter. Just start. I'm a good listener."

"Okay, today I found out my adoptive father, Patrick, is also my biological father. You see, when he was married to Hope, he knocked-up my biological mother, Grace, who was seventeen at the time. Hope didn't know Patrick was the father and when Grace couldn't take care of me, they adopted me."

"Hope is your aunt and your adoptive mother?"

"Yes. Patrick was maybe twenty-four at the time. Anyway, four years later his marriage is in trouble because he and Grace are still madly in love. I catch them in bed, tell my mom, and she throws him out. Grace and he take off for California. My grandparents disown them. Hope prevents them from contacting me. Now Grace has died and Patrick shows up to visit his mother—my grandmother—and they all thought it would be grand to surprise me with his presence and the truth."

"For real?"

"How could I make that shit up?"

"Why didn't Hope tell you before this?"

"She was afraid she'd lose me."

"Some things are difficult and risky to share, but that's freaking ridiculous!"

I laughed. "It is, isn't it?"

She picked up her glass. "Here's to having ridiculous parents."

"Here, here. So did you go to a movie?"

"Nah, I needed a good cry, so I rented *Titanic*."

"Cheery flick. Why did you need a good cry?"

She laughed. "Life sucks sometimes. Are you hungry?"

"Not in the slightest."

"Know what I hungry for?" she asked.

"What?"

She crawled over to me and straddled my lap. "You."

One minute later we were in her bed. After, we lay entangled—sweaty and panting. There was nothing gentle about what we just did.

"Wow. It's been a long time since I've had sex like that!" she said.

"Too much?"

"Oh no, it was perfect." We lay there for a time, then she sat up and said, "I can't get over your family lying to you like that."

"I asked my mom about Grace once and she said family wasn't as important to Grace as she was to herself."

"Well, considering she screwed her sister's husband, I'd say that's probably accurate."

"Patrick should have known better to mess with her. She was young."

"Look, at seventeen, Grace knew what she was doing. At that age I was all over my boyfriend. If I'd have gotten knocked up, it wouldn't have been his fault."

"I like your honesty."

"I tell it like it is."

I patted her flat belly and said, "And I'm sorry to leave you, but I have a dog to take care of. You like dogs?"

"My folks never wanted pets and I guess I never craved them like other kids."

I think that meant Bullet wasn't invited over. No big deal. He couldn't go to Adriana's either because pets weren't allowed in her building. I got dressed, went back to my place, and took Bullet out again and then stared at the phone with the message indicator blinking. I ignored it. I knew who had called. I picked up the two envelopes I'd left on the table, grabbed a beer, and got up the nerve to pry open the letter from Grace.

It was dated last August 15th on my thirtieth-first birthday.

My Dear Cal,

If you are reading this letter it means that I am gone. I want to apologize to you for so many things: the first was going along with the decision not to raise you myself. My only excuse was that I was young and easily swayed by my parents who said I was too young for such a responsibility. When you were born, I was barely eighteen and really didn't know how I was going to take care of you.

My memories of baby-sitting you are my only consolation.

When your dad decided that his marriage wasn't working and that he needed to separate from Hope, we decided to leave the state and not have our love thrown in Hope's face every time she saw us together. I cried all the way out to California.

Over the years when I tried to talk to you, my father rejected my phone calls. He told me to stop calling for your sake. I started to think he was right, but now I know I shouldn't have listened. I know I hurt Hope very much. Your dad and I didn't mean to fall in love, and after you were born, we tried to fight it. But as Hope and Patrick were unable to work through their difficulties and save their marriage, we realized we couldn't stay apart. It was selfish I know but we've had a wonderful marriage. I only wish we had been able to have you with us as part of our family.

I am grateful to Hope for taking you and loving you as her own child. I'm not expecting you to forgive me, Cal. I wanted to see you grown up before I die, but now I'm afraid I'm too weak to travel.

My beautiful boy, I have loved and missed you my whole life.

Grace

My face felt strangely cool. I touched my cheek and found it wet with tears and then a came the crush of sadness. I cried for all that never was . . .

Later, I opened the manila envelope containing the letters. I pulled them all out and, using the postmarks, sorted them by dates—August of 1982 through August of 1999. Inside the first was a child's birthday card with Mickey Mouse on it. Enclosed was a short letter and another smaller envelope containing a fifty-dollar savings bond. In the letter Patrick said he had moved to California and wanted me to come out for a visit so he could take me to Disneyland. He went on to say he loved and missed me and hoped I was doing okay.

All the envelopes contained a birthday card, letter, and a savings bond, which gradually increased in value, along with the sophistication of the cards through the years. If I'd received the August of 1989 letter, I would have discovered I had a new sister named Angelica. She was now twenty-three.

The mature bond value totaled $58,500. Obviously, Patrick and Grace had done well financially. I thought about my family, the one I lived with and the one I didn't dare to even think about when I was a child. What would my life have been like if Grace and Patrick had taken me with them? What if I'd known my little sister all these years? Not giving a kid his dad's letters was a shitty thing to do.

Before I went to bed I listened to the message from my mother. She just wanted to make sure I was okay. Seriously? "No, mom, I'm not okay."

I HAD THE NIGHTMARE. *I'm nine years old—playing video games in the den. My Grandma Dee left and tells me to mind Hank. He keeps pestering wanting me to help him build a rocket with Legos. I put him off because I'm really into Pac Man.*

When Grandma comes home she asks where Hank is. I don't know. We yell out his name, searching every room in the house. He doesn't answer, so I run outside to look for him. I look in the sandbox, the swing set, then run to the lake. Hank knows he's not to be down by the lake, but that's where he is—floating face down. I try to scream for help but no sounds come out. My Grandma runs up behind me, shrieking. She yells for me to call 911, then splashes through the water toward Hank. I'm frozen and that's where the nightmare always takes a hideous turn.

Suddenly, I'm pulled under the water. I can't see what's holding me down. I keep trying to kick to the surface, but remain under. Then I see Hank. I try to reach for him, but he drifts away. I'm out of breath. My lungs are going to burst. It seems to last forever. I'm kicking and thrashing and slowly—slowly—start moving upward.

I always wake when I reach the surface, breathing hard and drenched in sweat.

I'll never get that image of Hank floating face down in the lake and Grandma Dee's scream out of my head.

13

DAY FOUR

I WOKE UP AN HOUR before my alarm. At 5:00 a.m., I took Bullet for a run. Instead of mulling over the case, my mind kept flipping to my family. After I showered and dressed, I called Grandma Sylvia's home phone. She answered on the first ring. "Are you okay?" she asked anxiously.

"Not really. I'm really pissed at all of you."

She sighed. "I don't blame you. Just don't hate me. I couldn't stand that."

"I don't *hate* you. Can I speak to Patrick?"

"First, I need to confess something."

A dizzy wave swept through me. "Oh, Christ."

"Okay. I'm just going to come out with it. When I said I was visiting my cousin in Kansas the past few years, I really went to California. Hope and Dee didn't know about it."

Wow. "Anything else?"

"No."

"Then let me speak with Patrick."

I could hear the phone fumbling between them, then Patrick say, "Cal?"

"I read all the letters. I'm not saying I'm ready to forgive you or that what you did was right, but I think I understand your perspective."

"You don't know what that means to me."

"That's all I have," I said.

"If you ever need anything or want to contact me, my cell phone number is on the back of the envelope."

"What I need is time and lots of it."

"Take all you need."

"Thank you for the bonds and the insurance money. I wasn't expecting that."

"It's the least we could . . . Cal, I really hope to hear from you . . . when you're ready."

"Tell Grandma if there's anything else she's forgotten to confess, she should send it in an email."

"Right."

I hung up the phone, and said to Bullet, "They're all a bunch of lying bastards, Bullet."

He barked in agreement. I had to get my mind off my dysfunctional family and onto the investigation, but first I needed to stop at the bank.

At eight o'clock, Pam Udell, the receptionist at Prairie Falls National Bank, was unlocking the front doors. I followed her inside and asked about a car loan. With all the money I'd received yesterday, I could pay cash for a car, but thought I'd like to hang onto it, maybe use it to buy a house someday. Pam made a call, and a moment later, Hamilton Fairchild shook my hand a little too firmly as he introduced himself. Evidently, he didn't remember the time I helped him change a flat out on County 40 a few years ago while on patrol. That day Fairchild didn't want to get his fancy clothes dirty so he let me do all the work. I found that mildly amusing.

Fairchild, a distinguished-looking man in his early sixties, wore an expensive gray suit with a starched blue shirt and coordinated tie. Comb lines were visible in his thick gray hair. I'd wanted so badly to say, "Nice to meet you, Slick," but instead, I substituted "sir" and reintroduced myself.

"Deputy Sheehan? Aren't you on the team investigating my son-in-law's death?"

"Yes, sir, and I want to express my condolences."

His eyebrows turned down as his eyes sank into sadness. "Thank you. Making any progress on the investigation?"

"We're still gathering information."

"Well, I certainly hope you get to the bottom of this."

"As do we."

"Now, what can I do for you?"

"I need to purchase a new vehicle and thought I'd come in for pre-approval."

"Well, terrific. Do you have an account with us?"

"Yes, savings and checking."

"That'll make things easy, and we like to give our law enforcement officers in the community the best rate in town. My car loan officer is on vacation, but I can help you. Come on into my office."

I followed him into a large, corner office that smelled of furniture polish and leather. Fairchild sat behind a handsome, dark wood desk in a matching chair, and I sat on one of the two club chairs opposite him. His grief seemed to evaporate as he turned to his computer to gather my personal information. In a few short minutes, he said I had excellent credit and approved me for a loan of $20,000 more than I wanted to spend.

"Could you excuse me? I'll get a copy of this for you."

While he was out I took notice of the artwork on the walls. As I glanced at the professionally framed photos, one struck me. I got up to get a better look. *Holy shit!* It was a photo of Fairchild and Eleanor Kohler, brandishing rifles, standing next to an elk hung from a rafter.

Fairchild walked and said, "That was taken several years ago when we used to take family hunting trips to Montana."

"Eleanor hunts?"

Fairchild grinned proudly. "She shot that elk."

The implication must have suddenly dawned on him, because the back peddling began: "She hasn't hunted since she's had the kids. Doesn't even own a gun anymore." Fairchild sat back in his chair and said, " All right then, what kind of vehicle are we looking for?"

"Haven't firmed up that decision," I said, my mind stuck on Eleanor brandishing a rifle.

He looked at me for a moment then said, "I have a thought. As soon as the sheriff releases Ted's truck, Eleanor wants me to sell it. It's only two years old, low mileage, worth well over twenty-thousand, but I'd give you a really good deal on it—maybe eighteen."

"I was thinking something easy on gas."

"Well, think it over."

Buying a dead man's vehicle was a little too weird.

Fairchild walked me out into the lobby, grabbed a handful of pens just like the one under Kohler's truck seat from a basket, and handed them to me. We're always short of pens at the department.

"Coffee and cider over there. Think we even have some ginger cookies. Well, good luck on the investigation," he said.

I nodded. "I hope we can solve this quickly for your family's sake—and the Petersons."

"Yes, yes. Such a tragedy for all."

We shook hands and I stopped to deposit the insurance check and put the bonds in my safety deposit box. I left the bank with pre-approval and a fist full of pens, blown away by the fact that Eleanor was a crack shot. I also had a feeling that Fairchild wasn't deeply grieving his son-in-law's death.

Troy Kern was due back today from a vacation. He was not going to like missing being part of the case and I was hoping Ralph wouldn't think we needed him. Our personalities clashed. He thought he was a comedian and I thought he was an asshole who got off on making a guy feel like a fool. Every deputy started off with jail duty for a year or two. When I started ten years ago, Troy worked the control room in the jail. My second day of work, he arranged to have me process a guy by the name of Harvey Vann. Vann went on benders for days and finally ended up either in the hospital or in one of our jail cells designed for prisoners who were out of control due to drugs, alcohol, or mental illness. He had a habit of stripping when he topped off his tank, and that evening, patrol brought him in wrapped in a blanket. He was belligerent and smelled like shit. It took everything I had to keep that fat, naked, stinking man in control while I was processing him.

Later, Shannon, also a recent hire at the time, told me they usually had three deputies on Vann, and that Troy and his cronies were in the control room watching me on the monitors, laughing their asses off—all part of an initiation ritual. My initiation. Shannon said hers occurred on her first night, she mysteriously got locked in a cell with a prisoner and Troy didn't release her for an hour.

When I walked in at 9:00 a.m. Troy was sitting at his desk in our shared office. Divorced, in his early forties, about five-foot-eleven and 190 pounds, he has a distinguishing cleft in his chin, wore his brown hair over-gelled in the tousled look—thought he was cool.

"How was Vegas?" I asked.

He threw a pencil across his desk. "Why didn't someone call me to tell me about the double murders?"

"You were on vacation."

"This is the biggest case in the history of the department—I should have been notified."

"Not my call. Talk to Jack."

"You better believe I will."

I shrugged. Troy left for about an hour. When he came back in I was on the phone with Juanita Brutlag. I made a few notes, then made my way to the ten o'clock case meeting. Present were Sheriff Jack Whitman, Sergeant Ralph Martinson, Leslie Rouch, Betty Abbott, me, and as we were just getting started—Troy Kern showed.

Ralph began by asking Betty what she'd found on Kohler's computers.

Then I realized I should have checked Ronny's phone. I'd let myself get distracted with my family's bullshit.

When I refocused, I heard Betty say, "We found passwords in Kohler's desk drawer for both work computers. Samantha Polansky was able to work on them—nothing significant on messages sent and received. Internet history showed only work related searches or online newspapers. His secretary used her desk computer for personal emails but nothing stood out to help the case. Samantha will work on the home computer next. If anyone can find something, it'll be Samantha."

After only a year on the job, Samantha already had a reputation as our "kid computer genius." She looked sixteen but was in her early twenties.

"Okay, then. Now, let's move on to Leslie."

Leslie opened a leather folder case. She pulled out a few pages of notes. "We found nothing significant at Kohlers' or Petersons' residences." She rose and moved to the map I'd drawn on the whiteboard and pointed to different locations as she spoke. "Now, from the blood spatter and where the casings were found, we feel Mr. Kohler was shot from approximately one hundred fifty yards on the western edge of the clearing. He was facing south toward the shoreline.

"Mr. Peterson was shot in the back from approximately two hundred yards. Our docs pulled one bullet from Peterson's body. The five casings were found in two locations—two here and three here—and there were no fingerprints or smudges on them. So obviously they were handle with gloves. We figure six shots were fired, so we missed a casing. But I understand the scene was compromised last night, so no sense in trying to recover it." She sat back down.

"The shooter didn't pick up the casings because either he didn't take the time or we aren't expected to find the weapon," I said.

Leslie pointed at me. "My thoughts exactly. Also, we entered a number of items in the BRO Lab in line for DNA testing: the Bible quote note in Kohler's truck, a Pepsi can, two marijuana stubs, and a wad of gun. And with the heroin and marijuana find in the storage barn attic at the landing, it's certainly possible this is drug related."

Betty raised her hand. "We were able to lift prints from the containers. I haven't had a chance to run them through AFIS. Cal talked Bob Brutlag into surrendering his rifles and we obtained two .30-30's from the Johnston household, so we'll be conducting ballistics tests ASAP."

Ralph said, "We added Mike Johnston to our persons of interest based on a remark Bob Brutlag made in his interview. He said Kohler's secretary, Lisa Kelly, claimed Kohler made a pass at her."

Jack made a scoffing sound.

Ralph ignored it and continued. "Mike is Lisa Kelly's boyfriend. We figured he had motive right there. We obtained a warrant for firearms he had access to and pulled two .30-30 rifles from the Johnston household. And that brings us to Cal's interviews."

I opened my folder. "Okay. The Petersons gave me names of Ronny's friends. I was able to interview Max Becker, Chad and Todd Hackett, all of whom are roommates in a house on Fourth Street. All three had alibis and were not particularly cooperative—it was if they were distancing themselves. Peterson's brother, Kevin, says Ronny had a run in with Nevada Wynn and one of his buddies, Pierce Redding, last summer."

"Who're they?" Leslie asked.

Troy sat forward. "Wynn's a dirt bag dealer, street name, Snake. He moved back to Minneapolis when the task force turned up the heat on drug trafficking into our tri-county area."

"Are they persons of interest?" Leslie asked.

"Yep. They're on the list," Ralph said. "By the way, Cal, did you ever find Ronny's phone?"

Heat rose up my neck and face. "Yes, I found it in one of the Park Department's trucks. I dropped it off for Betty. Were you able to pull prints?"

"Yes, scored two good ones, but both Ronald's. It's back in evidence."

"Good, I'll be able to look into his call log after the meeting." I felt I covered my ass on that one, but no other prints means I couldn't prove anyone else touched the phone or how it got into truck #10.

"Also, when I picked up Brutlag's rifles, Bob gave me two phone numbers. I reached his wife, Juanita, this morning. She worked at Buzzo's and said Kohler used to stop for drinks there at least once a week and he was overly friendly, but that's it. To her knowledge, no one had any altercations with Kohler, including her husband. Ronny was a different story. She personally called the department on him more than once for bar fighting, and as a result he received two drunk-and-disorderly citations."

"Cal and I dropped in at Buzzo's yesterday afternoon. Man, were the rumors flying," said Ralph.

"Like what?" asked Jack.

"Oh, everybody had an opinion: gang shootings, foreign terrorists, mafia hit men. Rodney Teal said some guys who looked like Tony Soprano were seen having breakfast at the Sportsman that morning," Ralph said.

He continued. "Happens. Anyway, Hector pretty much substantiates what Juanita told Cal. We talked to Connie Hackett, she said Kohler was a charming man and Ronny was a doll."

Everyone laughed.

"No kidding, that's what she said."

"Yeah well, she likes anybody with a pecker," Troy said, getting a few chuckles.

Without reacting to Troy's remark, Ralph continued. "Now, I want you to view two interviews Cal and I conducted. The first is Kohler's secretary, Lisa Kelly and the second is her boyfriend's, Mike Johnston."

He opened up the file and projected the interview on the single clean space on the white board.

Everyone watched intently, occasionally making sounds or remarks. After, I noticed the smug look on Jack's face. "See, I told you Ted never touched the girl," he said.

I said, "But the thing is, *Johnston* didn't know that. So, he still had strong motive and his only alibi is his girlfriend."

"Betty, those ballistics tests are crucial," Ralph said.

"I'll get on it right after we adjourn and call you with the results."

Ralph gave a summary of his interview with Eleanor Kohler that added no significant information—which reminded me of the photo in Fairchild's office.

"Okay, something interesting. I stopped by the bank to get pre-approval for my car loan, and Fairchild himself helps me. On his wall, he has photos of family hunting trips. In one of the photos Eleanor is standing by the elk she shot. There's some time unaccounted for on the morning of the shooting—maybe enough time to drive out to Emmaline and back then run errands."

"Her alibi checks out," Ralph said. "Talked with the carwash and Nancy Martin—they confirmed her whereabouts."

"Maybe Rodney Teal's right and her old man put out a hit on him," Troy said. "Ronny's drives in, sees what's going down and takes off. Gets shot in the back."

"Troy, are you gonna go up to a pillar of the community and accuse him of putting a hit out on his son-in-law?" said Jack.

"Do I look stupid? I thought you'd do that, boss. The guy owns my house and car." He got the laughs he wanted.

"Actually, I don't think Troy's scenario is out of the question. Fairchild doesn't seem broken up about Ted's death. Kohler had week-old injuries—something was going on they're not talking about," I said.

Jack threw a pencil across the table. "Jesus Christ. Things are getting carried away in here."

"People do things when emotionally charged they'd never do ordinarily," I said.

"No shit, Sherlock," Jack said. "All I'm saying is that it is absolutely idiotic to think Ham Fairchild would put a hit out on Ted. What'd be his motive? We have no indication anything improper was going on in Ted's life."

No shit, Sherlock? Nice. He succeeded in embarrassing me.

"So what do the rest of you think?" asked Ralph.

Bodies shifting in chairs, a cough, and an "um" were the only responses.

"Go ahead. Investigate both Ham and Eleanor, but this department is going to look like horse's asses if we accuse but can't prove anything," Jack said.

Ralph and I looked at each other. Everyone else, except Jack, suddenly had something very important to study in his or her notebooks.

Ralph said, "This is the way I see it. We live in a small community and it can get uncomfortable when we have to investigate people we know. You know as well as I do, Jack, that the spouse and family are always looked at, and we can do it without creating a big stink. Now, back to the interviews. I spoke with Kohler's mother and sister. Neither knows of anyone who'd do Kohler harm and said Ted never mentioned any difficulty with clients or anyone else, for that matter. So, our only real unknowns are Wynn and Redding. Cal, see what you can find out about them today."

Jack didn't look happy. "Unless there's something critical I need to hear, I'll be returning to my office to attend to all the other business I've been neglecting. Ralph remains lead investigator so your reports should be submitted to him. Cal will remain on the case. By the way, the Kohler funeral is on Wednesday at ten o'clock at St. Stephens. Peterson's is on Thursday, same time, same place. Let Georgia know if you'll be attending either."

When the meeting ended, I heard Troy asked Jack if he could speak to him. He wanted to bump me off the case, and he'd probably win that one. I wasn't feeling so confident after Jack's cheap shot.

I headed straight to the office to do what I should have done when I found Ronny's phone. The lock hadn't been turned on so I was able to get into it. If the phone had been glued to Ronny's hand like his mother said, you couldn't prove it by the amount of calls.

October 7th

Two unheard messages: 1) Gus told Ronny he was on his way 2) Gus wondered where Ronny was and asked him to call back.

Received call: dental office at 7:03 a.m.

Calls made: To Gus at 7:18 a.m.

Missed calls: the two from Gus, three from my phone yesterday.

October 6th

Calls made: to Zach Whitman at 7:05 p.m.

Received calls: 1) From his home phone at 5:00 p.m. 2) From Zach Whitman at 8:04 p.m.

I found it interesting Jack's grandson, Zach, was one of our victim's recent contacts. I copied the number and left a message for him to call me ASAP. So, Ronny made a call from his cell phone that morning, which meant he obviously had his phone at that point.

Troy was wearing a smirk as he entered the office and sat at his desk. That meant he probably got Jack to assign him to the case . . . maybe even replace me. Why is there always an asshole in every group?

14

DAY FIVE

IT WAS A RARE MOMENT when Troy, Ralph and I were all in the investigations office. I was checking the incident involving the altercation between Peterson and Pierce Redding that occurred last summer. Shannon had arrested both Peterson and Redding for assault but the charges were later reduced to disorderly conduct. Peterson paid a small fine and Redding failed to appear and had a warrant out. After a bit of research, I found an Oklahoma address for Redding. He didn't have any priors in Minnesota nor did he have a drivers' license or vehicle registered to him. After I informed Ralph, my desk phone rang, I thought it was another reporter trying to get a lead concerning the case, but the display said Birch County.

"Sheehan," I answered.

"Hi, Cal, this is Naomi."

"Oh, hi!" I said. I glanced at Ralph and Troy. Both were watching me. I swiveled my chair to face my desk.

"I'm so glad you stopped by Sunday night," she said.

I pretended to write some notes. "Yeah, me too."

"But I didn't call to compliment you on your sexual prowess, although I'd certainly rate it as a ten plus, I called to find out when my guys can get into Emmaline Park to pull that dock, close up the park."

"Hold on, Ralph Martinson's right here." I put my hand over the receiver. "Ralph, Naomi Moberg wants to know when her guys can go in and close up Emmaline."

"Today, as far as I'm concerned," he said. "We're done out there."

I repeated what he'd said.

"Thanks, that's good news. Cal, I want to go out myself and see where it happened. Would you possibly have time to show me sometime?"

"How about if I meet you out there today . . . at twelve o'clock?"

"Perfect," she said.

106

When I hung up, I asked Ralph if he had a problem with Naomi's request. He shook his head. "Nope. So, you're going to meet her out there?"

"Yeah."

"I'm going with," Troy said.

"Oh, I got a call from Jack. He assigned Troy to the case too, part time," Ralph said.

Just as I thought.

"Uh, okay."

WE LEFT FOR LAKE EMMALINE at 11:45 p.m.

"So, how'd you manage that?" I asked.

"What?"

"Getting on the case."

"Jack thought you could use the help because you're inexperienced."

"Right."

"I mean why would Jack assign a rookie who has shit for experience to the biggest case we've ever had?"

"You wanted on the case—you're on—now shut the fuck up about my inexperience. How many murders have you investigated?"

He shrugged.

"Thought so."

He began prattling on about his wild weekend in Vegas with April Kadinsky, his intermittent girlfriend for six years. I volleyed my attention between him and my family's recent disclosures like I was flipping through tacky reality TV shows. I managed to say, "Uh huh" a couple times, which seemed to satisfy him.

We drove into the Emmaline Park at noon. The only evidence of a double murder was the yellow crime scene tape—trampled and flapping. We had just exited the vehicle when Naomi drove up in a county pick-up truck. All County Park vehicles were white with the green Birch County Parks logo on the cab doors. She was wearing a royal-blue suit with a skirt just to the tops of her knees—and running shoes.

"Funny to see a woman all dolled up hopping outta a pick-up truck," Troy said.

It was. Naomi and I shook hands and exchanged smiles like nothing was between us.

When Troy shook her hand, he held it a second too long. "Don't you look nice," he said.

She blushed and smiled at his flattery. When I showed them where Kohler had tied his boat, Naomi asked why the top of a dock post was sawed off. I explained.

"Good, so you have a bullet. I'll just have the boys replace the post."

Then they followed me to the location where Ronny Peterson's body was found. As we approached, we could see wasps buzzing the blood patch in the middle of the marked outline. Upon sight, Naomi started tearing up. We all stood there a few seconds before she said, "Ronny was kind of a soft guy underneath all that tough exterior. He cried at my mom's funeral—said he knew her from the shop and she was always so friendly."

"Yes, she was. Always had a big smile," I said. I pictured Neva Hunt behind the counter. Somehow I couldn't picture Ronny owning clothes that needed dry cleaning, but what did I know?

We stood there in silence until Naomi said, "I'll be glad to close this park this year."

"I'll bet," I said.

Troy said, "The only park open year round is South Birch, right?"

"Right. It's a revenue maker with the educational programs, cross-country ski rentals trails, and Minnesota Fare."

"The restaurant was your doing, Naomi?" Troy asked.

She nodded.

"The food's great," he said. "You've made great improvements to the county park system."

She seemed to be soaking in his schmoozing, when another county truck rolled in.

"Can your guys remove the tape?" I asked.

"Sure, I'll tell them. Thanks for meeting me out here. You guys get the son of a bitch who did this," she said.

"We're trying," I said.

She nodded and walked toward her park workers.

Troy asked where we'd found the evidence so I showed him. He whistled. "Man, we're lucky the shooter left the casings."

"I think he may have been too rushed to take the time to find them among the leaves, and we do have the three bullets. Now to find the matching rifle."

When we got back in the vehicle we both watched Naomi get into her truck. He nodded toward her. "She's mighty fine."

"Aren't you with April?"

"*With* her? No. Banging her? Yes."

"Do you usually *bang* more than one woman at a time?"

"Sometimes it just works out that way. Besides, April's a party girl and I can't see her as a mother."

"Huh. Never thought you'd think of women as mothers."

"Why not?"

"You're a player, Kern."

"I could settle down if the right woman came along."

"Wow. A new side to Troy."

"What can I say?"

I wasn't sure why I didn't tell him I'd been with Naomi. Maybe because I wasn't sure what we had going.

ON THE WAY BACK to the office, we stopped at Subway to pick up sandwiches, and who happened to be in line, but Naomi's husband, Jeremy. He stood five-foot-nine, had a medium build, copper red hair, thin lips and a massive amount of freckles. He turned and spotted us. He never seemed particularly happy.

"Hey!" he said without a smile, as we took our places behind him in line.

I wondered if he knew about Naomi and me. "Hey, Jeremy. How ya doing?" I said, trying to be nonchalant.

"Great. Troy, haven't seen you in an age," he said.

"Are you still working at the candy factory?" Troy asked.

"Yep, yep. I made vice-president."

"I don't think I could stand that sweet smell all day long," Troy said.

"You don't notice it in the administration office," Jeremy.

"That's not what I heard. I heard things are pretty sticky sweet for you in there."

Jeremy blushed and swallowed hard noted by the bobbing of his prominent Adam's apple. "Say Cal, what do you hear from Adriana?"

"Not much." I pointed forward, letting Jeremy know it was his turn to order.

While our sandwiches were being made he said, "I often wonder about her—if she enjoys her new position with that prestigious law firm," he said.

"Imagine so," I said.

"This guy was crazy not to follow that babe down to Minneapolis. Am I right, Troy?"

"Right. Your divorce final?" Troy said.

Jeremy sneered, curling his thin upper lip. "No. Would you believe Naomi called me this morning and wanted to know if I *really* wanted her to sign the divorce papers? Give me an f-ing break. It's not as if I haven't been begging her to sign the sucker for the last six months. Know what I mean?"

"Yeah," Troy said, looking smug and nodding.

So Naomi didn't want the divorce from Jeremy the Jerk-off? Then what was last night about?

We paid for our food and Troy said, "Well, see ya around, Jeremy. Good luck with the divorce."

"Thanks, I need it."

15

B ACK AT THE OFFICE, while I ate my meatball sub, I did a search on Nevada Wynn. He'd just been released from Minnesota Correctional Facility-St. Cloud two weeks ago after serving six months on a drug conviction. Both his parents were deceased, but he had an older brother, Carson, who lived on Bryant Avenue in South Minneapolis. I got hold of his sister-in–law, Shelia, who said she and her husband had no knowledge where he was currently living or working—and didn't care. Nevada was not welcome in their home. I could find nothing on Pierce Redding. Maybe that was an alias.

Next, I called the Whitman's home number to connect with Zach. His mother, Sarah, answered and told me he was working at Cadillac Jack's, so I decided to pay him a personal visit. The door to the bar was locked. The sign said they were open at 4:00 p.m. I knocked, and a minute later Zach opened it a crack to proclaim the obvious: "We're not open."

"I know. I just have a few questions about Ronny Peterson."

"What about him?"

"Can we talk inside?"

He opened the door and begrudgingly led me in to the dimly lit bar. No one else seemed to be around, which was what I was hoping for. The bar was located on the upper level of the building, and the restaurant on the lower. They'd recently painted the walls a yellowish gold and new photos of vintage Cadillac's hung above the dark wood booths along the wall.

"I'm going to get to the point. You called Ronny Peterson the night before he died."

"Did I?"

I nodded.

A fake look of enlightenment crossed his face. "Oh, yeah, now I remember, I returned a call from him."

The thought occurred to me Zach certainly could know the combination to the storage shed located so conveniently near his home. Maybe the drugs were his. He started wiping the clean counter.

"What did he want?"

"He asked if I wanted to hang out."

"Did you?"

"Ah, yeah. We had a beer at Beck's place."

"Beck meaning Max Becker?"

He nodded. *Why would Max lie about that?* "What happened that night?"

He shrugged. "Nothin'."

"Everything was cool?"

He nodded slightly. "Yeah, cool as a cucumber."

"Do you know anyone who had a grudge against Ronny?"

He shook his head a little too hard. "No, man." He started moving glasses from a dishwasher to a shelf.

"What about Ted Kohler?"

"Nope."

"Do you know Nevada Wynn and his pal, Pierce Redding?"

"I've heard of Wynn. He lived in Prairie Falls for a while, didn't he?"

"You ever hang out with him?"

"Nope."

My phone rang. V Lewis was on the display.

"Excuse me," I said.

"Sheehan."

"Cal, Victoria Lewis. How about dinner tonight?"

Jeremy's statement about Naomi not wanting the divorce flashed through my mind. "I think it could work. Cadillac Jack's at 8:00 o'clock okay?"

Zach and I exchanged glances.

"Perfect. See you then."

I turned back to Zach. "The reason I ask about these things is that we have prints on a drug case found in the storage barn on Emmaline."

He shrugged. "So?"

"So whoever's prints we have might be implicated."

He nearly dropped a glass. "Not my deal." His cheeks turned blotchy.

"Your grandpa know you hang around with the Hackett's? They're into some bad shit."

"Give me a break," he said as he gave me one of those looks I must have given my mother a thousand times when I was a kid. I let some seconds of silence pass.

"Something else?" he asked, trying to sound nonchalant.

"Yeah, were you and Ronny friends, or were you his dealer?"

He froze for a second before he broke into laughter. "You're joking, right?"

"Sure, call it that. Which was it?"

He pushed out an airy "Puh," as if I was stupid for even having such thoughts before he said, "Friend."

But he wasn't on the list.

I was content with making Zach a little nervous about his "association" with the Hacketts and drugs. I didn't see any point in continuing the verbal judo so I went back into town and drove down the alley behind Becker's on Fourth Street and parked behind the Focus.

Max just happened to be on his way out the back door. "I'm late for work, can't talk." He walked past me headed for his car and stopped when he saw his car was blocked in.

"You gotta move your car," he said. When he saw I wasn't moving, he added, "Please."

"This won't take long. Why didn't you tell me Ronny was at your house the Thursday night before he died?"

"'Cause I didn't know, dude."

"How's that?"

"I had classes that night."

"Did you know he'd been here?"

"Guess maybe Todd told me."

"What else did Todd tell you?"

"Nothing."

"Why's everyone minimizing their association with Ronny?"

"I dunno. I guess cuz he didn't come round very often."

"When he wanted to buy or sell drugs?"

"Dude, that's not my deal. I don't get involved with that shit."

"Well, somebody better start telling the truth, so Ronny can have some justice."

"I am telling the truth, man. Now, can I go?"

"Yeah okay, but we'll talk again."

Max was flustered. I'd touched a nerve.

"And, Max, don't call me dude."

WHEN I GOT BACK to the department I met briefly with Ralph to tell him about Wynn and my visits with Zach and Max.

"Betty just told me the fingerprints on the case don't match up with anyone already in the system. That means they weren't Ronny's."

"Zach Whitman's probably not in the system."

Ralph sat back in his chair. "If young Mr. Whitman is involved, things could get mighty sticky."

He handed me the copy of the Bible verse. "Ecclesiastes, 7:1-2. Do some calling. See if any church put it out there."

So, I pulled out the phone book, found churches in the yellow pages and phoned every single one in the county. Not one of them had made a flyer using the verse. I made some additional copies then returned it to Ralph telling him I'd come up with a blank.

"Think I should show this to our widow? See what she knows. Maybe run it by her father, as well," I asked.

"Go for it."

AFTER ELEANOR ASKED ME IN, I didn't waste time with small talk. I showed her the verse. "What do you know about this?" I asked.

She looked perplexed. After she read it, she lifted her eyes to me and said, "I don't understand."

"It was found in your husband's truck owner's manual."

"Really. Sounds like a threat to me. Is that what you think?" she asked.

"Could be. I saw an interesting photo of you in your dad's office. It was of you and the elk you shot. Good shooting," I said.

"Does he still have the old picture up? Geez, it's been years since I've been hunting. Funny how things change when you have kids. I won't even allow guns in my house."

"Is that so?"

She nodded.

"Well, thanks for your time."

I then drove directly to the bank where I found Fairchild alone in his office. I knocked on the open door and walked in.

"Sir, may I have a minute of your time?" I asked.

"Change your mind about Ted's truck?" he asked.

"No, just a quick question," I said.

"All right, have a seat," he said.

I stayed standing as I handed him the quote.

"Does this Bible verse look familiar to you?" I asked.

He looked it over and handed it back to me. "No. Why do you ask?"

"Found it in Ted's owner's manual."

"Hmm. I can see why you might read into it under the circumstances."

"Don't you think it odd that a quote concerning death and funerals ends up in a dead man's truck?" I asked.

Fairchild's eyes narrowed. "Just proves the point of the verse, wouldn't you say? One never knows when it's time to meet The Maker," he said.

"One thing I'm sure of is that Ronny Peterson and your son-in-law didn't see it coming," I said and turned toward the door.

"Deputy," Fairchild said.

"Yes, sir?"

"The sheriff was right about you."

"How so?"

"He said you were ambitious, but young and inexperienced. Do you know how preposterous it is to accuse me of murdering my son-in-law?"

I shrugged. "I thought I was just inquiring about a piece of evidence. My mistake." I forced a smiled and left feeling a surge of anger. Jack must have told Fairchild he was a suspect.

As I was walking to my vehicle, Ralph called. I replayed my encounter with Fairchild.

"Ya know—I'm not sure I like him," Ralph said.

"Why did you steer me to him for a car loan?" I asked.

"Gerry Hank usually does the car loans. Fairchild doesn't deal with the little guys," he said.

"Little guys?" I asked.

"You know what I mean," he said. "And I'd be surprised if Jack alerted Ham. Anyway, don't let the old buzzards get you down."

"I'll try not to," I said, appreciating how good Ralph was at diffusing situations.

"I called to tell you the ballistics results came back. None of the rifles tested were a match."

"Shit. I thought for sure it was Johnston. Back to square one," I said.

WHEN I ARRIVED AT Cadillac Jack's, Victoria was sitting at the bar next to Bob Brutlag. I took the stool on the other side of her. They continued their chummy discussion about her Toyota's problems while we drank a glass of wine and waited for our table. When we were called downstairs, I was thankful Victoria hadn't asked Bob to join us.

We were shown to a table by the fireplace. Evidently, Victoria had requested it. I didn't know if it was the glass of wine or the flickering firelight that made her look so good. Tamika was right—she did look like Snow White with her great facial bone structure, creamy skin, red lipstick, and perky little nose.

Our server, who introduced herself as Misty, was a buxom blonde with an oversized frizzy ponytail. I told her we'd just order our wine by the glass, but Victoria insisted on ordering a bottle of Stags' Leap Petite Sirah. I objected saying we had to drive back to town.

"We don't have to finish it all, but I want you to try it."

So she ordered the bottle and yes—the wine was excellent—but my usual was half the price and good enough for my taste. I might have a princess sitting across from me after all.

As Misty poured our wine, she took our food order. When Victoria ordered an oriental chicken salad—hold the chicken, Misty gave her a look that made me laugh.

"I never heard that one before. Are you vegetarian?" she said in her husky voice.

"Actually, I'm an ovo-lactovegetarian."

"Huh?" I asked.

"Besides vegetables, I eat eggs and dairy products. Occasionally, I cheat and order fish."

It looked as though Misty was biting her tongue. She turned to me. "And you, sir?"

"I'll have the prime rib—rare."

Misty grinned. "Very good choice."

When our dinners arrived, Victoria made an attitudinal face at my plate. Misty looked amused so I said to her, "Evidently, ovo-lactovegetarians don't even like to look at bloodied meat."

She laughed aloud and said, "Enjoy!"

After a few bites I asked, "So, what is Victoria Lewis doing in Prairie Falls working for a small daily paper?"

"It's family owned. Have to prove myself before I can advance. So, here I am, a city girl, bored silly in a small town. What on earth do you people do for fun up here?"

"What do you like to do for fun?"

"I love to go dancing. What's here? Skuzzy sports bars like Buzzo's? They have country bands upstairs here at Cadillac Jack's and only on Saturday nights. Then there's The Barn, which seems to me is a heavy-metal hang-out for bikers or underage drinkers."

"Yep, that pretty much sums it up."

"So have you always been in investigations?"

"Just recently switched from patrol."

"You're working the murder case." *Here it comes.* "Do you like it?"

"Yeah, it's like putting complicated human puzzles together."

"So, what are your scariest moments as an officer? Or do you even have scary moments up here?"

"This isn't going to end up in an article in the paper, is it? Because you don't have my permission."

She giggled. "No, it probably wouldn't even be interesting to anyone else."

I frowned. "Double murders aren't scary and interesting enough for you?"

"I meant your scariest moments while on patrol."

"Oh, it's definitely domestics. They can turn volatile in a second."

"Does that really happen that often?"

"We have all the same crimes as big cities only on a smaller scale."

"That could be a story—if you'd be willing."

"No, not me. Try the sheriff. He likes talking to the media."

"I'd rather talk to you."

"So, talk. Tell me about yourself."

"What do you want to know? If I've ever been arrested?"

"Have you?"

She grinned and shook her head. "But I bet you know that."

"Where'd you go to school?" I asked.

"Carlton College in Northfield. My Mom wanted me to go to Vassar like she did, but I wanted to be closer to my dad for a change."

"Where did you grow up?"

"Florida with my mom and stepfather. Did your parents stay together?"

"Ah, no. I lived with my mom and grandparents."

"Well, see, we have something in common. What's your mom like?"

"She's an old, liberal hippie, living in the good ol' sixties."

"I'd liked to have been young then. Does she have stories?"

"Not many she'll tell me. Her claim to fame is she met both Mick Jagger and Stephen Tyler."

"Wow, I'm impressed. So why did you become a deputy?"

"Back to that, are we?"

"I'm interested in why people select the professions they do."

"I've wanted to be a cop as long as I remember."

"Is it the gun? The power?"

"No. There's always something going on. I liked the action and excitement of getting a good arrest, and this may sound corny to you, but it is a service job. A lot of what we do is helping with medical emergencies or making welfare checks."

She eyed me. "You know what? I believe you. Only I must say you weren't very nice to me the morning of our crash."

"I was on my way to a murder scene and you rear-ended me."

She smiled. "Fair enough." She looked at her watch. "Look, I should get going. I have to take my place at the Sheriff's Department bright and early in case the old fart . . . er . . . I mean your boss, throws us a tit-bit. Did I just say that?" Giggle. "I meant tidbit."

I laughed then heard myself say, "I'd like to see you again."

"I'd like that too. I look forward to your call, and I need to use the restroom before I take off."

I watched Victoria walk with the exaggerated movements of a drunk—not surprising since she drank all of the Sirah but the one glass I had. No way would I let her drive home. I summoned Misty to pay the check and when Victoria returned I broke the news to her.

She didn't fight me. "I suppose you're right. I guess I was having too good of a time."

VICTORIA STUMBLED ONCE as I led her up to her front door. She leaned up for a kiss—a very long kiss that left us both breathing heavily. As I moved in for another, she put a finger on my lips and said, "I need to take this slow."

"I do slow. I do anything you like."

She smiled coyly. "No, I mean I need to take the relationship slow. The last one ended badly."

"Don't they all—if they're not right?"

"I guess so, but it's just too soon for me."

"How about tomorrow morning then?"

"Funny," she said playfully slapping my shoulder.

"No, I mean I'll pick you up so you can retrieve your car."

She kissed me on the cheek and said, "I'll take care of it. Thanks for the ride." She had trouble unlocking her door, so I gave her a hand, then watched her enter her house.

WHEN I GOT HOME and checked my email, I had a message from Victoria: *Okay, I think I blew it with Cal. I drank too much wine tonight. He is so damn hot-hot-hot! You say to play it slow. How slow do I have to play it? V*

How did she get my email address? Oh yeah, I'd written it on the back of my business card. Obviously it was intended for someone else—and I was going to classify that as an EWI—emailing while intoxicated—a thing to avoid in my opinion. The question was who was giving her advice on me?

16

DAY SIX

ATTENDING KOHLER'S FUNERAL was a good opportunity to observe those in attendance. By the time I got to St. Stephen's I had to park a block and a half away as the parking lot was full and media vans took up much of the side streets.

I considered myself a religious mutt—my mom gave God up when my brother died. She's declared herself an atheist, which riled Grandma Dee, a staunch Lutheran, and my Grandma Sylvia, a liberal Catholic. When I was a kid, both grandmothers felt compelled to give me fragments of religious training by hauling my little heathen ass to church on the occasional Sunday when they had "soul charge" of me—as my Grandpa Sheehan put it.

I'd been in St. Stephen's Catholic Church a few times—the last was when I attended Naomi Moberg's mother's funeral. I did appreciate the building: a beautiful brick church on the National Registry of Historical Places. It had four white marble pillars at the entrance, stained glass arched windows, and remarkable artwork on the walls and ceiling by an Italian artist. The church was divided into two main sections, split by one large center aisle. I sat toward the rear on the right side of the church next to a couple with two school-aged children. All four were really skinny and the children, sitting between the parents, were unnaturally still. I suppressed my urge to lean over and ask the kids if they felt safe in their home and were fed three square meals a day.

As I listened to the soft organ music, I looked around for camera crews. They must be in the choir loft because they were not on the main floor. I recognized a number of people in the congregation. Ralph and Troy were seated together five pews forward.

Dixie and Jack Whitman surprised me by squeezing in next to me. Jack put the kneeling bench down and he, and Dixie knelt for a few minutes. Dixie was a pleasant, attractive woman in her sixties. I wonder what she ever saw in him.

When the organ music stopped, I could hear chanting. A few moments later, while the priest led the procession down the center aisle of the church, a female song leader stepped up to the pulpit in the front of the church and began to encourage everyone to join the choir in singing *Jesus Walked This Lonesome Valley*.

I felt a hit of emotion when I saw Eleanor process in holding her two youngest children hands while the older three followed, also holding hands. Immediately behind were Ham and Ruth Fairchild and two women who looked like they could be Kohler's family.

Father Moran eulogized Kohler as a man who loved God first, his family second, and his business third. He extolled Ted for his generosity with money, time, and talent. Two friends told stories of his extended charity work. During the service, I surveyed the congregation for anything out of the ordinary, but could see nothing. After communion, a powerfully rich bass voice began singing *Amazing Grace* a cappella.

Dixie, touching her chest with her hand, whispered, "Oh, that's Ted. He sang this at many funerals."

What the hell? Personally, I thought it macabre for a dead man to sing at his own funeral. I half expected him to throw open the casket, sit up with arms outstretched, ready for an encore. The recording was effectively producing loud sniffing and nose blowing, as if written into the musical score.

In the middle of the third verse, Dixie Whitman poked me and whispered "Jack's not feeling well."

I bent slightly to take a look at Jack. He was ashen, sweating profusely, and rubbing his arms.

"Let's get him out of here," I said.

We exited out the right side aisle. By the time we were out the door Jack was rubbing his chest.

"Jack, I think you're having a heart attack. I'm calling dispatch," I said.

"Bah," he protested, "I just have the flu or something."

"No, Jack," I said. "We're checking this out."

"No ambulance!" Jack barked.

No sense in arguing with him, so while I ran down to get my the Explorer, I called dispatch, then drove right up to the side door of the church where they were waiting. After Jack and Dixie climbed in the back seat, I told Jack to give Dixie his wallet.

"Don't use the damn siren," Jack growled.

I used the lights.

A MEDICAL TEAM WAS WAITING at the Birch County Regional Hospital ER entrance and whisked Jack away. I walked with Dixie toward the registration desk. She was trembling as she looked for the insurance card in Jack's wallet. While she completed the process, I asked her if she wanted me to call Ben. She did and it wasn't long before he and his wife rushed into the waiting room. Dixie rose to receive comforting hugs from her son and daughter-in-law.

"How's Dad?" he asked.

"I don't know yet," Dixie said.

We chatted briefly about Jack's great stress level since the double murders, when a nurse came out and told Dixie Jack was being admitted because he was indeed having a heart attack. Dixie and Ben followed the nurse, but Sarah stayed in the waiting room.

"Well, Jack's in good hands. I guess I'll take off," I said.

"Thank you for all you've done," she said.

"Don't mention it. Are you and Ben close to the Kohler's?"

"Yes, we've been friends for years. He's also the accountant for Cadillac Jack's."

"Must be difficult to lose a friend. I'm sorry for your loss as well," I said.

Sarah was a pretty woman with curly, brown hair and large, blue eyes that were currently filled with tears. She took out a tissue and dabbed them dry, and blew her nose.

"Your in-law's car is still at St. Stephen's. Should we bring it here?"

"We'll take care of it, thanks."

"Okay then, I think I'll head back to work."

"Thanks again for your help."

When I got into my vehicle, I immediately called Ralph and filled him in.

"I wondered why I didn't see Jack in the lunch line here at church." He sighed. "The case is too much pressure for him. He told me this morning that he wanted it solve by the end of the week. When I told him that probably wasn't gonna happen, he got pissed off and flung his cup of coffee at the wall. I asked him if he felt better, and he said, 'No, and I won't until you figure out who f-ing killed Ted Kohler.' I added, 'and Ronny Peterson', and he said, 'Yeah, of course.'"

"It's obvious Kohler is his priority. So, when will you be back in the office?"

"As soon as I finish my lunch . . . then we can talk about what's next."

I stopped and picked up some chicken at the Save Rite and ate it at my desk thinking about what "next" would be.

When Ralph came back in about one o'clock, he said, "I just stopped off at the hospital. Jack wants me to take over for him. Says the commissioners will meet and make it official."

"Will you still be on the case?"

"Minimally. I'm moving Troy in full time. I left him a message on his cell phone."

"Well, Troy will be happy. He gave me shit because Jack assigned lil' ol' inexperienced me."

"Because I asked for you. You're smart and have good instincts. Besides, Troy's been so involved with the Drug Task Force I didn't think he needed anything more on his plate. That's where he is this afternoon. Later the three of us will sit down and talk about where we go from here."

I nodded.

"Troy's good. You must recognize that, whatever you may think of him personally."

"I do."

"Okay. I could use some help this afternoon looking through phone records."

ALL AFTERNOON WE PORED through a month's worth of phone records. Ralph had me take Peterson's and I found nothing significant in the home phone calls. On Ronny's mobile number, most calls were either family, food, or work related—calls to and from friends were few. But where his cell phone was found still troubled me.

"Ralph, October 7th, the morning Ronny was killed, he made a call at 7:18 a.m. He'd checked out #13 truck at 7:15, but his phone was found in #10, the truck Mark Norland later signed out. How would that happen?"

"Huh. Maybe Ronny switched trucks after he made the call."

"Possibly, or someone else used the phone."

Ralph pointed to a number. "I have something too. Kohler made a phone call to the Parks Department at 4:58 p.m. Thursday. I'd like to see what that was about. Why don't you take a run over there and check it out, then talk to Norland."

Joyce Baxter remembered Ted Kohler's call to the Park's Department that Thursday afternoon because it came in just as they were about to close up.

"He wanted to know if the dock was still out at Emmaline. I told him it was but should be taken in late tomorrow morning. The only reason I knew anything about it was because Naomi was annoyed they hadn't pulled the dock in the day before."

"All right, thanks," I said. "Can you track down Mark Norland for me?"

She made a phone call and told me he was in the maintenance garage. Gus Taylor was among the employees gathered just outside the garage office. As I approached the group, I told them I was looking for Mark Norland.

A lanky kid raised his hand. "That would be me."

I showed him my badge and introduced myself. His co-workers stood around for a couple seconds before they got the hint and walked off toward their own vehicles.

"Gus, stick around a minute."

Gus waddled back.

"How did Ronny's cell phone end up in truck #10? The information I have is that Gus drove it on October 6th, Mark on the 7th. Is that correct?"

"Yeah. I usually drive #10, and the guys know that," he gave Norland a dirty look, "and I had it on Thursday, but I didn't work with Ronny that day."

"He used his phone on Friday morning to call you, Gus," I said.

"Yeah, that's right, but I don't have a clue how his phone ended up in #10. Do you, Mark?"

"I dint even know it was in there," he said.

"You didn't hear it ring?" I asked.

"No, but I was in and out of the truck all day."

"Where were you before you came to work?"

"At home."

"Anyone substantiate that?"

"Sure, my wife and my mother-in-law."

"Do you want to talk to our boss?" Gus said.

"Yep."

The three of us made our way to the garage office.

Gus did the talking. "This here's Stan Haney, head of vehicle maintenance. Stan, Cal Sheehan from the Sheriff's Department."

I flashed my badge. Stan was an older guy with a hook nose and a generous supply of nasal hairs. His spine was half bent, and his fingers were stained dark from working on machines for years.

"What can I do fer ya?" he asked.

Gus spoke up. "Ronny's cell phone was found in truck #10—not the one he checked out. The deputy wants to know how it got in there."

I said, "I was wondering if on October 7th Ronny checked out #10 then changed his mind and took #13. Can you check on that?"

Stan shrugged. "I guess the vehicle he signed out would be the one we just got back from you guys this morning—which was #13," Stan said.

"Do you have a record of that?" I asked.

"Should have. They sign them out on the computer right there under the key box."

Stan moved to the computer. "Let's see here. Yep. Ronny signed out #13 on Friday at 7:15 a.m. and Mark signed out #10 at 7:55. Gus signed out #21 at 8:05, probably because #10 was already gone. Right, Gus?"

"Yep," he said, giving Mark another dirty look.

Mark said, "I won't take your truck again, okay? I didn't know it was such a big fricking deal."

Gus shrugged as if it wasn't.

I said, "We still don't have an explanation for how Ronny's phone got in truck #10, if he checked out #13. You didn't see him come back in and grab different keys?"

"No," Stan said. "I think I would've noticed."

"What about Harvey Kling?"

"Harvey always drives #20. Everybody knows that," Stan said.

"How secure is the sign-out process?"

"Everyone has their own password."

"What about the keys? Could someone pick up a set and take a truck without you knowing?" I asked.

"Unlikely," Stan said.

"But possible?"

Stan nodded. "S'pose so."

"Can you override and change the information?"

"As administration I can, but I've never done that."

"Can your employees?"

"Nope, just their own."

On the short drive to Norland's, it occurred to me that if the dock had been taken in on time and if the dental hygienist hadn't been ill, one or both victims might still be alive. I guess when you're in line—you're in line.

NORLAND'S MOTHER-IN-LAW was staying with the young couple because Mark's wife just had a baby. She said her son-in-law left for work at the same time everyday—7:45. I drove back to tell Ralph what I'd found out about Ted's call and Ronny's cell phone.

"Maybe Ronny was going to take #10 then changed his mind, and the phone accidentally dropped out of his pocket, or he grabbed the wrong set of keys and didn't bother going back in to get the right ones."

"Stan Haney said he most likely would have noticed if Ronny came back in for a different set, and I do think if he checked out one truck and drove another, someone would have complained."

"I bet Stan didn't notice Ronny coming back in . . . or the killer picked up the phone at the scene and threw it in #10 to implicate someone else."

"In that case it would have to be another park's employee."

Ralph shrugged. "More 'n likely he switched trucks."

"Whatever. We're not done with parks boys, are we?"

"Probably not, and we need to talk to Nevada Wynn and Pierce Redding *soon*."

ABOUT SIX O'CLOCK, Victoria called and asked me to come over for pizza. At least she didn't have a husband she *didn't* want to divorce. Ralph and I called it quits at seven-thirty and after stopping to tend to Bullet, I stopped at the liquor store, then drove to Victoria's house. When she answered the door in an open red silk robe and matching lacey thong, I about dropped the bag of beer and wine I brought. So much for taking it slow.

She pulled me in by my jacket collar and unzipped my jacket and snuggled into my body. We never made it out of the living room—Victoria had a *flawless* body and was the most uninhibited woman I'd been with—even had some toys I'd never tried.

An hour later, while we ate our nuked cheese pizza and drank beer, she sprung something on me.

"How about going to Vegas with me next weekend?"

I'm not the spontaneous type, so I made an excuse. "I have to work."

"Hear me out. I need someone to go with me to my dad's wedding and I can't bear the thought of going alone. What do you say?"

"I say no."

"Just like that? Won't you at least think about it?"

I put my index finger to my temple. "Hmmm. There, I thought about it. No."

She sighed deeply. "Well, I don't want to go either but I have to, and I really want someone to come with me that I can have fun with." She jabbed my chest with her finger. "That would be you. Come on! It's all free and it's Vegas, baby!"

"So why don't you want to go?"

"This is his *third* marriage. I asked him why he even wanted to marry again. He said, 'I'm the marrying kind—like Paul McCartney and Rod Stewart. Anyway, it'd do you good to get out of this place. Right? Tell me you'll think about it."

"No promises."

17

DAY SEVEN

WITH THE KOHLER/PETERSON case bouncing around in my brain like a racket ball, I had difficulty falling asleep. When I did finally manage to doze off, I woke panting and in a heavy sweat after a weird dream about Ronny Peterson and Ted Kohler. They were sitting together on bar stools in Buzzo's singing "Ninety-nine Bottles of Beer on the Wall." I'd felt relieved they weren't really dead. As I walked up to them, Kohler tipped his glass at me and asked, "Did you see him?"

"Who?" I asked

"Our killer. He just left."

Then they resumed singing. I ran out the door. All I could see was a shadow. I chased it for miles. Every time I'd get close, it'd ooze under a door or float upward.

I must have fallen back to sleep because I woke before five after having a dream about Adriana. She was helping me car shop and encouraging me to buy a red BMW convertible—her fantasy car. I was happy and ready to buy a car I couldn't afford when a huge great horned owl swooped down telling me to buy a Ford. That's when I woke up. I tried to get back to sleep and to my happy place with Adriana, but it was no use. I had to shake her off. The best way I knew was to go for a run.

Bullet and I did the six-mile loop along the Birch River that meandered through Birch County Park South. As I was pounding the asphalt trail at dawn, I mulled over the case: Kohler wouldn't have put his boat in if he'd interrupted something. He was shot first. Ronny probably drove in on the scene and was shot because he was a witness. Trouble was, all our likely suspects had witnesses to support their alibis. We still had no murder weapon. When I got to the falls by the Minnesota Fare I turned around and headed toward home.

I was ready for work an hour and a half early. I stopped at the Sportsman Café and picked up a half dozen cinnamon rolls for the eight o'clock meeting with Ralph and Troy. Tony, the owner, always threw in extra rolls. The warmth and aroma of the rolls radiated through the full white bag he handed me— I found myself salivating.

"Thanks, Tony. I think you over counted again. You and your cinnamon rolls are the best."

He winked. "Well, you're my best customer."

WHEN I WALKED into the squad room to grab a cup of coffee, Georgia was just making it.

"You're here early," I said.

"So are you. I'm here because Ralph has a press conference this morning at eight o'clock. The commissioners had an emergency meeting last night and appointed him acting sheriff until Jack comes back. They insisted the media be informed via a real press conference."

"Where is he?"

Georgia pointed down. "In the Sheriff's office. He's pretty nervous."

I hurried down the stairs to first floor to catch Ralph to wish him luck before he went on air, but I couldn't get near for all the lights and media personnel. So I went back up to the office. While I scanned my case notes, I ate two cinnamon rolls and sipped the liquid masquerading as coffee.

At eight o'clock I made my way to the squad room already crowded with staff ready to watch Ralph's news conference. Ralph looked scared and his hands visibly shook as he read from a large index card. It made me nervous just watching him.

"Good morning. My name is Sergeant Ralph Martinson. Yesterday, Sheriff Jack Whitman suffered a heart attack. He's expected to make a full recovery. The Birch County Commissioners have appointed me as a temporary replacement. As you know, along with the Minnesota Bureau of Criminal Apprehension in Bemidji, we're investigating a double murder, and at this time, we do not have a suspect in custody. We have two highly qualified investigators working full time on the case and will update you as we can. Now, I will open this up to a few questions."

"Sergeant Martinson, George Trent, *Minneapolis Star*. Can you tell us the manner of death of the two individuals?"

"Both died from gunshot wounds."

"Is there any evidence of more than one gunman?" Trent asked.

"Both victims were shot by the same weapon, so we believe we're looking for one individual."

Ralph pointed to another reporter. "Warren Bale, WCCO. What do the ballistics tests tell you about the weapon?"

"I can't share that information at this time."

"Do you have a person of interest in the case?" Bale asked.

"Let me just say, we have evidence in our favor and are following many leads."

Ralph pointed at Victoria. Oh, boy. She was Lois Lane wearing a navy blue pantsuit, red eyeglasses, little make-up and a ponytail. This was the same woman I'd had kinky sex with last night? Unbelievable.

"Victoria Lewis. *Birch County Register*. I understand a threatening Bible quote was found in Mr. Kohler's vehicle."

Ralph looked taken aback. I know I certainly was. But since I had called all over town asking about it, and showed it to Eleanor Kohler and Hamilton Fairchild, it's not surprising she found out.

"We don't know if it's related to the case, but we're testing fingerprints found on the note, just in case."

"Will you disclose what it said?"

"No, ma'am, not at this time."

Ralph called on Mac Simmons from the *Prairie Falls Times*.

"Sounds like you have no real suspects, Ralph."

"We're making headway."

"Do you have a possible motive?" Mac asked.

"We want to give you facts not speculation."

AFTER THE PRESS CONFERENCE, Ralph joined Troy and me in the investigations office. He sat in his chair with a thunk.

"Nice job, boss," I said.

"Did I look as nervous as I felt?" he asked.

"Not at all."

Troy laughed. "What are you talking about, Sheehan? He shook like a dog during a thunder storm."

Ralph's face dropped. "I was hoping it wasn't that obvious. I don't like the camera like Jack does."

"But the camera likes *you* better," I said, shooting Troy a *shut the hell up* look.

"How did the chick find out about the Bible quote?" Troy asked.

"Probably because I called all the churches in the county to find out the source . . . showed it Eleanor Kohler and Ham Fairchild."

"Why the fuck did you leak that kind of evidence," Troy said.

"Troy, we investigate what evidence we have, and that means asking questions," Ralph said.

Troy lifted his hands as if in surrender. "Well, that's how she got it. Ham Fairchild would give that chick an interview in a heartbeat. Who is she anyway?"

I leaned back. "Victoria Lewis . . . the woman who rear-ended me."

Troy sat back and belly laughed. "She could rear-end me anytime."

"Speaking of which, Cal, have you replaced your Civic?" Ralph asked changing the subject.

I shook my head. "Haven't had time."

"So make time."

"I'm going to Ronny Peterson's funeral at ten o'clock."

"Me too," Troy said.

"Do it after that. I have a meeting so its good you're both attending the funeral. So what will you boys focus on this afternoon?" Ralph asked.

"I want to go over everything we have so far, find out when BRO can get the DNA and toxicology test results back to us," Troy said.

Ralph looked at his watch and pointed at the door and said, "My meeting's starting in two minutes."

"And we better head out to the funeral," I said.

TROY AND I DROVE separately because I decided to go car shopping after. Compared to Kohler's funeral, there were only about a fourth the amount of cars parked at St. Stephen's for Ronny's. The media trucks had moved to the parking lot, so I easily found a spot right beside the church. Troy and I sat together near the back with the smattering of elderly women who attend funerals as a social event. I spotted a row of local reporters, including Victoria, sitting together in the very back row. A number of county employees, including Naomi Moberg, Joyce Dexter, and Gus Taylor, were seated mid-way in the church on the left side of the aisle. Hector Buzzo and Connie Hackett were seated several pews in front of us. I guess they were as close to him as anybody. Max Becker and Zach Whitman came in together and sat behind Hector and Connie.

The untimely deaths of young people usually make for huge funerals. But beside his co-workers, the only young people here were Max and Zach. The church was only about half full when the service began. A few voices from the choir loft guided the congregation in song as the family, about forty strong, processed in. They all seemed to have the same tank body style, even the women.

According to Father Moran's eulogy, Ronny and his brother mowed the church grounds every Saturday without pay. Huh. Never would have figured that one. The priest said when a young person dies tragically it's difficult to understand God's plan, but we must remember as lowly servants we are incapable of seeing it. Is murder really part of God's plan? Not in my mind, but someone definitely planned these cold-blooded murders and I have to figure out who and why.

During the service I noticed Troy's eyes on Naomi. He was definitely interested. After the service, we met up with her and Joyce in front of the church. Naomi looked sharp wearing a black dress with a beaded black cardigan. Her smile looked forced and her eyes bounced between Troy and me.

Joyce spoke up. "Isn't this just awful?"

We all nodded and uttered simple words of agreement.

"Did you go to Ted Kohler's funeral too?" Joyce asked.

"Yes," I said.

"I didn't know him personally so I didn't go. Hey, I saw Ralph Martinson's news conference this morning. Shame about the sheriff's heart attack—too much stress, I guess," Joyce said.

"I guess. So you gave your crew the morning off?" I asked Naomi.

"Actually, the whole day."

"We better get to the car if we're going to the cemetery, Naomi," Joyce said. As she and Naomi started walking away, I realized if I liked her, I better act.

"Hey, Naomi," I said and she turned and stopped. I pulled her aside. "Are you going to be home later?"

"I have my kids the rest of the week. So, sorry, I guess I'm not available."

"Oh . . . sure."

So, she doesn't want a divorce, and she has kids that prevent her from seeing me. Okay then. That's that.

When I returned to Troy he asked what that was about.

"Just asked if Stan had talked to her about the truck Ronny drove," I lied.

"Did he?"

"No."

A Vegas weekend with Victoria suddenly sounded appealing.

I DROVE TO DANIELSON'S FORD to find Rob Cornel, a golfing friend of mine who's a new car salesman. He greeted me with a fist bump.

"Hey, Rob, totaled the Civic and need to replace it."

"Heard that."

"Last night I had a weird dream. An owl swooped down and told me to buy a Ford."

He laughed. "You're shittin' me."

"Nope."

"Sounds like a good idea for a Ford commercial. Maybe I'll send it in. So would your owl approve of a red Mustang convertible? I have a beauty on the showroom floor."

He led me to the Mustang and proceeded to give me his sales pitch. I was even tempted.

"I'm thinking more practical. Would you believe Hamilton Fairchild offered to sell me Ted Kohler's truck?"

"Oh? I sold him that truck. It's really tricked out. Must be two years old, probably low mileage." He stopped and tapped his head. He leaned in and whispered, "Wait, am I fricking nuts? You want a new vehicle with better gas mileage. Am I right?"

Rob priced out a Fusion, Taurus and a Mustang, and then walked me over to used cars. There were a couple options that could work, but I wanted time to think about it. Before I went back to the department, I stopped at the hospital to see Jack. I wondered if he would mention Ham Fairchild.

18

WHEN I WALKED INTO JACK'S hospital room, Dixie was sitting in a chair reading a magazine. She said he was in the restroom. To make conversation I asked her if Dixie was her real name, if one of her parents had Southern roots.

She giggled and said, "No, my given name is Dorothy Jane Davis. One day my mother bought some Dixie cups, and from then on I told everyone to call me Dixie Jane Davis, because I loved the way it sounded."

"Great story," I said. She looked like a Dixie.

"What's a great story?" growled Jack as he walked out of the restroom rolling an IV cart.

"Oh, I was just telling Cal about how I got my name. And as long as he's here, I'm going to run home and get some things done. You two can have a nice visit."

"I can be alone, Dix. It's not like I'm dying, for Christ's sake, unless you know something I don't," Jack said.

"Oh, don't be silly. I just thought you two would like some time to talk. But remember—no shop talk—doctor's orders."

"Ah, what does he know?" Jack grumbled.

"And, Cal, thank you so much for your quick action at the church. We're so appreciative. Aren't we Jack?"

Jack gave a half nod.

After Dixie left, I sat in a chair beside him, waiting for him to bring up Ham Fairchild.

"This place is enough to drive a guy nuts," he muttered.

"I imagine you're being a perfect patient," I said.

"I don't do sick, so if you'd ask the nurses, they probably say I'm a perfect pain in the ass," he said. " Speaking of which, Cal, if I've been a bit hard on you lately, I apologize. I've been pretty stressed."

"Understandable." Nothing like a brush of mortality to let you know who's in charge.

"How's the department doing without me?" he asked.

"We're managing, sir."

"Ralph's a good man. He can handle things."

"I've always thought highly of him. "

"You getting close to solving?"

"Getting there. Troy's come aboard."

"You don't look happy about it."

I shrugged.

"He can be an ass. He asked me to dump you from the case—said it was too important to let a rookie screw it up. I told him if we're going to solve these murders, you all needed to work as a team."

Troy really did it, the prick.

"Dixie tell you I'm having triple-bypass surgery tomorrow?"

"No, wow."

"It'll be a while before I can come back. Yep, we just made the decision this morning when Doc Gage brought in the cardiologist. I'm going down to the University by ambulance tonight. Hate to see that bill—I told him Dixie or Ben could drive me, but my doctor nixed that idea."

"Too risky."

"I s'pose. So tell me the latest in the investigation."

"No shop talk, remember?"

"Ah, bullshit. Just tell me."

So, I did. He didn't offer an opinion, like I thought he would. With the first lull in the conversation, I bugged out, saying I'd let him rest and wished him good luck.

I STOPPED AT SAVE RITE and made myself a big salad and brought it back to the office. After I ate, I found Troy in the conference room working at the whiteboard. He seemed to be taking control of the case. I didn't like that idea.

"Buy a car?" he asked.

"Not yet. What are you doing?"

"Just trying to get a feel for where we need to go next."

"Is Ralph still the lead investigator?" I asked.

"Why? Oh, you don't want me telling you what to do. Is that it?"

"Just asking is all."

"Well, he didn't say."

And he was absolutely nuts on—I *do not* want to take orders from him. We spent the entire afternoon rehashing our data—until I was so frustrated I could have hauled off and cold cocked Troy.

THAT EVENING AS I approached my apartment I saw a note taped to the door. It said: *See me—Paris.* She was my twenty-year-old neighbor across the hall.

I knocked on her door. Three seconds later she stuck her head out. The first thing you noticed about Paris was her Mohawk—five-inch spikes of hot pink on the top, the rest dark brown and trimmed close to her head. She had multiple tattoos and piercings, and wore the alien type clothes she sells to teen girls in the mall boutique her parents bought for her, called Athena's Closet.

She blinked her eyes at me. "Whatsup?" she asked.

I showed her the note.

"Oh, yeah, you had a woman banging on your door looking for ya." I could see her green gum rolling in her black lipstick-lined mouth.

"What did she look like?"

"About my height. She was old, maybe your age. She wore a hat—a pink fuzzy thing, so I couldn't tell you her hair color or style."

Did she say old—maybe my age? "What time was this?"

"About six o'clock I'd guess. "

"Did you talk to her?"

"Nah, I just watched her out the peep hole."

"Well, thanks."

"No worries. Did you want to see her?"

"Depends on who it was."

Bullet greeted me with a whole body wag. After I took him out for a walk, I fed him, then sat at my table eating Chinese out of cartons while looking at my case notes. I kept thinking about the woman at my door—maybe Naomi.

I gave her a call. "Hey, Naomi, this is Cal."

"Oh, hi!" she said, sounding pleased I'd called.

"Thanks again for helping locate Ronny's cell phone."

"Oh, sure. Did it help you any?"

"Maybe. I may have to run some phone numbers by you."

"Sure, anything to help."

"Say, did you by any chance stop over at my apartment this afternoon?"

"No, why?"

"Just checking. My neighbor said a woman in a pink fuzzy hat stopped by."

"That . . . wasn't me." Her voice had changed.

"Didn't think so. How long are your kids with you?"

"For five days. That's how we alternate them."

"Seems like a plan."

"Works for us. So . . ."

"So . . . well . . . see you later."

"Bye."

That was awkward. Did I really like her? Or was it my ego? Maybe she just wasn't into me—or worse—she was going for Troy over me. So who's the pink fuzzy hat woman?

19

DAY EIGHT

FRIDAY MORNING'S *Birch County Register* ran the headline: "A CLUE IN THE KOHLER/PETERSON CASE." Victoria Lewis was listed as the staff reporter. The article covered Ralph's press conference and quoted the Bible verse found in Kohler's truck—unfortunate but foreseeable.

When I showed Ralph the paper he said, "We should have figured they'd find out and run it. Well, maybe if anyone knows anything they'll come forward."

"I just hope it doesn't spur copy cats."

LESLIE ROUCH ARRIVED for our scheduled case meeting. She promised the DNA evidence and toxicology reports by early next week. Ralph suggested I spend my time on Wynn.

Immediately after the meeting I checked for messages. Victoria had texted me: "Ready to go to Vegas? Still time."

I answered: "I'll get back to you."

I found Ralph in Jack's office and told him I'd been invited to Vegas, purposefully neglecting by *whom*. I said I'd interview Nevada Wynn in Minneapolis either coming or going."

"I'll go along with that."

"Great," I said.

But before I could get out of the door he asked, "Who's the girl?"

"Victoria Lewis."

"Oh, Cal." He stared at me. "Just be careful what you tell her."

"Hell, I'm hoping to pump her for information."

He shrugged.

When I called Victoria and told her I would go, she squealed so loud I had to hold the phone away from my ear. "You really will go with me? I don't believe it! This is going to be so much fun!"

"Where are we staying, by the way?" I asked.

"Dad booked us a suite at the Bellagio. I'll have your plane tickets. Can you be ready to leave by twelve-thirty for Minneapolis?"

"If I hurry," I said.

"Pack casual clothes. It's not formal. I'll pick you up."

"Sounds good," I said.

AFTER I DROPPED BULLET off at Larry's, who was only too eager to have "our dog" for the weekend, Victoria called to get directions to my place. She arrived ten minutes early and we took off for the Minneapolis/St. Paul Airport in her Toyota. On the drive down, I asked her questions about her family so I would know what I was getting into.

Her mother lived in Palm Beach, Florida, and had a successful realty company she procured in the divorce settlement. Victoria loved her father, hated his second wife, and wasn't sure about the bride to be. She had a brother that was always "up her ass" for one thing or another—most of it unwarranted in her opinion. Her grandfather made the family fortune, and it wasn't just the newspapers, but real estate and insurance companies.

"So if your family is that wealthy, why are you even working?" I asked her.

"Daddy's philosophy is the same as his father's—that the kids make their own way. We have money in trusts doled out to us at certain ages. My first will be when I'm thirty, but we can tap it if it's not for frivolous purchases. Dad doesn't want lazy, ungrateful children."

"I think I may like him," I said.

Courtesy of Adam Lewis, we flew first class. The free-flowing glasses of wine put me in the party mood. When we disembarked in Vegas, the warm air felt charged. We spotted the limo driver sporting a "Lewis" sign, and shortly after seven o'clock we were walking into the lobby of the Bellagio, where I saw Philip and Sheila Warner across the room. *Small world*, I thought. He was an attorney from Prairie Falls—and Adriana Valero's old boss.

Our suite had full-length windows with views of the fountain and strip. I was pumped for a kick-back relaxing time—weddings were fun, right? Victoria said we were already late and had to hurry. We showered together and after all that soapy fun it, not surprisingly, ended in a quickie.

After, Victoria rifled through my luggage and suggested I wear my white slacks and a light-blue Polo shirt. I found it mildly annoying she picked out my clothes, but obliged. Before we left, we both checked ourselves out in the mirror in the hallway by the door.

"You look very handsome," she said.

"That's because I have Snow White near me," I said.

She screwed up her nose. "Snow White?"

"That's what Tamika Frank called you. The deputy who handled our ... crash."

"Ohhh. Why did she call me Snow White?"

I pointed to her reflection in the mirror. "Look at yourself. Your hair, your creamy skin, you're gorgeous."

"Why thank you, kind sir." She turned and gave me a kiss that went on forever.

"I started reaching up under her pink sundress to feel her inner thigh.

"Later, baby. We need to get going now!" she said playfully slapping my hand.

By seven forty-five when the elevator doors opened onto the main floor, she said, "Ready to meet the old boy?"

"Sure thing," I said, as I suddenly felt nervous. Why did I care I was going to meet relatives of a woman I hardly knew?

Victoria grabbed my hand and led me to the private room where the party was being held. Strange. The Warners were standing in a small circle of people, just inside the door. Why would *they* be at this wedding? My eyes surveyed the room. Then I saw her—Adriana Valero. She was arm and arm with a man. *What the hell? Why's she here?*

Victoria dragged me through the crowd of about thirty people right up to the man with Adriana.

"Dad, this is Cal!" she said.

Adriana's eyes widened, and her mouth dropped. Dad? I expected to see an old dude, not a guy who could double as George Clooney. But with a closer look, I could see the crows' feet around his eyes and the start of wobbly neck skin. But I still didn't understand why Adriana was on his arm.

"Adam Lewis," the man said. "Nice to meet you, Cal. Victoria has told me so much about you. And this exquisite beauty is my wife to be, Adriana Valero," he said, lifting her hand to kiss it.

Wife? I don't know if I've ever been more shocked in my entire life.

Adriana flushed. She was gorgeous as ever, wearing a long, pale yellow silky dress, and a dainty diamond necklace.

"Adam darling, I know Cal. We dated while I was in Prairie Falls," Adriana said as she eyed Victoria.

"Really?" he said looking at me with newfound interest.

I couldn't find my voice, but mercifully, a couple not wanting to wait their turn to greet the couple, interrupted our conversation. Adam touched my arm and said we'd talk later. *Yeah, can't wait for that.*

As I turned away, a waiter with a full tray of glasses asked, "Champagne, sir?"

I took two, intending to drink both—one out of each side of my mouth, but Victoria grabbed one.

"What's wrong?" she asked.

"Did you know I was with Adriana for two years?"

"Two years? Oh, my gosh, no, I didn't."

"How long have they been dating?"

"Off and on for a few years. They started up again when Adriana moved back to Minneapolis."

Off and on for a few years? "How old is your dad?"

"He's fifty-one, and she's like thirty-four," she said.

"Thirty-two," I corrected.

He looked forty something—he must have had some work done—dyed his hair.

"You seem upset," Victoria said.

"I had no idea Adriana was getting . . ."

I felt a touch on my shoulder—Adriana's. "Victoria, can you give us a minute?" she asked.

"If that's *all* it is," Victoria said then walked off to greet some people in the corner.

I followed Adriana out into the hallway.

"Why didn't you tell me you were getting married?" I said.

"I tried to call you. Did you change your number?"

"Oh . . . my new phone," I said.

"I didn't know you were seeing Victoria—now I understand all her questions. You should know I didn't go into the details of our relationship with her."

"She said you've been dating *for years.* Did you see him while you were with me?"

"No, of course not. Cal, I told you about Adam the night we talked about all our past relationships."

"He's the man who wanted to marry you, but broke it off because you didn't believe in marriage?"

"Yes." At least she had the decency to appear rueful.

"Wow." I laughed. "It's just weird, you know? I go to a friend's father's wedding and it so happens *you're* the bride. What are the odds?" I sounded bitter—even to my own ears.

"Only in Vegas . . . I bet if you'd known you wouldn't have come?"

I smirked. "What was your first clue?"

Her brows furrowed. "So how long have you been seeing Victoria?"

"Not long. Coming to the wedding was a rather spontaneous decision."

"Then you've changed—I know spontaneity isn't in your comfort zone."

Adam Lewis interrupted us. "There you are, darling. I want you to meet the Harmons,"

"Just give me a minute, sweetie," she said.

Sweetie? Sugar Daddy is more like it.

"Sure, darling," he said kissing her on the lips—longer this time. He gave me a snarky look and disappeared back inside the room.

She hugged me. "I'm sorry, Cal. I hope this isn't too uncomfortable for you."

"Don't even think about it. Think about how you'll soon be Mrs. Lewis," I said.

"I'm keeping Valero."

"Good—easier when you divorce. Bet you signed a pre-nup," I said.

She smiled and patted my arm. "It's good to see you."

Victoria showed up to say, "Time's up, Adriana. Daddy's waiting for you."

"Yes, don't keep daddy waiting, Adriana," I said.

She gave me a look I knew well . . . it meant *shut the hell up*. She didn't look back. I excused myself and went to the restroom. I stood at the sink watching myself tear up. *Oh, get a grip, Cal.* I splashed water on my face, wiped it with a towel, and shook my head trying to clear the ghosts.

Phillip Warner took that opportunity to walk in. "Cal."

"Phillip."

"I take it you didn't know Adam's bride was Adriana," he said.

"Oh, I just noticed their names even start with the same fucking letters," I said.

He laughed.

I shook my head. "And, no, I didn't know."

"Complicated."

I shrugged. "Hey, Ted Kohler was a member of your club, right?"

He stood at the urinal and unzipped his pants. I looked away.

"Right. He was a client and a good friend."

"Do you know anything that could help find your client and friend's killer?"

"This may be nothing, but couple weeks before he was shot, my wife and I were having dinner at the club with him and Eleanor. He went to the restroom and didn't return. I decided to go myself and see if he fell in. When I walked by a smaller room, I heard Ted arguing with a woman."

"Who was it?"

"Couldn't see her—but I know it was Ted's voice I heard. By the time I came out of the men's room, he was back at the table."

"What did you hear?"

"He said that it wasn't his problem."

"What wasn't?"

"Don't know. I figured if he wanted me to know, he would have told me."

"Well, that gives me squat," I said.

He gave me a sly smile. "Always like to give a helping hand to the department."

"Right. See ya later."

I made my way to the bar then looked over the crowd. I spotted Adriana's mother, Magna, and her sister, Gina, talking with a small group of women by the bar. Adriana's father wasn't probably invited, as they hadn't had contact for years. Her parents divorced when she was young and her dad was always off in exotic places doing medical research.

Victoria was standing next to a man who was the male version of her. He was prematurely balding but shared the delicate facial features making him look effeminate. After I made my way over, she introduced him as Wesley, her pharmacist brother. His frumpy, thick wife joined us. She had broad facial features and large ears that protruded through her thin, straight hair. Her choice of dress was something my grandmothers might not even wear. When we were introduced, Melinda barely acknowledged me before she pounced on Victoria.

"So, *why* didn't you make your flight? You missed the rehearsal."

"Because I wanted to fly out with Cal."

"You aren't going to know what to do at the ceremony," Wesley said.

"What's to know? I'm sure it's similar to his *last* wedding."

"Don't even start," Wesley said. "Come on, Melinda, let's get the kids and take our seats."

As they walked away, Victoria giggled, "He hates when he can't control me."

"When was your Dad's last wedding?"

"Seven years ago—lasted three years."

Maybe this one will be shorter. "Was she a lot younger as well?"

"Only ten years."

Victoria pointed out the two children running willy-nilly through the reception room as her niece and nephew, Fanchon and Alston.

"Who?"

"Fanchon and Alston. Melinda didn't want common names for her *uncommon* children."

"Fanny and Al?"

She giggled.

Apparently the kids were not complying with their parents' request for them to be seated. Victoria and I took our places at a table near the wedding party. An elderly woman sat down next to me and introduced herself as the groom's Aunt Evelyn. You could tell she had been a beauty in her day.

"Cal Sheehan," I said, as I offered my hand.

Grasping it, she said, "Victoria's my grandniece." She kept hold of me.

"I see beauty runs in the family."

"Well, aren't you the flatterer?"

"I only speak the truth."

She smiled. "Victoria has always been extra special to me—lovely, smart child. Someone who goes after what she wants."

"Is that a warning?" I asked.

She chuckled, finally released her grip and moved her thin, veined hand to my forearm. Her huge diamond ring glittered in the candlelight.

"Is there a Mr. Evelyn?"

"My late husband, Hugo, died of a heart attack fifteen years ago. Couldn't have happened to a nicer man."

I must have looked confused.

"He was an ass," she said.

I broke into a grin, and she laughed raucously.

Wesley finally captured his children and forced them to sit on either side of the couple directly across the table from us. Even though separated, they still managed to interact. Wesley and Melinda's kids inherited the worst features from both parents—the ears, for one. Melinda ignored her children who were trying to outdo each by making farting noises.

I played nice and asked Melinda how old her children were: Alston was eight and Fanchon was six. Fanchon was big for six, almost as tall as her brother. My single question prompted a brag fest of how gifted her children were. Eventually, she ran out of things to say and asked what I did.

"I'm a deputy investigator for Birch County."

She looked amused. "And how did you two meet?" she asked.

Before I could answer, Victoria draped herself over my shoulder and proceeded to tell a complete lie. "We'd met during an interview on the double murder case Cal's investigating. You've probably heard about the two men who were brutally gunned down in a county park. Well, I'm covering the story," she said.

I guess she didn't want to tell them she'd rear-ended me. I understood that.

After dessert came the speeches proclaiming how *right* the couple was for one another. A friend of Adriana's (that I'd never met) toasted the couple "as two people who go together like champagne and caviar—espresso and chocolate mousse."

More like beans and weenies, I thought.

Aunt Evelyn chucked.

"Did I say that out loud?" I whispered.

"Mm-hmm."

"How rude of me."

She chuckled again. I liked her.

I caught Adriana's eye and lifted my glass to her. She smiled and returned the gesture. *Oh, Adriana, what are you doing?*

Eventually, those seated at my table all drifted off to speak to this person or that. I was left alone. Adriana's mother came from behind and sat in Aunt Evelyn's recently vacated chair. *Shoot.* She looked half in the bag.

"Deputy," she said in this tone of hers, which I liken to the snobby clerks in upscale stores who act like it's beneath them to wait on you. She thought she was hot stuff since she was an executive assistant for some high-powered executive—maybe it was Adam Lewis.

"Mugs," I answered, always wanting to call her that to her face, knowing full well she hated it. I enjoyed watching her stiffen. Oh ... come to think of it, maybe Adriana only calls her "Mugs" behind her back.

"Well, I was certainly shocked to see you here. You weren't on the guest list."

"You'll find me listed as *Victoria's* guest."

"Yes, I surmised that when I saw her hanging all over you at dinner. Interesting how you wrangled an invitation."

"Ironically, I came along to the wedding not knowing the bride was Adriana."

"I find that hard to believe."

"Doesn't matter to me one tiny bit *what* you believe."

Her jaw set tighter.

"Well, you must be happy Adriana landed a rich businessman," I said.

"Yes, quite. I've prayed so hard for Adriana to find true happiness, and my prayers were finally answered."

"I didn't realize you had a direct line to the Big Guy himself."

"I believe God answers all prayers."

"Is that so? Well, in that case, why don't you start praying for the end of hunger, poverty, crime? That type of thing."

She laughed. "Crime? Well then, whatever would you do for a living?"

"Maybe I'd apply to be your driver. You know, like driving Miss Daisy, only it would be driving Miss Mugs. I'm not sure it has the same ring though."

"Why Adriana appreciated your odd sense of humor, I'll never understand. Anyway, I came to say I wish you well and hope you find someone as right for you as Adam is for my daughter."

Before I could give her the finger, Adriana came up behind and said, "Mom, Adam wants to speak with you."

Magna shot out of the chair without a so much as a cackle and left. And I had so much more to say too, like: Try living your own life, instead of vicariously living your daughter's.

Adriana sat next to me in the chair recently vacated by her mother. "I didn't think you needed my mother needling you."

"Thank you," I said. "Do you call her Mugs to her face?"

She gasped. "God no."

"Oh."

She touched my arm. "I'm sorry you found out about my marriage like this," she said.

"It's okay. I let myself be hornswoggled into coming."

"Well, I'm glad you're here, and I hope you have a good time. You do know our time together was important to me."

I nodded. "Sure."

She patted my arm, smiled and left to join Lewis and her mother—who had to be about the same age as the groom.

Magna and I had gotten off to a bad start from the get go. She had a preconceived notion a law enforcement officer couldn't be a good husband or father. I tried to be nice in the beginning, but after the third hostile visit, I'd told Adriana she'd have to visit her without me. Then along came Sugar Daddy Lewis.

I considered walking out and taking the next flight home, but I decided I didn't want to give Adam or Mugs the satisfaction. I was under the influence pretty much the whole weekend and in an odd, almost out-of-body state—like I'd had a temporary lobotomy. I went through all the planned activities: the guys' golf game on Saturday when Adam beat me by nine strokes (and he was a crap golfer), the wedding ceremony in the atrium of the hotel, and the steak and lobster dinner, the dance, and gambling. Adam had given each guest two hundred in credit for the casino. Some of the night is a blank: all I recall is flashes of colored lights and the incessant music and ding-ding-ding of the slots. I'm not sure Victoria even noticed I was on autopilot, because I tried to act like it didn't bother me that my Adriana married her father five fucking months after we broke up. And she had been with him off and on for *years*?

I WAS GRATEFUL VICTORIA slept the entire flight home on Sunday night, so I didn't have to talk to her. After I sobered up, I grew increasingly pissed because she led me by the dick into the mother of all uncomfortable situations. So when she said we'd stay at "Daddy's" in Orono Sunday night, I told her I'd make my own way home. She must have known not to push it, and as we parted ways at the airport without so much as a hug, she told me she'd call tomorrow. I rented a car and made my way to the downtown Marriott. I slept fitfully, waking up frequently reliving the weekend.

20

DAY ELEVEN

ONDAY MORNING, I drove straight to the Minneapolis Police Department. After speaking briefly with Sergeant Karl Adamson, I was sent to Wynn's parole officer, Brian Day.

Day was about five-foot-eight, fifty-something and heavyset. He said Wynn had a job at a warehouse on Washington Avenue. We exchanged cards, and I drove over to North Cross Shipping.

The personnel director was a stocky woman, with curly, gray hair and a big rump. Her desk nameplate said HALDIS MOORE. I introduced myself and asked her if she could check if Wynn had been at work on October 8th.

After checking the computer, she said, "Yes, he was here that day. Why? This doesn't have anything to do with those killings up in Birch County does it? I like to think I'm helping parolees, but we have a no-tolerance policy. If they screw up once, they're out of here."

"No, ma'am, if he was here in Minneapolis at work, then he's clear, but would you mind if I had a word with him? He may have some information about another individual of interest."

"Oh, sure." She made a phone call and led me to a small room to wait for Wynn. Ten minutes later, Wynn "the Snake" strolled in wearing a tan work uniform unbuttoned enough to showcase a portion of his cobra tattoo, the head on the side of his face, swirling down around his neck and body to who knows where. I was happy to hear Minneapolis busted him on a felony. He was one bad dude.

I introduced myself.

"Sheehan, yeah, I remember you, and the unfriendly county you work for."

"Now, how can you say that? Didn't we give you a free night's room and board at a primo facility."

"Piss hole, you ask me."

"Well, I'm not here to get you to fill out a how-did-we-do card, I want to know about your friend that had an altercation with Ronny Peterson."

"Who's Ronny Peterson?"

"Don't play coy. I know you and Redding had an altercation with him last summer. He was brutally murdered last week. So where's Redding?"

"Dunno. Haven't seen him since summer."

"Is he living in Minneapolis?"

He shrugged. "Maybe he went back home."

"Where's home?"

"Oklahoma."

"What's his real name?"

"Dunno."

"Tell him I want to talk to him."

He glared at me. He told me the truth about Redding being from Oklahoma, the rest was bullshit. As I drove out of the parking lot I saw Wynn using his cell phone. I called Brain Day back and asked him what he knew about Pierce Redding. He said he'd check it out and get back to me.

I DROVE THE TWO HOURS home and went right to the office. As soon as I walked in, I checked my email messages. One was from Brian Day: *Didn't take me long track down Redding—full name is Fredrick Pierce Redding. He was picked up for assault with a deadly weapon in Tulsa and has been incarcerated in James Crabtree Correction Center in Helena, Oklahoma, since mid September. Good luck on your case.*

I took the stairs down and walked into Jack's office finding Ralph, Troy, and Leslie Rouch. As I walked in, I made the announcement that Wynn and Redding both had solid alibis.

Ralph sighed. "Dang it. I was hoping we had our man. Well, anyway, Leslie will bring you up to date."

"Toxicology report came back. To make a long story short—Kohler was clean of substances—Ronny had cannabis in his system. No evidence of Heroin."

"Okay," I said. "Oh, and when I was in Vegas I saw Phillip Warner, who told me he heard Kohler have an argument with a woman at the club. Didn't know who."

"Not helpful then."

"Nope."

AFTER THE MEETING, I called Kohler's to ask Eleanor about the conversation at the club Phillip Warner had overheard. A kid wailed in the background.

"I won't keep you. I just have a quick question. I have a witness that your husband had an argument with a woman at the club a couple weeks ago. I just wondered if he'd shared that with you."

"No, but it could have been someone getting some financial advice or someone who didn't like how their taxes turned out."

"You're right. It could have been anything. I just need to check on any little lead I get."

"Sorry, I couldn't help."

The crying got closer to the receiver.

"No problem. Sorry to catch you at such a bad time."

When I got home, I picked up Bullet from Larry's, then sat on my sofa feeling like shit.

"Bullet, you remember Adriana, the woman we loved? She married an old, rich dude. How could that have happened that fast?"

He sat in front of me, whimpered, and licked my hand.

21

DAY TWELVE

I WAS ALONE IN THE OFFICE Tuesday morning when my personal cell phone rang: V Lewis. I turned off the ringer, and returned to my paper work on Wynn and Redding. A half hour later Ralph called. "Thought you'd want to know—Troy's over at your girlfriend's house. She received a threatening Bible quote in the mail."

"What girlfriend?"

"Victoria. Is there another I don't know about?"

"Uh, no. Should I go over, too?"

"If you want."

I parked in front of her house behind Troy's Department SUV. I knocked on the door and Victoria answered. She threw her arms around me and said, "I'm being threatened."

I gently pushed her to an arm's length. "Where's Deputy Kern?"

Troy walked up behind her and said, "I've just finished up here."

"What do we have?"

He handed me an evidence bag with a note and envelope inside. Typed on white computer paper was the following:

The godly shall rejoice in the triumph of right;
they shall walk the bloodstained fields of slaughtered,
wicked men. Kyrie Eleison

The Bible quote found in Kohler's car also had Kyrie Eleison at the end— I didn't believe that was reported in the newspaper, which made me wonder if we had a nut job on our hands.

"I bet this is the same person who sent a verse to Kohler," she said.

"Possibly," Troy said. "If you're frightened, you might want to stay with someone for a few days."

"A friend at work perhaps?" I added.

"Maybe," she said.

"Come down to the Sheriff's Department today. I'll take fingerprints to eliminate yours," Troy said. "And I recommend you don't report this in the *Register*."

When I left Victoria, she looked so stricken, I sympathetically told her I'd be in touch. She said she was going back into work. A little after noon, while Troy and I were meeting with Ralph, she phoned and began screeching unintelligibly into the phone. She seemed to be hyperventilating.

"Victoria, calm down and take a deep breath."

I heard her inhale and exhale. "Cal! A crow . . . on my doorknob . . . hung with a noose. It reeks!"

"Don't touch anything. We'll be right over."

The two men looked at me curiously. I repeated what Victoria had told me. Troy cocked his head. "I told her I was handling the case. Why would she call you?"

Ralph shrugged and gave me the *you poor bastard* look.

"We've been sort of dating," I said.

Troy made a guttural sound in his throat. "You dirty dog. That's who you went to Vegas with. Isn't it?" Troy chided.

"Yeah, now forget it."

"No way am I forgetting this one."

Ralph put his hands up as if to say he was out of it.

"Let's get going, unless you want to handle this on your own," I said.

"No, no. I'll let you tag along. Give you a chance to see your squeeze."

"YOU DUMB BASTARD. That reporter's going to suck you dry and I don't mean your dick—I mean for information—even though I peg her as the type to be wild in bed."

I turned and faced him. "Shut the fuck up."

And he did. He parked in the driveway near the house and as soon as I exited the vehicle, I could smell the putrid odor of death. Dark goo had dripped from the bird's corpse onto her front step. Victoria had come around from the side of the house and with an envelope in her hand. She was about to hand it to me, but I pointed at Troy.

"He's your investigator," I said.

"Did this come in today's mail?" Troy asked as put on gloves before he opened it.

"Yeah, I saw the crow on the doorknob first. Freaked me out."

"I would imagine so," he said giving Victoria a lecherous smile. He read it aloud.

"'Take heed: The wicked man is doomed by his own sins; they are ropes that catch and hold him. He shall die because he will not listen to the truth; he has let himself be led away into incredible folly. Kyrie Eleison.' Holy shit that bird stinks," Troy said.

I didn't have my jar of mentholated rub with me to smear under my nose so I held my breath as I took a closer look. "There's a large puncture wound on the crow's breast—maybe from an arrow?"

After Troy looked at the wound, we got down to the business of taking photos and trying unsuccessfully to pull prints off the doorknob. "Don't think we need to bring this stinking bird in," Troy said, making a face. He asked Victoria for two garbage bags and we double bagged the crow and I threw it in the trash by the garage.

WHEN I RETURNED to the front of the house, Victoria said, "This is scaring me. I'm going to pack some things and stay at the Super Eight."

"Why don't you stay at Cal's?" Troy said. "Secure building would be safer."

She looked at me eagerly. I wanted to grab Troy by the neck and strangle him. He appeared oblivious to what he'd just done.

"I'm not sure that's such . . ." I said.

"I'd actually feel much better staying with you, Cal."

"Settled," Troy said.

What just happened?

"I'll call you later," Victoria said to me.

As soon as we got into the car I let Troy have it. "Are you fucking nuts? If I wanted her to move in, I'd have suggested it myself."

"You *said* she was your girlfriend."

"No, I said I had dated her. Don't you ever pull any of that shit on me again."

"What's eating you?"

"Last weekend she manipulated me to go with to her father's wedding—only she didn't bother to tell me the bride was Adriana."

"*Your* Adriana?"

"The one and only."

Troy burst out laughing. "So you're pissed."

"You could say that."

"Well, you're a dumb ass if you let that get in your way of doing that hot little mama. Hell, if it bothers you that much, she can stay with me. I'd like me some of that."

I shook my head.

"See? You've resolved it already." He laughed again. "So, now the case is complicated. Do we have a religious nut popping off sinners? If so, you'd better watch your ass," Troy said smirking.

"More than likely it's some copycat playing off the newspaper article she wrote," I said.

"Hey, there's a real threat in there—'*He shall die because he will not listen to the truth.*' You don't think we should take that seriously?"

"Of course, we do. I just don't want Victoria living in my apartment."

"I can't imagine why not with the bod on that one."

I ignored his remark and we didn't speak again until we found Ralph in his office. Troy showed Ralph the note and photos before he entered them into evidence. Ralph just lifted his forehead and said, "Geez."

"Yeah, dead crow smelled especially sweet," Troy said.

"Troy *invited* Victoria to stay at my place," I said.

Troy laughed. "Keep her safe. Don't you think that's a good idea, Ralph, even if he's mad at her for inviting him to her Dad's wedding? Did you know her daddy married Adriana?"

Ralph raised his eyebrows in surprise then dropped them in sympathy. "Seriously? You went to Adriana's wedding?"

"I didn't know Adriana was the bride until I got there. Victoria knew we'd dated. Can you now see why I don't want her to stay with me?"

Ralph made a face and shrugged. "Well, she is being threatened. At least at your place, she's in protective custody."

"That's one way to look at it," Troy said and laughed.

"Oh, one more thing," Ralph said. "Eleanor Kohler's was taken into the hospital this morning—overdose."

"Overdose? Suicide attempt?" I asked.

"Sounds like it," Ralph said.

"Whoa," Troy said.

LATER THAT AFTERNOON I picked up a message from Eleanor Kohler on my department landline phone. She wanted me to drop by the hospital. Could my question about Phillip's remarks set her off?

THE DOOR TO ELEANOR'S private room at Birch County Regional Hospital was slightly ajar. She was alone, sleeping peacefully. I stood near her bed and looked at her. A dim light above her bed cast a yellow glow on her skin. The room was warm and her skin was dewy. Her hair was matted to her face. It was tragic she'd attempt suicide. I decided to let her sleep and turned to walk out.

"Cal?"

"I thought you were sleeping," I said returning to her bedside.

"I guess I dozed off. Thank you for coming," she said as she wiped her eyes with her fist. "This is crazy—it was totally accidentally. I had wine with dinner, later I couldn't sleep so I took a couple sleeping pills. When I still couldn't sleep I took a couple more. Unfortunately, in the morning the kids couldn't wake me, so they called 911. Honestly, I didn't try to kill myself. But—I'm not sure I have any believers."

Her explanation sounded plausible. "I believe you."

She gave me a thin smile. "Thank you. You're probably wondering why I asked you to come by."

I nodded.

"I stopped by your apartment the other day to give you what I found in Ted's Town Car. I should have told you when you called yesterday, but I got distracted."

So it was Eleanor Paris saw outside my door. I wanted to ask how she knew where I lived, but in a small town, I suppose it wasn't difficult to find out.

"What was it?"

"A note—under the front seat. It was a threat . . ."

At that moment, Hamilton Fairchild's booming voice filled the room, "Hey, there, Deputy, did you buy your new car?"

"Not yet."

He kissed his daughter on the cheek and said," Hi, sweetheart, how're we feeling?" He didn't wait for her answer before he turned to me to say, "The truck's still available. Supercrew, six-point-five-foot bed, four-wheel drive. Heck of a deal. I'll drop the price to say . . . fifteen thousand. Now, that's a deal."

"Dad," Eleanor scolded.

"What?" he asked.

"Do not pressure him!" Eleanor said.

"What? I'm offering him a sweet deal," he said still smiling widely. Phony bastard.

It was a good price and the truck was in top condition. "Well, I could take a look at it, but I don't want to rush Eleanor," I said.

"She should be released today or tomorrow. How about coming by this evening?"

"Tomorrow would be better. Where is it?"

"The Sheriff's department was nice enough to deliver it to Eleanor's. What's convenient for you?"

"Before or after work."

"How about 7:45 a.m.? Then you can go directly to the DMV at the court house."

"If I decide to buy," I said.

Ham laughed. "Thirteen is as low as she can go."

"Take care. Save that item you told me about," I said and left.

She nodded and thanked me for coming. I heard Fairchild ask, "What item?" I didn't stick around to hear her answer.

Did Eleanor accidentally overdose like she said? Why wasn't the note found under the front seat of the Town Car?

I dropped by Richard Daniels's office at Daniels' Ford and asked him to search his records for Kohler's bodywork. He said they repaired a small dent in the front passenger door of the Town Car but didn't file an insurance claim. He brought it in on Monday October 3rd, and Hamilton Fairchild picked it up Monday the 10th.

WHEN I GOT TO THE DEPARTMENT I found Betty Abbot to ask her about Kohler's Town Car.

"Town Car?" she asked. "He had *three* vehicles?"

"Evidently the Town Car was in for bodywork when Kohler was killed. Eleanor says she found a paper under the front seat when she cleaned it out."

"So, what's on it?" she asked.

"Not sure, her father interrupted our conversation and evidently she didn't want to discuss it in front of him. I'll get it after she's released."

"I'm sorry. I didn't know about the Town Car."

"I should have caught it. I'll assume the blame."

"Was it another Bible verse? They're creeping me out."

"Yeah, makes me wonder what kind of a weirdo is behind all this."

My mind turned back to Victoria and the possibility she could be a third victim. I phoned her. "Hey," I said. "How ya doing?"

"I'm fine. Look, Cal, I think I'm just going to stay at my place."

Okay, now I felt guilty. "I'm not so sure that's such a good idea."

"I know you don't want me to stay with you. You're mad at me for not telling you Adriana was the bride, aren't you?"

"Because you knew we had a serious relationship."

"Actually no. Adriana had downplayed your relationship greatly to me. But I should have mentioned it regardless of what I understood your relationship to be. I'm sorry and I hope you can forgive me."

"Forgiven," I said, although it wasn't true. "And I guess I'd feel better if you stayed with me until we catch this whacko."

"Are you sure? I don't want to impose."

"Come over when you're ready."

"Have you eaten? I can bring Chinese."

"Perfect."

An hour later she walked through my door with a large red leather duffle bag slung across her shoulder and two bags in her arms that I immediately took from her: Chinese food and two bottles of wine. She dropped the duffle then immediately went on a self-guided tour of the apartment. I followed. She pointed to my safe in the closet.

"Is that where you keep your gun?"

"Yes."

"Can I see it?" she asked, her eyes bright with anticipation.

"No."

She made a pouty face. "Ahh. Is it a big one?"

"I'm not discussing my firearm with you."

She frowned and bounced out of the room.

Weird chick.

"Well, I really like your furniture. Pottery Barn?"

"IKEA."

"Your place is nice—granite countertops and everything. The house I'm renting is pure retro—and not in a good way."

"It's not so bad," I said.

WE WERE STANDING in the kitchen opening the white cartons of food when my doorbell rang. I rarely got visitors so I looked through the peephole—my mother. She's *never* stopped in unannounced.

I opened the door and her arms reached out and pulled me into a hug.

"Mom, what brings you here without a phone call first?"

"I'm just passing through. I was in St. Cloud picking up some pottery for the store from a gal who sells us pieces at a steal. Here, I thought this would look nice on your shelf!" She handed me a handsome black-and-brown vase then pushed her way inside.

"Thanks. Won't you come in?" I said to the now empty doorway.

Mom eyed Victoria and the duffle and said, "Oh, you have company. Hi, I'm Hope Sheehan." She extended her hand to Victoria who in turn introduced herself.

Victoria motioned toward the Chinese cartons and said, "Join us for dinner—we have plenty."

Mom quickly agreed and Victoria started moving the cartons to my square counter high table. Not quite believing this was happening, I grabbed plates and forks and set the table for three.

"So, how long have you been seeing each other?" Mom asked, not wasting any time. She was overly anxious for me to marry . . . she cried for a week when I broke up with Adriana.

"Not long," I said.

Victoria blushed. "Actually, I'm staying with Cal because I've been receiving terroristic threats and he'd thought I'd be safer here."

"Oh, my, terrorist threats? Tell me about it."

"Someone's been sending me threatening quotes from Bible scripture—like I didn't listen to the truth and I will die, that sort of thing, and today someone hung a dead crow from my doorknob. It was disgusting and kind of unnerving."

"I should say so. But you two *are* dating?"

Victoria grinned. "Yes, we went to Vegas together this weekend."

Mom cocked her head and gave me her Mona Lisa smile. I stifled a groan.

"Well, tell me all about yourself. What do you do? Where are you from?" Mom asked.

I sighed. Victoria and mother prattled on through the entire meal. Mom, as usual, had too much wine and so I offered to drive her to a motel. Victoria said she should sleep on the couch, and mom quickly agreed. So there we were, the three of us, watching *The African Queen*.

22

DAY THIRTEEN

WHEN I WOKE, the sun was peeking through the slots in the blinds. Victoria padded out of the bathroom wearing one of my T-shirts.

"You're awake," she said and sat on the bed cross-legged revealing she had nothing on under my shirt. "If you have eggs and cheese, I'll make us an omelet."

"That might be about all I do have," I said. "Ah, could you dress—with my mother here and all?"

As she stripped off the shirt and I saw her beautiful body, a twinge of desire shot through me. I didn't want to be turned on by her anymore. I got up, threw on some sweats, and took Bullet outside. When I returned, Mom and Victoria were talking about making breakfast. I showered and got dressed. After, they were chummily visiting like two old friends.

As we sat down to eat, Mom said, "Victoria said she'd loved to see the store. You two should drive over for dinner soon."

My response was, "The eggs are good."

Victoria smiled. "Thanks. It's one of the few things I can cook."

I was so uncomfortable with the situation I gobbled down my breakfast so I could get the hell out of there. I said I had to leave for work and thankfully mom said she did as well. I didn't want either one pumping the other for information. I walked mom out to her car and of course she was all excited about the new girlfriend.

"Oh, she's a pretty one, Cal—and so refined—of course, your Adriana was too. Do bring her with you next time you come home."

"Mom, we aren't really a couple."

"Didn't you sleep with her last night?"

I sighed. "It was over before it started. Okay?"

"Okay, whatever you say. Well, I'd better run!"

"And next time, call before you drop by."

"You're right. My bad."

I gave her a half-hearted hug and watched her roll out. I went back into the apartment, pulled out an extra key and gave it to Victoria.

"Come and go as you want. I'll tell the manager you're here and to keep an eye out for you. If you can ever take Bullet outside, that'd be nice."

"Can I take him for a run this morning?"

"If you'd feel safe. Look, I work late most nights, so just do your own thing."

"Cal, I have no expectations, if that's what you're worried about. I know that this—arrangement—doesn't mean anything to either of us."

Doesn't mean anything? "Well, okay then, see you later."

"Your mom is adorable."

I nodded. Not my adjective.

I STOPPED BY THE KOHLER'S to take a look at the Ford F150. Ham Fairchild and Eleanor were waiting for me in the driveway. The truck, at twelve thousand, was a sweet deal—one a cheap person like me couldn't pass up—even if the former owner was a dead man. I made out a check and handed it to Eleanor, which I think surprised Fairchild—he expected to get my loan business. She told her dad she could handle the title transfer at the DMV, so he took off to look important at the bank.

As Eleanor and I drove to the courthouse, I reminded her about the note she found in the Town Car. As she turned to respond, the bright light cast on her face revealed dark puffy circles under her eyes and the pallor of her skin.

"Yes, I plan to give it to you when we get back to the house. Truthfully, I didn't want Dad to see it. He over reacts to such things."

"Sorry to bother you with this truck sale today. I'm sure it's the last thing you wanted to take care."

"No, it's good to have this done."

After we transferred the title, we drove back to Eleanor's and she said, "Come in. I'll get the note."

When we entered, the house seemed too quiet. "Can I offer you some coffee?

"Sure, I could use a cup."

She pushed a basket of individual Kcups in front of me and told me to pick the kind I wanted.

As I handed her a Starbucks dark roast, I asked, "How are you?"

"Embarrassed."

"Why? You shouldn't be. You've been through hell and back."

"Oh, I don't think I've made the return trip from hell yet."

"It takes time."

She handed me one of the two individual brewed cups of coffee.

"Smells good—like Northwood's." I took a sip. "Taste's good, too. I might have to buy a Keurig."

"Let me get what you came here for," she said as she walked to the desk. She opened a drawer, pulled out a crumpled piece of paper, walked back and handed it to me. I grabbed it with a tissue.

"Oh, I've touched it," she said.

"Did Betty get your prints?"

"Yes," she said.

The message was written on the backside of the Cadillac Jack's menu in black marker.

LEAVE HER ALONE YOU FUCK
NEXT TIME YOU WON'T BE SO LUCKY

"Do you know who the 'her' is referring to?" I asked as I placed the note in a plastic evidence bag.

Her chin quivered. "I'm assuming Ted's secretary, Lisa Kelly. About a week before he died, Ted told me Jack Whitman stopped by one day and told him Lisa made up a story about Ted making a pass at her. Jack figured she either had a crush on him or wanted to make her boyfriend jealous. Ted asked me if he should fire her—I told him to talk to her and give her another chance. When I found the note, I had the thought her boyfriend killed Ted."

"He was cleared, but why didn't you tell me who you suspected?"

"Jack knew, so I assumed you did. Besides, I thought it had been resolved."

"Has anyone been over to examine the Town Car?"

"No, Dr. Madison, our dentist, bought it three days ago."

Three days ago? Shit! How did we botch that?

As I was about to leave, I realized I had to somehow return the rental. "Is it okay if I come back for the truck later? I have to return the rental first."

"To Daniels? I'll give you a lift. My mom still has the kids."

"All right."

On the drive over Eleanor asked, "Cal, had you ever met my husband?"

"No. Everyone said he was a good man."

"He was. You'd have liked him. He didn't deserve to be gunned down—like an animal."

"I'm sorry we aren't solving this quickly, but we will solve it." Who was I trying to convince?

IT FELT A BIT ODD DRIVING a dead man's truck around town—it seemed everyone I passed did a double take. I kept reassuring myself the purchase was a good decision. When I got to the department, I entered the note into evidence, then found Ralph to update him.

"I'll ask Doc Madison if we can have the lab look at the Town Car anyway. Can't hurt. So, how does the new truck run?" Ralph said.

"Good, but I haven't had it on the highway."

"Why not take it to Brainerd later this afternoon and have another talk with Johnston. All we have is his lying girlfriend's word and, as you said, anyone could get rid of a weapon."

MID-AFTERNOON, I DROVE to Brainerd to speak with Johnston. Bullet loved to ride so I stopped by and picked him up. He stuck his nose in the two-inch opening of the passenger window—he closed his eyes, luxuriating in the experience. But it was a wasted trip: the secretary at the tile plant where Johnston worked said he'd taken vacation days. She gave me his home address, mentioning he still lived with his parents.

The Johnstons lived in a large white house with black shutters in an older part of town. When a short, rotund woman somewhere around fifty answered the door, I introduced myself and handed her my card.

"I'd like to speak with Mike," I said.

"He's not home. My husband and sons went duck hunting right after work yesterday. They'll be back Sunday. Is there a problem?"

"I just have a few questions for him."

"He's not in any trouble, is he? He's always been such a good boy."

"Can you give him a message for me? Tell him we have the test results back for the Town Car."

"What does that mean?"

"He'll know."

I was blowing smoke but Johnston wouldn't know it.

ON THE WAY BACK, I stopped by the public landing on Lake Emmaline hoping whatever went down would appear to me in a vision or something. I parked in the lot, put in my ear buds, and turned on my iPod Nano to the fine trumpet sounds of Chris Botti, which always relaxed me. Bullet sniffed excitedly and moved through the edge of the woods, while I made my way to where the casings were found. I surveyed the area and stopped to focus on the landing—now without a dock. I imagined the shooter's clear shot. I turned and looked toward where Ronny's body was found. The shooter would have had to move several yards to get a clear shot. Witnesses reported a delay between shots.

As I made my way to where I thought the shooter stood then toward where Ronny's body was found, Bullet followed without my urging. Leaves were floating down with regularity now and soon the deciduous trees would be bare.

"Sheehan?"

I jumped and turned to see Ben Whitman. I pulled out my earphones. "Geez, Ben, I didn't see you come up behind me."

Bullet ran to him. He leaned over to scratch his ears. "We have a chocolate lab," he said.

Zach appeared from behind a tree.

"You know my son, Zach," Ben said.

"Sure."

I was uneasy as I watched Zach kneel to pet Bullet.

"Are you driving Ted Kohler's truck?" Ben asked.

"Yeah, I just bought it."

"It's just eerie for us to see it parked here."

"I bet."

"Nice dog you got here," Zach said. "Maybe you should have orange on him. He might get mistaken for a deer." A second later, he broke into a grin.

"It's not hunting season," I said.

"Poachers will shoot at anything. I wouldn't want this nice dog to get hurt."

Ben put a hand up silencing his son. "Let's go. We're already late," he said. As they started to walk away, Bullet started to follow. I had to whistle for him to come back to me. That was freaking strange. There's something about Zach I didn't like or trust.

WHEN I WAS ON MY WAY back into town, I received a phone call from Naomi Moberg.

"Did I do something wrong?" she asked.

"No, what do you mean?"

"Well, it's just that I thought we clicked and then you didn't call."

"Ah, you put me off—said you were going to have the kids."

"Well, the kids are with their dad now. Want to come over for dinner?"

"Yeah," I said without really thinking it through. "But I have some paperwork to do first."

"Anytime is fine," she said.

I felt a pang of guilt. I have Victoria living at my house—but she did say the relationship doesn't mean anything. There. Justified.

Victoria wasn't around when I dropped off Bullet, watered and fed him. So I made my way over to Naomi's. She answered the door, barefoot and wearing a pair of jeans and a striped knit top that hugged her body. An aroma of roasting meat filled the air.

"Mmm. Smells good in here," I said.

She smiled and moved in for a hug and kiss. "Pot roast with all the trimmings. Thought you could use a good home cooked meal."

"I have a woman living at my place," I blurted.

She stepped back and scrunched up her nose. "You're *living* with someone?"

"Victoria Lewis. She's sort of in protective custody."

"Why?"

"She's been receiving threatening Bible quotes."

"Like the one in the paper?"

"Yeah."

"Huh. So you think she's a potential victim?"

"That's what Troy thinks."

"She seems like an opportunist. She's probably writing them herself."

"No, she's genuinely freaked."

She turned her back to me and looked out the window.

"Don't worry about Victoria, okay? I have no future with her."

She turned and faced me, smiled. "I'm glad you're here tonight. Would you like a beer or a glass of Pinot?"

"A Pinot sounds good."

Over dinner I steered the conversation toward her work and kids—and not another word was mentioned about Victoria. Naomi and I had similar values: family, honesty, loyalty, and we both give our jobs two hundred percent.

Later, we made love slowly and tenderly, and as I held her in my arms, she said, "I don't want you to leave me tonight."

"But Bullet."

"Next time, bring him with you."

ON THE DRIVE HOME, it occurred to me she never asked if I slept with Victoria. I wouldn't have lied.

When I walked into the apartment, I found Victoria sleeping on the sofa. I covered her with a blanket and went to bed. At 1:13 a.m., I received a call from dispatch to report to the strip mall on the north end of town near Birch County Community College campus. There had been a burglary. Since I was on call for the week, I dressed quietly and slipped out.

23

DAY FOURTEEN

SOMEONE HAD BROKEN into a vacant store and sawed a hole in the wall to gain access into the hair salon next door. The burglars hadn't counted on the alarm system but managed to grab a new digital camera and cash from the till. They were long gone before patrol showed up. I spent a couple hours documenting the scene and talking to the salon owner then went back home and back to bed. When I got up at 7:00 a.m., Victoria was gone, along with her duffle.

At 8:30, I was already scheduled to participate in a conference call with investigators in neighboring counties about similar burglaries. None of us had any suspects. After, I spent time rehashing all the notes on the murder cases. There was a growing dissatisfaction in the community with how the investigation was going. Daily, the *Birch County Register* ran negative pieces concerning the unsolved murders in the form of editorials, letters to the editor, online blogs. I ran into Ralph as I was leaving.

"You're going home late," I said.

"Every night," he said. "You too."

"I'm so afraid the murder cases will go cold."

"They're not there yet. Heard you have nothing on the burglaries."

"Not a thing. They never leave a single print."

"You know our priority is the murders. There must be something we're missing."

"I've thought of some things we could check out."

"We'll talk tomorrow."

WHEN I WALKED INTO MY APARTMENT, I saw a white envelope on the counter in a plastic bag with a Post-it note on top. *This came in today's mail. I handled it with a tissue. Call me when you get home. I'm at work.*

I found some gloves and opened it. Inside was another quote:

CS: He that diggeth a pit shall fall into it

167

> **and whoso breaketh a hedge,**
> **a serpent shall bite him.   Kyrie Eleison**

A pit? Serpent? Not good. I called and left a message on Troy's phone. On my way to bring it in to evidence, Victoria called asking if I had been home.

"Yes, I'm on my way back to the department to enter the letter into evidence. How are you?"

"Scared shitless. I think I should move around. A girlfriend at work said I could stay with her."

More likely, she was punishing me for being out last night.

FIFTEEN MINUTES AFTER I GOT home, my doorbell rang. I glanced out the peephole. Victoria held a cardboard box. She must have changed her mind.

"You have a key," I said as I opened the door.

"I don't feel comfortable just walking in," she said.

"So what's this?" I said, as she put the box on the kitchen counter.

"Open it." Her arms were crossed—her lips pursed.

I flipped the flaps open and found among the loosely packed newsprint, another box with holes. When I took the inside lid off, there was a large, light-colored snake curled up inside. I slapped the lid back on.

"Snake," I said.

"I guess I can stop worrying how and when the snake would show up."

I wasn't afraid of snakes—but I knew nothing about them and this one could be deadly.

"Can it breathe in there?" I asked.

"Air holes in both boxes."

"Ah. Was this delivered to your house?"

"UPS delivered it to the newspaper office just after I called you," she said.

The return address on the box said: Reptile City, San Antonio, Texas. I pulled up Reptile City on my phone and found the hours. It was closed and wouldn't reopen until tomorrow at 10:00 a.m.

I called Troy to tell him we had something new in Victoria's case.

He said, "I'm occupied at the moment. Can you handle it?"

"Sure, just didn't want to step on your sensitive toes," I said.

He hung up.

Victoria had a finger in her mouth, her eyes wide with anxiety.

"Where are you staying tonight?" I asked.

"With a friend."

"Victoria, if you feel safer you can stay here."

"Let me make a call," she said. She went into the hallway by the bedroom and spoke softly—but I caught enough to know she canceled a reservation.

She rode along to the department, stayed in the car while I entered the snake into evidence. Then, since ketchup and beer didn't cut it for dinner, we went to the Sub Shop. As we pulled up to a stop sign on Central, Troy made a left turn in front of us. Naomi was sitting in the passenger seat. A crazy jealousy overtook me. Was it because Naomi was seeing someone else or because it was Troy? But with "Snow White" living with me, it would be illogical to expect Naomi to be exclusive. Still, I felt like a fool.

When we sat down with our meal, Victoria asked, "What's wrong?"

"Nothing," I said, as I crunched on a chip.

"No, you're definitely pouting. Is it still because of the wedding?"

"I don't pout, but speaking of the wedding, what was your *real* motive in taking me?"

She stared then blinked a couple times. "You still love her."

"I was totally blindsided. Adriana and I broke up only five months ago, and I certainly didn't expect she'd be the bride and marrying some old ..."

"How do you think I feel about a step-mother that's only seven years older than me?"

"How *do* you feel?"

"Who cares how I feel?

She has a knack for turning things around. "People in love can't care what others think, or no one would ever get married."

She picked up a pickle and pointed it at me. "Adriana's mother told me I should forget about you."

"She's probably right."

She smiled and shook her head. Then she reached across the booth to touch my cheek. "Look, I'm sorry. If I had been aware you were still madly in love with Adriana, I certainly would never have invited you."

We each ate a few bites of sandwich in silence.

Then she asked, "Are we okay?"

"We're fine."

I lied. At the moment nothing was fine.

24

DAY FIFTEEN

FIRST THING SATURDAY morning I checked the snake out and put it on Troy's desk. I made some calls, as I waited for him to arrive. As he entered the office, I smirked to myself at how clever I was giving Troy some of his own medicine.

"What's this?" he asked after spying the box.

I had an extreme sense of pleasure watching his reaction as he peered in the box—especially when he jumped back.

"Jesus Christ, Sheehan!"

"The *development* I spoke of last night. UPS delivered it to the newspaper office. Reptile City, the San Antonio company who shipped it, opens at ten o'clock this morning."

"Has it been entered into evidence?"

I nodded. "So, you were with Naomi Moberg last night?"

"How did you know?"

Just then Ralph and Betty walked in. "Matt from evidence wants me to identify a snake."

As she reached in and pulled out the snake, we three men stepped back.

"Oh, what a nice boy." The light-colored reptile curled around her arm. "It's a rat snake," she said. "Harmless. Your pet, Cal?"

"Ha," I said.

"Did you take pictures?" she asked me.

"Just in the box."

"I can do that. "Does it need a home?" Betty asked, grinning.

"I'm sure Victoria doesn't want it. Do you?" I asked.

"Sure, I have a nice big aquarium where he'd be happy."

After Betty left, Troy called Reptile City and put the call on speaker.

"Reptile City," a voice drawled in heavy Texan.

"Good morning. This is Deputy Kern from Birch County Minnesota Sheriff's Department. Could I speak with the owner or manager?"

"Speakin'—Billy Duran's the name."

"Well, Mr. Duran, one of our residents received a snake from your store. Trouble is the young woman is being harassed and the snake may have been sent to her for that reason. It shouldn't be too difficult to look up who the buyer was."

"Sure, I remember the sale because it was unusual."

"How so?"

"This fella said he wanted to send a snake as a *gift* and he used a prepaid credit card. Wanted it delivered UPS overnight."

"Did you happen to get a name?"

Billy gave a throaty laugh. "Said his name was Willie Nelson, but I 'spect it was an alias."

"I 'spect you're right," Troy said.

"Sam Houston is a nice snake. I hope ya'all enjoy him up in Minnesota. As I explained to the buyer, he'd just been fed, so he'd should be all set for a time."

"I'll pass the information along. If you'd give me that credit card number, that'd help."

After Billy gave him the number, Troy thanked him and hung up.

"None of this has actually caused harm to her." Troy started laughing.

"Victoria doesn't think it's so funny," I said to Troy.

Ralph said, "Neither do I. Even though the snake was harmless, it's threatening and escalating."

Troy called Visa and after about an hour on the phone he found out the purchase of the prepaid card had been made with cash at Walmart in St. Cloud, which was no help at all.

Ralph said, "Victoria's case is detracting from the murders. Today, I expect you two to put your heads together and come up with your plan to solve the Peterson/Kohler case because what you've been doing isn't working."

"Are you saying to drop Victoria's case?"

"I'm saying it's of lower priority. Solve the damn murders."

When Ralph left, Troy looked at me and said, "He's turning into a boss."

Just then Victoria called to say she'd received another envelope in the mail and asked what she should do. I sighed and suggested she bring it down to the station to give it to Troy.

We met her in the lobby. Troy read the note aloud.

God himself will shoot them down.
Suddenly his arrow will pierce them.
They will stagger backward,
destroyed by those they spoke against.
All who see it happening will scoff at them.   Kyrie Eleison

"Oh, great," she said. "Now I've got fuckin' arrows to worry about. I don't have time for this bullshit. I have a deadline." As Victoria stormed out of the double entry doors and into the lot, she looked over her shoulders, for flying arrows I supposed.

On the way back upstairs I said to Troy, "You may think this is all one big joke, but I'm concerned about how the arrow will manifest itself."

"Ah, come on. No one has been injured yet."

"Ronny Peterson and Ted Kohler were *killed* for Christ sake," I reminded him.

"True, but like you said earlier, this seems more like be a copy-cat."

"But why zero in on Victoria?"

"Someone with a grudge against her personally or the media in general, I suspect. How many of these have been sent?" he asked.

"Victoria's received four now, but we didn't find any evidence that Kohler received more than the one."

WE SPENT THE MORNING arguing about the best way to approach the Peterson/Kohler case. We'd decided while we waited for Johnston to return from duck hunting, we'd check further into Kohler's clients and his associations with his charitable work. Troy was taking the clients, while I would look into the latter. Eleanor gave me a list of his volunteer activities and I began to make calls. At 6:00 p.m., I left the office convinced we'd never solve the case.

LATE AFTERNOON VICTORIA had texted me saying she'd pick up pizza. I had texted back saying I wanted pepperoni on mine.

When I walked into my apartment, the pizza box was on the counter. Victoria was at the counter drinking a bottle of Sam Adams. She went to the fridge, then handed me a beer.

"I had them leave a one fourth of it plain cheese for me," she said. "I took Bullet out for a run and fed him."

"Thanks."

After I put my weapon in the safe and changed into jeans, I got out plates and started moving toward my counter-high table. Suddenly there was a piercing sound of glass breaking followed by a loud thud. Victoria screamed! Bullet was behind me barking his head off.

I yelled, "Down!" and lunged to pull Victoria down to the floor.

"What was that?"

"Look." I pointed up. An arrow with wicked point, the type used for big game, was stuck in my cabinet door.

Victoria gasped. "We were just standing there."

I grabbed Bullet to calm him and prevent him from cutting his pads on fragments of glass that littered the floor. I did a quick squat walk to the wall where the light switch was located and turned off the kitchen light. I put Bullet in his kennel in the bedroom, and pulled my Smith & Wesson out of the safe. I told Victoria to stay in the living room—but she followed me into the hallway. I flicked off the hall lights and slowly walked down the corridor hugging the wall. Victoria stood in the doorway. The outside fixture above the door cast enough light for me to see Larry Sauer fly down the front stairs, just as two figures neared the front door. I whispered for Larry to stop.

I had my weapon aimed at the figures.

"Why is it so dark in . . ." then a shrill scream. I could tell by their silhouettes that it was Paris and her skunk-haired boyfriend, Stoner.

"Paris, it's me, Cal," I said, lowering my weapon.

"Oh, thank God," she said breathlessly.

Stoner said, "Dude, I saw your gun, 'bout spazed out!"

Larry's words tumbled out. "I saw it all, Cal. A car pulled up. A guy got out of the passenger side with a bow, and the idiot shot an arrow toward the building. Did anybody get hurt?"

"Just his kitchen window and cabinet," Victoria said from behind.

"Did you catch the make of the car?"

"Maybe a Ford Focus—dark color," he said.

"Paris, did you see anyone around outside?" I asked as I went to the glass double doors and looked outdoors. Not a soul in sight.

"No," Paris said as Stoner hustled her through her door.

"Larry, can you stay here until someone from the department gets here? I'm going to see if I can find the vehicle."

"Sure," he said.

I called dispatch and explained to LaVonne why she also needed to get a hold of Troy even though he wasn't on call.

"Someone will be here soon," I said to Larry, who'd followed me inside my apartment.

"Victoria, this is Larry, the apartment manager. He'll stay with you until I get back. You'll need to tell the deputies what happened," I said.

She was right behind me as I grabbed my holster, cell phone, jacket, and car keys. "I want to go with you," Victoria said.

"Absolutely not. Not even remotely allowable," I said.

"Is Bullet okay?" Larry asked. "He seems a little nervous."

"Yeah, he probably is."

"I'll stay here until you get back," he said.

"Thanks, and don't touch anything, you two," I said.

"I won't," Larry said. Victoria's lips were pulled down in a pout.

25

I HAD AN IDEA WHOSE FOCUS it was and left for Fourth Street. From the street the Becker house looked dark, so I drove around and down the alley. Two cars were parked in the backyard: the black Ford Focus and a white Explorer. I got out and felt the hoods—both warm.

A light was on in the back of the house. Through a small window I saw Todd Hackett leaning against a cabinet. He appeared to be laughing hysterically. I walked back to where I parked, sat in my truck and called dispatch. Then I called Ralph. He'd already been apprised of the situation at my apartment and told me Troy and Tamika were on the scene. He said to go ahead and enter the premises and detain those present. He'd have units there shortly. I walked up a few steps to the back door of house and knocked. When Todd Hackett opened the door, his smile fell to the floor.

I flashed my badge. "You remember me? Deputy Sheehan with the Birch County Sheriff's Department. Mind if I come in? I have a couple questions."

Hackett hesitated a moment before he let me in. When I entered the small kitchen, Zach Whitman and Max Becker were sitting at an old Formica table with cans of Budweiser in front of them.

"What's this about, Cal?" Zach Whitman asked.

"Where have you been tonight?" I asked.

"We've been here," Todd Hackett said. He was a true punk: the body stance, the expression, the attitudinal tone—the kind you half want to resist arrest.

"Why lie about it? Hoods of the two cars out back are still warm," I said.

"We got back a long time ago," Todd said.

"You boys out bow hunting this evening?" I asked.

"Whatever are you talking about?" Zach asked.

I heard a car door slam. I hoped it was my backup, but soon Chad Hackett walked in. "What's going on?" he asked

"Evidently a warm car hood is a crime," Zach smirked.

Todd laughed. Max Becker looked pale. Chad lit a cigarette.

"Why are you really here, Cal?" Zach asked. "Need a little companionship?"

Ignoring the little shit, I repeated my question to the Becker kid, "Max, where were you tonight? " I asked.

He shrugged, but he looked scared.

"Well, maybe a trip down to County Correctional will jog your memory," I said.

"Oh, give me a break," Zach said.

I continued to ignore the little pissant.

"Max, how about we go take a look at your car?"

He looked like he could vomit.

"Ask for a search warrant, Beck," Zach said.

"Yeah, I want the search warrant," Max said.

I smiled at them.

At this point, Tamika Frank and Austin Spanney, the new guy who replaced me on patrol, arrived and entered without incident. Tamika told me Troy was on his way with the search warrant. I smiled. "It's on its way, boys."

As concern crept across the faces, the kitchen became quiet. I suggested we separate everyone into different rooms. Fifteen minutes later Troy arrived with the search warrant that included the Becker house, garage, and vehicles of anyone present in the home. One by one, we searched the premises, each kid, and the vehicles.

Spanney and I took Becker out to his vehicle where we found a BowTech Diamond bow under a blanket in his trunk. No arrows.

"What's this, Max?" I asked.

"How the hell did that get in there? It ain't mine."

I laughed. "Never is," I said.

When Spanney put Max Becker in the backseat of a squad, I walked back to the house to find Zach Whitman sitting in the dining room. He let out a little laugh. He was one cocksure kid.

"You think this is all a big joke? I have a strong feeling you are smack in the center of this, and you won't find it so funny when you're sitting in a jail cell."

He laughed. "You act like you don't know who you're talking to," he said.

"Are you kidding me? I guarantee you I'll find out everyone involved, and no matter who their granddaddies are, they're coming down."

I felt a firm hand on my shoulder. Troy told me to step outside.

When we were on the front sidewalk he said, "Look, this is personal to you and you need to step out of it now. Go home and see to your broken window and your hot girlfriend."

He was right. I drove home and when I got back to my apartment, I walked in on quite the scene: Victoria and Larry were sitting in my living room with their feet on my coffee table, listening to Van Morrison, working on their second bottle of wine. Bullet was on the couch, his head on Victoria's lap. When he saw me, he just lifted his head. Evidently, my dog forgot he wasn't allowed on the furniture.

When Victoria waved hello with her pinkie finger and her empty wine glass, Larry leaned over to refill it. One thing I was certain of—neither would pass a field sobriety test.

Larry said Troy and Tamika had finished up with the crime scene quickly so he was able to clean up and have maintenance board up the window. He said they'd be back tomorrow to replace it.

"Hey, Larry, thanks again for everything," I said expecting him to take the hint and leave.

"No problemo," he said not stirring from his position.

Larry refilled his own glass, and I grabbed the one remaining slice of cold pizza and downed it with a beer. I moved Bullet and sat beside Victoria.

"Did you find who did it?" she asked.

"Yeah, I think so."

"Who?"

"We'll see if it sticks."

"Can't you tell me names?"

"Not yet," I said.

"Yeah, Victoria's been telling me what's she's been going through," Larry said.

"Gotta keep it to yourself, Larry," I said.

"She's pretty scared," he said.

"So, what did you tell Troy Kern?" I asked him.

"That the car was a dark-colored Focus—could have been black—and the guy who shot the arrow was wearing a blue jacket."

I'd seen a blue jacket thrown over a chair.

"Good, that'll be helpful."

"Well, I just hope this is the end of it," Victoria said.

"So do I," I said.

"Is it the guy who murdered Kohler and Peterson?" she asked.

"Don't know yet." That would be too simple.

A HALF HOUR LATER Larry's cell phone rang and from the conversation, I surmised his girlfriend was on her way over, and I knew what that meant. Ten minutes later when Victoria and I went to bed we could hear the rhythmic creek of Larry and his girlfriend doing the horizontal bop overhead. I stared at the ceiling wondering if I'd ever get to sleep.

"Want to?" Victoria asked.

"No, I'm clearly not in the mood," I said.

"That's okay. It's been a big night for both of us. Can you at least hold me?"

She moved in close and I put my arm around her, but every muscle in my body was rigid.

"My boss wants me to write an article for tomorrow's paper," she said.

I sat straight up. "What are you talking about?"

"I know what you're thinking, but *he* called *me*. I told him I'd have to talk to you first, but he's pushing me to do the story."

"No, no, no. It could compromise the case."

"But it's my decision because it's happening to me."

"Shit. Trust me. It's not a good idea!"

"Okay, okay," she said. We lay in silence for several minutes before Larry finally got his happy ending.

"I guess he's not a wham, bam, thank you ma'am kind of guy, is he?" Victoria said giggling. It made me laugh.

"I've been tempted to record it for him or take a broom to the ceiling, but I don't have the heart."

Soon Victoria and Bullet were having a snoring duet. Sleep wasn't happening for me—my mind was going two hundred miles an hour. Why would Max Becker shoot an arrow into my building? It must have been about 2:00 a.m. when I dozed off, but my night was filled with vivid, violent dreams filled with pursuits, gunshots, and flying arrows. Max Becker lurked in the shadows. Why the hell was he involved?

26

DAY SIXTEEN

THUD! I OPENED ONE LID a crack to see Bullet's front paws on the bed, his brown eyes imploring *feed me*! My eyes spanned to the clock: eight-thirty, Sunday morning—late for Bullet. I got up and went into the kitchen, darkened with the boarded window. I relived last night's events. Bullet's nails clicked across the wood floor as he followed me around. When I ran a finger over the hole in the cabinet, he whined nervously, so I bent down to stroke his head and told him everything was okay, even though I didn't believe that.

I poured food into his bowl, then realized Victoria and her things were gone. *Don't blame her. She wasn't so safe here after all.* She hadn't told me she was leaving—and I knew why. She was going to write the article in the paper. I found my phone and texted her: *Don't do anything stupid.* She didn't answer.

I dressed in sweats and drove by the newspaper office. As I thought her car was in the parking lot. Then I drove to the department to find out how last night's interrogations went. I couldn't find Ralph or Troy so I went down to the gym to rid myself of the gripping tension in my muscles. Troy was on the treadmill. He was drenched with sweat and stopped when he saw me.

"You look like shit," I said.

"I've been up all night while you were home banging your babe."

I didn't take the bait. "What did you find out?"

"Watch the interrogations—see what you think. I'm going home to bed."

"You can at least tell me the gist."

"Okay. Becker said he was *hired* to shoot the arrow at the siding near the window as a practical joke."

"That's like saying, I meant to shoot him in the leg, not the chest. So, who hired him?" I asked.

"Said someone *anonymously* sent a letter and offered to pay him two hundred dollars if he ordered the snake from San Antonio and shot the arrow into your building. Half payment was included in the letter along and a Visa pre-paid card for the snake. The rest of it was to be delivered after he successfully fired the arrow."

"Let me guess. Becker claims he doesn't know who hired him."

"Correct, and I couldn't break him after an all-night session."

"Does he have the letter and card to prove it?"

"Both destroyed as directed."

"Of course. Want me to go round with him again this morning?"

"His dad hired Warner so we won't be getting any more out of him. He denies knowledge of the Bible verse letters."

"This is all such bullshit."

Troy shook his head and said, "Agreed, but when you can come up with proof and a motive, let me know. Now, I gotta get some shuteye."

He left for the locker room and I finished my workout, showered and dressed, then went to watch the interview. It took a good part of my afternoon and nothing Becker said or did convinced me the kid wasn't telling the truth. Maybe he's just that stupid to have someone manipulate him like that. I checked his record. He had a few juvie incidents: curfew violations, underage consumption but nothing since he turned eighteen.

I called Becker's boss at the Quick Stop. He told me Max quit ten days ago.

"For another job?"

"He took a part-time job with the newspaper."

"The *Register*?"

"Yeah."

My mind spun with the possibilities. I looked in my notebook. Ten days ago was October twelfth, three days after I'd first interviewed him. Victoria was connected to all this. I gave her a call. She didn't pick up so I left a message.

"Victoria, I need to talk to you as soon as possible. Looks like you moved out of my place. Look, I don't blame you, but maybe you should let the department know where you are. Call me. I have something about your case to run by you."

I also left a message on Troy's phone letting him know what I'd found out about Becker's employment. On my way home I stopped to pick up a few things at the grocery store and when I'd finished paying, I recognized Dixie Whitman's voice behind me.

I greeted her and asked how Jack was doing. "He's been released from the hospital in Minneapolis. He's waiting in the car—you should stop and say hello."

"He's doing well then?"

"Very well, but he's not happy. His surgeon says he can't return to work for another month. I only hope he can stay away from the investigation. He's stewing it hasn't been solved yet."

"We're trying."

"Oh, I'm sure you're doing your best. You know Jack—he's short on patience."

I nodded good-bye, grabbed my groceries and headed out hoping I could avoid Jack. I didn't want to discuss why his grandson had been pulled in for questioning. Unfortunately, his black Cadillac was parked next to my truck and as I unlocked my door he unrolled his window. He looked like shit—pale and old.

"Sheriff, nice to see you. You're looking good."

His brows furrowed in a frown. "That Kohler's truck?"

"Yeah."

"You bought it?"

"Yeah, feels a little weird."

"I should think so. Driving a victim's truck before you even solve his murder?"

I felt my face burn.

"Well, I better get going," I said.

He raised his right hand pointing a finger toward my chest. "Oh, Cal, maybe you should focus on the murder investigation instead of pulling kids in for some harmless pranks." His eyes narrowed. "Be smarter, Calvin."

I stared at him for a second then decided not to explain any of it. I got in my car and headed home. When I heard a horn honking, I realized I'd just driven through a red light. Fuck!

MY KITCHEN WINDOW had been replaced and a new wood blind installed, so I went upstairs to thank Larry.

"Larry, while I was gone, how was Victoria? How did she act?"

"She was pretty stressed. Glad I was there to calm her down."

"Yeah, thanks for that."

"She's a real gem. Hang on to that one."

"Yeah, right."

I went back to my apartment and called Victoria again. This time she answered.

"Sorry," she said. "I just noticed you'd left a message."

"Your things are gone."

"My dad and boss are insisting I stay at the Webber's. They say it'll be safer." Robert Webber was the editor of the paper.

"You okay?" I asked.

"Yes. Did they fix your window?"

"It was fixed when I got home today. So, tell me about Max Becker."

Hesitation, then, "Who?"

"Max Becker."

"I don't know him. Why? Is he the one who shot the arrow?"

"Says he was paid to shoot the arrow and purchase the snake."

"Oh, dear god, who would pay him to do that?"

"I thought you could tell me."

"Me? I don't know anything about this Max person. Look, I'm really busy working on something here and have a deadline. Thanks for letting me crash at your place. I'll see you soon." She hung up.

ON IMPULSE, I CALLED ADRIANA to see is she had any insight into her new stepdaughter. She answered on the first ring. "Cal? Is something wrong?"

"How are you?" I asked.

"I'm still on my honeymoon, so I'd better be good," she said.

The sound of her voice made me temporarily forget why I'd called. How idiotic can I be? "I'm sorry. I shouldn't have bothered you." I hung up and within seconds she phoned me back.

"It's okay, silly. Is something wrong? Is Victoria okay?" she asked.

"Tell me about her. Any history with a stalker or anything?"

She laughed. "From what Adam tells me, she's more likely to *be* the stalker. Why?"

"Did you know she's been receiving threats?"

"Then it's for real? Adam talked to her last night—but he used the word 'pranks' not 'threats.' He didn't seem too worried. Should he be?"

"They are threats and definitely escalating."

"I'll tell Adam. Cal, can I ask you something?"

"Sure."

"How did you meet Victoria?"

"She rear-ended me at an intersection and propelled me into another car. The Civic was totaled."

"She told us she met you at a press conference. You should know about the Minnetonka cop. She met him by backing into him in a parking lot, but when he called it off, she was furious and stalked him. That's why Adam insisted she move out of the Metro area to get a fresh start. So watch yourself. She also did the same thing to a campus cop while in college. Too much of a coincidence, don't you think? The girl has a thing for cops."

"Strange way to go about it. When did you learn this?"

"The day after the wedding."

"You could have contacted me."

"I was a little preoccupied with my honeymoon."

Zing!

"Why weren't the accidents in her record?" I asked.

"Adam paid the damages, and, in case you haven't noticed, Victoria uses her sexuality to get what she wants."

"Do you know the Minnetonka cop's name?"

"No, sorry. And now I think I'd better get going before Adam returns. I don't think he'd appreciate me talking to you. He's a tad jealous."

I smiled to myself. "Adriana, if you ever need me, you know I'm a phone call away."

"Same here."

VICTORIA'S AUNT EVELYN'S words came back—*she gets what she wants.* Could she have *orchestrated* this whole thing herself? She could certainly manipulate a kid like Becker to do anything.

I called Ralph and ran my thoughts by him.

"Right now we don't have a bit of proof, so don't say a word to her. We can get a warrant, but if what you say is true, I don't want her to know we're on to her. We'll meet with Troy tomorrow morning," he said.

"She's staying with the Webbers—Robert works for Lewis."

"We have to do this right. By the way, Jack's back home. He called pissed as hell we brought in Zach for questioning. Told him we did it to eliminate his involvement. I thought that might appease him."

"Not so much. I saw him in the Save Rite parking lot. He said I should focus on the investigation instead of hauling kids in for harmless pranks."

"Not to worry. What can he do?"

"Fire me?"

"That ain't gonna happen. By the way, Zach's prints were on the drug case in the county garage. I told Jack I'd hold it back because it wasn't pertinent to the murder case."

"That is the kind of information that could come in handy some day."

"I think he got my point."

WHEN I WAS LEAVING the building, I ran into the one person I could trust—Shannon. She was just coming off her shift. I asked her if she wanted to go out for a drink and she suggested I get Bullet and come to her place.

With a few glasses of wine in us, Shannon and I talked into the wee hours of the morning trying to solve the world's problems. When she was ready for bed, she brought a pillow and blanket and pointed to the couch. Bullet, the traitor, was already asleep upstairs with the boys.

27

DAY SEVENTEEN

B ULLET CAME SLINKING into the kitchen looking for his breakfast. He must have heard me making coffee,

"Oh, so now I'm good enough for ya, huh, boy?" I loved him up. When I took him out to do his business, it was sprinkling. Bullet never minded getting wet. I got the just-in-case-container of dog food I kept in my vehicle, picked up the newspaper wrapped in an orange plastic bag from the steps, and went back inside.

As I filled a pie pan with Bullet's food, the cats joined the feed-me dance, meowing loudly—all three animals staring at me eagerly. When Bullet finished in three minutes flat, I put him back out in the fenced yard so he wouldn't steal the cats' food. Shannon walked in and poured us each a mug of coffee.

"Sleep well?" she asked.

"Surprisingly well—after we solved the department's problems. What are you doing on your day off today?"

"I plan to get a lot done. How about you?"

"Work. I have a meeting this morning. It's only six, so I have time to get cinnamon rolls from the Sportsman Café."

Her eyes lit up, and that was all the encouragement I needed. When I returned Shannon had already showered, and was letting her hair air-dry. She looked good for only five hours of sleep.

"You should wear your hair down more often."

She rolled her eyes then pointed to the paper on the counter. "Did you read the headline?"

"REPORTER AND BIRCH COUNTY DEPUTY A TARGET"

"Shit! She must have been working on the story when I talked to her yesterday."

"Robert Webber wrote this one. Read it then look at page three.

185

Since staff reporter, Victoria Lewis, wrote an article about a Bible verse found in Ted Kohler's truck the day of his death, she herself has been harassed with similar Bible verses and related items. Last evening an arrow used for hunting large game was shot through a window in the home of a Birch County deputy sheriff investigating the Kohler/Peterson murder cases, narrowly missing the deputy and Lewis. This is the most recent in a continuing series of threats and physical attacks related to Bible quotes Lewis has received. Fifteen days later after the Kohler/Peterson murders, no names of suspects have been released and the case continues to remain unsolved.

BIBLE THREATS continue on page 3.

I turned to page three. Victoria's article was accompanied with photos of the crow, snake, the broken kitchen window and arrow in my cabinet. She told it all: from Kohler's Bible verse, to the dates she received each one along with each related object.

At the end of the article she wrote: "I'm not saying the Sheriff's Department is incompetent, but I do think they could use some expert help in solving the murder cases, perhaps from one of the metro police departments—before more innocent citizens get killed just doing their jobs."

"Damn it!" I said.

"She's one crazy bitch," Shannon said. "But I bet she had your dandy doodle at attention."

I smiled. "Cute."

"So call her."

I was so pissed off it didn't take much encouragement to dial her number.

Cal?" she answered in a sleepy voice.

"Congratulations on your full-page article," I said.

Silence. Then, "You're not happy with me, are you?"

"That would be an understatement."

"A girl's gotta do what a girl's gotta do."

"It was pretty stupid on so many levels," I said.

After a few seconds, she said, "Robert said we had to."

"And you had nothing to say about it?"

"Cal, I'm sorry. Can we talk later?"

"Nah, I'm done talking to you."

I touched off and Shannon gave me a fist bump.

I MET RALPH AND TROY at the department at eight o'clock. We laid everything we knew about Victoria's case on the table. I said, "In my opinion, she orchestrated the whole thing herself."

"Well, if you're right, at the minimum, she's facing felony charges for supplying false information," Ralph said.

"What's her motive?" Troy asked.

"The story," I said. "After she discovered the quote and reported on it, she plotted her own copycat scheme: sending herself the threats, putting the crow on her door, paid or coerced Max Becker into buying the snake and shooting the arrow through my window. He probably even got the crow for her. Then she wrote a grand article about it—what a great way to get her father's attention."

"Yours too. Do you like Max for Peterson/Kohler?" Ralph asked.

I shook my head. "I don't think he entered the equation until she needed him to do her dirty work."

Troy crossed his arms and leaned back in his chair. "Victoria has Max Becker by the dick. He's not going to give her up."

Ralph said, "Maybe so, and he's all lawyered up. You two need to find Victoria and bring her in."

ON THE WAY TO THE NEWSPAPER office, Troy said, "You picked the wrong one, Sheehan."

"What do you mean?"

"I mean *you* could be with Naomi. I know you two dated before you went to Vegas with Victoria."

I looked out the window.

"Look, Sheehan, I would never date a woman a friend was currently seeing."

"We're friends?"

He got a weird look on his face. "Aren't we?"

"We could be—if you weren't such an asshole."

He laughed. "You okay with me and Naomi?"

"Yeah—super."

THE MANAGING EDITOR of the paper, Robert Webber, said he had no knowledge of any plan for Victoria to stay with them, nor did he know where she was. He said, "She hasn't been in the office for a couple days."

"But the article?" I asked.

"She emailed it in."

"What's her contact number?"

"If you have her business card, you already have it."

I still had her number in calls received. Her phone rang six times before a voice came on saying the number was out of service. I replayed it for Robert and Troy on speaker.

"I hope she's all right," Robert said.

TROY AND I DROVE to Victoria's home. No one answered the front door and her car was gone. We went back to the office and while Troy did the paperwork for a search warrant for her house, computers, phone records, and vehicle, I checked her credit card activity—nothing in the last forty-eight hours. We went back to her house and used tools to gain entrance. For a while I thought maybe I was wrong about her and that something bad had happened, but when I saw that her personal items were gone, including her luggage, I knew she'd split. By now, she could be anywhere.

Ralph called Adam Lewis who said he had no idea where his daughter was, but she often took off on a whim. Ralph told him we were concerned for his daughter's safety and to contact the department when he heard from her. Lewis said *if* he heard from her he'd give her the message.

And we were at yet another standstill and no closer to finding the real killer in the Peterson/Kohler murders.

28

DAY EIGHTEEN

TUESDAY MORNING BEFORE TROY arrived, I found Ralph in the squad room having a cup of coffee. A white pastry box sat in the middle of the table, so I lifted the lid and picked up a raised sugar. I pushed the box toward Ralph.

"Nah, I'm on a diet."

"Again?"

He patted his belly.

"Gained five."

The doughnut was fresh—slightly crispy on the outside and soft in the middle just like I liked.

"Are they as good as Dixie's?" he asked, looking miserable with his decision to refrain.

"Nah, they're terrible." I grabbed another.

Troy walked in fully pumped. "Talked to Zach Whitman. Max Becker now works at the newspaper loading dock and knows Victoria Lewis. He didn't understand what she was up to until he saw the article in the paper and realized he'd been played."

"When did you talk to Zach about Max Becker and Victoria?" Ralph said.

"At Jack's last night."

Ralph and I exchanged glances. "You were at Jack's?" Ralph asked.

"Yeah, I dropped by for a visit. What's wrong with that? You both visited him in the hospital."

"Did Max admit to sending the verses?" I asked.

"Zach said Max didn't know anything about them."

Ralph placed both hands on the table. "I talked to Oliver Baken this morning. He doesn't think it's worth the time or money to pursue Victoria Lewis."

Baken was the county attorney, and if he wasn't willing to pursue Victoria, it was over.

Ralph said, "Since he lost his last two big cases, his evidence standards have tightened."

"The arrow could have killed Cal," Troy said.

"And we'll go for Max on that charge, but Victoria was right there and was in as much danger. It's her word against his."

Ralph's cell phone sounded. He'd changed his ring. "It's the old Dragnet theme," he offered.

"What's Dragnet?" I asked.

Ralph rolled his eyes then took the call. It was brief.

"Mike Johnston's waiting in the lobby. Asked to speak to Cal. Leave me a message on what's up with him. Troy, if you can get Warner to let us question Becker about Zach's comments, go for it. I'm late for a meeting."

Troy said, "Yeah, like that's gonna happen. I'm more interested in what Johnston's doing here, right now. I want to observe."

JOHNSTON WASN'T ALONE. Virgil Dodge, a local attorney, was sitting beside him, along with his mother and a man who had to be his father. Virgil was a small man with a concave chest who looked like his choice of weight lifting equipment might be a toothbrush. His pale complexion and gray comb over didn't add a thing to his look. He rose to offer a limp hand, then introduced Stanley Johnston whose handshake was a vice grip.

Virgil said, "Mike's come in on his own accord. Wants to clear things up."

"All right," I said.

Gone was the hostile body language I'd seen earlier. Something big was happening, and I was pumped. I asked the group to wait in the lobby while I arranged for his statement to be taped and notified Troy. I went up to the office and found my case notes. Fifteen minutes later, I joined Mike and Virgil Dodge in the interview room.

When I entered, the only sound was Mike's feet tapping on the tile floor. After noting the date, time, and his personal information, I said, "Mike, you've voluntarily come in to make a statement."

Without hesitation, he said, "I was in Kohler's Town Car and had a fight with him."

"When was this?"

Droplets of sweat formed on Mike's forehead.

"September twenty-ninth."

"Start from the beginning. Why did you have this altercation with Mr. Kohler?"

"Okay. Well, it started the day Lisa called to tell me Kohler trapped her in the file room and felt her up."

"State Lisa's full name please," I said.

"Lisa Ann Kelly."

"Go on."

"She acted upset, and I didn't want Kohler thinking he could get away with that, so I called him and told him I wanted to talk to him—to meet me out at Cadillac Jack's."

"How did you pull that off?"

"I left work, without signing out and drove over to Cadillac Jack's. I used the payphone downstairs by the restrooms to call Kohler."

"Did you give him your name?" I asked.

"No, and I disguised my voice so he wouldn't know it was me. Told him he'd want to hear what I had to say, or if he didn't, I was sure his wife would."

"No one saw you?" I asked.

"No one paid any attention to me," he said.

Johnston wiped the beads of sweat from his face with his hand, then sat back in his chair and began the foot tapping again.

"Go on," I said.

"Well, I didn't think he had the balls to show up, but he did."

"And if he hadn't?"

"I'd have found him."

"What happened then?"

"I watched him park the car and go into in the bar. That's when I climbed in the backseat of his car and hid. When he came back out, he didn't even notice me. After he drove a couple miles, I sat up and pulled a toy gun on him. Told him to pull over. I made him get out of the car. I punched him a few times to teach him to stay away from her."

"Did Mr. Kohler know it was you?" I asked.

"I wore a ski mask, so I don't think so," he said.

"Did you use Lisa's name?"

"No," he said.

"So, you wanted to teach him to stay away from Lisa, but you never used her name, you disguised your voice, and wore a ski mask."

"Yeah," he said.

"Seems like you went to a lot of trouble to disguise yourself. Why not just approach him at his office and have a face-to-face talk with him?"

Suddenly his expression changed—like he realized how stupid it sounded. But what he couldn't say was his intent had been to hurt Kohler, and he didn't want to be identified. But what I didn't get was why Kohler didn't report it.

"Did Mr. Kohler fight back?" I asked.

"At first, then he just curled up."

"Did you continue to assault him?" I asked.

His eyes widened and seemed to realize he may still be in big trouble. "No, I left."

"You walked away?"

"No, I drove his car back to Cadillac Jack's and left it with the keys in it."

"So you left Mr. Kohler out on the road, injured?"

"He wasn't hurt that bad."

"So you assumed. What happened next?" I asked.

"I drove back to work and finished up a small job, checked out, and went home to clean up. Then I drove back to Cadillac Jack's."

"Anyone know about this?"

"No."

"So, why come forward now?" I asked.

"I was afraid the evidence would show I was in his car, and you'd think I killed him, too."

"Did you leave anything in the car?"

"Just a warning note," he said.

"What did it say?"

"Leave her alone, or next time you won't be so lucky. Something like that."

"Meaning?"

"Meaning nothing. I wrote it just to scare him."

"What did you do with the toy gun?"

"I don't know. I lost it," he said.

"If there's anything else, now's the time," I said. "Like what happened the morning Kohler was killed."

He shook his head. "I didn't kill him."

"Beating him up satisfied you?"

"I guess you could say that," he said.

"But you warned him with a Bible verse," I said.

"Are you talking about the one in the papers?"

"Yes."

"The only thing I wrote to him was on the back of that placemat."

I went on for a couple more minutes trying to trip him up, but he maintained steadfast in his story. I excused myself and went to get Troy's opinion.

He said, "Johnston looks like one big, sorry kid."

"I suspect he's telling the truth, which slams the Kohler/Peterson case right back to square one."

I went back in and wrapped up the interview. When Johnston stood, I shook his hand.

"You did the right thing coming in, Mike. I'll discuss your case with the county attorney and see what he wants to do. We may have further questions."

Dodge shook my hand and said, "Okay, well, thank you for your time, Deputy Sheehan. Someone will get in touch with me?"

"You can count on it," I said.

I showed them back to the family lounge where his parents had been waiting. The Johnstons approached me.

"It was Mike's idea to come in," Mrs. Johnston said.

"That's in his favor," I said.

Mr. Johnston said, "We didn't raise our son to be violent but no self-respecting man is going to let a man touch his girlfriend like that. Too bad he didn't know she was such a liar."

Too bad I didn't know Victoria was one. We men can be such suckers.

LATER, RALPH FOUND ME in the office. "Saw Johnston's tape."

"I thought he was going to confess to Kohler's murder," I said.

"Do you think he's our shooter?"

"You saw the tape. What do you think?"

"He's believable and there's no point in arresting him without a ballistics match. The kid did himself a big favor coming in before the DNA showed up on the placemat."

"Now we know how Kohler got the bruises. So why didn't Ted report the assault?"

"Good question." Ralph sighed. "Maybe he did. Jack might have handled it on his own, like he did Lisa Kelly's claim."

"*You* ask him," I said.

Ralph laughed. "I will. Oh, and Webber called me back to let me know he's not happy with the prospect of Victoria's orchestrating her own harassment. He also told me something interesting: Bob Brutlag bought the old tire shop and is going to start his own business."

"Really? That takes capital."

Ralph nodded.

"So does his dad have money?" I said.

Ralph shook his head. "Not *that* much."

"He was my first suspect. And now he has enough money to buy a business."

"Remember, no ballistics match."

"There's got to be an angle we're missing."

"What could we possibly have missed?"

"It all goes back to that original Bible verse. Maybe it's church related."

"So do your research. What have we got to lose?" he said.

I woke in the middle of the night and found myself mulling over what a fool I was to trust Victoria. She paid or manipulated someone to harass her so she could write an f-ing story. And where did Bob get the money to purchase his own shop? Someone could have paid him to kill Kohler. It would be easy to dump a rifle around here.

29

DAY NINETEEN

I PICKED UP FOUR CINNAMON ROLLS at the Sportsman Café Wednesday morning before work, and as I drove by the old tire shop Bob Brutlag bought, I noticed a candy-apple '57 Chevy parked out front. I pulled up, parked, and knocked on a shop window. Bob grinned as he opened the door and I immediately smelled the strong odor of fresh paint and coffee sitting too long.

"Heard you bought this shop."

"Yeah, it's always had been my dream."

"So, how does someone your age go about getting enough money together to buy a business?"

I watched for signs of nervousness, but he just cocked his head and gave me a crooked grin, "Why do you ask?"

"Just curious. Takes a lot of money to start up a business."

He nodded. "I got a good deal on the building because it had been foreclosed."

"If I checked your bank records, what would it tell me?"

Now his eyes narrowed. "It'd tell you my old man set money aside for me from my mom's life insurance payout and that he also kicked in a good amount as my partner. I also got me a small business loan—some government deal."

Oh.

"Do you like the new paint color?" he asked.

"Depends on which is the new one?"

"It's called adobe clay," he said.

"Then yes. It's better than the color of urine."

He laughed. "I heard a rumor your girlfriend was terrorizing herself. Women, eh?"

"Who told you that?"

"Big Jack. Went to pay him a visit last night."

"What else did Big Jack tell you?"

He smiled. "He said with her looks she could make a fool out pretty much out of any man she wanted to."

"You're probably right," I said, as a few memories of how she used her feminine wiles on me passed through my brain.

I DROVE OVER TO the department, checked in, grabbed the bag of rolls from my truck, then took my assigned vehicle to St. Stephen's. Bag in hand, I rang the doorbell at the backdoor of the rectory.

The portly Father John Moran answered the door. He was dressed in a blue-and-black plaid shirt and black slacks. He had a full head of black hair even though he was probably well into his sixties.

"Good morning, Father."

"Good morning, Deputy . . . Sheehan, am I right?"

"Yes, sir."

"What can I do for you?"

"Do you have time for a few questions about Ted Kohler and Ronny Peterson?" I asked.

"Of course. Come in." He led me through the small porch into a kitchen that smelling of old wood and coffee.

He sighed. "Such a tragedy. We pray every day at mass for Ronald and Theodore and their families. I was having my breakfast. Care to join me?"

I lifted the white bag. "I have cinnamon rolls from the Sportsman."

"Oh, my. Well, the coffee's made. Cream or sugar?"

I shook my head. He told me to sit at the small kitchen table where he had a bowl of what looked like bran cereal. He methodically placed another plastic placemat and a white paper napkin on the small round wood table and then poured a mug of coffee and set it before me. He got two small plates and poured another mug for himself.

"I'll have to eat my bran before I indulge in one of those heavenly rolls."

"Go right ahead."

I opened the bag and took out a roll and placed it on my plate. Father Moran jumped up and took out a tub of margarine and a half-gallon of milk from the refrigerator. He pulled out two knives out of a drawer, and set one before me. He slowly poured milk over his cereal and took a few bites.

"I don't love the taste of the stuff, but at my age, it's necessary."

"Now, you said you had questions?"

"I understand Ted Kohler was quite active in the church."

"Oh, yes, very. He's been on our Parish Financial Board for several years and did our audits for free. He was a model Catholic. Practiced what he preached, so to speak."

"And what was it he preached?"

"He faithfully tithed and encouraged others to do the same."

"How exactly did he encourage?"

"On our stewardship Sundays I always asked Ted to do the homily. The giving always increased after his talks."

"What made him so convincing?"

Father smiled. "He had a sense of humor about him, but always gave a clear message: that you pay God before anyone, and that you should share your blessings."

"Pay God—meaning St. Stephen's?"

"Yes, and our charities."

I nodded. "Did Ted Kohler ever step on any toes here at church?"

"Everyone loved Ted," he said, grabbing for a cinnamon roll. "Oh, these taste just like the ones my mother used to make."

I pulled out the original Bible verse we found in Kohler's truck. "I know I asked someone from the parish about this before, but do you recognize this verse?"

"I believe he may have used this in his last homily."

"Really?"

Father Moran nodded.

"I'll leave the other two rolls for you. Thanks for your time."

I left Father Moran, his mouth stuffed like a chipmunk. I found the parish office in the new building that joins the church and the school that closed years ago. The plump secretary at the desk gave me a pleasant smile. She ran her fingers through her short dark-gray hair and asked how she could help me.

"I'd like to speak to Helen Marcus."

Helen was the parish bookkeeper. The secretary showed me to a small corner office off the lobby. Helen smiled when she saw me. I'd answered the call when her husband, attempting to sweep snow off his skylight, slipped off the roof. She was a large figure—almost six foot.

"Remember me? Cal Sheehan," I said as I extended my hand.

"Of course I remember you," she said, smiling.

"Your husband doing okay?"

"Oh, he's a little stiff and will never walk long distances again, but that's the way it is when you break as many bones as he did. We thank the Lord it wasn't worse. I bet you didn't come here to ask me about Jerry."

"No, I want you to tell about me Ted Kohler."

She sighed deeply. "Poor Eleanor and the children."

"He was on the financial board, so I imagine you worked with him some?"

"Yes, I take notes for the board and Ted did our monthly audits."

"What was the tone of these board meetings? Were there any disagreements over spending—the direction the parish was headed?"

"Oh, well, there's always disagreements, but things always settle down."

"Do you remember who he specifically may have gone round with?"

"Phillip Warner mostly, but the whole board argued about the land sale, and in the end they decided not to sell."

I showed her the original verse. "Did Ted ever use this verse in his talks?"

"This is the one that was in the paper that was found in his truck?"

"Yes."

"It was familiar to me. I think he used it in his last homily so he probably left it there himself."

"Probably." Maybe she was right, and the verse didn't have a darn thing to do with his murder after all.

"You know something just came to me, but it's probably not important."

"What is it?"

"When Norm Taylor was diagnosed with cancer, I overheard Ted tell Father that he'd go over and speak to him. After the funeral I heard his son have quite a heated argument with Father. I asked Father later what it was about, and he said Gus wasn't happy his dad had left the farmland to the church. I don't think he knew it was going to happen. There were others, too. Maybe Ted told them to keep it a secret so the kids wouldn't talk their folks into changing their minds again."

"It'd be helpful if you could write down the names for me, Helen."

"Don't give him a single name," Father Moran bellowed from the doorway.

I nodded and smiled at Helen, got up and walked passed Father Moran wishing him a good day.

I may not have names, but I had obituary records.

I CALLED WARNER'S OFFICE from my car. His secretary said if I hurried over I could probably catch him before he was due in court.

"Deputy," Warner said as he shook my hand.

"Counselor. This is the only office I've seen that surpasses Hamilton Fairchild's. Man, this is plush."

He snickered. "Have a seat."

I sat in a cushy black leather armchair, while he sat in a chair that looked like it did everything but fetch him coffee. He leaned back and rocked. "So, what's so urgent?"

"Murder seems urgent to me. Tell me about St. Stephen's finance board and Ted Kohler's role in the church finances."

He gave a half laugh. "You think the finance board has a murderer on it? Getting desperate, are we?"

I smiled, "Just looking under all the rugs for the dirt. Did Ted have a lot of power on the board?"

"He was a persuasive man, and I think he worked behind the scenes getting people on his side. He had an air of importance about him." *That's the pot calling the kettle black.* "People perceived him as the financial expert."

"Did anyone ever disagree with him?"

"I did—all the time. I felt he had a hidden agenda."

"An example?"

"He was pushing financing through his father-in-law's bank for the remodel. I wanted to sell some off land holdings to pay for it."

"And in your opinion, that was financially better for the church?"

He sat forward and gestured with his hands. "Of course. Ted and I never hid our differences of opinion, but we were friends and agreed to disagree. He was just more *persuasive* than I."

"He must have been. I know people he convinced to change their beneficiary to the church. Is it common practice to solicit people to hand over their life savings instead of giving it to their families?"

He shrugged.

"How do you feel about that?"

"I don't do wills. I have associates handle them. You know the client has the right to do whatever he or she wants with their wealth."

"Any family members get particularly angry when they found out that their inheritance went to St. Stephen's?"

He leaned back in his chair and grinned. "You know I'm not going to give out that kind of information."

"Well, if you're not going to help find your *friend's* killer, I might as well be on my way."

"Oh, low blow." He shook my hand and said, "It was good to see you again. I was certainly surprised to see you at Adam and Adriana's wedding."

"No more than I."

"I'd say we both lost out with Adriana."

I grimaced. "Say, you don't know where Victoria Lewis is, do you?"

"No, why would I?"

"You're a friend of Adam's."

"I don't keep track of his children. I must say she wrote quite the article in the paper."

"Yes, and now she's mysteriously vanished."

"Do you suspect fowl play?"

"Just her own. Let me leave you with a thought. Whoever killed Kohler might be crazy enough to take revenge on the attorney that changed a will. Something to think about, right?"

"I think you're making way too much of that connection."

"Maybe, maybe not."

"Well, good luck with that."

"Sooner or later, I'm going to run into someone who's willing to step up to the plate."

"You go with that positive attitude."

I saluted him and left to see Gus Taylor about a changed will.

30

I CALLED JOYCE DEXTER at the Parks Department and asked where I could find Gus Taylor. She told me he'd called in sick. I drove west to the Taylor farm. This time Spinner greeted me without a bark. I gave him a good ear scratch, and he followed me up to the front door. I knocked. No answer. I tried the knob. It turned and I entered his house still in disarray. I'd go crazy with the disorganization.

"Gus? Sheriff's Department here," I called. Nothing. I called out, louder a second time.

He poked his head around a corner looking like I just woke him—hair disheveled, eyes watery, face crinkled from sleep. "You scared the shit out of me!" he said loudly.

"Sorry. You didn't answer your door. I heard you called in sick and I was worried about your well-being."

"That's a load of crap. So, why are you here?"

"I need to talk to you—about your dad's will."

He looked taken aback, then said, "What about it?"

"You tell me."

He took out a red handkerchief and blew his already reddened nose. "You know my dad left the farm to the church?"

"Yes."

"I'm contesting the will. Virgil Dodge is handling it for me."

"So, I'm told you were angry when you found out."

"Wouldn't you be? I was betrayed. So, yeah, I was pretty pissed off."

He started coughing. Yeesh. I can't wait to get me some of that. When it subsided I asked him, "Whom do you blame?"

"The padre."

"Father Moran?"

"Yeah, it was his big plan to shore up the church's reserves. Man. I should have figured it out he and Kohler wasn't just visiting my old man—he never had time for him before. No, they were here to coerce my father—on his

201

deathbed, mind you—to hand his farm and *my inheritance* over to the church—they got everything but the buildings and the land they're on."

I nodded.

"Oh, wait—I see that look. I suppose you think I killed Kohler?"

"Sounds like a motive to me."

"He was shot, right?"

"Right."

"Well, I don't even own a gun. Never did. Hell, search the place right here and now."

So, I did. I searched the house and out buildings piled full of junk, but I knew there was nothing to find since he'd given his permission so freely.

I stopped back at the house and thanked Gus for letting me search. I said, "Just curious, Gus, why didn't you farm with your dad?"

"Tried it for a while but me and Dad couldn't get along, so I got the job with the Parks Department. A couple years ago when he hurt his back and sitting on a tractor even bothered him, I made the decision I would take over. But when I told him, he said it was too late, he'd already rented the land out."

"Was he punishing you when he bequeathed the land to the church?"

"Damn right. Now, I'm trying to reverse it. I'm told I have a good chance."

"Good luck with that."

"Thanks."

I WENT BACK TO THE OFFICE and sat down at the computer and started researching funerals held at St. Stephens. I started with the most recent and worked backwards after Kohler and Peterson. September was Peter Fillmore's. After a little checking, I found out his wife, Madeline, was a resident in the nursing home and their only child was a nun. I crossed off Fillmore.

In August, there were two funerals: one was a widow whose two sons were both deceased. I remember hearing about how one died in the Vietnam War and the other in a car accident. The other summer funeral was a child's.

The other two funerals were Gus's dad's, who passed away in January a year ago, and Naomi's mother's in April. I went back into the previous year and made a list of names. The previous year, only one family had willed money to the Church, but the son said the mother had consulted them before making the change. I looked at Neva Hunt's name. I'd been putting off questioning Naomi for more than one reason, but I knew it had to be done.

31

A LIGHT WAS ON AT NAOMI'S HOUSE. Now was as good a time as any. I knocked on her door and was relieved when I didn't get an answer. But just as I took a step down, the door swung open.

"Cal?"

"Oh, hi," I said.

"Come on in," she said, seeming pleased to see me.

I followed her into her living room and she offered me a drink.

"Ah, no, thanks."

"I'm so glad you stopped by."

"I'm just here to ask you some questions."

Her face dropped. "Oh, okay. I used to think you were a laid-back type guy, but you're really not. Your mind is always on the job, isn't it?"

"Pretty much."

"Mind if I pour myself a glass of wine while we talk? Had a rough day. Budget cut-backs."

"Always tough, I'm sure."

I took a seat at one end of the sofa and she returned with her wine and asked if I was sure I didn't want one. Again, I declined. She sat next to me and put her hand on my thigh. I should have chosen the chair.

"Well, what is it you have to ask me?" she said, with a slight smile.

I leaned forward and put my elbows on my knees. She responded by removing her hand. I scratched a non-existent itch on my forehead, looked down, then turned and looked directly into her eyes. "Did your mom bequeath anything to St. Stephen's?"

At first she looked taken aback—then nodded. "Yes. Why?"

"Were you aware she was doing that?"

She took a large gulp of her wine, sat back, and shook her head. "No, that was a surprise. Why?"

"How did you feel about it?"

"At first it upset me, but then I came to realize she could do anything with her money that she wanted."

"How much did she give?"

She picked at an imaginary piece of lint off her sleeve. "Two hundred thousand dollars."

"What?"

"Yeah." She nodded and took another sip.

"Was there anything left for you?"

"This house, which was paid for—and enough to cover her expenses and medical bills."

"Shit, I'd have been pretty pissed."

"What's your point?"

"It'd be upsetting, is all. Do you know who talked her into it?"

"I'm guessing either Ted Kohler or Father Moran—both visited her."

"I'm told Ted was very persuasive."

"Must have been because I never thought of Mom as a pushover. You sure you don't want a drink?"

"No. Have you done anything about it legally?"

"I doubt there's any use."

"Gus Taylor contesting his dad's will. He lost the whole farm. Couldn't hurt to try, could it?

"I don't want to."

"Why not?" I asked incredulously.

She looked annoyed. "Because it was her wish to give the money to the church. You sound like Jeremy. He wouldn't drop it either. Now, can I ask you a question?"

"Sure."

"Why didn't it work out between us? Was it because of the kids?"

"I heard you didn't want the divorce."

She looked shocked. "Who told you that?"

"Jeremy. I ran into him the day after we'd been together and he said you asked him if he really wanted you to sign the divorce papers?"

She made a scoffing sound. "That was *his* interpretation. I reminded him the divorce was *his* idea—and not to forget that. No, I made my decision when I realized he had big plans for my inheritance and wanted out when the money wasn't there."

"Nice guy."

"Not so much. At first, I was devastated, but now that he's actually out of my life, I'm much happier. He's an angry man and that rubs off."

"I suppose it does. Naomi, I need to clarify something: I also felt you put me off—more than once."

"Because I wanted to wait to introduce you to my kids until we had been together a while—I don't want them to get attached to a man if the relationship isn't going to last." She leaned into me. "Cal, I really like you. I hope you're trying to tell me you want to see me again."

"One word—Troy."

"I only started seeing him because I knew you were with Victoria," she said, and began to cry. I put my arm around her only to offer comfort when at that precise moment Troy burst into the room. We moved apart. I knew he would assume something was going on—especially when he saw Naomi wipe tears from her eyes.

"What the hell is this?" he demanded.

"Nothing," I said.

"Cal was just asking me some questions about Gus Taylor."

"You are fucking *crying* about Gus Taylor? Do you think I'm stupid?" he said.

"I'll leave you two lovebirds. See you tomorrow, Troy."

I half expected to be shot in the back as I was leaving. Naomi is one confused cookie. I'd have to set her straight and soon.

32

DAY TWENTY

I'D SLEPT POORLY and feeling damn grumpy Thursday morning as I went in to work—and ready for Troy's tirade. However, he came in acting as if nothing had happened. He said he'd spoken with Phillip Warner and Max Becker would not be giving any additional statements about Victoria or anything else. Although I intended on mentioning Naomi mother's will, I put it off to get a jolt of caffeine in my system. When I reentered the office, he was walking out. He told me was going to be interviewing Kohler's clients. He spent the rest of the day out of the office. I spent mine on the phone and computer looking into Kohler's other charitable associations. Nothing and no one stood out as contentious or murderous.

I left work earlier than usual, about five o'clock. I stopped at the Save Rite deli counter to pick up a chicken potpie, then the liquor store—as I was entering, I was surprised to see Adriana Valero leaving.

"What are you doing here?" I asked.

"Not even a hello?"

"Sorry. Hello. What are you doing here?"

"You're in your direct mode, aren't you? We're here for the Warners' twenty-fifth wedding anniversary party."

"Is Victoria attending?"

She looked amused. "No, I'm sure not."

"Where is she these days?"

"I'm not privy to that information. I assume it's because they think I would tell *you*—which I would, if you asked."

"Nice to know. If you do find out any information, let me know." I handed her my card.

She took it and said, "Weird, it's come to this."

"So how was your honeymoon?"

She gave me a forced smile. "It was fine. You look tired."

"You look beautiful, as always."

The compliment seemed to slide off like water. "Well, I'd better run. I just stopped to pick up some champaign."

"Where are you staying?"

"At the Rivers Inn. That's where the celebration dinner is as well, but we're having them up to the suite for a little pre-celebration."

I nodded. "Sounds like a hoot."

She gave me one of her little airy laughs and touched my arm. It was like a current flowing between us—but maybe I was the only one who felt it.

"Good seeing you," she said.

"Adriana, you handled wills when you were with Warner. Right?"

"You know I did."

"Were there any issues when someone changed their beneficiary to St. Stephen's? Like adult children upset when they found out their parents changed the will without their knowledge?"

"You know I can't talk about clients."

"You could give me a nod if I mention a name . . ."

"No, Cal, I can't. I have to go," she said started walking off.

"Be careful," I said after her.

She turned and shot me a disgusted look. "Now why would you say that?" she asked.

"Because the attorney who made the changes could be in danger,"

"Don't be so dramatic."

I shrugged. "Just saying."

BULLET WAS ALWAYS at the door when I come in, but tonight he wasn't. I assumed Larry had him. It was abnormally dark in the room. Then I realized the blinds were pulled in the kitchen and living room. I distinctly remember opening them before I left this morning. Alarm washed through me. I drew my weapon and moved slowly into the kitchen. I grabbed a flashlight from my cabinet and held it above my gun as I traveled around the corner. I could see a dark figure sitting in my recliner.

"Get down on the floor, now!" I yelled.

"Oh relax, Sheehan," said the figure. I recognized the voice.

I flipped on the lights and went around the corner still aiming my weapon.

"Troy, what the hell are you doing here?

"For fuck sake, put the weapon down. Little too jumpy, aren't you?"

"You're damn right, I'm jumpy, when someone gained access into my apartment. Lucky I held back on the trigger. How the hell did you get in, anyway?"

"Larry." Bullet sat at Troy's side gnawing on a real beef bone and still hadn't bothered to get up to say hello.

"I don't give my dog real bones," I said. "They aren't good for him."

"Sure likes 'em, though."

"What're you doing here?"

"Came to chat about why you're sniffing around Naomi again."

"I'm just investigating where the clues take me."

"What clues?"

"Kohler, under the direction of Father Moran, preyed on vulnerable parishioners—the elderly, the dying. Encouraged them to change their beneficiaries to St. Stephens. Most families never knew until the will was read. Naomi's mother willed a bundle. It's motive."

He pointed at me as he spoke angrily. "That's all bullshit and you know it."

"I'm just running down the list. I had to talk to her like everybody else. Gus Taylor could be our guy, but I have no proof and because he's taking legal action, I tend to doubt he's responsible."

"She told me about her mom leaving money to the church one of the first times we were together. She was disappointed but she's okay with it. No, this is all about revenge. I have Naomi. You have nobody. You're trying to ruin it for us."

"I'm only trying to solve the case," I said, trying to remain composed.

"Your thinking is remarkably flawed. What does anyone get for shooting Kohler? Not a damn thing. Stupid theory. Cal, don't make a fool of yourself and the department by playing *Miami Vice* or *Conspiracy Theory* or whatever the hell you're doing."

I stared him down. His attempt at humiliation only fired up my defensive instincts.

"Troy, we're through here. In the future I'd be careful about letting yourself into my apartment . . . with me being so jumpy and all . . . I may just shoot the intruder in my apartment."

Troy came in so close I could smell his beer breath, "Don't you—ever—threaten me—again. Why you're perceived as the golden boy is beyond me." He left, slamming the door behind him.

I wrestled the bone from Bullet's mouth and threw it at the door, then raced the dog to retrieve it. The very next thing I did was phone Larry to tell him never to let anyone into my apartment ever again unless the smell of death was coming from inside.

That night as sleep evaded me, my thoughts ricocheting between Adriana, Troy and Naomi, Victoria—and Ted Kohler's role in St. Stephen's campaign to obtain parishioner's inheritances. I got up and watched television on the couch and fell asleep watching an old Betty Davis movie.

33

DAY TWENTY-ONE

First thing Friday morning, I drove to the Parks Department to have a talk with Naomi.

Joyce greeted me with a big smile. "Hi there, Cal."

"Naomi in?"

"No," she said.

"Tell her I stopped by and to give me a call."

Then I drove directly to the department and found Ralph in the sheriff's office. He took one look at me and said, "You look like hell."

"Thanks," I said.

"You're not sleeping?"

I told him what I'd discovered about Ted Kohler and Troy's surprise visit, leaving out a few details.

"'Splain yourself, Lucy."

"You may not know I had a few dates with Naomi, and now Troy is hot and heavy with her. He seems to think my questioning her is about me getting some kind of revenge—because I picked Victoria instead of Naomi."

Ralph shook his head. "Hell, this seems like a mating battle to me. Personally, I think you both better cool it with Naomi. Here have a chocolate croissant," Ralph said, pushing a white bag in my direction.

"I thought you were on a diet."

"I'm having a minor-relapse. I'll start again Monday."

I hadn't thought to eat breakfast, so I grabbed a croissant and poured myself a cup of coffee from Ralph's pot into a Styrofoam cup.

"Naomi said Jeremy had big plans for her mother's inheritance—he asked for the divorce after the will was read."

"So what are you thinking?"

"I'm thinking Jeremy Moberg had money problems."

"A lot of people do these days."

Just then Troy bounded in. "This asshole telling you about his fucked up theory?"

"Sit," Ralph demanded.

Troy pulled a chair from the side of the room and sat on it backwards—cool dude that he was.

"You need to turn your baseball cap backasswards, too," I said.

"Fuck you," Troy answered.

"What this investigative team doesn't need is you two going at each other like a couple of kids on the schoolyard. If you can't control yourselves, then I'm gonna have to take the case over, and frankly, I don't have time."

"I can do it alone," Troy said. "Numb Nut here doesn't know what he's doing anyway."

Ralph put his hand up. "Shut up, the both of you, and get back to focusing on the case. Cal, tell Troy what you've learned."

Troy looked at Ralph and took a deep breath looking straight ahead, face scrunched in defiance.

"I know the St. Stephen's connection is a long shot, but we've hit a wall here. I found out there are a number of people who left land or money to the church."

Troy sputtered out, "So let's investigate *every* family member who lost out because of Kohler."

"I am."

"He started yesterday," Ralph said.

I lifted my arms in submission. "Hey, you can double check my work."

Ralph gave me the hand, so I shut up. "Jeremy and Naomi may have money problems," he said.

"They do. She's told me all about it . . . she also told me Jeremy had trouble letting the will thing go." Troy said.

Ralph had me recap what I'd learned about everyone on the list. Then he said, "Now, you two are going to have to put your heads together to figure out the best way to approach this, and before either one of you do anything, I want you to run it by me."

Troy let out a sound of frustration and said, "Oh for the . . ."

"Hear me?" Ralph said sternly.

"Yes, sir," I said.

Troy mumbled, and we exited Ralph's office. I told Troy I had something to take care of.

"Take care of this," he said giving me the finger.

"Back at cha," I said, refraining from returning the gesture. I went into the lobby and called Adriana.

After she answered I said. "It's me. What are you doing right now?"

"Why?"

"Come to Birch County Park South and park in the lot by the playground. I'll be in a department Explorer."

She hesitated but then said, "Give me a half hour."

FORTY MINUTES LATER she drove up in a red BMW convertible with the top up. I turned off my phone ringer.

"Nice car," I said as she climbed in the front seat.

"My wedding present."

"Whoops. I never did buy you a present. How about a case of Viagra?'"

"Ha, ha. Now what's this all about?"

"I've discovered that Ted Kohler was instrumental in getting parishioners at St. Stephen's to change their wills on their deathbeds, giving everything to the church. Most of the time the families didn't know and were counting on the inheritance."

Adriana examined her perfect manicure.

I said, "The biggest amounts were from Norm Taylor and Neva Hunt."

She sighed deeply and looked out the window. "I was the one who had to break it to both Gus and Naomi."

"And were you the one who changed the wills?"

She looked back at me and turned her body to face me. "Yes, but in both cases they got something: Naomi got her mom's house free and clear and Gus got the house, farm buildings and the land they were on."

"That seemed fair to you?"

"Cal, I don't tell clients what to put in their wills, but I always ask whether they are sure they want to make the changes."

"You sound defensive. Look, I'm not blaming you. When did Neva change hers?"

"About a month before she died. Ted Kohler called and said he'd just been visiting with Neva Hunt and she asked him to contact me because she wanted to update her will. She was too ill to come in so I met with her at her house."

"Was Kohler present?"

"No, Nancy Martin, Neva's nurse was."

"What were the Mobergs' reactions when they found out?"

"Naomi looked stunned but she remained calm—however, Jeremy was livid. I'll never forget his reaction. His face turned this bright pink—he picked up my crystal paperweight and threw it across the room."

"Anything said?"

"He sort of made a threat."

"Like?"

"Like I'd regret what I'd done."

"And you didn't take that seriously?"

"You know Jeremy's a hot head—remember how he used to throw his golf clubs when he had a bad shot? I assumed he'd get over it quickly like he did in golf."

"Okay. Was Gus as upset when he got the news?"

"After the shock settled in, the first thing out of his mouth was, 'I'm contesting this will.' I believe Virgil Dodge is handling the legal case."

"Thank you," I said.

"You're welcome. You heard none of this from me."

"Not a word."

She left leaned over and kissed me softly on the lips, leading to another—a passionate kiss that was like a sip of water to a man dying of thirst. We parted. She touched my cheek, then exited the car. I watched her drive away and wondered why I had ever let her go. I lay my head back on the headrest and closed my eyes willing the ache to go away. When I'd experienced enough self-pity, I opened my eyes, picked up my phone and turned the ringer back on.

I HAD A VOICE MESSAGE from Naomi: *Hi, Cal. I heard you stopped by this morning. I know Troy went to see you last night. Sorry about that. Um . . . I think he knows how I feel about you . . . and I'm still hoping we can work this out. Give me a call.*

Terrific.

I went back to the office and told Ralph and Troy what Adriana had told me. Troy ran a credit check on the Mobergs, while Ralph went to see Father Moran. The priest admitted to him that Jeremy had come by to see him about his mother-in-law's will and was very angry.

When Ralph came back in he said, "Bring Jeremy in."

"First, I think we talk to Tiffany Howard, his live-in girlfriend. See if we get inconsistencies in their stories," I said.

"Good thinking," Ralph said.

Troy screwed up his nose.

34

WHEN I ASKED TIFFANY to come to the department, she said she was home with Jeremy's sick children. We agreed I should drive over to interview her alone—less intimidating.

I forced my eyes to stay on Tiffany's narrow face and away from her double D's she shows off with low-cut tops. Tamika thought I had a type. I guessed Jeremy did too because Tiffany and Naomi certainly resembled one another.

I hadn't seen the Moberg kids in a while. They'd grown. Both had Jeremy's red hair and Naomi's eyes and chin. They were in the great room watching cartoons and seemed oblivious to my presence. Jackson, the five-year-old, was playing with Legos on the floor. He coughed then swiped at his nose with his pajama sleeve. Yeesh. Maggie, three, was lying on the sofa. In between her deep rattling coughs, she stuck her thumb in her mouth holding a tattered blanket under her nose. I wish I'd worn a mask.

"Those coughs sound awful," I said, wondering why Naomi would let Tiffany care for her sick children.

"Actually, Jackson's better, but Jeremy thought he should have another day home."

I nodded, thinking the sooner I got out of this germ-infested environment the better.

"I'm asking those who knew the Kohlers and Petersons a few questions," I said, turning on the recorder.

She looked confused. "I didn't know them."

"But Jeremy knew Ted."

"Yes."

I gave the case information, and then said, "Seems like everyone remembers where they were when shocking events take place—like 9-11."

She made a snuffling laugh and nodded.

"Where you were when you found out about the murders?"

"I was at work."

"Jeremy too?"

"Well, yes, a large crowd was in the executive lounge where we watched the coverage."

"What do you remember about the night before?"

"What do you mean?"

"How was Jeremy?"

"Preoccupied. Worried about some project that was due. I don't know what time he got to bed—got up extra early that morning for a run, but I met him for lunch and he seemed fine. Why are you asking this?"

"What time did he leave for work?"

"I don't exactly know, I was still sleeping."

"How do you know that he went for a run early?"

"Because he wasn't in bed?"

"You didn't see him in running clothes?"

"I didn't see him period."

"Did you hear him in the shower?"

"I heard him shower downstairs. He sometimes does that."

"The time?"

"I don't know. Early."

"Did he ever talk about Ted Kohler?"

"He was real sad he died."

"How about before?"

"Before? Well, he mentioned how Ted took advantage of Naomi's mom, talking her out of the inheritance. He didn't think Naomi did enough . . ."

"Did enough?"

"To let her mom know she needed the money. Shocking he was killed like that."

"Yes."

"Jeremy owns a rifle?"

"Yes, he has two."

"May I see them?"

"I guess so."

She grabbed a set of keys from a drawer and I followed her down to the basement to a gun cabinet in a room I could safely call Jeremy's man cave. Jeremy had a Browning 12-gauge shotgun and a Winchester .30-30 rifle. I thanked her and went back to the office.

WHEN I ARRIVED BACK at the department about ten o'clock, Troy already had Jeremy waiting in an interview room. Before he went in, he listened to Tiffany's interview. I observed as Troy questioned him. (Never mind Troy was bopping Jeremy's ex.)

Jeremy said Thursday, October 6th, he went to bed after Tiffany and got up before she did. The next morning, he went for a run, showered downstairs so he wouldn't wake Tiffany and the kids, and was at work by seven-thirty. No one, other than Tiffany, could verify his story. He says he knew nothing of the murders until he heard it on the news that afternoon. He denied throwing Adriana's crystal paperweight, being angry when speaking with her or the priest—all exaggerations, and he wasn't worried about anything, including financial problems. Yes, he had hunting guns, but hadn't used them for a few years. No, he wouldn't surrender them for testing. When Troy was tired of badgering him, he came out and we discussed our options. Until we had concrete physical evidence to back the charges, we could not make an arrest. Ralph said to release him.

But the inconsistencies between Tiffany and Jeremy's accounts convinced Ralph we should do the paperwork for a warrant for Jeremy's home, computers, and phone records. Judge Evans signed it—with reservation, and Ralph said we had better be right.

We drove over to the Moberg's mid-afternoon. Tiffany seemed reticent, but let us in. I'd just put the rifle in the Explorer when Jeremy arrived home, in a very foul mood. He ordered Tiffany to take the kids and leave.

"Where should I go?" she asked as he practically pushed her out the door with little Maggie in her arms.

"I don't give a shit. I don't want them here seeing this."

I followed her out. "The lab'll contact you, Tiffany, get fingerprints, etcetera."

She nodded. I looked at the kids and shook my head. He was protecting them from us? Two officers calmly doing their business while he was behaving like a lunatic? He really was an asshole. As we continued our search, he followed us through the house, growing more and more belligerent, repeatedly shouted, "You're violating my constitutional rights."

I walked up to him and whispered in his ear, "Shut the hell up, Jeremy. Your behavior will go in the report, and it doesn't look good when you act like a guilty asshole. If you're innocent, we won't find anything, right?"

I thought I'd gotten through to him because he temporarily shut his trap, but within a few minutes he again started up. I always knew he was a hot head, but I didn't expect him to carry it to this extreme. Eventually, Troy lost patience and had a back-up unit come to contain him.

In the end, we only took the Winchester .30-30, gloves, boots, one field jacket, and his home computer. If it contained anything criminalizing, Samantha Polansky find it.

The deputy who held Jeremy in his back seat said he settled down immediately—nothing like the threat of going back to jail. As we let Jeremy out of the squad, I said, "This evidence could clear you."

"Could? Are you *kidding* me?"

"We'll be in touch."

"Yeah, and I'm getting in touch with my attorney."

AFTER SUBMITTING EVERYTHING into evidence, Troy went to search Jeremy's office while I went back to Mobergs' neighborhood to question neighbors. No one noticed anything out of the ordinary or saw anyone coming or going at unusual times. I handed out cards and asked then to call me if they thought of anything. We would anxiously await the ballistics tests and Samantha's findings. I was sure this was going to be another dead end.

NAOMI WAS SITTING UP against the wall next to my door with a bottle of wine in her hand. *Oh, perfect.*

"That's not a happy-to-see-me look," she said

"Isn't that a line from a Michael Douglas murder mystery?" I asked, as I unlocked the door.

"Is it?" She followed me inside. "Joyce said you wanted to talk to me, but you haven't you returned my calls."

"Does Troy know you're here?" I asked.

"Ah . . . no." She smiled faintly and held up the bottle. "I brought wine. How about you open it and we have a talk."

"Okay," I said. I took the corkscrew and opened the Shiraz and poured us each a glass.

She took a gulp then smiled.

"Have a seat," I said, motioning toward the living room. She sat on the sofa, while this time I took a seat in the easy chair across from her.

"Have you spoken to Jeremy?" I asked.

"No. Why?"

He hadn't told her. "We've questioned him and obtained a search warrant for evidence in the Kohler/Peterson case."

She narrowed her eyes and wiggled her head in confusion.

"*What?* Is he under arrest?"

"Not at the moment."

"But you think he will be?"

"I'm not sure, Naomi."

"This is upsetting to me. I don't understand why he's a suspect. You know Jeremy, Cal. Surely, you don't think he could *kill* anyone."

"Then the evidence will clear him."

"Well, of course it will." She studied me. "Are you mad at me for some reason, because you look mad."

"No, I'm just leery—of having you here. You're with Troy now and I have to work with him."

Her fingers traced the edge of the couch pillow. "I'd rather be with you."

Oh, shit. "Naomi, You're a beautiful, smart woman, but you seemed really confused about what you want. I stopped by this morning to make it clear to you it wouldn't work for us."

"Because of Troy?"

"Mainly. He really likes you . . . but the truth is, I'm still in love with someone else."

"Victoria." she said with resignation.

"God no."

It took a few seconds before recognition crossed her face. She nodded. "Adriana? For gods' sake, Cal, she's married."

"Yeah, well, I guess I'm not ready for another serious relationship."

"I'll wait for you," she said, her eyes pleading.

I stood. "Don't."

Tears filled her eyes. "I thought when you'd stopped by this morning, that you . . . well, silly me." She wiped the tears away, picked up her purse, and walked out.

Shit.

"That didn't go so well," I said to Bullet. I fed him then refilled my glass. I needed a woman like I needed a root canal.

35

DAY TWENTY-TWO

I SAT AT THE COUNTER at the Sportsman's Café on Saturday morning, ordered coffee and two cinnamon rolls, and reached for the copy of the *Birch County Register* that lay nearby. Couldn't wait to see how Robert Webber was going to slam the department today. And there it was: the editorial entitled "THREE WEEKS AND COUNTING." Webber expressed *concern* about the pace of the investigation and the lack of experience of the investigators—now that pissed me off—even though a part of me was starting to question the very same things myself.

I'd eaten one roll before I realized I hadn't even tasted it. I shut the newspaper and savored the warm, soft cinnamon flavor of the bread smothered in frosting. I had just taken my last bite when I received a text from Ralph to come directly to his office when I got to work.

Ralph was sitting at his desk. He had the paper in front of him.

"Hey, boss, what's up?"

"Sit down," he said sternly. I was being taken off the case—sent back to patrol.

He pointed to the newspaper. "Tomorrow's headline's going to be a whole different story."

"Why so?"

"Just got a call from Betty. Ballistics tests confirm the bullets were fired from Jeremy Moberg's rifle and Sarah Polansky says the Bible quote found in Kohler's vehicle was created on Moberg's home computer one week before he was killed."

I did an arm pump. "Yes!"

But Ralph's demeanor remained dour—like the case really hadn't been solved.

"Why the glum look, Boss?"

"Jeremy's parents, Allan and Pat, are good friends. They're going to be devastated."

"Why didn't you tell me?"

"I didn't want to influence my investigators on the case."

"So what do you think of Jeremy? Did you ever think him capable of something like this?"

"Not at all, but I always thought he was a spoiled little jerk. Allan and Pat are good people, but they never let the kid suffer consequences."

"Unfortunately, he will now," I said.

He sighed. "Yes. This is quite the turn."

"So where's Troy? We need to make the arrest."

"I'll try calling him again," he said as he dialed then put the call on his speakerphone. After six rings Troy's cell went into voice messaging. Ralph left a message: "This is Ralph. Call me ASAP. It's important."

After continuing to try for ten minutes, Ralph said, "Screw it. Don't wait. Take two patrol units with you to Estelle's Candies and arrest Jeremy. He may not go easy."

I picked two of the youngest and strongest deputies on duty and we made our way in three different vehicles over to Estelle's Candies. After getting instructions from a reluctant young receptionist in the first floor lobby, we took the elevator to the third floor of the business office. As the doors opened, a middle-aged woman wearing a boxy navy-blue jacket looked up from her oversized desk. The nameplate said Suzy Hansen. She didn't look like a Suzy. She was a substantial, mean-looking woman.

"May I help you?" she asked, and not in a friendly way.

I flashed my badge. "Deputy Investigator Cal Sheehan. I'm here to see Jeremy Moberg?" I asked.

"He's *not* in," she said, her lips pursed.

"We'd like to check for ourselves."

When I told the deputies to start searching the floor, Suzy stood. "Stop! I *said* Mr. Moberg is not in today."

The deputies obeyed her and looked to me for instructions. I gestured to go ahead.

"Deputy, listen to this," she said. She went back to her desk and punched a button on her phone.

It was a recording of Jeremy's voice: "Suz, I've got to handle a family matter today so I won't be in today. Cancel my meeting with Edwin James. Thanks."

"I have a search warrant for his office," I said, showing it to her.

Big sigh. "Be my guest."

She showed me to an office down the hall. His nameplate was near the door. The office was empty. His desk and file cabinets were all locked. Suzy was in the doorway.

"Where does Tiffany Howard work?"

The corners of her mouth turned up. "She's down on *second* floor *now*."

"Was that a demotion?"

"Of sorts. Do you want me to send for her?"

"No, just give us directions to her."

I asked Suzy to keep this between us but I had a feeling that was like telling a coyote not to howl.

But second floor receptionist said Tiffany had also called in. I correctly assumed they wouldn't hand out her cell phone number, so we drove directly to the Moberg residence. However, no one was at home and neither car was there.

The thought crossed my mind that Jeremy packed up his family and made a quick exit to Canada or Mexico last night. Not wanting to hold up the deputies from their patrol duties, I told them they could check back in with dispatch. I could recall them, if need be. Curious where Troy was, I drove to his house on the north side. The small cape cod was dark and his Tahoe wasn't in the garage. Then I drove past Naomi's where I saw Troy's truck in driveway. I pulled up behind and went to the front door. I rang the bell, then knocked several times.

"Come on, asshole, answer!"

But no one did. I thought about kicking the door in but the door opened and Troy poked his head out. He looked like shit—hung over and angry.

"What the fuck you doing here?" he asked.

36

I HELD MY VOICE DOWN in case Naomi was in earshot. "We've been trying to get hold of you. Ballistics came back this morning: Jeremy Moberg's rifle was a match and his computer had the first Bible quote. We went to Estelle's to make the arrest but he's out of the office today. Drove by Mobergs. Nobody home."

"You asswipe! You have to be the big *hero* and arrest him on your own."

"That's your concern, *asswipe*? Why weren't you at work? And why didn't you answer your phone?"

Got him. He studied his bare feet.

"FYI, I had orders from Ralph to make the arrest. Bring Naomi in ASAP. Don't tell her about the evidence. I'll meet you back at the department."

I started the vehicle and pulled out leaving him standing on the front step. While I drove back to work, I called Ralph to tell him I'd found Troy and where—couldn't help myself. While we waited for them to show up, we set up an interview room. When Troy walked in he looked a sheepish and hung over.

"Where the *hell* have you been?" Ralph said.

"I was handling personal business," he said.

"In the future, call in to notify me if you have 'personal business.'"

Troy nodded. "Sorry."

"Did this 'personal business' have anything to do with our *suspect's* wife?" Ralph asked.

Troy glared at me. "I'm sure Cal already told you I was at her place. He could have checked *before* he went to arrest Jeremy."

"You're *supposed* to answer your phone," I said.

Ralph stood. "Both of you shut the hell up." He pointed at Troy. " First off, you need to break it off with Naomi *immediately*. Oliver is going to have a bloody conniption when he finds out you were *both* involved with Moberg's wife."

Naturally, Oliver Baken, the county attorney, chose that *exact* moment to grace us with his presence. He crossed his arms and an evil look glazed over his face. "Tell me you both weren't screwing our suspect's wife." He resembled a rooster—scrawny guy with a loud cock-a-doodle-do.

"We weren't screwing our suspect's wife," I repeated.

"Cal!" Ralph reprimanded.

"I said what he wanted to hear."

Ralph, obviously flustered, tried to explain the awkward situation: "These two, not at the same time, of course, were socially involved with Naomi Moberg. Neither realized what turn the case would take."

No proof it wasn't at the same time, I thought.

"How could you think it was *remotely* proper to get involved with a potential witness in the case? She's the fricking boss of one of your victims!" Baken hollered.

I watched a vein in his forehead pulse. Troy and I stood side by side with our thumbs up our asses. Troy stupidly tried to explain, "There was no way we could…"

"Do-not-ever-get-involved-with-a-witnesses-in-a-case!" Oliver screamed, his face bright as a tomato.

"I think we should call medical. I'm worried about your blood pressure," I said.

"Fuck you!" Baken said. "If this case goes sideways because of your dicks your termination is going to be my main priority."

It got very quiet in the room and I felt pretty stupid. I figure Troy felt even stupider. Secretly, I was pleased he was in deep shit, even if I was in it with him. Competition brings out the immaturity in me.

"Where's Mrs. Moberg now?" Oliver asked angrily. His blood pressure hadn't come down any.

Ralph pointed toward Troy.

"She's here—waiting to be interviewed," he said.

"Does she know her husband has a warrant out for his arrest?" Oliver asked.

"No," Troy said.

"Has she heard from him?" Oliver asked.

"She says not," Troy said. "They've been separated for months, only talk about the kids."

"So, she says. Find out if she knows anything," Oliver said pissily.

"We also want to bring in Moberg's live-in girlfriend, Tiffany Howard. If we can find her," I said.

"If … Oh! That's just terrific," Oliver yelled.

With all the blustering, Oliver still wasn't intimidating me. I said, "She wasn't at work, so she's probably with Jeremy wherever he is."

Oliver let out a sigh. "So ... you don't know *where* Moberg or his girlfriend are?"

"That about sizes it up."

"It was my decision to release him last night," Ralph said. "I should have held him over until the tests results came back."

Oliver said, "So why didn't you?"

"I didn't think he was guilty."

"And yet you obtained a warrant?"

"My investigators talked me into it."

"So, investigators, tell me his motive."

"Revenge," I said.

Oliver rolled his eyes and strutted out.

RALPH BANISHED TROY AND ME to the observation room while he took the interview. Once we were seated, Troy said under his breath, "I don't know what she can tell us—she didn't live with the prick at the time of the murders."

I gestured, *who knows?* I turned my attention to Ralph sitting across from Naomi. He has a gentle way with most witnesses: speaks calmly, smiles and always thanks them for speaking with him.

Naomi still seemed anxious. "What time will I be done here, Ralph? I have to pick up my kids."

I wondered how that was going to work, since Jeremy and Tiffany seem to be missing.

"It shouldn't be long. This must be quite upsetting for you to have Jeremy being questioned for Mr. Kohler's and Mr. Peterson's murders." He patted her hand. Naomi shoulders lowered.

"Yes, very."

"Am I correct in saying you are divorced from Jeremy Moberg?"

She hesitated looking down and away. "No, I haven't mailed the papers in yet."

Troy leaned forward. "What the?"

"Women," I said, shaking my head.

"Is it in the works?" Ralph pressed.

"I'm going to hold off now until this whole business is cleared up—and it will be."

"Why hold off?"

"Because then I don't have to testify against him. Right?"

"Jesus." Troy said. He sat back and crossed his arms over his abdomen.

"Might you have something to say that would incriminate him?"

Naomi thought about that for a few seconds. "No, I'm sure not."

"Then you don't have to worry. Naomi, we don't want to prosecute an innocent man." He let that soak in before he added, "I just have a few questions."

"Okay."

"Do you know where Jeremy is?"

"No. Troy said you were looking for him and he wasn't at work or home."

"When was the last time you talked to him?"

"Maybe three days ago."

"Let's talk about when he found out about your mother's will. I understand it was a surprise your mother left money to the Church. How did he handle the news?"

"Not well. He was upset—but so was I."

"How did he show this?"

Naomi hesitated for a few seconds. "He screamed at Adriana Valero, the attorney, then picked up a lovely, crystal paper weight from her desk and threw it across the room. It broke and I was terribly embarrassed."

"He has a temper then?" Ralph asked.

"Yes, but he gets over things quickly."

"How did he behave at home after the will was read? Did he get over his anger?"

"No, but this was such a tremendous disappointment to him. He thought mom's money was going to be the answer to our financial problems."

"How serious are these financial problems?"

"We have always carried a lot of credit card debt, but with mom's diagnosis, he made it worse by going on a spending spree."

"Who did he blame when he found out the money wasn't coming?"

"Me. He said I should have told my mom about our money situation."

"But you hadn't?"

"No, it wasn't foremost on my mind at the time she was ill, and I assumed I was the primary heir . . ."

"Did Jeremy talk about doing anything about it?"

"He wanted to sue everybody: Kohler, Warner and Associates, St. Stephen's, but for me, it was over. I refused to discuss it because it was mom's *choice* to leave the money to her church. Her mind was good. She knew what she was doing."

"How did you know Kohler had something to do with it?"

"Nancy Martin was Mom's day nurse. She's a friend of mine. When she learned about the will she told me Ted Kohler had come to visit mom and overheard him encouraging her to give to the church. After he left, Nancy told my mom to talk to me before she did anything.

"Did she?"

"No. I guess Adriana came over a couple days later."

"Did you tell Jeremy what you'd found out?"

"Yes."

"How did he take it?"

"He was very upset—as I was."

"Do you know if Jeremy talked to Ted about it?"

"I don't know. We separated shortly after and I try to limit our discussions to the children."

"Did you see him around the time of the murders?"

"I remember I dropped off the kids the night before, but he wasn't home yet. Tiffany was there."

"Tiffany is?"

"Tiffany Howard—his girlfriend. She's lived with him in the house a few months now."

"Was it unusual for Jeremy not to be home to receive the children?"

"Yes, I suppose so.

"Was Jeremy a hunter?"

"Yes. Isn't everybody in this area?"

"Was he a good shot?"

"He always seemed to get his deer."

"Have you ever witnessed him being violent?"

She hesitated a few seconds. "Not really."

"But you said he had a temper."

"Yes, but never violent."

"He threw objects."

"Yes, but . . ."

"Golf clubs," I whispered to Troy.

"Did he seem different after the will was read?"

"He was different towards me and within a few days said he didn't want to be married to me anymore. Since then, I've avoided unnecessary contact."

"He told his secretary he had some personal business to take care of. Do you know anything about that?"

"No. Maybe it's something for his folks."

"Do you have any idea where he might go if he wanted to get away?"

"Maybe out to the lake. He goes there to think sometimes."

"To his folks' cabin on Rodgers Lake?"

"Yes."

Ralph looked through his notes. "Anything else you want to say?"

"Just that I don't think he is capable of killing anyone."

"Would you write down Jeremy and Tiffany's cell phone numbers please?"

"Sure."

Ralph pushed his notebook in front of her and she wrote the numbers.

"We appreciate your cooperation."

37

AFTER A SHORT MEETING, Troy suggested we drive over to Moberg's to make sure Jeremy wasn't hiding there. Naomi's car was in the driveway and one car was in the garage. Tiffany answered the door. Where had she been earlier?

"May we come in?" Troy asked.

She seemed reticent, but let us in. Naomi was holding her little girl in her lap on the couch in the great room. Her son sat next to her wrapped in a blanket.

"I'm not supposed to talk to you," she said.

"We need to speak to Jeremy," I said.

"He's not here and Naomi just told me he wasn't at work."

"He told his secretary he had some personal business to take care of. Do you know anything about that?" I said.

She stared blankly at me. "No, and frankly I'm a little worried."

"May we check out your house to make sure he's not home?" Troy asked.

She extended a hand. "Be my guest."

With weapons drawn, Troy and I searched from the attic to the basement in vain. After, I spoke to Tiffany.

"When did you see him last?"

"Last night. He left this morning before I got up. I tried calling him but he's not answering his cell phone."

"So, you're not sure what time he left?"

"No, I'm not sure he even came to bed." She clenched her jaw.

"Okay. And you have no idea where he might be?"

"Last night he said he had an important meeting he couldn't miss today, and because the kids are still sick, he asked me to stay home and take care of them."

"I came by earlier. No one answered the door," I said.

"I took the kids to Urgent Care. They both have ear infections."

While Naomi was packing up the kids, Troy whispered to Naomi, "The press is going to be all over this. You might want to get the kids out of town. And you should know I am under orders to stop our relationship."

"Oh, well, we wouldn't want you to disobey orders," she said curtly.

Lots of unhappy people today.

"Tiffany, we want you to come into the department to answer a few questions."

"Why?" Tiffany asked.

"Jeremy may be in danger," Troy said.

She bought that.

TIFFANY WILLINGLY WENT WITH US, most likely because she didn't know what was going on. Troy placed her in an interview room then found Ralph. When Ralph said I was to take the interview, Troy swore and threw a pencil. No wonder Naomi likes him, he reminds her of Jeremy.

I asked Tiffany for her personal information. She's twenty-five years old and originally from Myrtle, a small community northwest of Prairie Falls, where her parents still live. She's worked in sales for Estelle's Candies for one year and has lived with Jeremy Moberg the past six months—they didn't waste any time after his separation.

"I have a BA in business administration from the University of Minnesota—lest you think I'm stupid," she added.

"I've never thought that," I said. But I sorta did—maybe because she dresses more like a hooker than a smart businesswoman.

"What's your relationship with Jeremy Moberg?"

"He's my fiancé," she said.

"You're engaged?" I asked, not hiding my surprise. Call me old fashioned but I think you should be divorced before you become engaged again.

"Yes, we're being married in December," she said.

"Even though he's not legally divorced yet," I said, trying to stir up a little mistrust.

She blushed.

"You didn't know?"

"No, I saw him sign the papers. Naomi didn't?"

"Nope."

She ran her hand across her hair. "Well, that doesn't surprise me."

"Why?"

"Because I'm not sure she wants the divorce."

Maybe not.

"Did he mention to you anything about a family problem?"

"No, nothing."

"No one seems to know where he is. We're concerned. Where might he go to get away?"

"Um . . . I can't think clearly right now. I'm too nervous . . . worried."

"Does he have a passport?"

"Yes."

"Where does he keep it?"

"In a lock box in our closet."

"We'll have you check it when we take you back."

"Do you think he left town?"

I shrugged. "We're just gathering information, Tiffany. Has he acted any differently the past few days?"

"He was upset. Wouldn't you be if someone suspected you of murder and took your computer and gun?"

"I want you to think back about his behavior the days before the murders?"

"I have thought about that and I really can't say he acted any different."

"Not agitated, grumpy, or distracted?"

She crossed a leg. "Maybe a little distracted. I thought it was work related."

"How about the day of the murders?"

"He gets up really early to run so I don't usually see him. But when I got to work he was sitting at his desk. We met for lunch. A guy who's just murdered someone doesn't act normal like he did."

"We have evidence, Tiffany. The ballistics match his rifle and your home computer contains documents that are linked to the crime."

She cocked her head and scrunched her face. "What?"

I nodded my head.

"That's just crazy. There must be some mistake."

"Did he ever talk to you about Ted Kohler?"

"Um, only once when we first started dating."

"What did he say?"

"He said he thought Ted was a snake for what he did to Naomi's mother, but that's it. Never mentioned him again."

I let a few moments of silence pass before I said, "I think you need to be honest with yourself, Tiffany. Your first reaction is to protect Jeremy, but now you're not really sure he's innocent, are you?"

Instantly her demeanor changed. She covered her mouth with her hand.

I continued, "Maybe little things bother you—things you ignored. And now you're asking yourself if you're wrong about Jeremy. The evidence doesn't lie. You're a smart woman. Put it together."

"Jeremy has two beautiful children and a good job. Explain to me why he would risk all that."

"He was obsessed with revenge."

She shook her head. "If that had been the case, I would have known. He's very transparent. He can't hide his emotions whatsoever. You must know that too, he told me you were friends."

I didn't skip a beat. "How did you learn about the murders?"

She sighed and rubbed the back of her neck. "Um, it was late Friday afternoon and we were still at work. Someone, I don't remember whom, said there had been a double murder in Prairie Falls. Everyone stood around the TV in the executive cafeteria and watched the news coverage. Jeremy seemed as shocked as everybody as I did. Things like this don't happen here."

"But it did, didn't it?" I kept eye contact a few seconds before I said, "Tiffany, Jeremy was counting on his mother-in-law's inheritance. He's in heavy debt."

Her face reddened. She shook her head in disagreement. "He makes good money."

"Maybe so, but he's tapped out."

"Even if you're right, how does killing Ted Kohler help his financial situation?"

"It doesn't."

"Well then?"

"He was enraged with Kohler because he interfered with his wife's inheritance—an inheritance that would have solve his financial problems. Think about it."

I remained quiet to let that absorb. When she started to fidget, I told her I'd be right back. I joined Troy and Ralph in the observation room. We all three watched her cover her face with her hands.

Ralph rubbed his chin. "Let her sit for a bit, then wrap it up. I don't think she knows anything about the murders, but she may know where he is now."

Tiffany cried for a short while, then fidgeted with her clothing while she looked around the room. She got up and tried to look out the small window in the door.

"She now knows Jeremy's not divorced and he doesn't have the money she thought he did. Maybe that will jar her memory."

"Something's going through her mind. How about if I give it a try?" Troy said.

"Go for it," Ralph said.

Troy went in and sat across from her.

"So, suppose you tell me everything in detail what happened with Jeremy the day and night before the murders."

"Seriously? I just told the other deputy."

Troy nodded.

Big sigh. She looked agitated as she began to speak. "When I got home from work, Naomi called and asked if the kids could come over a day early because she had a date. I said it was all right, so she dropped them off. When Jeremy got home, he was mad I let her change plans. He says she gets mad when we do it, but thinks nothing of it if it suits her. He sent her a text and told her from then on to arrange things with him, not me. Okay by me.

"Anyway, we fed the kids, gave them baths, read stories, then put them to bed. That morning, Jeremy went for his run, came home, showered, then went to work at the *same* time he does every morning. Is *that* enough detail for you?"

"What time did he go for that run?"

"I don't know. He usually gets up by five fifteen."

"So you really didn't see whether he was going for a run or not. Did you see him return?"

"No. But he's always at work by seven or seven-thirty, no one else shows until eight. There was absolutely nothing different about him that day. After I took the kids to daycare, I stopped in to say hi. We had lunch together in the cafeteria."

"Okay. Let's go see if his passport is in the lockbox."

We watched Troy and Tiffany exit the room.

Ralph stopped the recording and said, "I'm afraid he may be on the run."

Fifteen minutes passed before Troy called. "Jeremy's passport and luggage are at home. Nothing else seems to be missing. Also, Naomi left a note on the table. She said she was going to take the children to the Mobergs' cabin on Rodgers Lake."

38

I CHECKED JEREMY'S PHONE RECORDS while Ralph checked his bank and credit card activity.

"Credit cards haven't been used for two days," Ralph said. "No airline tickets or purchases of any kind. No cash withdrawals from any accounts. Guy didn't have much in savings anyway. What did you find out about his phone calls?"

"He had a few calls the days preceding from Tiffany and Naomi. This morning at 5:00 a.m. he received a call on his mobile from an untraceable number. Immediately after, he made one call to Estelle's Candies," I said.

"Something's going on," Ralph said. "Who in the heck would call him at 5:00 a.m.?"

"I have a bad feeling about this," I said.

"Me too. He's not answering his cell phone."

I updated Troy when he returned.

"We need to check if he's at the lake—especially with Naomi going out there with the kids."

Ralph said, " First, I'm going to give Allan Moberg a call. See if they've heard from him. They're already in Florida for the winter."

We listened as Ralph told Jeremy's parents of our suspicions. When he hung up he said, "Well, Allan was shocked. They haven't talked to Jeremy since they left five days ago—so they didn't know about any of it. They're going to fly back on the first flight they can get. They suggested I check their cabin before I do anything else. I'd call out there, but they drop landline phone service while they're gone."

"I say we head out to the cabin now," I said.

Troy said, "Maybe I should warn Naomi."

I opened my mouth to disagree, but Ralph put a hand up to silence me. Troy's call went directly to voice messaging, so he left a message for her to call him back ASAP.

"Are you worried about her safety?" I asked.

"Damn right," Troy said. "That man is a nut job."

Just then my phone rang. I was surprised to see who the caller was: Naomi. I could have handed the phone over to Troy. But I didn't.

"Sheehan."

Sobbing. Then she forced words out between gasps: "Cal! . . . Jeremy's dead! . . . I think he killed himself."

"Calm down. Breathe. Are you at the cabin?"

I could hear her take a deep breath. "Yes. Oh, Cal, it's so awful."

It was then I looked up and saw Troy and Ralph's eyes fixed on me. I lifted my index finger to indicate I'd tell them everything as soon as I'd hung up.

"Don't touch anything. Leave the cabin and wait in your car. Don't drive anywhere. Is there someone who can come and take the kids?"

"I don't know. I can't think." She was still sobbing in between words. "Maybe Nancy Martin."

"Okay." When I hung up I said, "Naomi found Jeremy at the cabin. Apparently, he's killed himself."

Ralph gasped. He folded his hands and put them to his lips.

"Why the hell did she call *you?*" Troy said, scowling.

Ralph and I exchanged glances and I shrugged. "I don't know, Troy. What does it matter? We need to get out there. Let's go,"

Ralph said. "I'll drive myself."

First, I phoned Nancy Martin. She said she'd be there as soon as possible. I noticed Troy also had his phone to his ear.

SINCE EARLY MORNING, the weather had turned bitter. It was raining hard enough to use the windshield wiper. As I followed Ralph and Troy's department vehicles, I was left alone with my thoughts. I guess it surprised me—I thought he loved himself too much to commit suicide. I guess you never really know what's inside people's heads.

As I turned into the Moberg driveway, I saw the so-called cabin. In reality, it was a beautiful lake home set on a hill surrounded by pine trees. We all exited our vehicles and made our way up the steep driveway to Naomi's Prius. I had the thought it would be a tough one to navigate when it got icy.

Naomi was sitting in the driver's seat, the two children strapped in back in their car seats. They were watching a video on a laptop. Her eyes were red, but obviously she had calmed down. Ralph asked her if the front door was unlocked, she nodded, then Ralph headed for house. Troy, who was standing at the driver's side, said he would stay with Naomi.

"The kids see anything?" he asked.

"No, I left them in the car."

"Watch what you say with the kids in the car," I whispered.

He pulled his hand behind his back and gave me the finger.

I leaned in, nudging Troy to the side. "Naomi, Nancy is on the way."

I walked away and toward the house. Once inside, I slipped on footies and gloves and made my way down the short hallway that opened into a large open space: the kitchen dining area to the left and the great room to the right. Ralph was standing in the great room, staring at Jeremy who was slumped in recliner located near the large stone fireplace where a fire was burning. On closer inspection I saw it was a gas fireplace with artificial logs.

"Should I turn it off?" I asked.

"Later," he said. "I want the scene intact when we take photos."

I turned to Jeremy. The entry wound was forward of his right ear, the left side of his head spattered across the room. His right arm hung over the stuffed chair, a stainless steel pistol with black grips on the floor under his hand, a half bottle of Johnny Walker Black and an empty glass on the end table beside him.

"It certainly appears to be a suicide," he said. "That's Allan's Ruger he bought at the gun show we attended a couple years back—a six-round 45."

"Is there a note?" I asked.

"I haven't gotten that far. Would you call Doc Swank and the lab? BRO, too. Use your mobile. I want to keep this quiet as long as we can," Ralph said.

I made the calls and came back to Ralph.

"They'll be here ASAP. They said they'll want DNA samples from the family and anybody who's been in the cabin recently."

"Okay."

I then walked out of the great room to the hall that led to the bedrooms. Everything was tidy in the three bedrooms and bathrooms. Glancing out one of the bedroom windows facing the driveway, I noticed Nancy Martin had arrived. Troy was helping transfer the kids, their car seats, and luggage to the Martins' minivan.

When I returned to the great room I said, "Everything is tidy and undisturbed. You could spin a quarter on the beds."

Ralph was sitting on the couch across from Jeremy, staring at him.

"He's their only child. I went to his baptism."

"That's a tough one. Sorry, boss."

I patted his shoulder, then I surveyed the room and kitchen: the refrigerator was off and bare, the cabinets had only a few can goods. In the corner of the kitchen cabinetry was a built-in desk with an Apple computer. I moved the mouse and the computer came alive.

I opened the computer's recent history: someone had been researching sites of attorneys in the St. Cloud area. Next to the computer was a piece of paper with phone numbers of plumbers and electricians, but near it was a paper containing only a short paragraph that simply read:

I don't know why I did what I did. I'm so sorry. Please tell those who loved Ronny Peterson and Ted Kohler, I have deep regrets. I only hope you can forgive me. Mom and Dad, I haven't been a good man and you don't deserve this. I'm so sorry, Jeremy.

"Found something, boss," I said as I walked over to Ralph and handed the note to him.

He read it then his hand dropped to his lap. "Here's our confession, and I've never felt so bad about solving a case."

"I know what you mean."

39

DAY TWENTY-THREE

SATURDAY MORNING I MET Ralph at Dotty's for breakfast. When I arrived, he was already sitting in the booth, newspaper spread in front of him. He folded it then pushed it across the booth 's table so I could read the headline: "ESTELLE'S EXECUTIVE FOUND DEAD CONFESSED TO DOUBLE MURDERS." I read on, it stated that a source close to the family reported Jeremy Moberg left a suicide note confessing to the Kohler/Peterson murders.

"Has that been officially released?" I said.

"Nah. They don't give a hoot."

"Who would the source be?"

"It wasn't me or Allan and Pat, I can guarantee you that. I talked to Allan last night and he said he wouldn't speak to the press at all. I told them they wouldn't be able to get into their house right away, that they wouldn't even want to. They'll stay with Pat's sister until their place is cleaned up. I advised them to have a professional service clean the place after we're done with it."

"Good idea. Must be terrible for parents to deal with the death of a child."

"The worse thing anybody can go through."

"What are you ordering?" I asked.

"A poached egg on toast."

"You on that diet again?"

He groaned and said, "Yeah, I s'pose you're having a heap of pancakes."

"No, I'm having Dotty's Saturday's Six-Dollar Special: eggs, bacon, hash browns, pancakes, coffee, and juice."

Ralph shook his head. "How the heck do you stay so trim?"

"Exercise."

"There's that."

After Ida took our orders she said, "All righty then," parked her pencil behind her ear, snapped her gum, and sashayed to the window to the kitchen and shouted "A bacon six pack and an ace on toast!"

Ralph rubbed his hands together. "If anyone would have told me the investigation would lead to Jeremy Moberg, I would've said their widgets were a few gears short."

"I agree. Just goes to show you."

"Guess he couldn't live with what he'd done."

"Or the thought of life in prison."

"Allan called me last night. They don't buy the suicide. He said he never really suffered from depression, even with his divorce and money problems. Allan said they told him before they left for Florida that for his Christmas present, they were going to pay half his credit card debt—one payment at Christmas, and for tax purposes, the other half after the first of the year."

"So his financial problems were over?"

"Yeah, pretty much."

"But one debt he could never erase—the murders."

I got a nod from Ralph on that one. It was profound, I know.

Ida brought over our plates. Ralph was given two eggs instead of one and mine was heaped with potatoes and bacon and I got three pancakes instead of two. Dotty thinks she's doing us a favor, so I think I need to do my part and eat it all. I'll skip lunch.

While we ate, Ralph told me about the Mobergs' plans.

"After Jeremy's body's released, he'll be cremated. His funeral will be private."

"I can understand that. Did they say when are they going back to Florida?"

"No, but I'd guess they won't hang around too long."

40

T HERE WAS PRESSURE from the whole community for a speedy ruling in the Moberg case. Only three days after his death, on Monday morning—Halloween day, Ralph made the official announcement in a press conference on the court house steps: Jeremy's death was officially ruled suicide and the Kohler/Peterson murder case was closed. Shannon Benson stood next to me in the squad room as we watch Ralph's televised conference. After everyone cleared out, she asked, "Want to buy me a cup of coffee?"

"The squad room sludge special or Northwoods?"

"Northwoods, of course."

"Let's take my cruiser," she said. "I want to show you something."

She drove down Fifth Street. We passed Kohlers' house, then on down past Naomi's. A small moving truck was parked in her driveway and a FOR SALE sign was in the front yard.

"She's selling her mother's house?" I said.

"I'm sure she's moving back into her old house," she said.

"That's pretty quick work. She's not wasting any time."

"She has the kids to think about—what's best for them. Have you talked to her since Jeremy died?"

"No. You?"

"Yeah, I saw her last night at Save Rite. When she saw me, she broke down. I'm not all that close to her, but it seemed she needed to talk, so I listened. I think she needs her friends right now."

"What did she say?"

"That she feels partly responsible for everything. Says she didn't treat Jeremy very well after her mom died . . . that she took out her anger on him and maybe that pushed him over the edge. She feels really guilty."

"People think they have the power to stop suicide—that if they'd only behaved differently they could have prevented it. It's all bullshit. We all do the best we can."

She drove on down Fifth to the river and turned south to Northwoods Coffee Shop.

"Naomi said she heard Tiffany Howard quit her job and moved out of the area."

"Already?"

"Yeah, most people think it was quite scandalous of Tiffany to move in with Jeremy in Naomi's house. So I'm not sure she got much support when he died."

"I thought it disrespectful to Naomi. Shannon, it's only been three days. How do you get your house on the market that fast?"

"I don't know. When our neighbors put their house up, it took almost two weeks before they got their sign."

WHEN I GOT BACK TO THE OFFICE, Troy was sitting at his desk with a pout on his face.

"Why are you so happy?" I asked.

He swiveled his chair around. "I'm exhausted. Sub Shoppe burglary last night."

"Yeah, I heard there was another one."

"Got the call at midnight and didn't get back home until five. Two hours sleep. Lucky me, to be on call, eh?"

"Have you talked to Naomi?" I asked.

His face turned sour. "Why?"

"Did you know she was moving?"

"Yeah, she had planned to sell her mom's house and buy a townhouse, but I guess she'll move back into Jeremy's house now."

"With the case solved, you two going to get back together?"

"Why? You want to put the moves on her?"

"No, Troy, I don't. You haven't answered my question."

"No, she says it's over. Ya happy?"

"Jesus Christ, Troy, let it go."

THE REST OF THE AFTERNOON Troy and I said very little to each other while we both completed paperwork. I know he blamed me for his break-up with Naomi and obviously thought I was still interested in her.

About five o'clock his phone rang. He listened briefly then said, "I'm on my way."

"What's up?" I asked.

"Nothing that concerns you."

At that moment Ralph called telling me he was with Allan and Pat Moberg at their place on Rodgers Lake.

"Is the place already cleaned up already?"

"The cleaners got in this morning as soon as the crime scene was released. Do you have time to drive out here and hear what they have to say?"

"Oh, come on, Ralph, I can't listen to what a wonderful man their son was and how he couldn't have possibly killed two people and himself."

"No, it's not like that. They found something."

"What?"

"You gotta see it."

I sighed. Although I had plans to meet Shannon and some of the guys at Buzzo's, I agreed.

WHEN SHE OPENED THE DOOR, Pat Moberg looked spent, heart-broken. She was a small woman, about sixty, black hair evenly graying.

"I'm so very sorry about your son," I said.

"Thank you. Allan and Ralph are in the great room."

Ralph introduced us. I'd never met the couple and I expected one of them to have red hair. I certainly didn't expect to see Allan with dark blond hair grown almost to his shoulders. Jeremy didn't look like either parent. Maybe he'd been adopted.

"What's up?" I said.

"Take a look at this," Allan said. He pointed to the fireplace.

"What?" I said.

I crouched down and looked at the artificial logs. They looked fairly realistic. Ralph shined a flashlight onto a rear log. "There," he said.

Allan and Pat were standing behind me as I looked for what they wanted me to see. Then I spotted it: a hole in a rear log.

"They just found it this afternoon when Allan went to turn on the fireplace."

"And behind it I found a bullet from my Ruger, the gun that was used," Allan said.

"Had Jeremy ever shot your Ruger?"

"Yeah, when I first got it he went to the range with me. Tell me why he'd fire a shot into the fireplace? He would have known he could have hit the gas line."

I shrugged.

"Ralph tells me the glass doors were closed when you got here and the fire was on," Allan said.

"Yes," I said.

Pat said, "Jeremy liked the doors open when we had a fire. He said he felt the heat more. He wouldn't have closed the fireplace doors."

Allan continued, "Besides, he would have had to fire the gun toward the fireplace, then close the doors. Would anyone in that frame of mine bother to close the doors to the fireplace? So I got to thinking: maybe someone shot him, then used Jeremy's hand to shoot into the fireplace to get residue on him so it would look like a suicide. I called the Larsens next door to ask if they heard more than one shot that morning. Bill says he thought he heard two pops that sounded like distant firecrackers about thirty seconds apart."

"Nobody from BRO talked to the neighbors?" I asked Ralph.

"Yes, but everyone was so sure it was suicide, they may not have asked how many shots they heard."

"Where did you keep the Ruger?" I asked.

"In a lock box in our bedroom closet," Allan said.

"Who knew about the it?"

"We didn't broadcast it, but Ralph and Jeremy knew, and I suppose whoever Jeremy told."

"Where was the lock box key?"

"On a key rack in our kitchen pantry."

"Is it there now?"

"No, it was stuck in the lock box and put back on the shelf."

"Anything else in that box?"

"Not that particular one."

"If your neighbors are home I want to talk to them," I said.

TWENTY MINUTES LATER I was back at the Mobergs, and by that time, Ralph had taken photos of the lockbox and key, removed and bagged the bullet and log and put everything in evidence bags.

I asked Ralph if I could speak to him privately. "Only Mr. Larson heard the 'pops.' He was still in bed but thought it was about six in the morning. There were at least thirty seconds and maybe as much as a minute between the sounds. Not hearing anything else, he went back to sleep."

"We do know Jeremy received a call at 5:00 a.m. Tiffany Howard didn't know what time he left the house. Allan says Jeremy's always been an early riser. He could have driven out here after the call," Ralph said.

I shrugged. "I'll be honest with you, I don't know what any of this proves. He could have shot of a round into the fireplace."

"But it's worth looking into it," Ralph said. "We'll check out these items for prints. If Jeremy's are on them, we'll have our answer."

We walked back over to Allan and Pat.

I asked them, "If you're right about this, do you have any thoughts on who might be responsible?"

Pat said, "Well, we think it was the person who killed Ronny Peterson and Ted Kohler. Maybe the phone call was this person and Jeremy knew he was coming out and got the gun out to protect himself—it could have been taken away from him and used against him. You hear that happens all the time."

"I think his murder was staged as a suicide," Allan said. "Maybe the real grudge was against Jeremy in the first place. He was promoted over others, you know."

That was a stretch. "You think a co-worker broke into Jeremy's house stole his gun, went out to the park, killed two people to get revenge for a job promotion?"

Allan sighed. "Well, when you put it that way."

"Look, you can't discount the evidence we have against Jeremy in the Kohler/Peterson case, and the note is an admission," I said.

Pat rubbed her husband's hand then looked at me. "*If* he was the one who wrote it. Cal, I understand you knew Jeremy. Do you think it even sounded like him? Because we don't—he wouldn't choose *those* words."

"I don't know. When people are distressed they get pretty serious."

Ralph put his Twins cap back on and said, "Okay, well, we'll see what we can do. Can't promise you anything."

"That's all we ask," Allan replied.

Ralph and I left the Moberg house and stood beside our vehicles in the driveway.

"What do you think?" I asked.

Ralph said, "I don't know. Whatever, we need conclusive evidence before we reopen. I can't bring this to Oliver unless it's so clear that no jury would find reasonable doubt. If we can't do that, we won't make an arrest."

"If they're right, and that's a big if . . . we'd be negligent not to proceed."

Instead of going to Buzzo's, I went to the conference room across from the investigations office and wrote on the white board.

Jeremy Moberg

Guilty	Not Guilty
•Known to have temper	•No witnesses
•Revenge motive/threatened	•Those around him didn't see a change in him before, during or after murders
•Murder weapon is his	
•Note in victim's truck written on his computer	•Revenge motive—weak. May have temper, but not one to carry grudge.
•No alibi	•He moved on with his life.
•Note at suicide	•Claimed innocence
	•Evidence circumstantial
	•Set up possible by someone with access to his house keys
	•R.P.'s cell phone ends up in different truck.

Did he commit suicide?	Was he murdered?
•Investigated for murders	•Parents said he wasn't depressed, note didnt sound like him
•Left note	•Parents giving him monetary help
•Father's gun	•Bullet in fireplace: doors found closed. Jeremy liked them open. Could have been shot to make sure gun residue was on victim's hand
	•Call at 5:00 a.m.

Nothing there proves he didn't commit the murders or kill himself. But I underlined what gave me pause. I left work, stopped to water and feed my dog, then drove to Buzzo's for a beer and pizza—and to get Jeremy Moberg temporarily out of my head. I didn't mention one word about the case to my colleagues.

But later as I lay in bed, the facts in the case whirled round and round in my head. At one point I got up and made some notes. I may have managed a couple hours of sleep.

41

DAY TWENTY-SIX

O N TUESDAY MORNING, I wrote my notes to the side of what I wrote last evening on the white board.

QUESTIONS:

- Who had access to Jeremy's rifle/computer?
- Who may have had a grudge with either Peterson or Kohler?
- Why did Ronny's cell phone end up in a truck he didn't sign out?
- Is there a drug connection? (Jeremy's blood panel still not back)
- Who called at five a.m.?
- Who would Jeremy let in his parent's house?
- Was there someone he felt he needed protection from?
- Who knew about the Ruger?
- Who had a motive to kill Jeremy?
- Who is smart enough to carry out a perfect murder?

Troy poked his head in.

"What are you doing?" he said.

"You know about Mobergs' contention their son didn't commit suicide or murder?"

"Yeah, but what parent wants to believe their kid is capable of either?"

"I hear ya, but Ralph promised the parents we'd check it out."

He stood before the board and took time to read the whole thing.

"So who do you figure fits all these points?"

"Maybe not all, just most."

He reread my words. His head turned slowly to face me. "You think it's her?"

"Interesting you came to that conclusion. I believe she's the only one who fits the criteria."

"Bullshit," he mumbled and walked out. My thought was the big baby was going to go run to Ralph. I went to the investigations office and waited for the call. And a call did come, but it wasn't from Ralph. The sound of her voice always gave me a rush.

"Where are you?" Adriana asked.

"At my desk. Where are you?"

"At *my* desk ... in Minneapolis."

"Are you wearing a skirt?" I asked.

"Stop it. I have something to tell you."

"What?"

"I just got a call from Phillip Warner. He said the life insurance company is holding back on Jeremy's premium payout after they talked to the sheriff's office about his case. Seems you guys are thinking about reopening?"

"Maybe. So what does Warner have to do with it?"

"His office is handling Jeremy's estate."

"You handled his will?"

"Yes, his and Naomi's, but I didn't remember all the details. Philip says his beneficiary is still Naomi since the divorce papers were never filed or the beneficiary changed. She stands to receive a million dollars."

"Holy shit! What about Naomi's policy?"

"Hers was for one hundred fifty-thousand."

"Who's the agent?"

"John Parker. Parker Agency handles Estelle's executives' life insurance policies. He told Phillip that the suicide clause was in affect for the first two years, but since this is the third year, it shouldn't be a problem. Want me to call if I hear anymore?"

"Please."

RALPH ENTERED the Investigations office.

"Miss your old job?" I asked.

"I do. I'm ready for Jack to return."

"Man, I'm not. I'd rather work under you. You should run against him."

"No way," he said.

"That's what I was afraid you'd say."

"I saw your notes on the white board. It seems to me you think it's Naomi."

"Interesting you and Troy came to the same conclusion."

"Something else that's interesting: John Parker called to tell me the underwriter of Jeremy's life insurance wants him to verify the cause of death before the payout is released. He said Naomi is the beneficiary of one million big ones."

I didn't let on I knew. "What did you tell him?"

"The truth: that we have new evidence and may reopen."

"Naomi's not going to be happy—keeping a million bucks from her."

"I had to tell the truth."

"Of course. Do you think Allan and Pat would come in? I'd like to ask them a few questions."

"I'm sure. Hey, the real reason I came up here was to tell you only Jeremy's prints showed up on Moberg's pistol and his prints were on the top but not the bottom of the lockbox and no prints whatsoever on the key."

"You know what that means."

"How do you handle a lock box by just touching the top. Cal, we need physical evidence that proves Naomi did it. We need to tie this up tighter than a drum."

"Did you talk to Troy?" I asked.

"No, why?"

"When he read my notes on the white board, he took off."

"Well, he better not be talking to Naomi about this."

He punched a number in his mobile. "Where are you? ... Okay, after you're done, come directly to my office."

When he hung up he said, "He's interviewing the owner of the Sub Shoppe."

Ralph got another call. He listened then said, "Bring her down to my office." After he'd hung up, he wrapped his knuckles once on the desk. "Naomi Moberg's here to talk to me. Dollars to doughnuts it's about the insurance settlement."

"Huh. I think you tell her we're reopening but don't let on we suspect her—see what her reaction is."

"Good idea. I'll call Allan and ask him to come in."

WHEN THE DEPUTY BROUGHT Naomi into the interview room, she looked surprised to see me.

"Naomi, have a seat. Would you like some coffee?" Ralph said.

"No thanks. I'm fine."

After everyone was seated, I leaned back and crossed my arms and let Ralph handle things. I was so curious what she would say.

"I thought we would meet in your office," she said.

"Oh, well, this room was available. So what can we do for you?" he said.

"My insurance agent tells me Jeremy's life insurance company needs more than the certificate of death. I guess they want proof Jeremy's death was ruled as a suicide. Can I get that from you?"

"Not exactly."

"So who can help me?"

"The insurance company was informed the case could be reopened because of new evidence."

Narrowing her eyes, she dropped her head slightly and said, "What new evidence? Wait. Is this all about Allan and Pat's contention that Jeremy would never kill himself?"

"That's only a small part of it."

She looked to me for help. I didn't give it. "What's the rest?" she asked.

"We believe the individual who killed Peterson and Kohler set up your husband, then murdered him."

She stiffened in her chair. "Really? That seems farfetched. What makes you think that?"

"We're not at liberty to say at this point."

"So why haven't you made an arrest? Or don't you know who this mysterious person is?"

I couldn't resist. "Oh, we know who it is. We're just pulling the details together before we slap the bracelets on."

She rubbed her hands together. "Are you going to tell me who killed my husband?"

"You're one of the first people we'll notify," I said.

She made an airy sound through her nose and looked like she didn't know if I was being sarcastic or not. "When's this all going to happen?" she asked.

Ralph leaned back in his chair and crossed his leg. "Can't say exactly. But I think we have it about wrapped up. Right, Cal?"

I nodded and stared her down. "Absolutely."

Naomi chewed on her lip and looked between Ralph and me. She broke the few seconds of silence. "They're wrong about him not ever being depressed. My guess is he hid it from them."

I crinkled my brow, showing how interested I was in what she was saying. "Tell us about that."

"He called me crying more than once."

"Is that so?" Ralph said. "Did you share that with your in-laws?"

"I didn't feel it my place."

I sat forward. "Don't you think it was *your place* to share that with us the day he was found with half his head missing?" I said.

She winced, which turned into a look of disgust. "My, how sensitive of you. Anyway, I was too upset to think clearly."

Ralph tapped the desk with his fingertips. "Well, we'll be in touch. Shouldn't be long. Cal, will you show Naomi out if she has no more questions?"

She shook her head. "No more questions. I just want to know when this is settled."

"We'll let you know," I said. "You're good to go then."

When in the corridor her eyes were ablaze with anger. She asked, "Is this your doing?"

I shook my head. "No, no. Actually, everyone on the team came to the same conclusion. See the problem was the M.E. felt pressured for a quick ruling, and well, that was just wrong. Is there some reason you're troubled over finding the truth?"

"No, of course not. I want the truth as much as anybody."

You want your prize money.

After I lead her to the lobby, I smiled and shook her hand. I said, "Okay. See you later, then."

She stomped out.

THE MOBERGS WERE WAITING in Ralph's office. He said he'd sit in, but he wanted me to handle it.

"How do you get along with Naomi?" I asked.

Pat said, "Very well. She's always been like a daughter to us. Even after the separation we still spoke frequently."

"What were you told about their separation?"

"Jeremy told us they hadn't been happy for a long while, but Naomi was the one who told me he was seeing someone else. When I saw Tiffany I knew why ... Jeremy was just going through an early mid-life crisis or something. I told Naomi not to give up hope."

"Have you seen Naomi since Jeremy's death?"

"Sure, every day. She wanted us to stay with her at the house," she said.

"She's moved back in then?"

"We told her to. Silly for her to buy a townhouse now," Pat said.

"When they separated, did she keep the keys to Jeremy's house and your place?"

"Yes."

"You're positive about this?"

"Sure. Naomi told me when Maggie forgot her blanket—she can't sleep without it—she had to go into the house because Jeremy and Tiffany weren't home."

"Are you sure Jeremy wasn't depressed?"

"I'm positive," Pat said. "Why? Does someone say otherwise?"

"Naomi."

"Really? She never mentioned that to us," Allan said. "Are you saying you think he *did* kill himself?"

"No, there's evidence he didn't," I said. "If Jeremy didn't kill himself, whoever did, had a motive. Do you know Jeremy's life insurance situation?"

Pat said, "We know he had a good policy. He updated it—must be three years ago now. He asked if we thought he should increase the amount. We told him he had to consider what would be enough to raise the kids if something should happen . . ."

"Did you know the policy had a suicide clause for two years? This is year three. Naomi is still the beneficiary. She inherits one million dollars."

They looked thunderstruck. Eventually Pat found her tongue, "You think it was *Naomi*? But she and Jeremy had recently talked about reuniting. He admitted he'd made a mistake."

"Did Jeremy tell you that?" I asked.

The couple looked at each other. "No, Naomi did," Allan said.

"What did Jeremy tell you about Tiffany?"

Pat continued, "That we would learn to love her like he did."

"So he was in love?"

"I suppose he thought he was."

"Did he tell you they were planning to marry in December?"

"He mentioned it once," she said.

"Have you had contact with Tiffany since Jeremy's death?"

"Yes, she came by this morning. She wanted to know what we were planning for the service."

"Did she tell you where she's staying?"

"With her mother in Myrtle. She says she's moving to the Cities to find a job."

"It's just so hard to believe Naomi would do such a thing," Allan said.

I said, "Unless we find physical evidence to link anyone to the shooting, we have no case."

Ralph sat forward. "You need to keep this to yourselves."

"We won't say a word," Pat said.

When they left, Troy was waiting to speak to Ralph.

"I want to talk to both of you," he said.

I responded with a nod.

When we were seated around Ralph's desk Troy said, "Cal, I think you're right."

"Sweet Jesus. About what?"

"The morning of the murders I bought doughnuts for Naomi."

"Doughnuts? What's that got to do with anything? Besides, I thought you went to Vegas that morning with April Kadinsky."

"I did. After I bought the doughnuts, I took off for Minneapolis."

"So she wanted doughnuts?"

He flicked something off of his shirt and said, "I was with her the night before the murders. I cooked her dinner at my house, and she went home about eleven. She called that next morning to thank me and to tell me she had a good time. Then she said she'd overslept and was running late and still had to pick up doughnuts for a meeting. She asked if I could possibly pick them up and bring them to her place."

"What time did she call?"

"Seven thirty."

"Notice if it was her home phone?"

"It was her cell."

"What time did you bring her the doughnuts?"

"She needed them at seven fifty."

"Did she have a county truck at home at that time?"

"No."

"So tell me, why was your dating a secret?"

"*She* wanted it that way."

"And that didn't give you pause?"

"Her divorce wasn't finalized. She was being careful."

"Jeremy had been shacking up with Tiffany for months. Why would Naomi dating you be a problem?"

He twitched his shoulders then looked at me for the first time. "I don't know. I was just respecting her wishes."

"Are you seeing how she manipulated the *both* of us—putting us right in the middle of this shit?"

He rubbed his whiskers. "I'm beginning to, yeah."

"If we could just put her at the park that morning."

Troy asked, "Why did you ask me if a county truck was at her place? You think she drove one out to Emmaline."

"It would be least conspicuous, now wouldn't it? Why don't they have a damn security cameras in that county parking lot?"

"I don't know that they don't," Ralph said. "Let me give Stan Haney a call."

After a lot of "uh huh's" and a "sounds good," Ralph ended the call. A grin crossed his face and he shot up from his chair.

"There *is* a fairly new camera in the parking lot, behind the security lights—it was programmed to record only after hours from 5:30 p.m. to 7:00 a.m. I'll run over and pick up the discs while you boys continue to work on your reconciliation.

Reconciliation?

After Ralph left the room, neither of us said anything for a time. Finally, I broke the ice. "Did you know she asked me out the night of the murders?"

He looked at me blankly. He'd been with her the night before.

I said, "So why did she do that? You two were already dating."

"She knew I was with April in Vegas and one date didn't mean we were exclusive."

"Did she tell you we had been together?"

He looked out the window. "Eventually, yeah."

"That wasn't a problem for you? Because it is one hell of a problem for me. I don't share women with guys I know."

He looked out the window and didn't respond. Disgusted, I got up and left to use the john.

42

TROY SAT NEXT TO ME at my computer as I scrolled through the two-county garage security discs for October 7th. The date and time were recorded in the lower right hand corner. The camera had been installed last summer, and Stan told Ralph he'd never had a reason to even check the discs. I could see why. The only things the camera caught meandering through the lot were rabbits, cats, birds, coyotes, and even a lone fox. Just when I was starting to think this was a waste of time, at 6:30 a.m., a figure wearing dark clothing and a black baseball cap entered the screen from the left sidewalk, and walked toward the camera.

"Here it is," I said. "Look like a small adult to you?"

"I'll be damned. Pause it," he said.

"Shit, the visor's pulled down so we can't see the face, but it could be Naomi. Looks like her walk."

"Yeah, maybe."

The figure walked out of view.

"She's going to the office to get the keys," I said. "And how many people have keys to that place?"

"Probably very few."

About five minutes later the figure came back on screen, walked over to a pick-up, got in and drove out of the lot.

He said, "Rerun that. Stop."

When I did, I noticed the number on the side of the truck and pointed to it. "Look there. It's #13, the truck we thought Ronny drove out to Emmaline."

"That's definitely not Ronny. So what are you thinking?" Troy said.

I said, "This is how I see it: Naomi knew Ted Kohler would be out at Emmaline the morning of the 7th and she drove #13 out there. Ronny and Gus were scheduled to bring the dock in later in the morning, so when his dentist appointment is canceled Ronny calls Gus and is told to meet him out at Emmaline. For some reason Ronny decides to go early, takes #10, drives out to Emmaline and sees #13 there already. He wonders what's going on, leaves his cell phone and keys in the truck, and unwittingly becomes a witness to a murder. Naomi shoots him too. When she goes to leave, Ronny's truck #10 is blocking #13, so she drives #10 back into town. But by that time, the camera is off. She had plenty of opportunity and time to manipulate the truck sign-out after the fact, but I don't think she knew it was a problem until I found Ronny's cell phone in #10."

"She calls me to pick up the doughnuts because she's running late: Ronny was a complication she wasn't counting on."

"It also gives her an alibi. I'm calling Ralph up to see this."

IN SHORT ORDER, Ralph viewed the footage beside us. "Dang it. The face isn't visible, but I'll get Samantha Polansky on it to see if she can help us enlarge the image. You know the number of people who have keys to that building is limited."

"That's what we were saying," Troy said.

Ralph gave us each a pat on the shoulder. "Good work. We're darn close to proving our case."

"She set him up, waited for us to figure it out, then after we questioned him, she manipulated him out to the cabin and killed him, then set up the suicide so she, the poor widow, could get a million bucks. Sweet revenge for two men who wronged her."

Troy's phone rang. Before answering he looked at the display. "It's Naomi."

"Take it," Ralph said. "Just don't let on about any of this."

While Troy took the call, Ralph got hold of Samantha, and I busied myself burning copies of the disc.

When Troy's call ended, he said, "She wants to know if I could get her a copy of the cause of death. She also said she went to see you, Ralph, and you mentioned new evidence."

"What did you tell her?" Ralph asked.

"I pretended I didn't know anything about it . . . that you two left me out of the loop and I was pissed."

I gave him a nod of approval. "She probably believed that."

"She wants me to come over to her place at seven o'clock for dinner tonight. I told her I'd get back to her. What do you want me to do, Ralph?"

"Go. See what she's up to."

"Problem is, I'm not that good at pretending. I think she'll suspect something's wrong."

"You have to do this, Troy," I said.

"Wear a wire," Ralph said.

We sent an email to Samantha asking her to take a look and get back to us. She called within minutes.

"Because of the camera angle and visor of the cap, I can't get a good still of the face, but I enlarged a shot so you could see the clothing. It's a black Northface jacket, black jeans and black ballet slippers. I'll send you the enlargements."

"Why ballet slippers?" she asked.

I said what came to mind, "They're small and maybe could be worn inside boots or something."

Troy reluctantly agreed to accept Naomi's invitation and wear a wire. While he went home to change, Ralph and I set up the Tech van, normally used for drug surveillance. We parked around the corner, a half block away. Before Troy went in, he stopped in the van so Samantha could tape a wire under his shirt.

"If I'm gonna get laid at the end of this I'm taking off the wire."

"Yeah, we don't want to hear that shit," I said.

"Speak for yourself," Samantha said.

I laughed but Ralph, remaining serious said, "Getting laid isn't part of this deal. Restrain yourself."

FROM WHAT WE HEARD of the conversation, Naomi's kids were at her in-laws, and she'd roasted a chicken for dinner. While they ate, they made boring, small talk, but my ears perked up when out of the blue Naomi asked, "So tell me what new evidence you have that makes you all want to reopen Jeremy's case?"

"I told you I didn't know anything about it."

"Don't you hold team meetings and discuss those things?"

"Yeah, sure, but I've been busy with the burglaries. I don't know, maybe they don't trust me not to tell you."

"Why is it such a big, friggin' secret?"

"I haven't a clue. You do know, I'm not even supposed to be here because of Jeremy's case."

"I wish you would've been there when I talked to Ralph and Cal. They were totally weird. It was like they were playing cat and mouse with me. Why would they do that?"

"Beats me. They're assholes."

"I'm just saying it's funny they're not telling you anything. Do they not think Jeremy shot Kohler and Peterson?"

"Yeah, I don't think Cal likes him as the shooter."

"Why? With all the evidence they have."

"They must think if Jeremy was murdered it means he probably he was set up for the murders."

"Oh, for god's sake. Who would set him up?"

"You tell me . . . Assholes."

"No seriously, Troy, who would set him up?"

"Someone who could benefit from his death."

"Like who?"

"Like Tiffany. She must be his beneficiary. I'll run that by them tomorrow."

"Oh, let's not talk about this anymore. I want you to fuck me."

Fumbling sounds. "Wait . . . what is this?

"A pager."

"Nobody wears a pager under a shirt. Is it a wire?"

More fumbling. "Fuck!"

"Don't," Troy said.

"Get the hell out of my house!" Naomi screamed.

43

OXICOLOGY REPORTS SHOWED Jeremy Moberg had no alcohol or drugs in his system at the time of death—indicating the bottle of Johnny Walker had been staged—but his case was never officially reopened because we didn't have enough evidence to arrest Naomi or anyone else. Therefore, Naomi was granted her million dollars insurance payout. The three of us investigators vowed to keep tabs on her as best we could, but I could tell the interest was waning.

It was the morning of December 1st, and in a team meeting, Ralph told us the Mobergs were afraid they'd never see their grandchildren again if they didn't treat her as if she was innocent. After a simple memorial service in Florida, they released their son's ashes in the Gulf of Mexico. Then to show their loyalty and faith in their daughter-in-law, they took her and the grandkids to Disneyland for five days.

"So basically, they're letting it go. Are you willing to do that, Ralph?" I asked.

Ralph said, "If we don't have the physical evidence or a confession, there's not much any of us can do about it.

"Did you ever consider that Naomi actually told the truth, Cal?" Troy said. "The only real evidence we have that Jeremy didn't kill himself was the lack of prints on the bottom of the lock box and key."

"And the staged bottle of Scotch, and the fact Naomi said he called her crying. *When* did she have those conversations? I studied his phone records—a few short conversations—not the kind where somebody carries on crying—and she tells his parents they're reconciling, but Jeremy and Tiffany are making fricking wedding plans. It doesn't add up. She committed the perfect murders."

"Maybe you're right, but until we have physical evidence or a confession, our hands are tied," Ralph said.

"What about the film of the person entering the garage to get the keys to the truck. We have a good shot of the ballet slippers, if nothing else. See if Naomi purchased any."

"Shoot," Ralph said.

"What?" I said.

"A bag of clothes found at the community college was turned in—had some black slipper shoes. I didn't think much of it. Thought they were probably just some co-eds," he said.

"Where is it?"

"In the evidence room . . . just . . . in case."

I raced up to the room to check the bag out. Troy and Ralph followed me. I took it to the investigations office and pulled the items out with gloved hands. The shoes were black ballet slippers. Troy opened up the file with the film to compare.

"They look the same to me," I said. "And see the blood smear on this sleeve? Jesus, we could have our physical evidence, Ralph!"

"Oh, I didn't see the blood. But does the saying *too good to be true* ring a bell?" Ralph answered. " Do we even have DNA samples from Jeremy's family members?"

"The lab should still have the samples taken when Jeremy died. We need to send this in for DNA top priority testing," I said.

"All right, I'll give Leslie Rouch a call, but I hope you're not disappointed with the results."

"It's a long shot," Troy said. "Some random bag, thrown in a garbage can at the college? It's probably contaminated."

Yeah, maybe it was a long shot, but I was absolutely sure Naomi had planned and carried out the murders down to the smallest detail—after all, she was a *perfectionist like me.*

44

DAY SIXTY-FOUR

I T WAS THE NINTH OF DECEMBER and the dusting of snow on the lawns sparkled in the streetlights. I'd volunteered to pick Shannon up for the department Christmas party at Cadillac Jack's. On the drive to Bensons' I muttered to myself about the DNA tests not being back yet. The two cases haunted me—day and night I found myself mulling the details, trying to figure where Naomi had tripped up—and second-guessing if I was wrong about her.

As I drove by the Super 8, I noticed a family walking in, struggling with their kids and luggage, but still looking happy. The Kohler and Moberg kids wouldn't have both parents to vacation with anymore.

I pulled into Bensons' driveway feeling like it was a date, but I knew better than to call it that. I was about to get out and walk up to the door when Shannon stepped out of the front door. Good god, she was wearing a dress and heels. I hopped out and went around and opened the door for her, and supported her elbow as she stepped up onto my running board.

"You look nice," I said. "You should wear a dress more often—show off your legs."

"Right." She pulled her long coat closed.

"I think your legs are sexy."

They were strong and muscular. I did think they were sexy.

"Oh, shut it," she said.

I grinned. I loved to compliment her—watch her get flustered.

"I can't believe you bought a dead man's truck. God, I think it might be bad luck or something," she said.

"Yeah, like that's what I want to hear."

She giggled. "I'm kidding ya, Sheehan. It's a real nice truck. I hardly notice the aura surrounding it."

"Shut up."

She giggled again.

WE TOOK SEATS at a table with Troy, April, Austin Spanney, and his date, Lauren something. Since the conversation centered on department business and gossip, April and Lauren, sitting side by side, disconnected and engaged in their own conversations.

After the meal Sheriff Wittman got up to speak. He abruptly announced his retirement and the special election in May to elect a new sheriff. He said although he encouraged Ralph to run, he said he wasn't interested, but would continue until that time. Now that depressed me. I liked working under Ralph.

I needed to go to the restroom, and as I walked in, I ran into Bob Brutlag.

"Hey, did Jack make his big announcement yet?" he asked.

"Yeah. You knew?"

"Yeah, he told my old man. Say, guess who I ran into at the airport in Minneapolis."

"Who?"

"Naomi Moberg."

"Okay?"

"She was with her kids and . . . wait for it . . . Tiffany Howard."

"Tiffany? No shit?"

"Yeah, and she fell all over herself explaining why Tiffany was with her."

"What did she say?"

"That Tiffany had become important to her kids and she wanted to maintain the relationship."

"Wow, so they travel together? That surprises me."

"Juanita says it's way too weird."

"When was this?"

"Couple of weeks ago."

"Where were they going?"

"Chicago."

I couldn't wait to tell Troy what I'd learned, but upon hearing it, all he said was, "Strange."

"Something's wrong with that."

"I'll talk about it Monday morning but tonight is party time."

At eleven o'clock, Shannon mentioned she'd like to get home to her boys, so we left shortly after.

On the drive back in to town she said, "I overheard what you told Troy about Naomi and Tiffany. What do you think's going on?"

"I don't know. I just don't think Naomi would befriend Tiffany now unless there was something in it for her."

"What would that be?"

"I don't know. I'm going to go talk to Tiffany's parents tomorrow."

"It takes a lot of patience to be a good detective."

"I guess."

She gave me one of her killer smiles. I let a couple seconds pass before I gathered the courage to say, "Shannon, I really like spending time with you. Is there anyway you'd be willing to move our relationship forward?"

She turned to face me. "It scares me."

"I know, me too. But we can proceed slowly. Maybe start with coffee dates, that kind of thing."

"If it gets weird, we stop. Okay?"

"Okay."

"And I don't want my boys to know. I don't want them to get their hopes up."

"I hear you."

When I pulled up in her driveway, I leaned in to give her a quick kiss on the lips, and she didn't haul off and hit me. Progress.

"See you tomorrow," I said.

She smiled sweetly. I felt all warm and fuzzy inside—Benson and me—dating.

On the way home as I passed a strip mall on the west side, I saw a flash of light inside the auto parts store. That wasn't right. I pulled around to the back and saw an unoccupied black Dodge Ram beside a door that had been jimmied open. The truck bed was loaded with boxes of auto parts. The driver had left the engine running. I got out trying not to make noise. I turned the Ram's ignition off, put the keys in my pocket, and called for back up—no lights no sirens. I also mentioned to dispatch I was off duty and unarmed. I had the license plate run and smiled when I saw who the registered owner was: Kent Silva's, the Hackett brothers' sperm donor. I love to nail scumbags. I hoped he wouldn't come out before my backup arrived with firepower.

Within a minute, two squads silently rolled up and boxed the Ram in. Greg Woods handed me a shotgun and he, John Odell, and I waited behind our vehicles, weapons trained at the back door. When Chad and Todd Hackett burst through the back door, they stopped in their tracks to the sound of all three of us shouting versions of "Get down on the ground!"

Silva's arms were loaded with boxes, so he couldn't see. He ran smack into one of his sons. I expected them to bolt, but they didn't. They dropped the items in their arms including a cash register, and complied with our commands.

When Woods patted Silva down, he pulled a nine-millimeter Glock off him.

"Oh, nice. Having a little bonding time with your boys, Silva?" I asked.

He grunted.

After all three were searched and cuffed, I said, "So, what are you doing with this merchandise and cash register?"

"This is my buddy's store," Sylva said. "We're doing some work for him."

Odell groaned. Woods chuckled.

"Yeah? What's the buddy's name? Let's give him a call see if he wants you to move his cash register and sell off all these auto parts for him," I said.

Of course, Scott Wagner (the owner) didn't know Kent Silva or his boys. While the deputies took the three off to county to process, Scott met me at the store and needless to say he was grateful I just happened by. Maybe the dead man's truck was good luck after all.

Because I couldn't get over Tiffany and Naomi traveling together, I drove by Moberg's. A FOR SALE sign was in the front yard. Naomi was selling both houses. Why?

I got home after two o'clock. Larry had left a note that he'd watered Bullet about ten o'clock, so I loved up my dog, took off my shoes, sat down, put my feet up and had a beer. I reveled in the satisfaction of solving the burglaries. Troy was going to be pissed. I smiled.

I set my alarm for seven o'clock so I could call and meet with Tiffany Howard's parents.

45

DAY SIXTY-FIVE

THE HOWARDS LIVED in a brown split-level on the southeastern edge of Myrtle. Mrs. Howard was a round, short woman who didn't look one bit like Tiffany. She said her husband was downtown playing cards.

"You said you had some concerns about Tiffy's safety?"

"Do you know where she is right now?"

"Sure, she's moved to Chicago."

"Alone?"

"With Naomi."

"Does that concern you at all?"

"Why would it?"

How could I put this delicately? "Don't you think it's strange she would live with her dead boyfriend's wife?" Not so delicate.

"Not really. The part I thought strange in the first place was her involvement with her mother's husband—and I told her so."

"Come again?"

"Oh. You must not know Naomi is Tiffy's birthmother. We got her when she was only three days old. What a blessing—such a good girl, smart as a whip. But like I said, when she started dating Jeremy, I told her I thought it would cause trouble. She said for me not to worry and to trust her."

For some reason, I felt like puking.

"You know Naomi?"

"Yes, she was only fifteen when she got pregnant. The adoption was handled through a lawyer in town—it was all kind of hush-hush."

"Did Naomi keep in touch with you—Tiffany?"

"Yes. She would only agree to the adoption if we let her have a relationship with Tiffy and keep it a secret from her parents, because they wouldn't have approved."

"Jeremy's not her father, is he?"

265

"Oh, good lord no. Poor Jeremy, killing himself like that. Tiffy said he'd been depressed."

"Do you know who Tiffany's birthfather is?"

"Sure, Sal Newhouse."

"And where is he?"

"St. Charles near Chicago."

"Did Tiffany have a relationship with both her birth parents?"

"She knew who her birthfather was but only saw Naomi." She chuckled. "Sal's been a big help to them. We're flying there for Christmas."

"Would you do me a favor?"

"Of course."

"Don't mention I was here. I don't want them to know I was worried. I feel a little foolish about it."

"Oh, sure."

"Naomi is a good friend, and I'd like to send her a Christmas card. Could I get their new address?"

46

DAY EIGHTY-SIX

THIS WAS TO BE AN IN-AND-OUT TRIP for us, but the traffic was ridiculous, and if Shannon and I didn't stay on schedule, we would miss our return flight. I drove the rental from O'Hare to St. Charles, Illinois, Police Department. Since we needed their PD's cooperation, we had two officers accompanying us: one male—one female. With warrants in hand, I knocked on the front door of Sal Newhouse's historic two-story home along the Fox River. My breathing quickened, my heart thumped.

Tiffany answered. Perfect. Her initial expression of surprise quickly turned to dismay. With a look of resignation, she let us in, and we followed her down a short hallway into a kitchen/family room. The house was quiet except for the sounds of our shoes on the wood flooring. Newhouse had tastefully decorated his home using both antique and modern touches. The Fox River was visible through the glass patio doors to the backyard.

I gestured for Tiffany to sit at the small round table off the kitchen. She picked up an orange from a bowl on the table and rolled it in her hands. She looked nervous.

"What weapons are in the house?" I asked Tiffany. "What? Like guns?"

"Yes."

"I don't think there are any."

We wouldn't take her word for it. Shannon and the St. Charles officers disappeared down the hall and upstairs.

I pulled out my small recorder, turned it on, and said, "Why don't you tell me how you and mommy killed her husband?"

"What?" She looked terrified.

"Your DNA was on the suicide note."

She burst into tears. I handed her a tissue from a box on the counter and read her the Miranda rights. Then hoping she wouldn't exercise her right to remain silent, I asked how it all began.

Sniffing, she said, "It was his own fault. He hit on me."

"Are you speaking of Jeremy Moberg?"

"Yes, I'd been working at Estelle's only a week before he asked me out, and when I told Naomi, she was so devastated. She told me to accept, to see how far he'd actually go."

"Were Naomi and Jeremy still living together then?"

"Yes."

"And he didn't know you were Naomi's daughter?"

"No one did but my parents . . . and Sal and Naomi."

"Then what happened?"

"The situation kept progressing . . . and . . . and when Naomi went to stay with her mom when she was dying, he really pushed hard."

"What do you mean?"

"He said he wanted to leave Naomi to be with me. When I told her she said it would help us get him good, but I guess I didn't know what she meant."

"Did you ask?"

Sniff. "No."

"But did you know she was going to kill Kohler?"

"Not at first, but later she told me her idea how to murder Kohler and pin it on Jeremy."

"What was your part?"

"She asked me to type the Bible verse on his computer."

"Why did she kill Kohler?"

She spit the words out. "Because *he* was the *one* who took our *inheritance* away. Big, rich man. He was toxic. We had to equalize things."

"And how did you pin it on Jeremy'?"

"She used his gun, gloves, and boots."

"What do you know about Jeremy's death?"

"She made it look like suicide."

"But she killed him?"

"Yes."

"How?"

"She shot him with his dad's gun. He agreed to meet with her because she told him she was moving the kids to Illinois and knew he would fight it. She said it worked like a charm. She told him she had to go to the bathroom so she could get the gun from the closet, then came up along side him and shot him. He didn't see it coming."

"Did you type the suicide note as well?"

"Yes, but Naomi composed it."

"Why did she kill Jeremy? For revenge or the life insurance money?"

"Both, but he owed us the insurance money."

"So you knew when he left that morning, you'd never see him again?"

"At the time, I hoped it would work out that way, yes."

"And now?"

"Now I know it was really wrong."

"So why did you go along with Naomi?"

"I just wanted her to love me." She started sobbing.

The power of a parent's love . . . Patrick and Grace. Don't go there.

I cuffed Tiffany, hands in front.

I heard footsteps down the stairs and the male officer accompanied a dark-haired man wearing a pair of navy shorts. His hands were cuffed behind his back. He was maybe five-foot-ten, medium build. He asked, "Will someone please tell me what's going on?"

"Are you Sal Newhouse?" I asked.

"Yeah, and who are you?"

We identified ourselves and I explained the situation. He looked shell-shocked. I had Shannon take him to the dining room where she would ask him questions we had prepared.

Soon, the female officer brought Naomi down, also cuffed, wearing only a man's T-shirt. She had bed-hair, no make up. I hardly recognized her.

"What the hell, Cal?" she said.

"The jigs up," I said to her.

"You've got no right to come in here like this. Get-out-of-my-house!"

"Your house?"

Panic crossed her face as she noticed Tiffany. "Tiffy, do *not* say a word to them."

"Too late, she already did, mama," I said. "You have the right to remain silent . . ."

AFTER NAOMI'S RIGHTS were read, she was taken back upstairs to the bedroom so she could dress.

Tiffany asked, "Are you taking us back to Minnesota?"

"Yes."

"What about my parents? They're flying here tomorrow."

"Call 'em." I let her use her cell phone. She cried pretty hard during the call.

As soon as Naomi returned, she asked, "Where's Troy? Why isn't he in on this?"

"He's out of town."

"With April?"

I shrugged. *That* was her concern?

"So what about my kids?"

This was the first she'd mentioned them. Mommy of the year.

"Do you want them to be with Jeremy's parents or the State?"

She glared but eventually said, "His parents. But who'll take care of them now?"

"Fox County will have them in their care until Jeremy's parents arrive."

"Oh, that's just great," she said bitterly. "Can I at least say good-bye to them?"

I took her up to the bedroom where they were still sleeping. They barely noticed her kisses on their cheeks.

When she said good-bye to Sal, she said, "You are the love of my life, Sal. We were going to live happily ever after."

He looked distraught, but my thought was maybe now he won't be another one of her victims. After questioning him, Shannon concluded he knew nothing about the murders. He thought he was starting life anew with an old heartthrob. A Fox County social worker arrived before we left. They were to release the children into the custody of Jeremy's parents that afternoon.

The women were transported to O'Hare in two different PD squads. During the flight, Tiffany was cuffed to my wrist, while Shannon took Naomi. Tamika met us at the Minneapolis/St. Paul airport so we would have separate vehicles to transport the women individually.

Because I hoped Naomi would talk during the drive, I switched women with Shannon. After a restroom stop at MSP airport, I placed her in the back seat of the squad Shannon and I had driven down and parked in the short-term parking lot. Tamika had bag lunches for everyone for expediency.

I purposefully made no attempt at conversation. I wanted everything properly recorded. We rode in silence until about an hour into our trip, when Naomi said, "You think you've won, don't you, Sheehan?"

"You think there are any winners here?"

She looked out the window for a while before she asked, "What did Tiffany tell you?"

"If you like, I'll play the recording for you when we get back to the department."

"Damn it!" she said. In the rear view mirror, I could see tears streaming down her face.

"You don't have any evidence," she said. "It's my word against hers."

I smiled recalling the day I spoke to Teresa Gibbons, a maintenance supervisor at the community college and her underling, Jan Hagen. Jan was the woman who found the white garbage bag in a trash bin where they usually find only small items like cups and fast food bags. Jan was curious so she looked in it finding black ballet slippers, socks, black jeans, and a gray sweatshirt. All the items looked in fairly good shape, but there was blood on the back of one of the sweatshirt sleeves. With all that had gone on lately, she thought it could be something and turned it in to the Sheriff's Department. Even though Ralph never mentioned it, thank God he logged it into evidence.

"We have more than you think," I said.

And we did. The DNA test results had came back yesterday: the blood on the sleeve was Jeremy's, the socks and shoes carried Naomi's DNA.

She looked out the window for a while. "Cal," she said crinkling her nose. "You could let me go—for my kids' sake."

"Ah, for your *kids'* sake. Now that's ironic—it was the *kids* who cinched it for me—when I knew for sure that you killed Jeremy."

"What are you talking about?"

"The day Jeremy was shot. You didn't take your kids or the luggage in the lake house—because you *knew* what was in there. And just so you know, I think they're better off with people who have souls, so, no, there's not a chance in hell I'd let you go for 'the kids.'"

Her eyes grew watery. The ice princess just felt sorry for herself because she was caught. "I want to call my attorney."

"When we get to Prairie Falls."

She stared out the window. "You don't have a shred of evidence."

"Don't we? We found the bag of clothes."

"I don't know what you're talking about." But I had caught the flicker in her eyes.

"Was he surprised?"

"Who?"

"Kohler."

She held my glance for a couple seconds then looked away.

I chuckled. "Kohler totally underestimated you, didn't he?"

She looked at me and smiled. At that moment I saw the cold, calculating woman she was. "Fucker."

I don't know if she was referring to Kohler or me.

THE NEXT DAY, RALPH told me Naomi retained an attorney from St. Cloud, and that Tiffany was cooperating with Oliver for a deal. He convinced her Naomi's intention all along was for the evidence to point to her if and when the suicide was discovered to be staged.

I watched Oliver's interview with her. Tiffany told him if Kohler had been cool when Naomi went to see him about the will, he wouldn't have had to die. If he'd apologized or told her he'd see what he could do to reverse it. But he was dismissive. Naomi asked him if he was going to leave all his money to the church instead of his family. He said he had young children . . . they weren't adults like her. He suggested she pray for forgiveness for being greedy. And poor Ronny? He just got in the way. Tiffany said Naomi felt bad about that.

I just couldn't get over how Naomi duped her own daughter into shacking up with her husband just to plant evidence. It would have worked too—if she'd disposed of the clothing in a different place. One simply mistake is all it took for that last puzzle piece to slip into place.

47

MAY 19

Late Sunday morning I took Bullet along for a run in Birch Park South. It was a beautiful day. The sun's warming rays felt good on the skin. I felt strong and happier than I had in a long while. As I neared the playground, about to cut north out of the park, I saw a female jogger approach. Bullet started whining before I recognized who it was—Adriana. *What was she doing up here?*

"Hey," I said, stopping.

"Hey! I thought I'd find you out here," she said.

She looked fantastic and like she'd lost a little weight, not that she needed to. She got down on one knee, and gave Bullet a good scratch behind the ears, then kissed him gently on the nose. He swiped his tongue across her face, hitting her lips square.

Smiling, she wiped her mouth on her sleeve. "I miss you," she said.

"Obviously, he misses you, too."

She stood and faced me with her hands in her pockets. "Not Bullet, dummy, *you*."

"Oh."

"So how are you?"

"Great, great."

"Do you like having a woman sheriff for your new boss?"

"It's all good."

"I was surprised to hear Troy ran for the job. How did he take the loss?"

"Not well. I think he's looking for a different position."

"But you—you're quite the hero these days."

"Ah, shucks, lady, I was just doing my job."

"So Tiffany is Naomi's kid?"

"Yeah. Who would figure that one?"

"Pretty awful she actually encouraged her own daughter to live with her husband. That's just wrong on so many levels."

273

"I'll say."

"And Tiffany cooperated for a lesser sentence?"

"Thanks to her we have a solid case on Naomi, and Tiffany will only serve six years."

"When does Naomi's trial start?"

"Not until September. The judge wouldn't grant bail. Flight risk."

"She really thinks she can be acquitted?"

"Guess so."

She titled her head and looked at me with those big brown eyes. "So, what would you say if I moved back to Prairie Falls?"

I eyed her suspiciously. "Why would you do that?"

"Back to you."

My heart skipped a beat. "Why?"

"Because I've been miserable ever since I saw you at my wedding—I knew I shouldn't have gone through with the ceremony—I was too stupid to even listen to myself."

"Does Adam know you're thinking about this?"

"Yes, he suggested it. He said he wanted me to look at *him* like I looked at *you*."

"What does that mean?"

"That I love you."

She moved closer but I put my hand up stopping her.

"But you love him too, right? Maybe you'll find that when you're with someone else, you'll want to be with him."

"We both agree our marriage was a mistake."

"What about your career? Your wonderful, exciting life in Minneapolis?"

"Phillip says I can come back to my position anytime. He's says you've been giving him a lot of work."

I took a deep breath. "You know, I saw my father recently. He told me not to settle for anyone that didn't knock my socks off." I pulled up my pant leg and pointed to my feet. "See? My socks are still on."

She looked confused.

"I just can't take the chance on you, Adriana," I said.

Her face dropped. "You don't love me anymore?"

"Of course . . . and I always will, but I don't trust you. Some day you'd look up at me with those big brown eyes and tell me you've made a mistake about us. Deep down, you know that's true."

Tears began to form in her eyes. "That's it then?"

"Yeah, I'm sorry."

The tears rolled down her cheeks and I pulled her into my arms. I kissed her on the cheek, and said good-bye. Six months ago, I would have welcomed her with open arms. Looking at my watch, I realized I needed to hustle to get ready to go to Shannon's parents' house for lunch. Our families were meeting today to discuss our August wedding plans. I think I'll wear loafers with no socks.

Acknoweldgements

Special thanks to my family and friends, especially my husband, Tim, for the ceaseless encouragement and support, and to the Orono Police Department and every other police officer I cornered to answer a few questions. Any procedural errors in this novel are my own. Also, I wish to express my appreciation to Corinne and Curtis at North Star Press for their great work in giving *The Equalizer* life.

CPSIA information can be obtained
at www.ICGtesting.com
Printed in the USA
LVHW030739011218
598846LV00005B/8/P